I0562040

tales of the
ÖCTAGON
BY **JIM MARCUS**

Tales of the

Octagon

Six stories that tell the history of the first one
hundred years of the Octagon,

By JIm Marcus

June 2025

This book is set in Lato Regular 9/13
Titles in Lato Heavy 16/20

Thanks to Hilary Shroyer

ISBN 979-8-9924718-3-0

©2025 Pulseblack / Jim Marcus.
All Rights Reserved
www.pulseblack.com

Chapters

12:3: ‖" 9D 18 : 4:
■ ‖ PULSEBLACK ‖■

Advisory

This book contains extensive descriptions of often
extreme sexual acts.

....

"Even if I now saw you
only once,
I would long for you
through worlds,
worlds."

--Izumi Shikibu

1 - Yum - 2082

"That show was great." Ed was tall, with short dark hair. He pushed the sleeves of his black hoodie up higher, over his remarkably thin forearms, as he took off his headphones and set them on the counter.

Kari lifted the electronics and handed them back to him, without missing a beat, as she continued to clean the top of the countertop and sink. She was at least a head shorter than him, with a lion's mane of blonde hair over an affable and consistently smiling face. You wouldn't say she was chubby, but, let's face it, compared to Ed, who wasn't?

"Thank you, Mr. Sevegny. It felt good, you know?"

Ed tried to find something to do with the headphones without putting them back on his head, unsuccessfully clipping them to the belt of his black jeans. "I'm going to make those meatballs."

"Do you think upstairs liked it?" She nodded toward the area upstairs where the showrunners sat. As time went on, Kari thought she had less and less access to them.

"Well, who knows. But you do have some fans here. Waiting to see you."

"Wait– people to see me, now?"

"Yeah, like the you know…" Ed made a motion as though he were drawing on his forehead. "People."

"I do not know."

"On their foreheads." He looked around and whispered. "Octagon people. Do you have Octagon friends and you didn't tell me?"

Kari laughed and her face lit up. "No, I don't have Octagon friends. But if they're fans, let them in."

Ed smiled like a kid and whispered into the walkie to send them back.

The thing is, that Kari was probably more excited than he was. The most surprising thing about this adventure into being a streaming chef personality for her was just this:

She had fans.

Kari had started the Yum Show less than two years ago, just to get some ideas out. At first, all by herself, drawing in more and more viewers until finally, she discovered, she had viewers all over the world.

And beyond.

Just six months ago, her new showrunners had informed her that her show was streaming on other worlds, places she'd never been – places she could never imagine going. It was both humbling and insanely ego-boosting at the same time.

And it had really caused her to up her game. She was representing Earth.

Well, in a way that a five foot four, thirty eight year old, chubby little Polish kid from Newark could. She laughed a little under her breath and wiped her hands.

And the room went quiet.

A young intern was ushering back three people from the Octagon – a tall dark woman, a blonde man and a younger Filipino girl.

Kari tried not to stare. All three were human, but that's where the similarities ended. The tall woman was model beautiful. Her skin was Arabian dark and smooth and covered all over in mystical tattoos. Her black robe was open in front, nearly revealing her breasts, with a range of brilliant jewelry arrayed across her neck and arms. And on her forehead, something all three shared – a beautifully stylized tattoo of an octagon.

The other two followed her as she made her way to Kari and shook her hand in an effulgent and friendly way. Kari couldn't help but feel like this woman was one of the most physically present people she'd ever met. She threw herself into the handshake, and it seemed warm and strong and adoring.

"I am such a huge fan and it's so great to meet you in person." Her voice was lilting, the kind you should read poetry with.

Kari beamed up at her. She struck her, more than anything, as a kind of goddess. She looked around. Who were these people? "Oh, my god, thank you."

She turned to the blonde man, who stepped up and took her hand as well, cradling it in both his warm palms . His smile was infectious and inviting. "Ms. Lourdes, It's really great to be here, on this set where so much great art is made." He winked at her and she laughed. His hair was short and perfectly groomed. The symmetrical line art tattoos running down the side of his face only seemed to accent his cheekbones, pulling his face into a kind of perfect squared off oval, offset by stunning long silver earrings falling deftly into a black robe, like tiny waterfalls.

The man continued. "My name is Priest. This is Master Reylan, and this young lady," he said, pointing to the younger girl, " is Gossamer."

Kari looked at the Filipino girl. She smiled and held her hand. She was the only one of the three not in a robe. Her black hair was in an unkempt but pretty fringe. She wore a stylish black tank top surrounded by mesh wraps under a pair of black jean shorts and black combat boots. Her clothing was sexy and strong-looking but she herself matched her name better. Her skin looked nearly translucent. She couldn't have been more than 25. She looked like she could fly away.

"I love meatballs. I'm sorry, I had to tell you that." Gossamer laughed conspiratorially.

Kari was excited. "Oh, you saw."

"This was my favorite episode in a while," Ed said, reaching out to shake Priest's hand.

"I'm so sorry, this is my production guru, Ed."

"My friends just call me Seven."

"You do good work, Mr. Seven," Priest shook his hand, pulling him in a few inches.

"It's just Seven. My last name…" He trailed off, shaking the others' hands. Honestly, he thought, nothing he had to say would match what would come from these three. He looked at Gossamer and smiled.

"So what can I do for you?" Kari had finished cleaning the counter. She placed containers in the set's large fridge as she talked. "It's a long way to New York."

"It absolutely is. Honestly, I'm just here to touch you in the flesh, smell all the smells here, and then visit with my sister." Reylan smiled.

"Your sister is in New York?"

"She is only a few blocks away. She's a writer, she lives here. Etangiel Corroba."

"I know her. Very powerful. She's quite good. She wrote Ghul." Kari felt a strange kind of connection. She was a big geopolitical buff.

"That's right." Reylan beamed.

"But," Priest intoned, "There is something that we would like to talk to you about. Maybe in private? Seven, maybe you could keep the young lady company?"

"Oh." Ed looked over at her. She smiled at him and he felt his temperature rise. He tried to say something consequential as the three talked.

He could smell Goassamer, as she seemed to drift closer to him. He couldn't place the smell at first, but then decided it was chai.

He remembered how he and his sister used to drink that before going to bed at his grandmother's house. He held that memory in his back pocket and smiled back at her as the others walked over to the breakroom.

Kari spent most of her time in the breakroom when she wasn't shooting. It was the closest thing she had to an office and people tended to leave her alone there. She opened the door and ushered the two cloaked shapes in.

"So, what could you possibly have to discuss with me?" Kari walked over by the breakroom sink and leaned back. It seemed so strange to stuff these otherworldly people into the regular old breakroom. She tried to resist the urge to clean. This was a big part of Kari's life – resisting the urge to clean.

"Ms. Lourdes, I am not sure if you are aware completely of what we do at the Octagon," Priest began, sitting in a chair at the table.

Kari slid to her right and let Reylan lean next to her. "I know as much as anyone does. You have…intercourse with alien species to sort of keep the peace. Is that…uh…"

Reylan nodded and squeezed in closer. Even leaning, she towered over Kari. "That's a pretty good assessment. We mediate issues that might arise between different groups."

"Of aliens," Kari offered.

Priest interjected, "They actually prefer being called yolcu – or Voyagers. We are all yolcu somewhere, at some time."

"Right, yolcu." Kari tried to look casual.

"And then, once we have a plan – a contract, we help officiate it." Reylan shrugged and smiled. She seemed much younger than she likely was because of her playful mannerisms.

Kari tried not to look as lost as she was. "Officiate?"

Reylan put her hand over hers. Kari looked down. "Which can be different for different species, but is generally through physical intimacy." She thought about what she knew about the Octagon. This didn't make sense. How could these people be here?

Priest opened his hands as if in summary. "And we facilitate that."

Kari realized that Reylan would just keep holding her hand as long as she wanted. She put her other hand in hers and they held hands. It felt really good. "That is amazing. What does that have to do with me?"

Reylan held tight. "Well…"

"Ok, I'm sure you've noticed that your popularity has grown." Priest was trying to move a drone through a tiny window, verbally. It would be easy to scare her.

Kari felt like kissing Reylan's hand, but then disposed of that as silly a second later. "Yes."

Priest pointed out, "deservedly, really. Off world, as well."

"Oh." Kari did know. And it was eerie.

"Have you ever heard of the Vigo, or the Encantada?" Reylan asked.

"I have not."

"These are two very old species, each inhabiting a number of worlds. We've been working on a trade relationship between them. Well, I have been. Negotiating it."

Reylan lifted her hand and kissed it playfully, almost as though she sensed that Kari had wanted to do that. She seemed really passionate. Kari laughed and Reylan continued. "You will be excited to know that much of it revolves around food, both cultures being passionate foodies. They have exceptional taste."

Kari laughed. "Ooh, people after my own heart."

Reylan laughed back. "Yes, actually, more than you even know. We recently discovered one of the only real things these cultures have in common."

Priest interjected, "one of the things that they both love, more than anything. Is... well. You. "

Suddenly, the floor fell out. Kari felt really lost in this conversation. "What are you talking about?"

Reylan lifted her hand with Kari's in it. And then cupped it with her other hand, warming it as if in illustration. "Both of these cultures adore your show."

Priest looked up. "And they trust you."

Kari felt warm leaning into Reylan, "Oh, my god. Are you serious? That's really flattering."

Priest nodded. "Well, you have fans all over. "

"Am I missing something?" Kari felt like they had approached the point. Maybe she had just missed it.

Reylan clearly tried to be serious. "They trust you. They're close to officiating this deal."

"And they want to do it with you." Priest stood up and smoothed out his long black robe. "In three days."

***

While they talked, Ed grabbed the rest of the set to store for the weekend. Along the way, he tried his best to keep Gossamer occupied.

"So, you don't have a robe?"

She lifted a box to help. Talking about her outfit, Ed noticed how little she was actually wearing. "Nope, I'm still a novitae. In training."

"Ah. But you do have the…" He made the same drawing motion on his forehead. Gossamer picked up on it a lot faster than Kari had.

She smiled. "Yes, I earned my t'kau two weeks ago."

"And it means?" He tried not to be offensive. In some ways, she seemed so much like the people he knew, In some ways, though, she was alien, magical. "I read that it means you are open to having sex with anyone."

"More or less." Gossamer tried to reach up and place the box. Ed was one of those tall people who never realized how much being tall made things possible. He grabbed the box.

"Even out here? Away from the Octagon?"

She nodded.

The two wandered across the back of the set. "And you would?"

"Well, I didn't wear a headband and cover it up."

In his head, Ed tried to figure out how this worked. "So, if someone on the hypertrain just wanted to…"

"We teleported here," she interjected.

"What if someone wanted to have sex with you who didn't… You know, deserve you?" He fumbled.

She shrugged. "You know, none of us deserve any of us."

He opened the door to the lot, trying to shield her eyes from the light. He still had to lock up all the edit suites in the next building. "I mean. Would you have sex with me?"

She stopped and looked up at him, squinting slightly. "Do you want to?"

Ed rubbed his hand through his hair. "I don't know how to answer that."

"You're a smell person, aren't you?"

He looked at her and began walking again. "How could you know that?"

"I've been watching you sniff me." It took Gossamer an extra step or two to keep up with Ed. He slowed down and hunched a bit as he realized.

"Yes. Geez. I'm sorry."

Gossamer grabbed his sleeve. The big black hoodie was like a handle. "Stop. I like smells, too. Do you want to smell my neck?"

He stopped again. "Yes, I do."

"Ok. Now, the way you answered THAT makes me think you really want to." she stepped into him. He could feel her breasts against him behind her slight tank. She put her hand on the back of his neck and pulled his head down into her neck.

Ed inhaled. Without thinking, he wrapped an arm around her waist. "Oh my god, you smell good. Ask me again."

Gossamer whispered, "Do you WANT to have sex with me?"

"More than anything in the world."

She pulled back to look him in the eye. "That was cute. I would love to have sex with you."

He opened the door to the suites in the next building as she squealed.

"Is that an editing room?"

She grabbed his hand and pulled him into the building, toward the suite. "I've always wanted to see one of those…"

Gossamer ran into the messy edit suite. It was surrounded by audio cancelling padding. She stood in the middle, waiting for Ed to open the door. She unhooked her black jean shorts and let them fall to the floor. She wore nothing underneath and he could see a tiny line of black rising up from her root, perfectly groomed. She pulled off her tank.

He realized that these two articles of clothing were all she wore, except for the fishnet pieces and boots, and that she wore them on top, over the mesh. She was nearly naked so quickly. Her breasts were the same olive white as the rest of her, full and pointed upward. They bounced slightly as she walked toward him, still in her boots.

"Oh my god, you're beautiful." Ed struggled to open his jeans. She dropped to her knees in front of him and pulled them down in one motion, reaching for his cock and sliding it, seamlessly, into her mouth.

"A lot of that going around," she laughed, trying to pull his shaft into her throat. He was almost entirely hard already.

Ed moaned a little, whispering apologetically, "I'm not that big.."

She continued to suck him, putting her hands on his ass for balance, "Seriously, do I look like I have a Tardis in me?"

Ed almost tipped over laughing. "Wow."

"Did you just get harder because I made a Dr. Who joke?"

"I definitely did." Sure enough, he was rock-hard now.

She looked behind her for a moment, letting herself fall into the plush sectional couch piece that was being used as a chair. Spreading her legs, she grabbed his hands and pulled him in, aiming his prick directly into her open, waiting cunt.

"Look at all the things I'm learning about you." She pulled at him and he slid inside her.

Ed moaned. "You smell sooo good."

"Yeah?" She spread her legs wider as they began to get into a rhythm. " Do you like the way it smells when you're fucking me?"

"Fuck, yes." Ed was nodding in rhythm as he pumped himself into her. She seemed to open up wider with each motion.

"I love that. I love how you use my little pussy." She lifted her hands up over her head and put them on the back of the chair.

He pushed up on her thighs. Magically, her legs kept moving after every little push. There was no resistance as he felt her legs easily slide backward, so that her knees flanked her head. "Is this ok?"

"It's all okay. Just don't stop. Don't stop until you fill me up. Can you do that?" Ed wished he had another hand so as to grab hers tightly and crush them together, holding her down. The fact that she was still wearing her boots hit him in a wave, turning him on even more.

"Yes. I want to fill you up." He could feel it rising inside him. The rhythm was becoming more primal – more intense.

"Can you fill my hole up?" Gossamer moaned, bringing that moment ever closer.

Ed let himself look at her. She opened her mouth widely for his kiss. He was afraid that if he tracked too closely the lines of her face or the gentle swell of her breasts across her chest, velvet brown tipped, he would cum too quickly. "God, yes. You're so fucking perfect."

"This is perfect. I can't believe your name is Seven, it should be fucking Ten." She laughed as the rocking motion of the chair slammed into the desk behind, sending an award trophy skittering to the floor along with some pens and notepads. "That's not important."

"Nope." To Ed, nothing was important. He heard the sound of the two of them slapping together and it became the most beautiful sound he ever heard.

Gossamer wrapped one hand around his throat to pull him in. She needed to feel more of him against her. "Yes, like that. If you do that, I'm going to cum." He tucked in his head. She grabbed his face with the other hand, drilling her eyes into his.

"Yeah, look at me. Ed, I'm cumming. I'm cumming."

"So am I. Fuck." They came, forcing the chair to upend the desk entirely, knocking out one of the supports and sending the entire contents of the table to the floor in a loud crash. As they lay there laughing, Gossamer wrapped her hands in Ed's hair, moving his head in closer to lap at her nipples.

Ed held on tightly and tried to remember forever how the room smelled.

***

By the time Gossamer and Seven got to the teleport room, Reylan was ready to go, and Kari and Priest were saying their goodbyes. Smiling, Priest looked over at the younger novitae "I see you won a hoodie"

"I'm a winner. Ed wanted to keep my shorts." She lifted the hoodie, showing her bare pussy below and shrugged. "So..."

Reylan waved from the teleport pad. "Well, I think the hoodie thing is one of Earth's most profound rituals." She stuck her tongue out at the young girl and disappeared in a blue flicker of light.

Gossamer giggled as Ed picked her up and placed her on the teleport platform, moving his head in for a long, slow kiss. She wrapped her arms around him in that way that shorter girls do to show how much they enjoy the towering height of their partner. Kari crossed her arms and leaned in to whisper to Priest.

"Did they...?"

Priest smiled and leaned in. "I think so." Kari thought that his face seemed particularly suited for smiling. The sharp jaw and cheekbones that initially looked hard and square to her now looked like a toy machine for smiling, a children's toy, designed to make all children smile back.

Kari breathed in. "See, I can't do that. I can't do what she did, what you all do."

Priest pressed his hand against hers and she automatically held it, like she had done with Reylan. This was very odd for her. She wasn't someone who casually just held hands with people In this case, it just seemed normal. "If you don't want to, no, you certainly can't."

She turned to him. "What if I say no?"

He squeezed her hand comfortingly. "Then it will be no." He leaned in to whisper, "I'll probably still watch your show."

Kari laughed. "Thank you. I only do it for you fans."

Priest looked a bit more serious. "Look, If you say no, we will do what we can. You aren't obligated to do anything." He fished in the pocket of his robe. It suddenly occurred to her that he wasn't wearing anything under his robe either, any more that Reylan was likely wearing anything under hers. It struck her how close she was to a very handsome, nearly naked man who smelled, in reality, like clean teakwood and lemonade.

"Here, take this. It's our internal teleport code. Come by tomorrow and look around. You might get a better idea of what we do." He handed her a thick black metal card with an octagon shape on one side and a four digit number on the other. She'd never seen a teleport code that short before.

She slid it into the pocket of her jeans. "None of you get paid or anything?"

Priest made his way to the platform, still holding her hand. "No. it's one of our rules. But, hey, did you know that this was the first gift ever given to the Octagon?"

Kari looked around. "What was?"

Priest nodded. "Teleportation. From a species called the Ahreee. In appreciation for our very first negotiation."

Kari looked up at him on the platform. It was only an inch or two off the floor, but it magnified their height differences. "I never knew that. And you sold it to the world?"

Priest rubbed her hand and handed it back to her. "We gave it. We don't keep the gifts to ourselves. They are freely given to Earth."

Without thinking, Kari leaned in to hug him goodbye. Priest hugged her tightly, then called out to Ed with a grin. "Seven, bring it in, shorty."

He hugged him, smoothing out his hair.

Kari looked up. "Tomorrow, what time?"

Priest and Gossamer looked at each other. "Anytime you like," he responded. The two faded into a shock of blue light, leaving Kari and Ed standing to watch. Kari could feel the card in her pocket, thick, unyielding metal. For a second, she wondered how long a card like that might last if left outside.

Definitely longer than a person.

***

Kari appeared on the teleport platform at the Octagon a little before six o'clock the next day. She had spent much of the earlier part of the day trying to figure out if she would come or not.

Eventually, her curiosity had won out.

Reylan, Priest, and Gossamer were there, waiting for her arrival. Alongside them was another girl, about the same age as Gossamer. She was a little taller, with long dark hair, and striking Italian features, beautiful pouty lips, covered in obsidian jewelry. Where Gossamer's skin was nearly untouched by tattoos, except for her t'kau, this girl was heavily tattooed with images of birds everywhere.

She also had a t'kau, and wore a black wrap around her neck and another beautiful black wrapped shawl, below her bare breasts, opened to expose a thick pretty triangle of hair between her legs.

Gossamer was holding her hand, dressed much like yesterday, just without the shorts and tank top, exposed as well. The goal for both the girls, it seemed, was to wear beautiful and expressive clothing, just not clothing that actually covered anything.

And while Priest and Reylan each wore their robes, there had been no effort put in, today, to keep them closed. Kari was aware of Priest's barely confined nudity even more vibrantly than the day before.

As soon as Kari faded in, Reylan stepped over to her and held her hand, helping her down from the platform. "Be careful, this one's a little higher than the newer ones."

Kari stepped down into hugs from the entire group. Priest grabbed her other hand and pointed out the new girl. "Kari, this is Zoi, she is also a novitae here. She has a beautiful voice. And of course, I'm sure you forgot everyone else."

"I did, all gone." she smiled. The new girl, Zoi, flashed her a wink.

Gossamer seemed to be the only one worried she wouldn't come. She rubbed her shoulder against Kari's. "I'm really glad you came."

"Seven – I mean – Ed, he says, and I quote, 'tell her I have more hoodies.'"

Gossamer laughed and shot back, "well, tell him that the exchange rate is three shorts per hoodie. Or four. We'll work it out."

Priest continued, "Master Reylan wants to make sure you're settled. Everybody here is available to you the whole time you are here. But we can show you where you will be staying?"

Kari looked up. Before she had stepped on the teleporter, she wasn't sure if she would be leaving or not. By the time she had gotten to the thula where she would stay with Gossamer and Zoi, she had resigned herself.

What was a day or two?

Moving through the hallways of the Octagon was a unique experience.

The building itself was huge. It felt airy and alive. Gray and colored stone walkways opened up to big mosaic balconies that looked down on gardens and pools. All of it seemed bound by white tipped mountain ranges.

And throughout, men and women in long black robes moved back and forth, often accompanied by naked novitae, all exposed somehow, but in their own unique ways. She saw a young man, unmarked in any way by tattoos, clothing, or jewelry walk by, speaking to another man wearing nothing but boots and metal rings around his neck, with a metal chain seemingly connecting the tip of his penis to a black metal belt. She saw a few yolcu, one woman bright orange, covered in elaborate jewelry in a white robe, and another, a tall green man, naked, walking next to a beautiful bald black woman in a red robe with a dark octagon-shaped crystal on her forehead.

The variety of dress and people itself was nearly overwhelming. Throughout it all, Kari wondered about what she didn't know.

What was their story?

The thula was large and it seemed to go on. It reminded Kari of a sort of Greek home. The thulas had five bedrooms and were each occupied by two kezmaki, in the black robes, and three novitae, the ones in training. The bedrooms were large and had their own bathrooms, arrayed around the outside of the space. But the common area of the rooms themselves was based on an interior circle, with a large, heated pool in the center. Kari realized that even though the Octagon didn't pay anyone, there was also nothing here to buy.

The Octagon was a sovereign market socialist nation.

"So, like the Vatican, the Octagon is its own country?" Kari asked as they looked around the thula.

Priest became more animated when he talked about the specifics of all of this. Kari could tell he was a history buff. "It is. It occupies about a third of what was once the city of Bursa, in Turkey."

"So, wait, we're in Turkey?" Kari took all that in. She was used to teleporters. In fact, she herself still lived in Arkansas and only traveled to New York for the show. But this felt so magical.

"Yes, and about a million people live in the nation that is the Octagon. This group of buildings, though, is where all the Officiants live."

"It's really beautiful. And the leader of the Officiants is the head of the country?"

"Yes. Shukkat. She is one of five gerekmaki that provide leadership for the country. They are the ones in red robes, usually. A council."

"All women?"

"Well, it doesn't have to be. And it's complicated. But this entire place was founded by women. It's fairly matriarchal. Are these really the things you want to know?"

"I think I want to know everything. This whole place is crazy. That thing on your head. I could just walk up and kiss you or do what I want to you and it would be ok?"

"Do you want to?" Priest asked.

"That's not the pont. I mean, is that the point?" Kari cocked her head.

"I'd love to kiss you. I like holding your hand. I'm glad you're here. Could you do what you want? Sure. But that still means you have to figure out what you want. It doesn't make it completely easy for you. "

"It's not easy. You know I've had sex with two people in my whole life. One boyfriend and one girlfriend in college. I'm a lost cause."

Priest looked interested, "Did you want to have sex with them?"

Kari thought back. "oh, god, yes."

"And did you enjoy it?"

Kari remembered back through the awkward discomfort, the anxiety.

But the feelings. And the feeling right afterward.

"I really did."

"So, you're batting 100. How is that losing?" Priest smiled.

Kari stepped toward him and put her hands on his chest. She slid his robe open a little and shifted them inside. She lifted her lips and bent her head slightly. Priest met her more than halfway, pressing his lips against hers. As they met, they seemed to relax, to meld and blend in with each other. Kari's mouth opened and she licked at the inside of his lips while he lazily let his lips kiss her back, shaping to her mouth. And when she pulled back, he followed her the last few inches, extending the kiss. She looked up at him.

"You're a really good kisser."

"So are you, Kari Lourdes. You know what the big difference between us is?"

Kari scrunched up her brow, thinking. "I do not."

He whispered, in as sultry a voce as he could muster. "I can't cook a noodle to save my life. Not a pot of water, nothing."

"Oh, a tragedy." Kari pulled back, still holding his hand. "So Reylan lives here, too?"

"She does. She is Vasmek, a little higher than me. I used to be her novitae."

"So you walked around naked after her doing what she wanted?"

"I did. She actually helped me get more comfortable being naked. You might notice that sexually, I'm a bit submissive. So is Gossamer."

Kari swung Priest's hand and moved into the common area.

Zoi and Gossamer were kissing casually in the pool in the center while the taller girl held Gossamer's hands behind her back.

"Zoi is on the other side." He looked at her and laughed.

"So, is there an authority thing? Could they do anything they wanted to you?" Kari pointed toward Gossamer and Zoi.

"Yes, of course. It's not about authority. It's about acceptance." Priest nodded at the pool. "Is it okay if i take my robe off?"

"Sure. it's your place. Is it cool if I leave some things on?"

"Of course. It's your body."

"Woo. Get in here, chef." Gossamer splashed her as Zoi laughed.

"This is the weirdest vacation ever."

"No shit," Zoi yelled out, diving under the water .

"How long has she been here?" Kari asked Gossamer.

"Same as me, about two years. May I introduce you to my college roommate?"

"Holy shit."

Zoi came up for air. "Is everyone talking about me?"

Priest playfully pushed her back underwater. "Yes, continue."

Kari smiled. The truth is, it did seem like a vacation.

Zoi slowly rose up and climbed into Priest's lap. She wrapped her legs around him, pushing his arms back against the edges of the pool as she rode him. Her face came down hard and she kissed him roughly.

Kari realized that she liked him. But she didn't know what way. And nothing here felt like it was meant to or could make her jealous. She felt for his hand and held onto it as Gossamer slid in next to her and cuddled.

She watched as Priest came in Zoi after a number of loud orgasms from her.

Zoi pulled herself up on the edge of the pool like a dancer and sat, leaning back on her hands as Gossamer swam over and began to kiss and lick her between her legs as if in ritual. Behind the thick, curly shock of hair, Kari could see the darker lips of her pussy, almost purple, opening to show the bright pink inside. Gossamer licked away the cum dripping from her, the result of her quick tryst with Priest.

Kari wished for a second she knew what it tasted like. She realized how easy that would be. All she'd have to do is to give the animated little short-haired girl a kiss, quickly.

She looked at Priest and squeezed his hand. She put her other hand on the back of Gossamer's neck, who silently turned and, as if reading her mind, slowly moved in to kiss her. Kari moved in and opened her mouth, kissing the smaller girl softly on the lips. They felt round and wet and impossibly smooth, and the taste was electric and sparkly, slightly salty and more than anything, warm. It was the taste of body warmth, the taste of security, being wrapped in people, defended, swaddled, surrounded. It tasted like the opposite of loneliness, the multiple of togetherness.

She leaned back and Gossamer went back to servicing Zoi's pretty cunt. Kari wished that she had taken her bra off. She wished that she'd been giving something. Why didn't she? She knew what would happen if she did.

Acceptance.

She put her arm around Priest's naked belly and felt his cock graze her arm. She pulled him in a little closer. He wrapped his arm around her. She kissed him again. What if this were a vacation? What if that was all this would really be? A vacation. That would be ok, wouldn't it?

She let her tongue swim in his mouth, taking in the sleekness of his mouth and teeth. Then she leaned over and said, in his ear, "what happens if I say I'll do this?"

"Well," he said, trying his best to keep his lips on her cheek as he spoke.

Kari realized that when he did that, she could hear his voice half in her head. "We take a couple more vacation days and learn a few things."

He moved down and kissed her neck. "And meet some people."

***

They walked down a different path than the one they'd been on earlier. This one was even wider, although less populated. At one point, it curved into a huge garden, half indoor,s half outside. They walked through. Kari looked up, confused as to where the ceiling ended and the open air began. One day, she thought, she'd like to have the blueprints of this place.

They passed an open library space, books lined up for meters in every direction. The ones right out in the open here seemed like fiction. But not human fiction. She paused in front of one showing three orange yolcu in front of what looked to be their home, defending it against some distinctly unfamiliar beasts. The title read, <u>The Consequences of Night</u> and a review next to it pointed out it was a classic bestseller on Narimi Seventeen.

Books from other worlds.

She looked back at Priest. Gingerly, he pulled her forward a meter or so and she looked into an open archway. The library space went on, seemingly forever.

There must have been millions of books. Shakespeares from all over the universe were in there. Kari felt her knees give a little as she moved forward.

A group of novitae walked past, decked out in elegant microclothing that covered nothing. She saw a girl with bright red dyed pubic hair, and a youngish man with an elaborate tail snaking out from an exposed buttplug behind him.

A transgender man had a brilliant copper chain extending from his navel to his clitoris and running through rings in his labia.

"Is it okay for me to walk around like this?" She stopped and looked down at her jeans and linen shirt.

"Sure." Zoi said. Gossamer nodded.

"Technically, you are a guest, you can dress any way you like." Priest explained.

"Technically, nothing is mandatory. It's a tradition that novitae are exposed and that kezmaki wear black robes and stupid clown noses like that one." Zoi pointed to Priest's nose.

"Exactly." Priest twitched his nose, making Kari laugh.

Gossamer grabbed her hand. "Do you want us to dress you up later?"

Kari looked up and realized that no one had ever dressed her. No one had ever kissed her in a warm pool. No one had ever jumped up to hold her hand walking somewhere.

"Yes, I really do." She smiled at Gossamer and felt the sun on her as she smiled back. The rest of the way Gossamer made her squeeze her hand whenever they saw an outfit she liked. And each time she giggled and squeezed back. It became a game to see who could squeeze harder.

"Finally," Priest pushed Zoi down a hallway, making her giggle. They seemed to have a kind of physically aggressive way of being affectionate together. Priest's attitude toward her was different than with Kari, or Gossamer. Where other people she'd met here were playful, Zoi was almost primal. And he treated her that way. It made Kari feel like anything could happen next.

Which was probably good preparation.

A giant blue door opened in front of them and they all moved in. Moving down an interior hallway, it became clear that this was someone's home.

This was where someone lived. It didn't really resemble the thula that they had been in, though. It was about the same size, but sparse, except for a wall of foliage on one side, with a waterfall down the center. In front of this was a long wooden table, simple, but looking as though it had been built from one piece of a massive tree. Looking up, it seemed as though there was no ceiling. A close look showed that it was interactive – a kind of screen. And it showed four moons.

As they approached the table, Kari could see a man in a white robe. The closer she got, however, the more she realized he wasn't any kind of man she'd ever met.

Priest hugged him and so did the girls. He was at least a good head taller than Priest, which made him far taller than Kari. His skin was dark blue, with strips of lighter blue wrapping down his neck, like cable. He seemed to have almost no fat in his face, only thick, harsh cheekbones and orbital ridges that pushed up into his skin, rendering it taught and leathery-looking. He was not from Earth and, to Kari's eyes, accustomed to science fiction novel covers, that much was clear. In the middle of his forehead, though, was a tattoo of an octagon.

Kari felt a strange weight. This was the first time she'd ever been in a room directly with someone not born on Earth. It felt strange and huge and it seemed to twist her around. This man was from another planet.

He smiled widely at her, still hugging Zoi. "This is Kari Lourdes. I haven't seen you since yesterday over some meatballs." He reached out to take her hand. Kari leaned in to hug him. He felt like a series of fiber optic cables wrapped around wood. He was hard and unyielding. But there was something so inviting in his voice, which was deep and resonant.

Priest continued the introduction. "Kari, this is Kerada. He is Vigo. And he is a Kheirobos here."

Kerada looked at her. "And you are not expected to know any of those words."

"Yes, sorry about that. We'll explain it all." Priest looked over at Kerada, "Do you want me to set the table?"

He moved toward a wall that had been nearly invisible to Kari.

"That's great. It's almost done." Kerada bowed slightly to Kari. "tonight, I have the honor of making YOU dinner."

Kari looked around. "Wait, me?"

"With some of your own recipes, but, also lots of love and surprises." Kerada held up a finger and followed Priest.

"Thank you." Kari raised her eyebrows at the girls.

Zoi was leaning over the table, cocking her head. "Is it dress up time yet?"

Gossamer nodded. Kari smiled as the two girls pulled her through an open space in the foliage wall into another room. It was spare as well, looking like a rocky garden.

"I know there is stuff here we can use," Zoi said under her breath as she opened the small closets built into the rock. Kari couldn't see any of them until they were opened. Clearly the girls had been here before. She looked at them. Suddenly, they didn't really seem as naked anymore. Zoi was on her knees, bent over, trying to reach a box in the back. Her ass and pussy were on full display. It was absolutely pornographic but, somehow, not. Gossamer came up behind her and placed her foot under her, so that it was rubbing against the purple lips of her pussy. Zoi pushed back and grinded on it.

Everything seemed like a game. Kari wondered aloud at Zoi, "Hey, how come you didn't come to New York?"

Zoi grabbed the box and shot up. Placing it next to Kari, she ran one hand over herself, much like Vanna White. "Because this…" she made a little flip with her hand, "isn't for covering up."

Kari laughed. "I guess New York has laws about excessive hotness."

Gossamer floated over to her with a beautiful beige and crimson wrap she placed around her neck. It had tassels that drifted casually over her breasts, hiding nothing. "Well, they're not going to let you back in, bitch."

Zoi pressed a spot on the wall and it dissolved into a mirror, lifting Kari over to it by the hand. It really was a beautiful piece.

"Yep, I like it. We lean into the pretty beige with the red trim." Zoi reached around to take off her shirt. Kari nodded. It seemed to her that the younger girl lingered maybe a bit longer than she needed to.

Gossamer pulled Kari's bra off and arranged the tassels. "No black. It's like a nordic goddess. Like this is how Frigga dresses for sex parties."

Kari giggled at that. Her breasts really did look good. And the red was unexpectedly cool. Zoi pulled out some bracelets that went up Kari's arms and snaked through her fingers in the same theme. "We stay away from the hair."

"Right, don't touch the hair." Gossamer agreed.

Kari slipped off her pants and underwear. "Wait, why?"

"It's kind of fucking perfect." Zoi shrugged.

Gossamer wrapped some small thin chains around Kari's waist. "You, you have 'fuck me' hair."

"It's just like, people want to see it move around while fucking you." Zoi shook her, and Kari watched her hair tussle in the mirror. Gossamer attached a series of charms and connecting chains to the ones around her waist. She seemed very serious.

Kari had never been dressed up like a doll before. Suddenly this wave washed over her. These two absolutely stunning girls were just treating her like a life-sized Barbie doll. And they were doing it with so much joy that it was impossible for Kari to miss.

"And this shapes here. Open in front." Gossamer wrapped something around her torso, right under her breasts. At first it seemed like a scarf. It was thin and beige and so pretty. She wrapped it so that it lifted her breasts and then surrounded her belly, opening to expose her pussy, which Kari had kept shaved.

"Wow. I usually hate my belly."

"You look like some kind of hot fertility goddess. I love it." Zoi came up behind her and wrapped her arms around her, kissing her on the cheek. She put her hands over Zoi's, leaning back into her.

She really loved how she looked. And somehow she didn't really feel all that naked. She looked at Gossamer and smiled.

"Now, I'm ready for dinner."

As they stepped back through the green wall opening, they could see that Kerada and Priest had set the table. And there was a good deal of food on it for five people.

Priest stood up and surveyed Kari's new outfit. "That's... Wow. And that's all I have."

Kerada was smiling. He stood until the girls had sat down. He winked at Kari, holding up a glass. "To a woman of beauty, taste, and civility."

They all drank. Kerada sat down as the rest started putting food on their plates. Kari looked confused.

Priest looked over at her. "So, this is a story. Kerada will sit out the first course of the meal."

Kari asked, "how come?"

Priest looked over at Gossamer. "Do you know why?"

She nodded, putting her hand out and holding Kari's. "So, the Vigo, Kerada's race, originally were born on a nearly dead planet. It was almost impossible to grow food there. In fact, often people had to choose to not eat so that younger people, or sickly people, or people in the most need could eat first. The job of the chef first evolved as someone who could cook to make the food last enough to feed everyone."

Zoi took a drink and continued. "And to make sure, the chef would sit out the first course, only eating when it was clear that everyone else was able."

Kari looked over at Kerada. "That is so sad, and beautiful."

Kerada smiled at her. "You see why the idea of the chef is elevated on our planet. And why you are so beloved."

"I'm flattered, but I'm so sorry."

"It's fine, Ms. Lourdes. My people now live on 17 different worlds, manipulated and formed to grow food copiously. None of my people go hungry anymore."

"And I will eat to that." Priest dug into a beautiful dish in front of him.

Kari dipped her spoon into the soup. "This is so like a cremini mushroom. It's spicy, though. And something like thyme?"

"This is really zesty." Zio seemed to enjoy it.

Kari looked over at Kerada. "Ooh. that has a bite. But I really like it. What kinds of peppers?"

Those are Zaharie root peppers from one of our worlds. It's a little modification that we often make to Earth recipes. Our people have a predilection for intense spices."

"Do you dry them, as well?"

"Absolutely." Kerada really seemed to enjoy talking recipes and food with her. And about halfway through the fourth course, it was hard for her to see him as an alien at all anymore.

Kari recognized the sixth course immediately. She looked over at Kerada. "Is that an Osobucco with creamy polenta and gremolata?"

"It's your recipe, with the pork shank instead of veal." Kerada was eating a bit, but more than anything, he was watching.

Kari pulled the dish closer. "Look at that just fall off the bone. And the polenta is so smooth it looks whipped." Kari took a bite. "This is wonderful. It's a very full and complex pepper remoulade here. I am really loving the yolcu additions."

Priest took a drink and smiled at Kerada's delight.

"You seem to be picking up the language here very well.

"I'm trying. So, you are yolcu, but you have a t'kau. And a white robe?"

"The people here in white are Kheirobos."

"They're like tester perfume at the store." Zoi made a face at Kerada.

"I don't know what that means, but if I could catch her, I'd spank her." Kerada and Priest began clearing the plates.

"It's kind of true. Kheirobos are voyagers from various species who live here and help us with information about their people so we can work with them better," Gossamer explained.

"And they help you be intimate with people of their race?" Kari leaned back in her seat. As the conversation moved back to sex, she suddenly realized again how naked she was.

"Among other things." Priest was grabbing her empty plate. She looked up at him. He stopped for a second to continue. "There are over 20 different classifications for genitals for the people that we know across just this arm of the galaxy. Humans have nine. And they are?" He looked at Zoi.

Zoi slid herself up on the part of the table that had been emptied in front of her. She sat crosslegged and sounded off, pointing with both hands to the parts of her body as she called them out, first in English:

"Mind, Vagina, Penis, Anus, Urethra, Mouth, Breasts, Limbs, Skin."

And, then, again with their Octagon names:

"Aatma, Yoni, Lingam, Gudam, Mutramargah, Mukh, Stanam, Angam, Charm."

Kari made a mental note of Priest's teaching style. He tried, when possible, to make the novitae into teachers.

She gave Zoi a rough push, tipping her over on the table. Zoi got up on her hands and knees and glared back at her with the most fervent naked desire she'd ever seen. The darker girl crawled on the table over to her. Kari leaned in to kiss her, falling into the kiss. It was open and wet and alive. She heard Zoi's heart beating through her skin. She lifted her hand to place over her heart. The beat was strong. Her chest was hot and smooth. Kari had never felt this powerful and sexy before. There was something dark and complicated on the other side of it, but she felt like she could be open with this girl. With that one push on the table, Kari felt like she was part of her pack.

The kiss broke off and Zoi smiled, sitting back on the table with her legs spread, hands behind her. Priest and Kerada had cleared it all. The blonde man looked at Gossamer. "What best describes what we just saw?"

"That was a knot." Gossamer shot back.

Kari put her hand on Zoi's and she held onto it tightly. "What's a knot?"

Priest stopped wiping down the table for a second. "I wish I had some props for this. No matter, it works. When you meet someone, the things you like about them are like little soft ropes, pulling you together. This one is their smile. This one is how they pronounce that word you love. This one is their eyes, how they smell, etc. The ropes are floppy and soft. But when you keep adding them, they don't just pile together next to each other. They intertwine. They wrap around. They start to form a knot. And then, one thing might happen. Someone sees you and recognizes your primal energy, for example, and pushes you over. And it pulls it all together. All the ropes. Like a knot."

Zoi squeezed her hand harder as Priest continued. "And a knot can be impenetrable. It can stop a bullet. After time, it can fuse whole. It can feel like one of the strongest things in the world."

Gossamer spoke up. "That's what we try to build here. What we do for petitioners – well, what I'm training to do – is not just about celebrating a contract through sex. It's about building the biggest knot possible - A knot of desire – it's about real acceptance."

Kerada smiled at her. "Here in the octagon we have these 12 principles, broken into six couplets. The fourth is "perfect acceptance is acceptance," and "all rejection is perfect rejection."

"I get that. True acceptance." Kari looked at Zoi. Zoi smiled and looked at her with a look that seemed to slam the point home. Zoi behaved like she wanted every part of her, exhaustively. Kari thought she could get lost in that look.

"If I do this... can I learn everything I need to in two days?"

Kerada stepped over to her and knelt next to her. "in a way, you're ready now. I've watched your show. You're kind." He looked over at Zoi. "What's the third couplet, puppy?"

Zoi leaned in to Kari and cradled her face with her hands. Kari couldn't help but remember Reylan telling her that Zoi had a beautiful voice as she whispered, like a love poem, "With Kindness, there is Wisdom. With Deprivation, there is atrophy," and kissed her. Kari reached under her and pulled her closer by the globes of her ass. Zoi's legs parted around her and the kiss sunk in deeper.

By the time Kari came up for air, the other three were ready to start. She looked at Kerada, kneeling in front of her. "The Vigo are my people. You will learn a lot about them. But IF you decide you want to do this, you should know what the experience will be like."

"Do we have sex? You and me?"

Priest jumped in. "You absolutely don't have to. You decide what you do. We thought you should at least see what this is about."

Kerada stood up. "My people have most of the same genitalia as yours. Except for the reproductive ones."

Zoi clarified, "They have a class 14 and class 15, instead of a Class 2 or 3."

"What is a 14 and 15?"

Priest looked around the room. "Do you want to see?"

Zoi leaned in to her. "You really want to see, trust me."

Kari absentmindedly put her hand near Zoi's pussy. Zoi sucked in a breath and moved forward, pushing two of Kari's fingers inside. Kari could feel Zoi squeezing her fingers. "Ok, I would like to see."

Kerada pulled open his white robe and slid it off, folding it and tossing it on the table. Kari felt like some strange decadent queen with her fingers inside Zoi while this man paraded nude for her.

She looked at him. The cables of light blue spanned his entire body. They were like hard tubes wrapping around and through his darker blue flesh. Just like in his face, he appeared to have virtually no fat. As she ran her eyes down toward where his legs met, it seemed, for a moment, as though there was just a smallish bulge, much like you might find on a ken doll.

Priest played the part of narrating to explain what she was seeing. "Here, we call it a Sarpaah when any species has a collection of smaller prehensile extensions that can work together. In Vigo culture, theirs is called R'kash."

The area between Kerada's legs seemed to open up and Kari could now see 12 distinct tentacles thicken up and extend themselves, waving like cilia in water. It was beautiful.

"Oh my god." This was becoming more and more real to Kari.

"Would you like to see how this works?" Kerada asked.

Kari felt how wet Zoi was. She grabbed her by the hair and pulled back, kissing her ear. "Can you show me on her?"

Zoi breathed in and nodded. She held her hands out for Kari. Kari pulled her hand out and held onto both of Zoi's with one hand. With the other, she held tight to her hair. "Where do you want her?" It was hard to think about anything else but how Zoi must be feeling. Kari wondered if she was being primal enough. She looked down to see the shimmer of liquid pooling between the darker girl's legs and concluded she was.

Gossamer moved down to the other side of the table. "Drag her over here."

Kerada positioned himself at the other side of the table as Kari dragged the girl toward him. Kari wasn't sure what had come over her, but she KNEW in her heart that this would be more fun for Zoi if she was pretending to force her. She leaned in to whisper at her.

"Will you tell me if I go too far?"

Zoi snorted, letting out a quick laugh. She leaned into Kari's ear. "I'll give you a medal if you can go too far."

Kari flipped her over so that she was on her back, her head facing the edge of the table where Kerada stood. She dug into Zoi's pussy with her left hand and pulled her by the neck with the other, until her face was right near the place where his legs met. Kerada leaned down and grabbed Zoi's breasts while he placed the area over her mouth.

Zoi reached back and clamped her nails onto Kerada's ass, pulling him in. Priest and Gossamer watched as his r'kash grew, the tentacles becoming thick as fingers. They played over her face and, one by one, dug down into her mouth, and into her throat. They seemed to be able to operate independently or together. Six of them tightened into a thick corded rope, the girth of a large cock, and he began to fuck her face.

Zoi spit up and choked for a moment, taking in the large, now unified, rod. But she held on tight with her hands. Zoi spread her legs backbreakingly wide as Kari pushed her fingers in and out of her cunt, pressing down on her belly with the other hand, how she liked to masturbate herself at home.

"A Vigo can use the tendrils one at a time or in groups." Priest explained. "And ejaculate from any of them at least a few times per session. And there is a lot of ejaculate."

Priest looked up at Kerada who pumped harder into Zoi's open mouth. He pulled hard on her breasts as Kari could feel the girl's pussy begin to spray. Zoi seemed to loosen up and move like a wave as the pool on the table thickened. Suddenly Zoi arched her back and came in one solid gush, reaching up Kari's arm, as she pulled Kerada's coiled members deeper into her throat. Pale blue liquid poured from the sides of her mouth and over her lips. It ran down her face and onto her breasts as Kerada finished deep inside her throat.

Zoi hugged his body to her, trying not to let go until both of their waves were over.

Priest continued to narrate. "A Vigo like Kerada here could now ejaculate again immediately with the other six khas, and then again right after with the first. He has a low refractory time and each one could, technically, cum separately."

Zoi lazily pulled herself up and crawled back over to Kari. Kari leaned in and licked at her lips and face, tasting the blue liquid. It was actually kind of spicy. Not salty at all. She kissed Zoi, trying to get accustomed to the taste. She was eating the cum of a man who was born on a different planet.

Zoi whispered in her ear, "do you want to try? It's ok if you don't…"

Kari dug her tongue into Zoi's mouth. Zoi tried to open it as far as it would go, giving the blonde woman full access.

"Do you want to make me?"

Zoi instantly changed. In a split second, she went from a responsive puppy to a bear, strong, vicious, every movement thick and relentless. She shot up, wrapping her right hand around Kari's throat and resting the other between her legs, fingers just touching the inside of her cunt. She pushed her down and pulled her to the end of the table.

For a moment, Kari felt hyper-aware of herself, her body, scared. But that seemed to vanish under the intensity of Zoi's assault.

Kari looked up and saw Zoi's belly over her face. She licked at it, tasting her sweat dripping into her mouth. She rubbed her face into it, trying to get more of her to swallow. Gossamer unhooked the simple little chain between Kari's legs – the only thing covering her shaved cunt, and spread her legs at the end of the table. Zoi swung her right leg over, placing her ass directly over the blonde woman's face, as she grabbed at her ankles, pulling her legs open.

Kari felt the hard wood digging into her back as her legs lifted up over her head. For a moment, she was self conscious about her belly, folding up as she bent. She felt exposed and wild and made herself not think about it.

The hair between Zoi's legs dripped excess cunt juice onto her face. She opened her mouth, moving her head up to clamp it onto the Italian girl's open pussy. She dug her face in, letting her nose comfortably slip into the wet space made by her asshole as she sucked. Kari had a sense she could make Zoi squirt again just like this, right into her mouth.

Through all this, she had almost forgotten what was about to happen. Kerada's r'kash tendrils played over her pussy, touching her everywhere. She felt one specifically seem to wrap around her clit and pull on it, pulsing up and down, almost as though jacking off a tiny penis. They moved independently in a way that felt completely alien and jarring to her. She felt like someone had dropped her cunt into a box of garden snakes, each about the thickness of a finger, but growing, moving.

Kerada's body seemed to run hotter than hers and she could feel it. Everywhere her skin touched his felt like a heating pad, warming, wet, electric.

She felt one of the tendrils slide into her asshole, feeling more like a long tongue than anything. It ascended into her, past the place where her nerves were, into the abyss inside her. It made her panic for a moment. Another one slid in to follow it, and another.

The three in her ass now merged, corded around each other, building what felt like a ridged, undulating device, pumping over and over.

Kari had never felt anything like it before. She felt her belly shake and contract from the dual sensations in her clitoris and ass, sucking harder at Zoi's juice filled holes. She moaned, leaning into the beautiful pussy in front of her. She wanted Zoi to cum in her mouth as she was cumming. Calling out, she sucked harder, wrapping her lips over Zoi's clit and pumping it, her face slipping in and out of her, covered in her.

Kari's pussy felt so empty as she came, wet jets pushing out in rhythm on the table. Her legs spread even wider, trying to make room for her pussy to be filled. She called out, "please, please" as her ass lifted, pushing her cunt up and out. Kari imagined Zoi watching as Kerada's remaining tendrils formed a ridged phallus and slid into her wide open bare hole, rotating and reaching in her. The tip of it spread open and began to massage the places inside her as Kerada pushed it in and out in an escalating rhythm.

She felt a group of tendrils inside her play up against her g-spot, while a group seemed to press deep into her. A part of her brain that wanted nothing more than to submit to this was triggered, causing her to drop her arms on the table and stop controlling her legs, Zoi grinding harder and harder on her face while Kerada moaned and bucked, riding her holes.

She felt the last of his tiny tendrils enter her urethra and it was psychologically the last straw. He was inside her everywhere. She screamed and came, gushing onto the blue tendrils inside her everywhere, invading every part of her. Kerada heard her and bucked, cumming inside her from every tentacle.

This sensation was like nothing Kari could have ever imagined. It felt like someone had turned on a hot water faucet pouring into every hole in her body. Hot blue cum poured into her pussy, up her ass, even into her urethra, filling her everywhere, while Zoi let loose on top of her, grinding her own cum into her mouth. She imagined the need from both of them as they clamped on to her, riding the waves until they finished.

There was so much cum. She let her knees fall outward, relaxing her core, letting the blue liquid seep into her everywhere, hot and invasive.

Finally, after Zoi had finished, she wrapped her arms around her, holding tight to her ass, and slowly made out with her cunt, wishing the warmth inside her would stay that way forever.

***

The stars were out when they made their way to the balcony. Gossamer tossed little bits of wood into the fire burning in the stone pit in the center of it. The balcony was wide open, but surrounded by a diverse range of flowers and plants. Kari was told that they were all of Earth origin, but they certainly didn't seem like it as they filtered the moonlight onto the stone floor.

Priest and the rest sat around the edges of the fire while Kerada tried his best to detail the situation with his people. "This you should hear from someone a little more objective." He looked up and raised his voice slightly. "Dorothy...?"

"Yes, Kerada, how is your night?" Kari could hear a woman's voice, soft, with a slight accent she couldn't place, come from all around her. It was hard to determine the source.

"Where is that coming from?"

"Hello, Kari. I'm Dorothy, the primary intelligent interface of the Octagon. And you aren't technically hearing me. I'm a mnemonic primary lobe transference tool that communicates directly to your brain."

"Ok, thank you." Kari realized now that the sound didn't change when she moved her head. At the same time, Dorothy SEEMED sort of human.

"You are very welcome. Kerada, you wanted something?"

"Yes, I did. Would you mind giving us an objective account of the history of the Vigo and Encantada peoples. "

"I would love to. Objective?"

"Don't worry about my feelings, Dorothy."

"Ok, Kerada. Thousands of years ago, the Vigo fought to remake their home world, Virugar. Experiments to render it more opulent, thought had backfired, causing many more on the planet to starve. They poured their remaining resources into interstellar travel, managing to bring nearly 10% of their planetary population to a nearby M-type world. The colonists on this new world of Voru thrived and began sending food and materials back to Virugar that enabled them to restart the ecology of their homeworld. But nearly half the population had died in the process and the remaining people became cold and warlike."

"The Vigo became obsessed with finding new worlds and struck out to find 22 new ones. Of those, 10 were clear of dispute. The remaining 12 were also being colonized by the Encantada, a race that had also undergone extreme deprivation. Wars were fought for over 200 years for the rights to those 12 planets. In 2052, a peace was declared here at the Octagon, officiated by Shukkat and Zehra. During those negotiations, it was determined that six of the planets would be ceded to the Vigo and the other six to the Encantada. "

"It was also decided that the Vigo had been punitive and criminally violent in their execution of the engagements. The treaty called for a reassessment of the situation in 20 years. If a normative trade relationship could be established, the races agreed to live amicably and trade. If that proved impossible after 20 years, The Vigo agreed to allow the Encantada to take, by right of conquest, the outlier planet Kallistae."

"It is speculated that the taking of this planet would result in the deaths of over a billion people."

"The normative trade pact is due at the end of the 20 year assessment period, which will be in 46 hours from now."

It was unnaturally quiet as Dorothy's voice faded from their heads. The night was lit up with shifting reds and oranges, colors pulled from the fire as it flickered across all five faces and painted the stone around them.

Gossamer looked over to see Kari with her head in her hands. She got up to put her hand on her shoulder.

Kari pulled away, shooting up on uncertain legs. Tears ran down her face. Her voice cracked. "A billion people. This is insane. This is... I can't do this. I'm sorry."

Priest stood up as she ran to the door. Outside the front door he called out. She pulled away.

"I'm so sorry. I know that's a lot."

"It's a billion people, Priest. Anyone in the world is more qualified than me." Kari felt like she was hyperventilating.

Priest reached out. "It's ok. Can I hug you?"

For a second, Kari processed the library they had passed. It was everything. Entire worlds of information. Great minds and thoughts and experiences from everywhere in the universe. From places she would never even be able to pronounce.

She knew nothing. A billion people.

"Please. Can I go home? Please?" Her shoulders shook as she sobbed. Her breathing was heavy and labored. She could hear her heartbeat.

Priest tried his best to make his voice calm and soothing. "It's ok. C'mon. Let's get you home. We'll get you home, ok?"

Kari avoided his eyes all the way to the transporter. She tried to drown out the sounds of people laughing and having fun in the corridors.

She didn't raise her eyes again until she was sitting back at the studio on the breakroom floor, covered in a t-shirt and a tablecloth.

And that's where she slept.

***

Kari lifted her head and shifted uncomfortably. Maybe the floor wasn't the place to sleep. Seven was sitting next to her in a red hoodie, his hair looking likely worse than hers. He was quietly bouncing a ball off the wall. She took a deep breath and sat up.

He smiled at her. "Hey, Bizarro"

She liked his warmth next to her. She didn't feel much like she deserved it. "Oh. Hey. I'm sorry."

Ed sent the little black rubber ball to the far wall and caught it. "You know we don't have a show for another two days?"

"I know. I didn't want to go home. Why are YOU here?"

"Oh, I pretty much live in the edit room. We're neighbors. It's smaller than this. But it has charm."

"Is that a handball?" Kari tried to catch it on its return this time. Ed caught it, handing it to her so she could throw it.

"How did it go at the place?"

"Have you talked to Gossamer?" The ball bounced off a wall corner, forcing Seven to scramble to grab it under the table. She looked up at him.

"I have. Not about anything important. Just when we're getting together and something about the very complicated economy of shorts to hoodies."

"Ha. Very nice."

"It seems like it leans my way, so…" He slid down the sink and sat back next to her.

She took a deep breath. "I don't think it went that well."

"I'm sorry." He leaned in. "That'll make the showrunners happy. They are a little freaked by all this. I think they don't want you connected to something they think is a sex cult."

"The Octagon isn't a cult." Kari grabbed the ball from his hand and lofted it, catching it again.

"I know that. Did you get to hang out with Gossamer? I bet she's having sex with an alien right now."

"I did. I like her." She turned in to him and tried to fix his hair. It hit her that she never realized Seven was one of her best friends. His hair was not playing along, though. "She's amazing. Oh, and it's not alien. It's yolcu. Voyager. We say yolcu – voyager – out of understanding that travel broadens you, it lets you grow. When I call someone an alien I am saying that all I know about them is that they don't belong. When I call someone yolcu I'm saying that all I know about them is that they have grown, learned."

Ed hung on every word. "That's... really cool. You talked to them?"

"I did."

"Can I ask?"

Kari thought. It seemed like a strange place to start lying. "Yes. Yes, I did have sex with a... voyager. I guess."

She could feel Ed's excitement. "Oh my god. How was it?"

The night before flashed in front of her. Not just the joy of it, or the release. This morning, there was something different, as well. She was so fearless last night, but today all she had was fear. "It was... it was really good." She put her head down on Seven's shoulder and cried." It was nice."

He pulled her in close and petted her hair. "I'm sorry, you don't have to talk about anything. I'm sorry. I've never seen you like this before.

I mean, you're always so… are you ok?"

She nodded. "Do you want to just sit with me?"

Ed made a point to settle in. He pulled her close. "Of course. I can sit here with you until the next show if you want."

She slid in and put her head down in his lap. He put his hands on her hair and tried to make her feel safe, handing her a napkin to wipe her eyes."

She shifted and rested her head on a small lump in his hoodie.

"You have her shorts in your pocket still?"

"I do."

"Nice."

**

She spent the rest of the day cleaning the studio. Seven was nearby, also refusing to go home. It seemed like he was afraid to leave her. She wished she could figure out how to talk to him about all of this, but all of it was so outside anything they ever experienced. How could she foist that on him? Did he have the tools to think about a whole planet dying? Hell, did she?

After dinner, Kari made her way up to the rooftop. The roof for the main studio building was where most of the events happened at night. There was a bar and a suite of padded conversation pits. The view was remarkable, the river to one side, stretching out with a subtle mystery, the dark greens of the park to the other. The warmth of the night framed Kari leaning against the chest-high brink embankment that surrounded the rooftop on one side, trying to see as far into Manhattan as she could.

It was beautiful here, too.

She turned and saw Zoi step out of the stairwell and move directly to the right of her. She was wearing a black Mickey Mouse shirt many times her size. She slid closer, breathing a little hard, leading Kari to think that she had taken the stairs the whole way.

"Your friend Seven said you'd be up here."

Kari turned to her. "You crazy bitch. You're wearing a shirt."

She looked down, as though just now noticing. "For exactly five minutes." Pulling off the shirt, she tossed it as far as she could over the edge. She was completely naked underneath. "And there it goes." She looked at Kari. "That was probably a bad idea."

Kari followed the shirt down with her eyes as it swam to the ground in the warm air currents running along the massive brick building. "You hate the outside world."

"Well, YOU'RE here…"

"Let me guess, you want to try to make me come back and do this?"

Zoi turned to her and leaned. "No. I get it. I've been a novitae for two years. I've read every book in that library, twice probably. And I don't think I'd be ready. Why would I expect you to be?"

Kari took her in. "YOU would be."

Zoi reached over to take her hand. It was warm and Kari felt a kind of electricity that didn't happen with other people or objects or, really, anything. "Look, I get it. If you didn't freak out about a billion people dying, you'd sort of be a shitty person."

"Then why are you here?"

The darker girl shook her hair as if to establish her place here in the real world, in the warm Manhattan night. Maybe she was here to make this place magic, too. It all tumbled out of her mouth. "I thought we'd make out a little, I could listen to you. Maybe suck your pussy for a while but you try not to cum so I can be down there for a while."

She went on. "Maybe piss all over me. Maybe we wrestle. Talk, I dunno. You could feed me. I wouldn't say no. I'm not proud."

Kari's stomach rippled as she laughed involuntarily, pulling her hand closer. "Oh my god, that sounds amazing. I'll definitely end with that last one."

Zoi paused. "I know this hurts. I want to be something you can lean on to make it better. "

"Even though I can't do this?"

She moved in and spoke right next to her ear. "Even still."

Kari leaned into her, feeling her breasts rub against her. She suddenly wished she were naked, too. She remembered the tiny chain that hung from her waist yesterday, rubbing up against her clit, reminding her it was there, every minute. That she was alive.

"So you really came just to be with me?"

"Is that so hard to believe?"

Kari pulled Zoi's long hair back and looked at her face. It was perfect, the way humans are almost never perfect but a cat's face can be. The way it reminds you that perfect things happen. She kissed her forehead. "I think your octagon ruined me forever."

"How so?" Zoi put her hands on Kari's forearms.

She leaned in. "Because of you, I'm too turned on to think straight when I see that stupid shape on your head."

"Oh yeah?"

Kari whispered. "Kiss me."

Zoi pulled her in closer and opened her mouth, devouring Kari's lips, pulling them in. Her hands explored the back of her head, creating a seal.

Kari pulled back and whispered louder, "harder."

The darker girl pulled at her, forcing her tongue down Kari's throat, pulling her mouth open.

"Now, get my pants off as fast as you can and get your tongue in my ass."

"Yes." Zoi yanked at her pants, ripping the waistband, shoving them down and off. She pulled aside Kari's slight pale mesh panties and tore at them, pushing her down into the nearest conversation pit, pulling the cheeks of her ass apart as she tore the underwear into strips, digging her tongue into Kari's open asshole and fucking it.

"Fuck. Yes. Suck me," she moaned. Zoi sucked on her ass, slapping the bright white globes with her fist as she pushed her face deeper inside her, into Kari's root. Kari leaned forward onto her hands and knees and slipped, falling over the back of the overstuffed pit couch, her legs spread, imprisoned. She pushed back.

Zoi growled. "I like how you fight. Let me see how strong." She flipped her over and slapped her breast over and over, pushing her knee into the space between Kari's legs, feeling the wet, sloppy intensity of her.

Kari taunted her. "C'mon. Can you get in there? Do you want it?" She pushed up her pussy for Zoi to jam her fingers in it, pressing her lips down hard on her mouth. Kari bucked against her hand, pushing down, trying to swallow it with her pussy. She slapped Zoi across the face, driving her harder, deeper. Kari could feel Zoi's fingers on her G spot and all she wanted was to whip her into a frenzy so she would push past everything into her. She breathed harder, grabbing Zoi's breast with a claw-like hand and yanking her in closer with it.

Kari was close to cumming, faster than she ever had. She looked up at Zoi, whimpering. "Harder. Come here. Hit me. Fight me."

Zoi punched her chest, letting her hand run up to the nipple, grabbing it and twisting it in her fingers, pulling her closer while her other hand violated her cunt, digging at her little spot. Kari opened her mouth and Zoi spit into it, pumping her fist in Kari until her legs fell open and she gave up, a stream of liquid pouring over Zoi's hand, lost in the swell of her contracting hole.

Zoi slid down, collapsing into her. Kari lifted her hands to her head and laid there, wishing she could be crushed flat.

Zoi whispered, "are you ok?"

"That was wonderful. Why can't it just be that?" She sat up, holding Zoi's hands. "I don't know how to do this, but I don't know how to not do it. What if I give up and they die anyway?" Her eyes welled up.

"It's not your fault."

"What if I do try and I fuck it up?"

Zoi pulled at her hands, drawing her in closer. "It's not your fault."

Kari stood up, pulling the remains of her panties off and moving toward the red ridge at the end of the rooftop, wiping her eyes. "No matter what, people are going to die. It's more people than I've ever seen in my life. I'm never going to see a billion people."

"It's. Not. Your. Fault."

Kari stood there in the glow of the toy lights of the rooftop bar and waved her arms. "But it WILL BE MY FAULT." she yelled into the night. "Being there, in your home, it IS like a vacation. When you touch me, I feel like I'm on vacation. I feel lucky, I feel like I'm something privileged."

Zoi looked up. "That's good. That's great."

"But I'm just some tourist. I don't know what I'm doing. I don't belong with you. I don't belong there. You said it yourself, you've read every one of those books."

"I'll tell you now, some of them sucked." Zoi stood up and pushed the couch section back where it belonged.

"I didn't earn this from you. I didn't earn it from them." Kari turned around and looked off the roof. Zoi moved over next to her.

"What are you talking about?"

She turned. "Your t'kau. You are free use. I could be anyone."

Zoi crossed her arms and shook her head. "I don't think you understand how any of this works."

Kari needed to be wild. She needed to experience that so she could let go. She had things to say. She realized that what Zoi had just done for her opened a floodgate. And there was something riding that wave.

"You're right. I don't. That's why I don't deserve this. I can't do it. I'm not some evolved super sex Jedi."

She paused. "What if I'm in love with you?"

Zoi smiled, moving in closer. "Fine, then we'll fall in love. If that happens, we'll be lucky."

Kari pushed her. "How can you just say things like that? Just give up control?"

"Oh, I'm all about control, man. I control me. And I DO love you. I'd like to find out if I could love you in different ways, too." She stopped for a second and pushed her back in such an intentional way that it made Kari smile.

The smile dropped as Kari looked down. "And how will you look at me if I let those people die? Or, even worse, if I cause them to die?"

Zoi lifted her head and looked Kari in the eye. "I will look at you just like this and tell you. It's not your fault." Kari's lips pulled up in the center and she began to cry. Her voice was softer, as though all of the adult had fallen away, leaving only the little girl.

"You won't want me anymore."

Zoi stood up straight and put her hands on her waist. "That's not true."

Kari wiped her eyes. "I see you. All you want to do is to give yourself to make the world better. If the Octagon didn't exist, you would fucking invent it."

Zoi shook her head, even as she agreed. "That's not untrue. I'm a poly sci drop-out who spent every day in school waiting for the weekend so I could slut it up. I had a boyfriend who let four of his friends run a train on me and then said I'd never be anything useful because of it, while he copied off my homework so his dumb ass could fucking graduate. Yeah, I hate the outside world. I'm exactly where I fucking belong." She put her hand on Kari's neck, pulling her closer.

Kari looked defiant. "Then why are you here? In a Mickey Mouse shirt?"

"Because maybe I belong with you, too. Is that ok? Is that something you can deal with? And maybe that was the only shirt I could find. I do want to do something good. And so do you. And if all you can think about is a billion dead babies, not the good you can do, all I can do is take your mind off it and love you." She kissed Kari hard, wrapping her arms around her. Kari leaned in until she could feel her heartbeat.

"To be clear, they wouldn't all be babies."

Zoi smiled. "No, I don't think people predominantly send babies to war." They rocked back and forth.

Kari kissed her neck and whispered, "they fight like shit."

***

It was 2AM when Kari and Zoi returned to the thula and opened the door to Priest's room. It was sparse and clean and covered in plants, with a massive fishtank as the only light, glowing from an internal lamp, filtering and projecting flickering waves of icy blue on the walls around them. They padded in naked, reveling in the womblike warmth of the room.

Kari pushed Zoi into the bed next to the sleeping kezmek and leaned in, kissing her full on the lips. Zoi pulled her in, opening the sheets and moving the blonde woman so she was positioned over Priest.

Kari reached down and put her hand on his half-ready cock, placing it in the groove of the entryway between her legs. She moved back and forth on it, watching him shift, giggling with Zoi.

Once it had hardened sufficiently, she slid it between her pussy lips and sat down, pulling his member inside her. She held Zoi's hand as she slowly moved back and forth, feeling Priest grow harder inside her.

He began to moan a little in his sleep as Zoi kissed his shoulder and neck, finally letting her lips brush against his. His eyes opened and he saw Kari.

He smiled. "Oh. You're back. Oh, damn. That's good."

Zoi placed his hands behind his head and kissed him harder.

Kari looked down, drilling her eyes into his. "I'm going to do this. But I only have eighteen hours to learn everything." Kari was surprising herself with her own directness. She wondered for a moment if being surrounded by a matriarchal organization was making her more like...well, like this.

Priest looked up at her. "Are you sure?"

She pushed down harder, moving back and forth. She felt Zoi's hand under her, playing with his balls. "What can I learn in the time I have left?"

He breathed a little faster. "A lot, really."

"Will you help me?" She pressed down, feeling the tip of his prick push against her spot.

"Of course," he responded, his hands still over his head.

Kari was in complete control, moving to place his dick right where she wanted it. "This feels really good, by the way."

He seemed partially hypnotized by the power exchange. Kari thought about how she was using him. His breath was following her movements, "It really does."

She smiled at Zoi, giving her a quick kiss, speaking to Priest without looking at him. "Can you hang in there while I cum a few times on you?"

Zoi bit his ear, pulling at his hands to stretch him out. "I'm a professional. But you know. Maybe don't say that word."

"Cum?"

Zoi whispered in his ear, "Do you like the feel of that pussy? I mean, I love that pussy."

Priest was clearly trying to control his breathing as Kari increased her rhythm. "Maybe not that one, either."

The dark haired girl smiled and looked up at Kari. "This seems really restrictive."

She was moving back and forth hard and fast now, pushing his cock deep up inside her. She spoke in rhythm. "Like my free speech is being impinged upon."

Zoi squeezed his balls, pushing even more of him up inside Kari's cunt. "I probably can't even play with his balls like this."

Kari rubbed her clit on Priest's root as she felt his dick slam into her g-spot again and again. She closed her eyes. "It's a goddamn human rights violation."

Priest moaned under his breath, "fuck."

"How about this? If you cum before she does, I get to peg you." Zoi pressed down, kissing him hard. He looked up at her, half over the top. Kari could see he was about to cum.

"You're actually evil. She's redeemable. You're a lost cause." Priest smiled at her.

Zoi grabbed his face and squeezed. "We probably have to peg you anyway for this demonstration. Do you want to get bent over and fucked?

"That's good. Good boy. I'm cumming. Zoi, I'm cumming." Kari felt him rise up inside her.

Zoi cheered her on. "C'mon, baby. Use that fucking dick." She climbed up and placed her pussy directly on his face, pressing down.

Kari wrapped her arms around her as Zoi's breasts bounced from the rhythm of riding his face. "You look so good."

"So do you, baby. Just get what you can." Zoi rode harder, aware that priest could still hear her, even as his face was jammed in her open pussy.

Kari twisted her nipples until Zoi breaked in sharply. "Are you going to cum on his face?"

She shook and leaned into the torture. "Yeah. His tongue is all the way in. Fuck this is good."

Kari was suddenly overwhelmed with a desire to know. To know this girl from top to bottom. She realized that every new thing she learned was like a little gift. "Tell me something about you."

"I always wanted to be a singer when I was really little," she blurted out.

"Would you sing for me, sometimes?" Kari pleaded.

"I will. Right in your ear." Zoi looked as though she was close to cumming. She dipped her head and moved. "Tell me something about you."

"Well. Technically," Kari smiled. "And this is a true story. Technically, I had sex with someone from another planet before I had my first human threesome. I'm all over the place."

Zoi thought for a moment about Priest suffocating under her as his mouth worked on her cunt hungrily, and it put her over the edge. "That sounds like a great story."

"I'm going to cum again."

"Ok, me, too." She locked eyes with Kari.

"Oh. I feel him cumming inside me. That's so nice."

"You're beautiful." Zoi put her hands on Kari's cheeks and kissed her.

Kari leaned into the kiss, wishing the moment would drag out. "So are you." Both of them slowed until the room was so quiet you could hear the slight movement of water in the fishtank, microcurrents built by the flex of tiny tails and fins in an ecosystem still spraying electric blue light around a room filled with foreign air and forms. Priest would say that the tank was his favorite way to feel the energy of minds that evolved so differently, in their own homes, inches away, and each was a tiny voyager, far from the place it was born but comfortable in a home that he lovingly cared for. Zoi thought about how far from home both of them were.

"Are you ready for the rest of this training?" She whispered.

***

The alarm woke them up at seven and the three of them moved into the dining area. They'd spent a few hours more talking about the couplets, inspiration, ideas, and the specifics of the trade agreement between the Vigo and the Encantada while falling back and forth into sleep. Kari felt a little more capable. She understood a little better.

She knew she was still not prepared.

Reylan and Gossamer were both seated nude, crosslegged around the table that was recessed into the floor. Gossamer jumped up to hug Kari.

"You're back. I heard you all early this morning." Kari wrapped her arms around her and smiled at Reylan.

"How is your sister?" Kari dragged Gossamer along with her comically to greet the other woman at the table. Reylan stood up and hugged them both.

"She's wonderful. She's a fan of yours, too, you know."

"I'm trying to imagine the two of you just hanging out in New York at a bar somewhere." Kari sat down, sliding her legs into the hole in the floor that ran around the table. Gossamer started to put a plate together for her full of fruit from containers on the table.

"Well, for the purpose of your fantasy, while we are not biological sisters, we look disturbingly alike." Reylan laughed and handed her a mug of some warm tea. Kari noticed that she was likely more covered in tattoos than even Zoi, her skin darker, too, by quite a few shades. She was a few years older than Kari, but was considerably taller. She was magnificent, if she had to admit it to herself. As the woman got up to bring a few more items to the table, Kari noticed a few deep scars on the backs of her legs. Somehow, on this beautiful woman, every tiny imperfection was just a mystery making you want to know more. The fact that she had lived made it easier to sit next to her and listen.

And between her and Priest, they seemed to have a lifetime's worth of knowledge on mediation, conflict resolution, achieving compromise. Even on holding yourself together as you waded through it all.

She looked at Priest as he slid in next to Zoi, nearly pushing her off the floor-level bench and stealing a banana from her plate. She laughed and pushed back. She imagined at this point he owed her a few pushes.

"You went over the basics of the deal?" Reyland asked Priest. He nodded, grabbing some fruit as well.

"Yes. We discussed the original deal, what's expected, what has been agreed to. We talked about the essentials of what is going to happen."

"Great." Reylan smiled. She seemed to have a natural authority that she didn't have to cover up here, either. She looked over at Kari.

"One of the things we need to remember is that it's not necessary that we agree with the compromise or that we like it. It's not ours to like. And it certainly won't be your fault if it doesn't end up where we hope."

Reylan had clearly been let in on the details of the previous night. She slid her hand over and held Kari's, like she did before. It felt familiar and comfortable.

"Right. I guess I get that."

Priest interjected, "you're going to go in that room and you are going to celebrate with them, or mourn with them, or some bizarre combination of the two."

"Mourn?" Kari wasn't sure if she understood his use of the word.

Reylan explained, "letting go of anything, even to get something better. Leaving a bad situation, changing for something better. There is still mourning that comes with that."

Kari nodded. Reylan Leaned in. "Rather than try to pour a million things into your brain that will only make you nervous, we're going to depend on the fact that they really like you, that you are essentially a kind person, and that they probably wouldn't be here if they didn't want to make this deal. How does that sound?"

Kari hoped all of that was true, honestly. "I like it."

Priest reached around Zoi for her hand and explained, "We are due at eight o'clock for the start of the ceremony. Before that we need to make sure you are rested. And we have one more thing to go over at the Zucaro."

Kari looked over at Zoi sitting next to her. The darker girl winked at her as she shot up. "It's kind of a sex gym." She leaned in. "This will be fun."

***

Zoi had dressed her up before they made their way to the Zucaro. She was wearing a pretty white wrap with blue fringes around her neck and a blue and white shaping wrap around her waist that opened in front and back, leaving her exposed. She wore more jewelry than she ever had but it didn't feel wrong. She felt pretty. Zoi told her to wait and stepped back into her room to get dressed.

She walked out and Kari saw why.

Every item she wore, Zoi had matched, except where hers were white and blue, Zoi was covered in blacks and greens. But they matched. Kari had never felt more beautiful in her life, having been dressed up to match her. It was something she hadn't expected to feel.

Gossamer was covered in see-through mesh, red this time, torn to expose her, and her boots. Reylan and Priest wore their robes, fluttering open to expose them, as well. Kari realized suddenly how inured she had become to the pornographic displays around her. Any one of them would have been the only thing anyone looked at back in a New York sex club.

And yet.

Kari paid special attention to the yolcu she saw walking through the Octagon. The entire place was huge, big enough that they could have teleported around it. She was glad they didn't, though. It seemed like every fifty meters or so something changed, something new popped up, more beautiful than the one before.

They passed another library, even larger than the last one she'd seen. The entryway was covered in vines and plants and, as she peered in through the door, she could see that there was a hologram in the center, showing loops of anatomical imagery of various yolcu. She stopped, fascinated.

One day she would wander through this. She would sit in libraries with books written all over the universe about people with experiences she couldn't begin to imagine.

A few minutes later, they arrived at the Zucaro. All her life, Kari had thought of herself as an open-minded, if cautious person.

If, however, you would have told her just last week that she would be excitedly walking mostly naked into a "sex gym," she would have doubted that very much.

As she expected, it was large. It was easily as large as a Soccer pitch. The walls were white and shockingly clean. And, all over were hexagon shaped areas, black pads rising up from the white floors. Ropes, cabinets, surfaces, all could be invoked to drop from the ceiling or return.

It was all so open, exposed. As she looked around, though, at small groups of people in each hexagon shape, she could see that some were enclosed, surrounded by a white screen.

She had no idea what they were here to do, and, if she had to be honest, it was exciting. If anything, the mystery was taking her mind off of the mysteries of tonight.

Reylan pulled Priest by the hand into the center of the closest hexagon and started to swing him around, dancing. Priest smiled and followed her lead immediately. She pulled him in and he spun her perfectly. He was good. Was he a dancer in a previous life? After just a few moments, he extended his arm and smoothly rotated her into his chest like a yoyo rolling up, as they fell to the mat, laughing. Kari remembered that Reylan was the one who trained Priest. And she did seem to pull him around like something she was proud to show off. She imagined the two of them dancing around their thula when he was just a novitae. Did she push him off of benches and into doorways and make him laugh, too? What was their thing?

Reylan sat crosslegged and pulled Gossamer over to her on one side like a little doll and Priest on the other. The two of them sat on their knees. Zoi ran over and dragged Kari down, sitting next to her. They made a half circle, open on one end.

Kari looked at the open area of the circle. "Are we expecting anyone?"

Priest looked at her and winked, "A couple people."

"But first, let's talk about what we know about the other species participating in the ceremony. The Encantada." Reylan squeezed Gossamer's hand.

The young Filipino girl started. "Gender is very complex. For reproduction, it's a tiny bit easier. In the galaxy, there are four classes of genders, generally, Givers, Receivers, Catalysts, and Hosts. Givers tend to inject others with genetic material, Receivers tend to take in genetic materials, Catalysts tend to kickstart reproduction, and hosts tend to use their bodies to grow offspring. In humans, Men are often Givers, while women represent the other three genders."

That was a different way for Kari to think about it, but it made sense.

Priest smiled at her. "Well said. But, Zoi, what about the Encantada?"

Zoi looked up, remembering. "The Encancada have four different genders, two are givers, one is a receiver/host, and one is a catalyst. The ambassador who was here twenty years ago was a type one giver, technically an ovipositor. The one coming tonight, Mekari, is a type two giver, one of the two 'male' genders – an inseminator. We don't know a lot about the type two giver. But we believe, based on the anatomy of the previous ambassador, that their penetration tool may be large."

Kari looked up. "How large are we talking about?"

"We actually don't know." A man with a wave of dark hair sat down next to Gossamer, hugging her. He wore a black robe, again, open at the front, and his t'kau was cobalt blue on his forehead, over deep dark olive skin. Kari could easily believe that he was native here, Turkish, or maybe Spanish, Dominican, anything. He wore a big smile, centered within a well kept casual black goatee. As she followed him, she could see that all his tattoos were the same deep blue, making him look for all the world like an ancient piece of ceremonial pottery.

At the same time, a girl sat down next to Kari. She was definitely Arabic, or possibly Turkish, nude except for a beautiful cornflower blue headwrap matching her shockingly blue eyes, and elaborate metal rings up and down her arms and neck.

She was heavily tattooed in foreign, seemingly mystical letters. She was about Zoi's height, and just as beautiful. She smiled at Kari.

Priest introduced them. "This is Gadd, he is a kezmek like me. And this is one of his novitae, Qerici. They are here to help."

Kari looked confused for a moment until she looked down. Qerici's mystical tattoos extended down her breasts, her beautiful belly, and then across the length of her very large and thick penis.

"Qerici is four-gendered. For the purpose of reproduction, if she wanted, she could act as giver, receiver, catalyst, or host." Priest continued.

"And," Reylan added, "she has one of the largest members here of all the human contingent."

"Now, before we go on, do you want us to close the screen?" Priest seemed 100 percent invested in her being comfortable.

Kari looked around. "That's not necessary."

Priest went on. "We're all going to get undressed. Remember, we are all under t'kau here. You know that that means, right?"

"You are all open to intimacy?" Zoi slid her hand under Kari's butt as she answered.

Priest continued, "Right. We are all accessible to you. In any way to do anything. Any curiosity you have, this is how we meet it."

"And it's important." Reylan slid her robe off handed it to Gossamer, who tossed it comically behind her. "Because when you walk into that kurge-to officiate, you have to be accessible to the petitioners, completely. Anything they want to do. "

Priest tossed his robe aside as well. "This is how officiant duties work– it's about complete acceptance. There is one place in the world where what you need, who you are, is accepted completely. The kurge."

Gadd had folded his robe beside him as he looked over at Kari with kind eyes. "And we want to be that here, now, for you." She realized that something about him reminded her of Ed.

"Wow. Thank you."

He turned to her. "Qerici here is a built a little differently. She has a very large penis, but behind it is a vagina. That won't be the case for Mekari, the Encantado petitioner. Do you want to feel?"

Kari looked at Qerici and she smiled widely. The girl spread her legs, putting one up so that Kari could touch her more easily. Kari dropped her hand and began to run her fingers over Qerici's beautiful cock. It was warm and pulsing. "Ok. But he'll be about the same size?"

She heard Zoi from her right. "We don't know. When one giver is an ovipositor and another is an inseminator, the first is usually bigger. But it's all up in the air. Biology is weird."

"So weird," Gossamer cut in.

Priest continued, "so, the overwhelming amount of sex in the universe is done for joy or pleasure, connection, community, etc. So often reproductive agents who are givers can act as pseudoreceivers for the purpose of non procreative sex."

Qerici put her right arm around Kari's waist, pointing to her parts with the other. "My penis and vagina function procreatively, but my anus, mouth, and urethra don't, and can act as pseudoreceivers."

"Ok, that makes sense now." Kari was getting it. She slid one hand under the darker girl's cock, pushing three fingers into her wet pussy under it. Her prick widened under her touch and the head rose up while Qerici moaned and half closed her eyes. She let her face rub against her neck. "My fist or fingers would be pseudogivers."

Reylan lowered her voice a bit, trying not to ruin the mood building. "Perfect. Yes. They still work. Because, remember, most sex isn't procreative."

Kari looked at Zoi, who mouthed, "kiss her," pointing to Qerici. She leaned in and kissed the girl lightly, her lips sinking into Qerici's open mouth. Kari tried to merge into her a bit. This was about acceptance. Something Priest was just getting to.

"Seeing someone's t'kau is seeing them. In fact – and you've shown you understand this – There is no greater way in the universe to show someone that they are seen and valued than to share intimacy."

Gadd agreed. "When you are in the kurge, that is what you need to project."

Kari was becoming very turned on by the process. "I will. I want to." She slid down Qerici's body and sucked at her nipples. She massaged the girl's dick with her left hand while moving her fingers in and out of her wet pussy with her right. Qerici arched her back and leaned backward, pushing her cock in the air. Kari put her head down and licked at the head of the prick in front of her. She could taste precum from the tiny hole in front but knew she'd never get the whole tip in her mouth. It was thick and apple shaped and warm under her tongue. But there was still something vaguely feminine about it. She opened her mouth wide as Zoi put her tongue in her ass, massaging her little hole. Kari spread her legs wider and pushed her ass into the air. She couldn't believe she was doing this in front of people. Reylan's voice was soft and sensual in her ears.

"What we know about Mekari, the Ambassador for the Encantada, is that he is a very studied man, a type two giver, an academic. Kol, the representative from the Vigo, was a general. He is also a giver, although their species tends to be hermaphroditic, like Kerada."

Kari licked the shaft of Qerici's thick cock, feeling her cunt start to contract, liquid dripping from it onto the matt. She hadn't realized Kerada was male and female, too. She started to wish she had payed more attention when Kerada had fucked her.

"Yes, behind the r'kash are two holes. Both have to be entered and ejaculated in so as to impregnate a member of their species. A larger one and a smaller one." Reylan sounded almost like a teacher.

She continued. "Depending on the size, you may find that the anus is a better option for you. We can help you stretch. Here if you get close, you can see that Priest is effective at stretching and allowing his ass to be used." Priest moved to the center of the circle and Gadd followed him. He layed down on his back and let Gadd kiss him. The two looked as though this wasn't their first time. Gossamer and Zoi had gotten some oil. She could feel Zoi's hands massaging it into her ass as Gossamer did the same for Priest. Kari tried to not let the sensation distract her too much from her work on Qerici's thick cock. She licked in all over the head and did her best to open her mouth wide enough to take it.

Gadd lifted Priest's legs and made his fist into a rocket shape, sliding his fist into him, right at the spot where Kari could see if she only slightly turned her head. Priest bore down on it as hard as he could. Pushing in deeper, Gadd turned and threw his left leg over Priest's body, aiming his cock into his mouth. It slid immediately all the way down his throat, to the balls, seemingly without any obstruction. Gadd breathed in and moaned a little as he continued to pump at the other man's ass.

Kari felt Zoi's hand behind her. She tried to open, pushing at it. She wanted Zoi inside her. She lifted her head and kissed Qerici, grateful to her for being so close. She pulled at her dick as she played her fingers inside the dark lips of her pussy. Qerici was disturbingly beautiful and the smell of cinnamon was seemingly nearly dripping from her pores. Kari looked into her eyes as Qerici let out a moan and whispered, "oh, you got me. You do. Kari."

Kari felt the cum pour from the tip of her rod, spilling over her hand. She dipped her head down and tried to clean it all up, licking and drinking it in. She slid her tongue into the open hole at the top of the darker girl's prick and felt the pressure of her cum just as she felt the pop of Zoi's hand inside her.

"You will be with two givers so you may have to be creative anyway." Reylan intoned brightly.

Kari pulled Qerici close, burying her face between her legs as she heard Priest cum next to her.

Zoi's fist slammed deep into her, giant and thick, like a challenge to anything the Encantada might bring between their legs. She slid onto her stomach and Imagined the sweat falling down Zoi's breasts from her exertion and what that would taste like right now.

***

They wandered through the Zucaro holding hands. It was huge. They made their way to a massive room filled with black tile everywhere and a large pool. Jets from above mimicked the action of a waterfall, dropping water through dense green and purple foliage. The lights created a series of rainbows on the mist above them, turning the room into a mythical seat of Grecian decadence.

She sat in the pool with only a couple of hours left, water dancing down from the overhead waterfall on top of her. Her body felt alive and ready. All six of the others splashed around except for Zoi, whispering to her in the corner, playing with her hair, focusing on her.

"I'm going to dress you and make you up. I'm your Apriya. I'll use some oil to massage your places to try to make this easier. I'll do your hair and paint on a t'kau."

"Paint?" Kari put her arms around Zoi's waist and pulled her in.

"The very first t'kaus on earth were done with henna. It won't last. But I'll make it pretty."

"What does Apriya mean?"

Zoi paused for a minute. "It means 'loved one.' It's supposed to be the person you are closest to. When Priest officiates, I am his Apriya. Either Gossamer or Priest are Reylan's. Qerici is Gadd's"

"Loved one."

"Is that ok? You can choose anyone you want."

"No. I choose you. I would have chosen you, anyway."

"I know. Will you remember when you get home?" Zoi winked.

Kari looked into her eyes. She would never forget it. "Remember?"

"What Apriya means?"

"I absolutely will."

"Distances don't matter. You have a teleport code, anyway. And I can find more Mickey Mouse shirts."

Kari's hand steepled with Zoi's. "It's going to be silly for me to tell you that this is the most remarkable experience of my whole life."

"Well, Im afraid to tell you that this matters. I don't want to scare you." Zoi said, kissing her full on the lips, as she pushed back against the edge of the pool. Kari felt the pressure and realized how badly she wanted to be crushed by her.

"Zoi. I'm done being scared."

Gadd swam over and hugged them both, trying to lift them from the water. Zoi laughed and did her best to make it hard for him. "Did you tell her the one thing?"

"I was just about to. You can…" Zoi stepped back.

"No big deal. In the kurge, the most important thing. All three of you have to connect. The intimacy is for you all, the two petitioners and you, the contract. You are the contract. You are hope."

"Ok, all three of us."

He looked her up and down and smiled. "Do you like being one of us?"

"Am I?"

Gadd had a wink in his voice. "In every way that counts."

"Then, I do. A lot."

He grinned at her and dropped below the water to swim away.

Kari looked at Zoi. "Apriya."

"You aren't going to let that go, are you?"

"I am not."

***

The next two hours were a blur, and, for the first time, Kari used the internal teleporters, nearly invisible recessed pads in the corners of the rooms, to get around. They arrived at the kurge, built nearly like a stylized hospital operating room with seating above for the audience and a circular room below. Rooms around the diameter of the main space were there for the participants to get ready, and for their apriyas to wait for them until the ceremony was done. It was a beautiful room, made to be art itself, with a wall of yolcu sculptures and green and white flowering plants running down the oppposite wall. The fountains made it smell like a freshwater pond.

Kari felt the familiar twinge of panic looking up at the observer area, realizing people would be watching. But then it occurred to her that the people in the front watching would be Gossamer, Priest, Reylan, Gadd, Qerici, people she had come to think of as her team. These were people who saw her with different eyes.

There were no rules as to how long the ceremony would be or exactly what would happen after the ceremonial opening. It was about building acceptance and connection, and that might differ with different participants.

She walked around, ready, waiting, getting used to the space. She went back into her private space and let Zoi massage her with oil again. On the bed, in the room, was a black robe. She looked at her apriya, who put it on her, over her jewelry. Kari looked in the mirror. For a second, she thought she was looking at Priest. Her own blonde hair was longer, though. And her shape was very different. She shook her head.

They gave her a robe, she thought.

Zoi kissed her as the lights flickered.

She walked into the space. Three circular pads rose up from the floor. Kari moved to the centermost one and kneeled. The words came easily.

"Hello. My name is Kari Lourdes and I represent the Octagon, Earth. I welcome you all in love. I have read the agreements and am prepared to defend them or deliver them to my people as law. I stand before you without deception or artifice." She pulled her robe off and folded it, placing it in front of her.

She could feel Zoi beaming at her from the doorway. She smiled and looked down.

Kol and Mekari entered. Kol looked strikingly similar to Kerada, but with a slightly harsher face. He seemed stern and even businesslike as he mounted one of the large pads and spoke.

"Ugaru. My name is Irrikas Mah Kol and I represent the people of the unified planets of Vigo. I welcome you all in love. I have read the agreements and am prepared to defend them or deliver them to my people as law. I stand before you without deception or artifice." He removed his robe and folded it quickly, placing it on the floor in front of him.

Mekari was hard looking, with white skin that resembled ceramic or horn. There were horny protrusions on either side of his mouth and his eyes were large and insect-like. He looked like the pictures Kari had seen.

"Fiaca'kr. My name is Thrace Mekari and I represent the people of the Encantada. I welcome you all in love. I have read the agreements and am prepared to defend them or deliver them to my own people as law. I stand before you without deception or artifice." He slid his robe off, folding it perfectly, placing it on the floor in front of him.

Kari took a deep breath. "Irrikas Mah Kol, Thrace Mekari, millions of years ago, as officiant, I would have offered my life to you as defense of this contract. But we are a people changed and guided by love, by compassion, by joy. I offer you my ear if you wish to contest it. I offer you every other piece of me, in passion and acceptance, if you wish to make it live."

Kari couldn't believe how easy it had been to memorize that. The last part was supposed to come from her heart. That was a little harder.

"You know me. I'm so honored to be asked by name to be a part of this. I'd say be gentle with me, but I think we all know that's probably not the most fun."

Mekari and Kol seemed to smile. Kari realized that Kol was not so daunting as he first appeared. She heard the laughter from the observation area and it lifted her up.

Kol went next. "We do know you. And we know that this must have been a shock for you. I appreciate your being a part of this. And, if I can say, you are even more yummy in person."

The observation booth laughed as one, with the Vigo contingent leading the way. Kari smiled and waved her hair, drawing even a few more. She looked over at Mekari.

"We know you as well. We are humbled by your participation. This has been hard for us and your rare presence makes it easier."

Kari raised her hands and from the floor came a larger pad that fit into the three raised ones, connecting it into one circular bed. She was shaking as she crawled over to Mekari and curved her body next to his.

She reached up and touched the t'kau on his forehead, drawn in just for today as well. And buried her head in his neck, kissing it.

"Thank you for your honesty."

She turned and crawled toward Kol. He leaned forward and put his hands on her shoulders, pulling her in. She kissed his chest and then neck. He lifted her head and kissed her hard. His skin had no give, but his lips were smooth and round and soft. She let her tongue move in his mouth for a moment, dropping her hand down to his R'kash.

"Thank you for your honesty."

Kari looked over at Mekari. He opened his legs and she saw the member between them. It hung, only semi erect, but it was already as large as Qerici's. For a moment she was shocked. But as her eyes moved to his face, she felt something different.

Was it the fact that she had never been in the same room with a member of his race? But she felt something. Something disconcerting.

"Irrikas Mah Kol, I ask for your indulgence to speak to the other petitioner in private for a moment." She took his hand and looked at him in the eyes. Suddenly, she realized that he wasn't hard at all. His professionalism was possibly a front.

He adored her. He was one of the reasons she was here. He was putting on a show for her.

She squeezed his hand and he smiled at her. "Of course, Kari Lourdes."

Kari mouthed "thank you" to him. And stepped off the bed. She took Mekari's hand.

"Will you speak to me alone for a moment?"

There was some grumbling from the observation area but the look he gave her was clear.

It was gratitude.

The two of them moved to one of the unused rooms around the diameter of the kurge. Kari pulled the curtain shut and turned to him. She kissed his neck again and sat down in a chair next to him.

Mekari took a deep breath and pulled out the other chair. He stared into her eyes and began. "My wife and I have two children. They are beautiful. Do you have any children, Kari Lourdes?"

Kari hadn't considered that for a while. She was under oath now, though, to be absolutely honest. "I want them one day. I think. I have an oath of honesty here so I may need to add that I don't see it."

"We lost both our husbands. My children's eggfather and spark. In this war, thirty years ago." Mekari seemed tired. He dropped his hand on the table between them.

"I'm so sorry. I can't imagine how that must feel." Kari placed her hand next to his, nearly touching. She wanted to be what she could be, but only when needed.

He looked at her. "If I can't do this? If I can't put aside my anger, am I a monster? I ask myself that over and over."

"Are you a monster if you can't let go of anger?"

"If I won't. If I won't go back in that room. I could let those people die. I could walk away."

Kari paused. She put her hand in his. "What does your wife think?"

"She is a fan of yours. She says you are kind. She says that you would know how to do it. The kindest thing."

"She puts too much faith in me, I think."

"In me, too, usually, " he chuckled. His face opened up a bit talking about her.

"I bet she's wonderful."

"She wants me to let go, she says, but I wonder, deep down what she wants."

Kari played with his hand. Without thinking, Mekari put his in a little web with hers. Kari was overwhelmed with the idea that these two hands were made on opposite sides of the galaxy and yet they fit together. "Can I say something?"

"Of course."

"I'm not sure that I hear anger." she put her other hand on his leg. He was warm and softer than she first thought.

"I've lived with it for so long. I shouldn't be here. I wasn't the soldier. They were. My husbands."

"I hear pain. " Kari whispered.

"Maybe I don't know the difference anymore." He turned to her and dropped his head. Kari was becoming very aware that he was naked. And that he needed something. She felt inside her and it felt like it was something she could give.

"Maybe the difference doesn't matter."

"Do you forgive people who take away what you love?" She looked at him and realized that it was time to be maybe even a little more honest.

"I don't know. You know, I almost didn't do this."

"I'm sure it must have been insane for you. Your culture, you can't have wanted to come here and have sex with us."

"Hey, hey." She lifted his head up with her finger under his chin. "The sex part isn't the hard part. That kind of blows my mind still. The sex is the easiest part of this."

"Yes?"

"And as I stand here talking to you – trust me. it gets easier and easier."

She kissed him. His lips pulled in slightly and the bones on the side of his mouth wrapped around her. It felt enveloping, protective. Suddenly, he didn't feel hard. He felt protective. He was a shield. He was a living barrier safeguarding the things he loved. He looked at her and moved her hair aside. "You are beautiful."

"Thank you. So are you." Her hand moved against his member, larger now than before. It was the width and length of Gadd's arm. "If I can be honest, though, that thing is huge."

He smiled, "I suppose from your perspective, it must be."

"But, I mean, that isn't the issue. It's kind of the main attraction, but not the issue."

He kissed her forehead. "I understand. I think."

"I'm so afraid of failing. I'm afraid of changing, I'm afraid. I tried to learn everything. It just made me more afraid. A billion people."

"It's more than anyone's brain can wrap around." She hugged him, her hands roaming across his back. "I just cook things, you know?"

"And I talk. It's what I do. All of the doers are dead, leaving the talkers to run the universe."

"I don't think that's true. You are here, doing."

"Or not." He kissed her cheek.

"Someone told me recently that all change, even change for the better, can make you mourn. And it's ok."

"Even peace?"

"I want to celebrate with you or mourn with you. Either way, I'm here. Either way, you have me. I promise. I'm right here."

He took a breath and looked at her. "I meant it when I said you were beautiful."

She took him by the hand and pulled him toward the main room. "Yeah. I meant it when I said you were a doer. Do I need to be wearing my apron?"

"I was sort of imagining that." He laughed softly.

Kol stood up as they walked out of the room. She looked at the large blue man and tried to read his energy. "Do I need to be wearing the apron for you, too or are you going to fuck me?"

He paused for a moment and then began laughing. The observers above laughed as Kari pulled them both to the bed. She pushed Mekari down and kissed him deeply, placing her right hand on Kol's r'kash. She could feel the smaller tentacles begin to thicken and wind around. She arched her back and lifted her ass in the air, pulling him behind her.

Before she had been in this room, she imagined it might be a clinical thing. The idea of perfect acceptance was something pretty and sensuous. But her experiences over the last couple of days wiped that idea away. For her, perfect acceptance was about need. She looked at Mekari, below her. He was a champion, a protector. He was a man who mirrored her own thoughts, her own misgivings. He was built of the most perfect stone, brilliant, eternal, a man so immersed in the people he loved. She wanted to give him that back. Her mouth moved down his body to his massive prick, while she spread her legs for Kol.

She licked at Mekari's dick, trying to get her tongue into the hole at the tip as she massaged him, pulling it up against her. She reached behind and opened her ass for Kol, who sent a number of tentacles on exploration inside, deeper until they disappeared into her core. She moaned and pushed back, sucking at Mekari's cock.

Just as Kerada had, Kol wrapped six of his tendrils into a thick pulsing cock and let it slide into Kari's pussy, She let out a loud moan and sucked harder. She felt like the connector between the two men. "Oh, yeah. Fuck me in every hole. Everywhere."

Mekari put his hands on her face roughly and tried to dig his cock into her mouth.

She worked as hard as she could to open her mouth, licking at it. Her hands played across his chest and then dropped to his ass to try to help pull the massive rod into her tiny mouth. The tip of his dick began leaking violet colored clear liquid. Kari let it drip into her hand and licked it off, staring him in the eye. She pulled up and kissed him, placing his rod at the entrance of her pussy and rubbing it back and forth.

Mekari seemed turned on by her desire for his cum. She leaned in and began to beg him to cum, rubbing his prick against her wet pussy. As she looked down, she saw Kol's arms wrap around them both, His R'kash buried in her pussy and ass. She looked back at him and begged. "Yeah, fuck me. Oh, those are good."

Six of his tendrils were now coiled inside her cunt, pumping in and out, while two dug deep into her ass. As she stared, she saw the other 4 whip up between her legs and wrap around Mekari's massive dick, massaging it in rhythm.

"Yeah, gimme that cum. I want to drown in cum." She said to Kol, "help me get him off." She kissed Mekari sweetly on the lips. "Please. I want all your cum."

He reached down and pumped his cock only a few times, letting the soft wet motion of Kari's dripping pussy and Kol's r'kash jerk him off all over her belly. He moaned and closed his eyes as wave after wave of thick violet liquid poured all over Kari. She collected it with her hand and lifted it to her mouth, sucking her fingers while she kept riding, sliding up and down his prick. It tasted slightly like ginger, the same feeling of being cleaned on the inside. She licked and ate it off of him everywhere like an animal.

Kol exploded inside her, in a hot wet wave of blue slightly milky liquid. Kari pushed Kol down to kiss him as she tried to collect the dripping cum. She ran her face down his body, to his r'kash, and then behind. She remembered Reylan telling her the larger of the two holes was the one that stretched the most. Kari reached for Mekari's cock and slid it into Kol's larger hole as she pulled his legs over his head. Mekari was surprised by how well he fit.

She threw her leg over Kol's body, placing her ass over the center of Kol's r'kash. She rubbed against it as the Encantada began pumping his dick harder and harder into the blue man beneath her. Blue and violet cum dripped down Kari's face as she smiled up at Mekari, his dick rubbing against her clit as it slammed into Kol's hole.

"Kol, can you fuck my ass while he fucks yours?" Kol nodded and she felt a rope of tendrils dig its way into her posterior hole. She pulled Mekari in, harder and harder, feeling the cord of ropelike tendrils slide deeply into her. Mekari reached up to grab her tits. She smiled at him.

"If you do that, I'm gonna cum."

He laughed, moving his hands closer to her nipples. She could feel Kol below her nearing another orgasm and hoped Mekari was, as well.

"I'm warning you." she laughed, pressing her asshole down on the blue alien's ridged dick below while Mekari's massive prong slapped against her clit. He dropped his hands, squeezing and teasing her nipples, holding them between his fingers as she screamed. "I'm cumming I'm cumming." Kari closed her eyes and laid backward, pushing her clit up against Mekari's body. Kol held her as he pumped his own cum into her ass.

Mekari slid off and flopped himself next to the two. Kari rolled off Kol's body and began kissing both of them. The room was warm and had darkened a bit. She looked up, breathing heavily, to see stars above the observation space. They must have opened the roof up while she was occupied. She tried to place any of the stars, but it was impossible. For a moment, she imagined people on planets around each one of them.

People who felt like they were where they belonged.

***

Kari woke up in her room back at the thula. Zoi was asleep next to her, her hands wrapped around her.

Reylan was sitting on the bed nude, seemingly waiting for her to wake up on her own. She looked up into the taller women's eyes. She wondered if people could see that kind of kindness in her own eyes.

Reylan smiled. "Hey, Superstar."

Kara started to sit up. "Oh, I knocked out."

"I know, we need to get you back at some point for your show tonight." Reylan held her hand.

"Did I...did it...?" Kari pulled herself up, letting Zoi begin to wake up.

"We have a shiny new agreement, better than we had hoped. A beautiful peaceful trade agreement."

Kari breathed out. "Oh my god..."

"And it's all because of you. So we let you sleep in." She looked at Zoi, who kissed her neck and chest animatedly.

Kari laughed. "Is everyone gone?"

"They left messages for you. And gifts. This is from Kol. He left a copy for our library, too." Reyland handed her a letter and a small computer drive.

"What is it?"

"It's a cookbook, written by one of his great grand parents. Their own recipes. Never seen before. He says he expects to see one or two of these on the show."

Kari felt an outpouring of gratitude for Kol. If he hadn't been so staunchly supportive..."Wow. This is..."

Reylan handed her a few small boxes. They had two slots as if for an electrical plug to fit. "And a bunch of these. From Mekari."

"A plug?" She thought about what that must mean.

"It's an eternal power supply. Never needs to be recharged. He made this himself with standard plug ports for the U.S. You could plug your phone in that forever."

"It's so small." Kari rolled it in her fingers.

"We'll get this science figured out and donated to Earth within a year. Imagine the lives this little guy's going to save." Reylan stared at one intently.

Zoi rose up on one arm, "Hospitals…"

Reylan nodded, "Anywhere on earth they need power."

"That is so cool" Kari held it in her hand.

Reylan kissed her on the forehead and got up. "When you guys are ready, come sit in the pool with us for a while, before you have to be at your show."

"We will." Kari thought that she might make a pass at Reylan.

She turned to Zoi. "Should I fuck her in the pool?"

Zoi giggled. "Yes, 100%." She put her hands between Kari's legs and Kari snapped them shut, trapping her.

Zoi placed the tiny box on her chest. "You did that."

"I thought we were a team…"

"We are. But I couldn't do what you did. One day…."

"You could."

"You look good in that t'kau. You should keep it." She kissed her hard, pushing her hand inside her.

Kari breathed in sharply. "Maybe I'll come back and earn it sometime."

They spent some time in the pool before Kari had to return. A few hours later, after scrubbing the henna from her forehead and putting on a linen shirt and a pair of jeans, standing in the studio kitchen, Kari felt like she was still back there, sparring with Zoi, conspiring with her.

She cleaned the studio with a little less effort than usual. She took the little box and placed it on the counter behind her, plugging her phone in it. Taking two steps back she looked, nodding.

No one will notice.

She'd read the letters as soon as she'd gotten back. Mekari's was short, just asserting that his wife, as usual, was right. Kol's was a bit longer, essentially going on about what a good sport she was.

And what a big fan he was.

Kari blushed a bit, against her will, thinking about his watching tonight. She put the letters in a drawer as Seven came in wearing a dark blue NASA hoodie.

"Ok, are we good for takeoff?"

She smiled. "Oh, yeah. Are you ground control?"

"You like it, space lady?" He shot back.

"I do." She looked at him. His hair was brushed, suggesting he might see Gossamer later. "Seven, I appreciate you."

He looked up. "I appreciate you. Are you ok?"

"I am. I'm good."

Seven pulled out a piece of paper from his clipboard like a parent might with a present on Christmas. "You're better than that."

"What are you smiling about?"

"We're streaming the last episode to lead in, like we always do," he said.

"And right now, you have more extraterrestrial viewers than any show in Earth history. I'm checking now but I think it's true. The numbers."

"Really, let me see that." She reached for the paper.

He pointed over her shoulder. "And a shit load of people from here, too."

She looked at the page. It added up. "Wow."

He paused. "Are you going to talk about the place at all? The Octagon?"

"I'm guessing the showrunners say no." she said, handing the page back to him.

"I say fuck em. This piece of paper tells me you're the boss."

"Right?" Kari laughed.

"You good to go, boss?"

She turned back to the counter. "Yeah, let's light it up."

Ed smiled. "I don't know what that means, but I dig the enthusiasm."

He leaned in and started counting with his fingers, miming the last four. "In five…"

"Hey, everyone. Welcome back to the Yum Show. I have so much for you today I can't even stand it."

She looked out at the camera. There was a little red light glaring back.

"First, over this last week, I had the honor of…working with great people, the Encantada and the Vigo. I was officiating, helping to build a peace. It was the biggest thing I've ever done, I think. And I'm still kind of flying. This recipe here is my gift to them, my new friends. It's got a bit of a kick to it, so my earth bound friends may want to pull back on the spices. Or, maybe just dive in and do it, you know."

She let out a deep breath. And everything seemed the way it was supposed to be. She thought about the people on those planets who were where they belonged. About Zoi, who was where she belonged. And about the new worlds that she belonged in now.

"If you're on the site, you see the full list of ingredients, posted since last night. So... let's get to it. "

2 - First - 2050

Archie stood in front of the biggest mirror he'd ever seen and fiddled with his hair. Archie Benjamin was a ginger and his hair had been relatively sparse since he was in his twenties, a reddish brown patch kept mostly short playing up against his forehead like the shore at night, always looking ready to bear off, to spill in the other direction and evade the beach forever. Now that he had recently passed 35, his faith in that tide had disappeared.

He called out to the bathroom of the Emperor's suite. "Shar, is my hairline receding?"

A tall Turkish girl of 24 or so poked her head out from the bathroom, with a toothbrush in her mouth. She wore a starched clean white t-shirt with "Bahamas" on it and nothing else, revealing a set of smooth dark legs whose curves seemed nearly impossibly mathematically precise rising up to a bare, beautiful pussy, darker than the skin around it.

"Archie, I've known you for four years. I think it's holding its own pretty well." She stepped toward him, running the toothbrush over her gums. Sharla Tuk alwayds mixed a fresh concoction of toothpaste, mouthwash and mint into a little cup and ran it over her teeth in the morning as she got dressed. Archie had to admit that it worked, every time he saw her smile.

Or was it something else?

He sighed, touching his roots. "The little soldiers are fighting so hard."

She kissed him on the forehead. "They really are."

The truth is, she thought, Archie would still be a handsome man if he had shaved it all off. The core of Archie Benjamin, everyone would agree, was his smile and lit up eyes, that seemed to flash for everyone. Archie made you feel like there was a horribly impolite inside joke and you were in on it.

Shar slipped behind him and grabbed his chest. "Are you sure it's ok for my friends to be staying here, especially now?"

Archie looked behind him. "Do they need more room? We can go take over the Canadian Embassy? They left last week."

Sharla took a second to take in the mirror. It really was ridiculous. This entire room was. The Embassy building was large and opulent, old, dignified, from a time when British/Turkish relations were something worth investing in.

"I'm serious. Are you going to get in trouble?" Her voice wavered slightly.

He grabbed her around the waist, causing her to giggle a bit unintentionally. "In trouble? I'm not even sure I have a job anymore."

She pulled out the tooth brush and kissed his nose. "Well, that makes me feel better."

Archie wrapped both arms around her waist and leaned back, looking at her. "Look, What's your name again?"

Without thinking, Shar shot out, "I'm Cleopatra, the queen of Egypt." She looked for a white button down to put on over her Bahamas shirt.

He continued, businesslike, "I should have remembered that. Cleo. As soon as these visas clear, you and your friends will pack up, we'll steal all the silverware we can and we're headed to London and they'll just have to figure out what duke to marry. They should start with the less inbred ones. Look for chins." He leaned in and kissed her.

She laughed, putting on a thick official accent. "That's right. Ambassador Benjamin, here are all the papers for your porn star girlfriend and her hooker friends to come to live with you in England. Good luck and I hope they marry well."

He lifted her shirt and played with her tummy. " Are you really a star, though? I mean you are to me." He pouted at her.

Shar tried to be even slightly angry with him. It was not working. "I'm serious."

He held her hand, looking around on the floor. "Shar, it's fine. The papers are coming."

"Before THEY do?" Sharla stepped over to the window and looked out. Throngs of people had assembled, requesting, and not too nicely, that they go home. She held the curtain and motioned him over. He stepped up, shaking his head.

"These are your people, can you talk some sense into them? Maybe with a megaphone? Or a brick?"

Archie resumed his search on the floor, bending over as Sharla raised her voice,. "Those are not my people. This isn't even my country anymore." She looked over at Archie who was on his knees on the ground, handing her a small box.

"Good. Here, hold this."

She didn't need to open the box to know what was in it. He looked up at her from one knee. She smiled, pulling him up. "Oh my god. Get up. Stand up."

He got to his feet. "I thought I might get that past you if I did it quickly."

"Put that thing away." She handed him back the ring box. If she were being honest, she did wish she knew at least what it looked like.

Archie returned it to the drawer under the mirror. "You already said yes in your sleep, you know. Actually, it was 'oh yes. Yes. Fuck, yes.'"

Shar started buttoning her shirt up. "I do sort of remember that. I don't know that's binding at all, really."

The massive door swung slowly. Dorothy slid in before it was fully open. She was Turkish, as well, about 25 years old and petite. She was slightly lighter than Sharla and her very innocent look is what made her and her sister Zehra so successful as escorts with tourists. Her English, like Sharla's, was impeccable. Between the three women, they spoke nearly twelve languages, which Archie, an avowed language geek, brought up whenever he could.

Dorothy shook her head. "This is really getting scary"

Archie waved her in. "I know. Come on in. Let's all stay away from the windows. But it's going to be ok."

"What are you two up to?" Dorothy looked at them mischievously. Sharla and the two sisters had been close for years, sharing the same men, the same beds, and often the same crises. They were a matched set.

Archie looked up. "Dot, She's telling me she can't marry me because my penis isn't large enough."

Dorothy crossed her arms and played along. "Well, let's see it."

Shar lifted her arms in resignation. "I didn't say that."

He pulled it out and let it lay against the front of his pants. It flopped over, red and thick and unafraid of the air. This is where Archie lived. He was comfortable with his prick out, waving around.

Dorothy was pleased to have her mind taken off the impending crisis for a bit. She loved ribbing the two of them about their relationship. "It's pretty good. Good size. I remember now. You should probably do it, Shar."

"Right? Thank you." Archie laughed. the truth is that Dorothy had seen it a lot. If there were a group sex opportunity, she was in the middle of it, goading it on.

Sharla waved at his exposed cock. "Archie. Put that thing away, too, it'll escape and crawl into the walls."

Zehra came in after Dorothy. She was a little shorter than the other two women. And while she was just as pretty, she had a condition that meant her eyes might have been a millimeter or two too widely set. Archie thought it made her look mysterious and cool. Almost like an alien here on earth. She closed the door behind her and pointed to the window, "What if they try to burn the place down?"

"It won't catch. This place is made of Imperialism, pain and stupidity, dear. Inflammable all around. Ladies, just hang on until morning. I'll keep watch." Archie hated that everyone was so up in arms. He knew that the turnover in government was bad news and the vastly more regressive incoming Red Party had excited the people around an isolationist platform that meant all of them had to go at some point.

Zhera's family was part of this new regressive movement. She hadn't spoken to them in years. The sisters knew that their family would reject them if they knew anything about them. So why let that happen? "I'm not sure we have that long."

"Zehr. It's ok. Why don't you all stay in here with us tonight. We'll get this cleared up by morning. We'll stick together."

The door swung open again, this time fast enough to make even Archie jump.

Riley pushed his way in. The embassy coordinator was a black man with short, well groomed facial hair and a buzz cut. He was nearly always in his own personal uniform, a dark blue suitcoat over a black turtleneck. He walked quickly and, besides Archie, was the only senior staff member of the embassy remaining.

"Arch, you need to see this."

"Riley, what's up?" Archie stepped over to talk.

"People. Trying to get in." Riley appeared a bit behind the room in terms of information.

Archie let his head dip. "Yes, we see that,. All over the front. They'd like to hang us, I suspect."

Riley shook his head. "Not them. The back."

They all followed him to the communications center, where Rey was standing, her arms crossed, observing the master monitors. Rey was an intern, smartly dressed in a pencil skirt and black suit coat over a white button down. Archie thought she might have been 20. She had a good sense of humor and he loved how she tolerated his constant play. She had missed the last helicopter for some reason and more than anything both Archie and Riley wanted her out of here before things got ugly. She shook her head as they entered, pointing to the screen.

"I count 42 people."

Archie took a breath. And exhaled. There was a mass of people in the back of the embassy, clamoring for entrance.

For sanctuary.

Sharla shook her head. "That's two full football matches"

Archie pointed to her. "I like where you're going with this."

Riley put his hands on his waist. "They want sanctuary. Some sex workers, other people at high risk under the new government."

"They'll be the first to go in this war." Shar looked at Archie sadly.

"Sh. We don't say the 'W' word in front of the 'K.I.D.'" he shot back.

Rey spoke up, half smiling, "I'm an Oxford educated intern for a British embassy in a sovereign foreign nation. In what world do I not know how to spell?"

Dorothy shrugged. "The little illiterate one has a point."

Sharla turned to Archie and Riley. "We have to let them in."

The Ambassador nodded. "What she said, Riley. Let's get it done." They started to move out of the command room. Riley stopped and faced them.

"The crowd in front is going to go crazy."

Archie pushed past him. "And what, want to kill us more? Twice, maybe?"

Riley followed him into the hallway. "Shouldn't we discuss this?"

Archie picked up speed. He began to jog to the elevators. "No. I'll go. We need to speed this up."

Riley looked at Shar. "How does he make these decisions so quickly?"

Rey rushed after Archie. Sharla grabbed Doroty's hand and followed, looking back at Riley, "When you do the right thing, sometimes it's just faster. "

Riley stopped, calling out behind them. "That's insane. And not true." he looked at Zehra.

"Wait for me." She ran after them, meeting up with them at the service elevator. They were all piled in, still leaving room for 30 more people. It was clear that this facility could handle the influx without stress. Archie hit the ground floor button twice, uncharacteristically annoyed. Rey thought for a second that she had never seen serious Archie.

She wasn't sure how she felt about that.

Until it passed. Archie stood by the back door with everyone. It seemed safe to open the door and let everyone in .

He looked at Rey. "Look at that girl and boy. They're your age. Maybe you can talk to them in that teen slang you do."

Rey tried to stop from laughing. "Oh my god, I will smack you."

Archie ran out the door to keep watch behind them. Sharla bolted right behind, calling out to the women. "Zehr, Dot, can we get a bunch of rooms assigned? We have years worth of military rations, but they'll go down better in the main hall, with some fruit."

Rey started pulling people inside. "I'll get the hall ready with this group."

Sharla looked at Archie, a bit more afraid of the night air than she'd like to admit. "Just stay in sight, Captan Ginger."

They moved the last of the people inside. "You're just afraid I'll try to propose."

She looked over at him as they barred the doors. "What's your name again?"

He shook her hand, "Robert. The Bruce. Nice to meet you."

Sharla smiled and shook her head, "Just get your kilt on and get to the hall, Bob."

Archie pulled the people behind him, grabbing a child from a woman's arms. He kissed Sharla. "Got it."

They made their way to the hall through the massive corridors. Sharla looked to her right and saw the opening of a massive library, filled with books. "Hey, how is there a whole other library here that I've never seen before?"

"Because you spend all your time copulating with me and various other fun people." Archie put his hands on the ears of the young girl in his arms, "I mean, I'm not complaining, just commenting."

"I think I had no idea how big this place really was."

"I think Great Britain gave them a plane for it." They rounded the corner to the hall and followed Rey and the others. Sharla stopped Archie as he put the young girl down to run inside.

"This puts some big holds on those plans. We can't get papers for all these people. And we can't leave them."

"I've been thinking the same thing. What we need is back-up. We need soldiers that can stand outside and frighten people until Parliament figures out what to do with us."

"But we don't leave these people, right?"

He kissed her. "I promise. Look, this isn't what you expected, I know, being with me…"

"I don't care about that. We're on the same page, that's all that matters."

Archie put her head in his hands. "We're on the same page."

They moved into the room and caught up with Rey holding a piece of paper in front of her. She looked cover at Sharla and Archie. "ok, there are, right now, 51 people in this entire building. Me, Archie, Riley, and Mera, the other intern…"

Shar was counting, "That's four."

Rey continued, "Sharla and her two friends, Dorothy and Zehra."

"That makes seven"

Rey nodded, "the two guards downstairs, Sean and Ricky."

"nine"

"forty-two locals. Including at least thirty-two sex workers and trans people who will likely be murdered if they are sent away." Archie nodded.

"Fuck me." Riley walked up with his head in his hand.

"Riley, get on board and help me or go sit in the corner, I swear to Christ." Archie waved a single finger at him.

"I'm here. I'm helping. What do you need me to do?"

Archie took him aside. "First of all, I need you to make sure you are treating all these people with respect. I don't care how you feel about what they do, Comprende?"

"Why are we speaking spanish?" Riley cocked his head. Archie glared. "Ok, all right, respect. Absolutely."

Second, we need a consolidated area. We both know this embassy can hold 40 times this many people. We don't need people wandering off and disappearing. We need to know who they are and what they need. Help Rey with that, please."

"Ok, I'm on it."

"Thank you, Riley." Archie put his hands on the other man's shoulders.

Rey brought over a couple of girls. For a second Archie thought he was seeing double. The girl to her right looked so much like Rey it was scary. He shook his head.

"Archie, This is Tanji and her sister, Eren. They, uh, work this area. And Eren is…" She turned to the girl and whispered "hakkında konuşmak uygun mu?" Archie caught it and looked at her, smiling. "It's ok. If you don't want. konuşmana gerek yok." Her Turkish accent was seamless.

Eren smiled at him. Rey continued. "Eren is transgender."

"Ok. What do we need here?"

"No matter what, they're safer here in my clothes. I have a ton. So does Mera. And we have more that other people left behind."

Archie stood up. "This is why your mother and I say you're our favorite. Good idea. Let's get as many at-risk people looking like the shabby British"

Rey looked down at her clothes and shook her head. She turned to Eren and Tanji. "o benim gerçek babam değil." They laughed.

Sharla came up behind him. "Did she just tell those girls you aren't her real dad?"

"Parenting is thankless."

"Everyone is eating. People are getting settled. I think we can duck out." Sharla grabbed his hand and moved back toward their room. In reality, it was his room. She was never an authorized person in this Embassy, from the first night he brought her here, along with a bottle of whiskey and a credit card he could never find an atm to use.

She drank with him and laughed and they had sex until the morning, him promising to pay her the going rate at some point. Every once in a while one of them would comment on how large the bill was getting, as she stayed, night after night, sharing his bed. Her friends visited and stayed as well. And still, it never seemed like the right time to find that ATM. And on nights when Sharla had other dates, other opportunities, she found herself finishing quickly and rushing back to the embassy, smiling at the guards at the front and sliding into bed with Archie, still smelling of other men. He didn't care. He could smell her through anything.

Tonight it felt familiar as she slid into it again, pulling his pants off in one seamless movement as they rolled around in the bed that was many times too large for them. She pulled her panties aside and slithered down his body, impaling herself on his cock as they tried to keep their lips fastened together, as if sutured by some expert surgeon. She rubbed herself against the ginger patch of pubic hair at his root over and over, feeling the warmth of him inside her.

The door slid open and Zehra padded in, running to the bed. "You guys said I could stay in here tonight."

Sharla shifted and rose up, sitting back down on Archie's face. She teased the other woman. "Oh, are you scared, little Z?"

Zehra sidled up to the bed and pulled her dress off. She pulled out a condom and ripped open the wrapper, sliding it onto Archie's prick. "I'm just horny, actually."

Sharla pushed down on Archie's mouth, reaching behind her to spread her ass open. She felt his tongue invade her everywhere. She pulled Zehra up to slide on top of his dick. Zehra sighed and fell into a groove, moving back and forth on top of him.

Sharla felt herself finishing what had been started rubbing against his cock, as her clit sank into the area right above his chin, grinding over and over. His tongue dug deep inside her and she reached over to hold hands with Zehra.

"It's so weird for Archie to be quiet." She shifted back and forth slowly, squeezing Sharla's hands tightly.

"I know." Sharla loved the heat between her legs from his breath as he worked to devour her. There is nothing like being on the face of someone who tells you constantly how good you taste.

"He proposed to me twice today." She started breathing a little harder.

Zehra tried to match her movements. It was becoming a game. "How many times until you say yes, already?"

Sharla tried not to look down at his prick, moving in and out of her friend. She tried to keep the orgasm away for at least a few more minutes. Looking down would lead to her losing it.

"It's an even number, I think. Yes. an even number of times." Sharla loved the idea that he could hear every word.

Zehra's voice was rising as she came closer to cumming. "I'm so glad you have a plan."

Sharla laughed. She remembered what a shy thing Z was when they first met. How they had worked together to wipe it away. She remembered hitting on men together and dancing naked for parties, bachelors tossing money. And, in the back rooms, roughly loving each other for the edification of guests, on pillows in the center of the room, the taste of her all over Sharla's face.

And that was it for both women. Sharla grabbed her friend and kissed her hard as they both came all over Archie. Sharla could hear him swallowing her and she knew she had been able to squirt in his face. She smiled, sucking on Zehra's lips and whispering.

The three of them spent the night trying to take each other's minds off the mountain of refugees downstairs, and what it meant to their speedy exit to somewhere safe. It was terrifying. But there were a number of ways to ensure that at least one of them would be quiet for a time, and that was good enough.

***

Archie woke up to Riley standing over the chair in the corner of the room. He wondered why he never bothered to lock the door. He looked down at Zehra and her perfect breasts, lying next to him, wrapped around Sharla pretty legs, and remembered.

That's why he never locked the door.

He got up and went to the bar, pouring two drinks. The look on Riley's face suggested he'd be drinking them both. He tossed on a robe and motioned for the darker man to join him on the balcony.

It was sunny and warm outside, forcing Archie to shield his eyes. The protestors had dispersed but he was pretty sure they'd assemble again in a few hours.

Riley picked up a rock from the plant box next to him and tossed it onto the street. "You see, this is why you got stationed out here in the first place, Archie."

He looked down at himself and pulled the robe shut. He took a drink. "Because I like to drink and fuck sometimes?"

Riley turned to him. "We're in an official building you've stocked full of prostitutes and street people."

Archie took a breath. "The people who are safe right now because we opened the doors?"

"Safe for how long, Archie, for how long, exactly?" Riley threw another rock. He was angry.

Archie shook his head. "Riley, Why even have a job if I can't enjoy my life a little, and help some people who need it?"

Riley threw his hands up in the air. "I can't talk to you."

Because you're so insufferably British you can't live your life." Archie said loudly. He looked around and lowered his voice. "It's not my fault."

"I'm here to do my job, not have threesomes with hookers all night."

"Then do your goddamn job. Help me keep these people safe and get them out of the country somewhere they can be happy." Archie finished his drink and considered throwing the glass. He dropped it into a planter and looked right at Riley. "Help me."

"Do you even know what your job is?"

"Do you, Riley? Do you know what an embassy is?" Archie turned, frustrated.

"I know it's meant to be a place of order, not what this shitshow is." Riley waved at the room behind him.

"Fuck order."

"Fuck order? Right. Good motto, Arch."

"Those people don't need order. They need to be living their fun, disorderly lives in a place that's not about to be a war zone."

Riley's response was cut off by a rumble that shook the entire building. Archie had never experienced anything like it.

It seemed like the room moved ten centimeters up and down.

Archie looked up. "That came from the roof."

The two men ran back inside the room. Sharla and Zehra had been woken up by the rumble and were pulling themselves out of bed. Archie thought quickly. "Zehra, call Sean to have him meet us armed on the roof, then try to calm people down. Riley, get to the armory and grab three rifles. Meet me on the roof as fast as you can…"

"I'm coming with you. Sharla started pulling clothes on even as Archie got his pants on.

"I know, I don't have time to argue with you." He started toward the stairs. It was only three flights to the roof and this would be faster.

Sharla bolted out after him. They entered the stairwell. "How did they get on the roof?"

"I don't know. There's a goddamn helipad on there. Maybe they have a helicopter?"

Sharla took three stairs at a time. "That's insane."

As they rounded the stairway leading to rooftop access, they could hear sounds coming from behind the door.

Archie leaned against the door. Sharla ran up next to him. "What's going on out there?"

"No idea." Archie whispered. "This door stays shut until I have a gun in my hand."

Sharla listened to the door. "They're saying 'help us.'"

"No, they aren't and I don't care." Archie looked at her.

Sharla pushed against the door. "They need help."

"Stop it." He tried his best to hold her back, but Sharla slammed the door open.

What happened next seemed to go by in a blur. Sharla and Archie stumbled onto the rooftop, shielding their eyes from the light. A giant metal object that looked more than anything like a prawn sat in the center of the roof, long articulated feet digging into the tar. Four shapes emerged from the belly of the prawn, one carrying a blue bundle. Sharla ran to them as the man fell. Archie came up behind her. The wind seemed to pick up as he realized that the object was a ship, and its slowly dying thrusters had whipped the air up around them. He looked down and saw the blue thing on the ground.

It was a nude woman, painted blue all over. She was spitting up what looked like some kind of blue poison, seizing and choking violently. Archie picked her up and ran with her back into the compound. Sharla was right behind him, followed by the other men. He exited the stairwell on the top level and ran to the infirmary, the rest not far behind him. Kicking open the door he placed the woman on a cart. She was seizing up. Was she being poisoned by the blue paint all over her body? Was this some kind of strange torture? She rolled over and vomited. The floor filled with dark blue liquid as Archie hunted.

"Diazepam, help me. We're looking for Diazepam." He called out to Sharla. Archie didn't know much beyond having been a field medic, but he knew he didn't have much time.

Sharla grabbed his arm. "Archie, no."

"Shar, I need Diazepam. Help me." His voice cracked.

He looked back. She shook her head. Next to her were Sean and Riley holding weapons out to one side.

Archie followed the barrels. Standing there were four alien creatures staring at the table.

He looked down. The seizure had slowed. He could see it now. The blue wasn't paint.

It was the natural color of her skin.

Archie stepped back and put his head in his hands. He looked up. "I could have fucking killed her."

Sharla turned to Sean and Riley. "Put the guns down."

Sean looked at Riley who nodded. They dropped the guns.

Archie looked at the aliens. "Do any of you know what's wrong with her?"

One of them, a woman with a greenish hued face, filled with lizard like scales spoke in English. "We don't know. This happened once before and she was fine after some water, hydration."

"ok, " Archie looked at Sean. "Sean, can you get me some water, ice chips, a tube?"

Sean tried to tear his eyes away from the aliens. He nodded and moved to the adjoining bathroom.

Archie looked back at the woman. She was wearing a white robe that only showed her face. "What caused this, do you think? Now, before, anything?"

A taller alien, with dark insect-like skin, lifted himself up. He also wore a white robe. The way he moved, Archie suspected his body looked very different from his. "Are you a doctor?"

Archie smiled and chuckled to himself. "No. I was a medic. We are a bit short staffed here. I think you picked a bad time to visit."

"We know." The first woman spoke again. "By about 500 years."

Sharla was feeding water to the blue woman who had stopped seizing and looked better, although her eyes were still closed.

She looked at Archie and laughed.

Archie turned back to the aliens, confused. Sharla's laughter ripped across the room. Even as the blue woman's eyes opened. Sharla held her hand, sliding hers into the woman's three fingered palm.

Sharla stopped laughing. "500 years ago, this place we're standing. Bursa, Turkey. This was the most powerful seat in the world."

Archie sighed. "the Ottoman Empire."

The blue woman coughed, pulling herself up with Sharla's hand. "I'm sorry to have panicked you all."

Archie looked down and tried to get her blood pressure. He shook his head. What would it tell him. "Is there anything we can do to make you comfortable? Do you need anything?"

"No, thank you. I didn't want to admit this, but it looks like this is the K'smia. I should be fine, but my body is going to go to sleep soon."

Sharla shot up. "You don't mean, like, permanent sleep?"

The woman looked at her kindly. "No, no, I'm so sorry. I don't have a lot of control over these translators. Just a temporary sleep. To repair myself. Maybe a few solar cycles."

"Oh. ok." Sharla looked up. She had never felt more out of her depth.

Riley was rubbing his forehead with his hands, "Arch, can I talk to you for a minute?"

"Sure. Sean, mate, you can go back and keep watch. And let's not talk too much about things none of us understand yet?"

"Got it, Mr. Benjamin."

Archie and Riley moved over to the wall near the bathroom. "Ok, let me consolidate, here. Five aliens, featuring what looks like four different species, including a woman so sick she's about to go to sleep casually for a couple of years, just landed in a giant metal shrimp on a roof that I'm not 100% sure can hold it. Do I have this?"

"A bit reductive, sure, but yes."

"What the fuck, Arch."

"Yes." One of the aliens, a man shaped person who looked, for all the world, like he might have just been wearing a lizard mask under a mop of average looking brown hair, spoke up."

Riley looked over, "I'm sorry, what was that?"

"Yes, we are about 500 years off. The ship is a gift. I'm not sure how it compensates for time dilation when we view far away events. So I miscalculated before we jumped here. I apologize.

"Exactly. So they were far off and the light reaching them was 500 years old, they miscalculated, and now they're here. Could happen to anyone." Archie tried to rise to this occasion, no matter how bizarre. He slapped Riley on the back.

"Sure. Anyone." Riley wasn't feeling so inclined.

Sharla stood up, "My name is Sharla Tuk. It's good to meet you all. You're certainly welcome here and we'll do our best to take care of your friend."

Archie reached out his hand to the alien who had spoken. "I'm Archie Benjamin. This is Riley Adams. It's our job to kind of keep this place going." He touched hands with all of them. None had the presence of mind to shake, but that was ok, Archie thought.

The blue woman on the stretcher kept hold of Sharla's hand, reaching out her other one to Archie. "It is good to meet you. I am Vorun Ekel, Officiant for the Forsa." Sharla sensed, as she said the word, that "Forsa" might represent the odd shape she had tattooed on her forehead – a shape bound by an eight sided figure. An octagon.

The door swung open and Rey stood in the doorway. She looked around the room.

"Holy shit."

Archie responded without looking. "Swear jar, young lady." Rey stepped past him and punched him playfully in the arm, still staring ahead.

Sharla called her over. "Vorun, this is Rey. She's very smart. She works here as well." The two shook hands.

Archie turned to Sharla. "Do you mind, you and Rey stay with Vorun until she's feeling a little better. It's getting a bit...crowded in here. Riley and I will take the rest to the meeting room at the end of the hall. Just yell out if you need anything."

She nodded and kissed him as Archie and Riley walked down the hall briskly with the other four aliens. He knew Sharla had her concerns about why Vorun was wearing no clothing and seemed so ill. He had faith that she could find the truth in that room, even as he looked for his own.

The aliens sat around the table with Archie. He looked up and Riley shook his head as he sat down. He sighed.

The man seemingly wearing the lizard mask spoke up first. "Well, I am Katel-ko-ra. I am from a species known as the Form. I am a witness. I was the unfortunate pilot for this adventure,so…"

Next to him sat the two other women with greenish skin. They were smoother, however, more like the face of a snake. The largest one spoke, "I am Plasri No and this is Kivak Atel. We are from the Ahreee. I am a petitioner and she is my Apriya." She pointed to the smaller woman beside her.

The last man spoke. His skin was darker than Riley's, pulled back into a carapace like thickness across his elongated skull. His eyes were eerily human. "I am Symkere and I represent the Velios Unity, comprising over 60 peoples. And I am petitioner, too."

"Ok," Archie started, standing up. "I'm very glad to know you, all of you. This is, technically, first human contact with aliens so you probably understand we know nothing. To understand, we may need to go over a few things."

Symkere shook his head. "no."

Archie smiled awkwardly. "You don't want to talk and go over things?"

"Oh, I'm sorry. Again we have translators that don't always deliver the more accurate… What I mean is that this isn't first contact."

Riley perked up, "I don't understand."

Symkere continued, "people from various Velios planets have frequented Earth for thousands of years. Forsa has representatives here."

"Wait, there are blue people here?" Archie tried to find clarity.

"Of course." Plasri No dug into the pocket of her robe and pulled out a book. On the cover was a blue person with many arms, resembling Vorun dramatically. She passed it to Archie. He looked around the room, picking up the book. One one side it was written in a dense alien language. On the other side, the even pages, it looked like Sanskrit. Archie flipped through the pages of images and text.

It was the Kama Sutra.

***

"So, you've been here before?" Sharla had taken out a notebook back in the infirmary to write down everything Vorun had to say. She propped it open in her lap with her other hand still in the blue one. Rey was doing her best to make Vorun comfortable.

"She is sweet. And, yes. I thought it must have been a couple hundred years ago, but it looks like a bit longer."

"So, your people live very long."

Vorun smiled. "It doesn't seem like long enough."

"You'll be asleep by this time tomorrow?" Sharla shot Rey a panicked look.

"Yes, but I'll be fine."

Rey put her hand in the blue woman's other hand. "I'm sorry if we are so full of questions. We want to get to know you and know what to do."

"It's ok, Rey. Your friend here is Shukkat."

Sharla looked up. "What is that?"

"Oh. the translator didn't catch that. In my culture, in Forsa, 'Shukkat' is a complement. It means 'someone who wants to know.' We consider it a sign of love to want to know about someone. If you want to know everything about them, no detail is too small. It's kajere, the second one, actually."

Rey smiled at Sharla, "I like that."

"Me, too."

"The first kajere, sign of acceptance, is to see someone. The second is to want to know them. The third is to hold their hand." She lifted both her hands, showing how Shar and Rey had automatically held her hands to comfort her.

Vorun had a way of explaining things that made you feel smart for even asking the question. It was hypnotic and Rey noticed right away that it played into Sharla's fascination with people in a way she'd never seen anything ever do.

This woman was hundreds of years old, born across the galaxy. And she was willing to tell them anything they wanted to know.

Sharla was filling her notebook. "You are an officiant. That's your job?"

"It's not my job. It's what I do. And it has to be done on neutral ground, which is why we traveled here. The Velios Unity covers so much of space. Finding a place outside their jurisdiction is a daunting task."

"What has to be done?"

"There is a negotiation. The Ahreee, whose worlds number in the hundreds, wished to join the Velios Unity, whose 60 races sit on thousands of different worlds. We are near a contract."

Rey shrugged. "I can see why it was so hard to find a neutral place."

Vurun nodded. "We have been here before and found Earth to be a pleasant place to negotiate. The food is good."

Sharla looked at Rey, "Hey, Zagats, a four star review."

"I'll take it," Rey shot back.

"So you negotiate and have a little ceremony and the contract is signed, right?"

"In essence, yes."

"So we can do that before you start your healing sleep. We can set it up for you." Sharla felt a new kind of excitement. In the middle of the mess outside, something good could happen.

Vorun smiled wanly. "I'm in no shape to officiate. I contacted the Forsa and asked them to send another."

Rey was confused. "but you seem ok."

"I am. I will be. Do you see this symbol on my head?"

Sharla nodded. The tattoo had fascinated her from the start.

"It's called a t'kau. It represents the eight aspects of gender and shows how my own unique gender works."

"Ok," Rey believed she understood.

"It's necessary. Because of my duties as an officiant are acceptance, I am open to being freely accessed for the enjoyment of anyone. It's why I chose to be naked on board the ship, so that no one felt I was inaccessible."

Sharla asked timidly, "sexually?"

"Yes. Forsa members must be open and accepting. It's how we create the pure acceptance necessary for officiating."

"Where you have sex with the petitioners?" Rey whispered.

"Yes. Where we open ourselves up completely, as the contract, to show the petitioners what absolute acceptance looks like."

"And you won't be in the right shape to do that?"

"That's right. I feel terrible. I feel like I've let them down. And now I feel like I've let you down."

Sharla squeezed her hand. "Shh. absolutely not. How long will it take them to send someone else?"

"It should take no longer than six months."

***

Sharla slid into the conference room next to Archie. The aliens all seemed more comfortable.

"How is Vorun?" asked Katel-ko-ra, addressing Sharla.

Shar looked around the room. "She's good. She's starting to drift in and out of sleep. It's how she is going to heal, so we don't want to keep her up. Zehra and Rey are keeping an eye on her."

Archie nodded. "Riley went to join Mera and Dorothy to pass clothes and food around and calm everyone downstairs."

"We appreciate your efforts so much." Symkere looked around the room. "The Velios Unity won't forget this graciousness."

"It's not a problem, Simmy." Archie looked over at Shar, "What did she say about a replacement officiant?"

Sharla mouthed, "six months."

"Ok. You are all welcome here as long as you like, really. In all honesty, we would prefer for you to stay. This is more exciting for us than you, for sure. We're just not sure if WE'LL be here in six months."

Plasri No stood up. "We are grateful for your help. If it's not possible, we can leave." The others grumbled at her. There was something else here, making this more difficult.

"Is there a time constraint on the contract?" Sharla asked.

Symkere looked around the room. "Yes. I represent 60 different people, different species, different…everything. They have given me authority to make this deal within a time frame."

Sharla turned to Archie. "Join me in the hall."

"If you'll excuse us for a second." Archie stood up as Sharla dragged him by the hand to the hallway.

Archie turned to her in curiosity. "Ok, you clearly have an idea?"

"I do. WE do it."

"Just like that?"

"Yes, just like that."

Archie put his hands on his head. "ok, you know what this entails, right?"

"I do. I've got a whole notebook full of what we do." Sharla handed him the book.

Archie paged through the book. "Symkere's species are arthropods. They are insects, basically. Are you prepared to have sex with an insect?"

"They are people. The rest doesn't matter."

"Ok, ok. So we do it?" Archie handed her back her notebook.

Sharla opened the book and pointed to an image. "In order to be a forsa cadre – an Octagon, we need four of us, pledged to mediate and...oficiate."

Archie thought for a second. "Ok. You, me, Zehra, Dot. Four people"

"You?" Sharla cocked her head.

Archie put his hands on his waist. "Yes. I think it's rude how you always think you're a better prostitute than I am."

"It's literally what I do for a living."

"What do you think I do for a living?"

Sharla scrunched up her face. "I actually can't debate that."

He put his hands on her shoulders, like Archie always did when he delivered his pep talks. "We can do this."

"I think so."

Archie leaned in and kissed her.

"See. That's why we belong together."

"Seriously?"

"C'mon, we've only boinked a fraction of each other's friends. Let's tie the knot and make it 100%" he spun her around.

Sharla laughed, "Well, that sounds like a reception for the ages."

He held her and moved back and forth. "Open bar, too. Little sandwiches. Oral sex."

"Look, you had me at boink, but this is not realistic. I love you, but your parents are never going to accept me."

Archie tried to dip her. "Those old things, they're vestigial."

She thought, "Oh, god I love your accent. Say 'vestigial' again. Vestigial. Swoon."

"Do you really want to marry your escort?" Sharla whispered.

"You only live once. I'm just saying I'm not going to do it even once without you."

"That was good," she thought. That worked.

"And for the record, you may be other people's escort, but I haven't paid you yet even for the first time."

She grabbed his hand to move back into the room. "It's because I gave you credit."

He stopped her and put his lips on hers before they entered the room. "What's your name again?"

Sharla didn't pause. She cocked her head to one side and looked into Archie's eyes, laughing. "Mrs. Benjamin."

Archie stepped back and shook her hand. "It's good to meet you, Mrs. Benjamin. That's a pretty name. It rolls off the tongue." They moved into the room. The alien contingent stood up.

"You think so? Maybe you should take my last name."

Archie made a face. "Archie Tuk? God, no, that sounds like a venereal infection."

Sharla looked out and addressed the room, still holding Archie's hand, "ok, everyone, we're going to do this the right way. And we're doing it today."

Faces in the room lit up. Sharla listened to the sounds of joyful back and forth. Until it was drown out by a boom.

Archie looked across the room. His stomach sunk as he moved to the window. The protesters were back and burrowing through the front foyer. He watched as they pointed up toward the roof.

They had seen the ship.

Rey ran into the conference room holding the rifles. "We have to get down there."

"All of you, stay here, please." Archie was terrified about what the small-minded crowd might do if they caught sight of an actual alien. He made his way to the elevators with Sharla and Rey right behind him.

The elevators opened to chaos on the ground floor. Riley was holding back the crowd with a rifle, ushering their people. into the elevators.

Dorothy was right beside him. "That's my father and brother." she pointed to two Turkish men near the door. "I can talk to them." Dorothy's belief in people overlapped with her desire to DO SOMETHING, sometimes leading to bad decisions. this was one.

Sharla lifted her gun. "No, you can't, Baby."

Rey found Tanji and Eren. Both were dressed so like her. She tried to shoo them into the elevators, but they stood behind her, instead.

They weren't going to leave her.

"Riley, secure the first floor with all the people there. If anything gets up there that doesn't belong here, fucking kill it."

"I'm not leaving you, Archie."

"Just do it, Riley. Ok? For once, do what I say."

Riley heard Archie's tone and grabbed the stragglers, stuffing them in the elevator. A rock from the protestors hit him in the head, drawing blood. He shook his head, sending blood everywhere, and pushed a button. The elevator closed.

Sharla turned her attention to the crowd advancing. Somehow the gate had been raised, the one securing the front doorways. She looked at Rey, who nodded, running to the entry desk, the other two following, and hit the close button, reversing the gate.

There were still people inside, but the fence was slowly coming down, the spikes at its base aiming for the holes in the floor that housed them.

Dorothy was hit by a stone, right below her eye. As Archie looked, she was hit again, in the head. She wobbled and yelled out "Gökhan!" At the entryway her brother stood with a handful of rocks, throwing them as hard as he could at her. She took a step and Archie grabbed her. He shot the man in the leg as he charged at them.

Dorothy's brother fell, slipping in his own blood, coming down hard near the entryway desk. Rey raised her gun and advanced on the crowd, shooting another man crawling under the gate.

Dorothy's father stepped up beside his son as if to grab him. Rey stopped as he lifted him. Suddenly, he dropped him and spun his hand around, blindly stabbing Eren in the neck. He followed Eren down to the ground, stabbing the girl over and over like an enraged animal. Rey pulled up her gun and shot him in the head. Tanji stepped back, staring into Eren's open dead eyes. She screamed and ran toward the door. Sharla shot two more people who were crawling under the gate as Archie pointed out targets, shooting with precision while holding Dorothy like a rag doll with one arm.

Tanji tried to climb under the gate, in panic. Rey reached her and dragged her out, holding her, crawling over her to protect her. Hands reached for the young intern, pulling her under the gate. The sharp spikes at the bottom stabbed into her legs, driving downward, pinning her. Tanji tried to free her. Blood pooled under her as she struggled to get back inside and pull free from the spikes.

Rey's screams sent Sharla running toward her. She looked at Archie. Tears were falling down his face.

"No, Dot, no. Please, no." Dorothy was dead in his arms.

He pulled her body in close and looked back at Sharla. He opened his mouth as a small dark spot in his forehead grew and he fell to the ground. A man in a black and white mask behind him lowered his gun. Sharla screamed and shot him over and over, dropping to her knees.

She looked up to see another man advance on her and raise a gun. She clicked the empty barrel of the rifle.

She heard Rey's screams in her head as she closed her eyes.

Suddenly, the sounds shifted toward silence, except for a feral growl. Shar opened her eyes to see Rey panting, looking over her shoulder. Symkere had dropped his robe. He was moving toward her with inhuman speed on four thin insect legs, ripping the gate from her and hoisting both her and Tanji in his thin, articulated arms. He held them close and protected them with his body, returning to stand with the two Ahreee.

Katel-ko-ra lifted Sharla up in his arms delicately as Plasir No held a weapon out in front of her.

"You are trespassing. This facility and everyone in it is under the protection of the Ahreee and the planets of the Velios Unity. And additional aggression will be dealt with immediately. Prepare to be transported back to where you belong.

Suddenly, noiselessly, the invaders disappeared.

Sharla put her arm on Katel's shoulder unsteadily and dropped to the ground. She crawled over to where Archie laid, still holding tight to the woman he had tried so hard to save.

She slid in their blood as she tried to wrap her arms around them and sobbed. The walls closed in and she stopped feeling anything.

***

Sharla woke up in the infirmary across from Vorun. She walked over to the sleeping woman and kissed her on the forehead. She was warm, but not feverish. Sharla realized she had no idea what a fever would be for a Forsa. Katel and Zehra were asleep in chairs in the room. The lizardish man woke up as she ran her hands over Vorun's palm.

He spoke up quietly, "She would like to know that you were touching her like that while she was asleep. "

Sharla sat next to him. "I'm glad that the violence didn't make it up here."

"She's fine. I think she already looks healthier." Katel wasn't wrong. Her skin looked more vibrant, brighter.

Shar took his face in her hands. "Thank you for rescuing us."

"We're working on that now."

Sharla cocked her head, confused. She looked over beyond Vorun and saw Rey in bed. Tanji was asleep next to her. Shar grabbed Katel's hand and padded over to her.

"Hey, kiddo."

Rey's eyes opened. Suddenly she started crying. "I'm so sorry."

"I know, baby. I know."

"Archie. I'm so sorry. And Dorothy."

"I know, baby, I know. I'm sorry about Eren. Is Tanji ok?"

Rey smiled at her through her tears. "I can't believe you know their names."

Katel moved to the other side of the bed. Sharla whispered to Rey, petting Tanji. "She's going to need you."

Rey sniffled and took a breath. "You need us both."

"What do you mean?" Shar grabbed Rey's hand and she held tightly back.

Rey went on. "I know what you're going to do. You need four people. You, Me, Zehra, Tanji."

"No way." Sharla dropped her head and pressed her forehead against Rey's. "Not you. And not her. We'll get by."

Rey was adamant, "Well, I'm not leaving."

"What do you mean?"

Riley stepped in, his head bandaged. "She means she is leaving. Along with everyone else."

"What are you talking about?"

"Shar, I'm so sorry about Benji." Riley hugged her. She remembered that Riley called him that on good days, on days they were a team.

"I wish he were here to see this."

Katel leaned in to her. "That is what I was saying. Teleporting all your people downstairs all the way to Britain would not be possible without an accepting telepad. But Symkere identified an old telepad in Athens, Greece that was left there on a previous visit. It is still functioning."

Riley continued, "we can teleport all the refugees there and the British government has agreed to send a helicopter and visas. They'll be safe."

Zehra came up behind Shar and hugged her. "Archie would be so happy."

Shrla looked out into the room. "Yeah. Thank you, all of you."

"We're not going." Rey pulled herself out of bed. Her legs were still wrapped and covered in tall white stockings, but she seemed able to walk easily.

Riley looked over at her. "Yes, you are."

Rey looked through the pockets of her gown. "I quit. You aren't my boss." I guess there's nothing to hand over. They should give us badges."

Sharla sat on the bed. She pulled Rey down in front of her and ran her fingers through her pitch black hair. She had forgotten how beautiful the younger girl's skin was. "What are you, 20?"

Rey put her hands on Sharla's waist, shaking her head. Part of her didn't want to have to say this. "Shar. How old were you when you met Archie?"

A tear came down her cheek. "I was twenty."

Rey pulled Sharla in and kissed her neck. She whispered in her ear. "How old were you when you fell in love with Archie?"

She held Shar and let her cry. She smoothed down her hair and rocked her back and forth. Zehra put her arms around them. The room was quiet except for her sobs.

"I was twenty"

They stayed that way for a while. Sharla felt like she really had no one left to say goodbye to. Both Sean and Ricky came up to say goodbye to Rey before they left. Riley's final goodbye was a blur. Mera helped gather people and left without saying goodbye.

By the time it was dark, there were only nine people left in the Embassy.

It only seemed right to gather around the unconscious Vorun as they prepared. Katel brought a small box with a paddle attachment. He demonstrated it on his own arm as the four women shook off their clothing in the bright light of the infirmary.

Zehra had brought Rey some black stockings to wear over her bandages. She pulled them on, sliding her black panties and bra off and moved to the mirror. She rubbed the spots where her clothing had left marks watching it bounce back. After a minute or so, there was no sign she had ever worn clothing.

She helped Tanji out of her clothes, stripping her down to a pair of red shorts and matching underwear. With every touch, Rey tried to remind her that while one sister was gone she had another. She pulled off her underwear and draped a few necklaces around her neck.

Zhera and Shar kissed slowly as they pulled each other's clothing off, stripping for the younger girls' enjoyment. As they moved back and forth, Katel told them stories about the great officiants he had witnessed. And about how many t'kaus he had applied himself.

As a professional witness, he had seen things that other people would do anything to be a part of. He had seen the intimate ceremonies of some of the most mysterious species in the world.

Sharla read from her notebook, explaining rituals, as the women became more comfortable with each other. Rey stepped over to Sharla and kissed her on the lips, holding her tongue in her mouth for a long time before letting go.

"I guess you're my boss now."

"Really. You know what I like about that?"

"What?"

Sharla put her hand down between Rey's legs and dipped her fingers inside her. "No HR department."

Sharla explained to them that acceptance happened in joy.

And then Katel took over.

"First of all, these are called 'Leeir' They normalize your system. Once a year or so means no bacterial issues, no disease, no reproduction. These are from Vorun. I'm sure she would want you to have them as gifts." He handed them the pills to take.

Then he stood in the middle of the room and held up his device.

"When different peoples get together, the connection can be thanotic– death-dealing, destructive. Or it can be erotic – creative, building, growing, even reproductive. Vorun has dedicated herself to the second path. This device places a t'kau on your head. It's an external shape representing the four gender classes and the four gender drives. It's up to you to one day fill in the t'kau with your own identity. Even as it shifts and grows. "

"The t'kau means you are available. You are open. One of the things the Forsa do when receiving a t'kau is to visit someone with whom they have argued or had hatred and make themselves open to them. "

"It's a rite of passage we don't have access to here, but remember, a t'kau is not ever in a final state. It is always a chance to grow. To become more. Gender is a verb, not a noun"

"The name you choose when you take your t'kau is your name. Who you are is up to you, being built always. Never shy away from who you can be because of who you were."

He slid his robe off. As expected, there were patches of lizard-like skin arrayed across his entire body, on his belly, under his arms. The area between his legs was smooth with what looked like a long, split reptile cock, boh pieces prehensile, moving on their own. Shar remembered from biology that many snakes had this. It was called a hemipene and it was split in two, each side growing out of one side of the cloaca.

He moved to Zehra, who was sitting cross legged on a white table, nude. He stepped up in front of her. She looked up and kissed him. She sighed and recited her oath, as he applied the tattoo to her forehead, loud enough for everyone to hear.

"I am called Zehra, and I pledge myself to the Octagon, to listen in faith, to connect in love, to give myself in joy as contract."

He finished and stepped away. Sharla saw the black octagon on the smaller woman's forehead and it felt real. Katel stepped toward her. She pulled him close and wrapped her legs around him. She looked him in the eye and smiled, cocking her head slightly. She kissed him and he nodded. She reached down and pulled the two parts of his cock together, slipping them into her pussy. She moved forward, breathing in. For a moment she realized that she was being penetrated by an actual alien, letting the idea wash over her. She closed her eyes and leaned back, pressing her clit against him. She spoke slowly, copping the rhythm of his movements, letting herself feel every part.

"I am called…Shukkat." She paused, listening to the sound of Katel's breathing. She put her hands on his ass and opened herself up. "And I pledge myself to the Octagon," She moved faster, catching his eyes and kissing him again.

He laughed and finished her tattoo, putting the machine down and pumping inside her cunt. He smiled. It was a race now. She whispered in his ear, "c'mon, you fucker," laughing as she leaned into his fuck. He smiled and put his head down pushing, harder and harder. She lifted her ass from the surface and felt his prick slam into her again and again. "To listen in faith, to connect in love, to give myself in joy." He pulled back and dug himself into her. Sharla felt the warmth of his cum as she held him and whispered the final words. "As contract." She kissed him on the nose and raised her arms.

The girls cheered and clapped for her, trying to grab onto the joy in the room. They let the last 24 hours fall away in a kind of sardonic frenzy. Rey reached her hand out to Katel and pulled him over between her legs. There was something freeing about the pill she had just taken – almost as if she couldn't be harmed, like she was unstoppable. She kissed Katel widely on the lips, feeling his lizard-like tongue invade her mouth and open her up. She reached between his legs and gathered up the wetness, lifting it to her mouth. She tasted Shar – Shukkat. And she tasted Katel. She kissed his neck as he lifted his device.

She felt the light trail of the device on her forehead. This would be her first tattoo. She leaned in, feeling Katel against her naked breasts and belly. She wished, for a moment, that the pain were more intense. She spoke to him. "I am called Reylan Corroba and I pledge myself to the Octagon, to listen in faith, to connect in love, to give myself in joy as contract." She kissed him again as he lowered the device and kissed her back.

She looked over at Tanji, her body so similar. They were the same color, the same shape. Both looked as though they still had time to grow into themselves, to be bigger than life. But today, pert but round breasts rose over taut little bellies. But where Rey was untouched by tattoos, Tanji was tattooed all over already. Rey reached for her hand.

Katel began her tattoo. Tanji closed her eyes, familiar with the feeling. Her accent was simple but beautiful. When Tanji spoke, you could imagine long lost poetry and belly dances, nights touched with saffron and cinnamon.

"I am called Etangiel…" Rey held her hand and nodded vigorously. She needed Tanji to say it out loud. Tanji looked forward. "Etangiel Corroba. and I pledge myself to the Octagon, to listen in faith, to connect in love, to give myself in joy as contract." She opened her mouth for Katel, running her hands over his back. She'd lived on the streets for so long, done so many things with so many people. This was her choice and she realized she loved the smooth, cool feel of the scales on his face.

Rey cheered and the rest joined in.

Shukkat's notebook explained that the ceremony happened in a place called a kurge. While the embassy had no kurge, obviously, it had a space very similar. On the third floor was a large and spacious gym. In the gym was a large wrestling area with a number of smaller rooms around it– changing areas for participants.

As Rey stepped over the matts in the main wrestling areas, she felt powerful. A wrestling area was a good idea. It allowed her to think of this as a playful event. This was an athletic event, something they could feel convivial about.

Like the Olympics.

Zehra and Rey entered one of the rooms as Shukkat and Etangiel made their way to another. The Ahreee and Velios Petitioners were already in their respective rooms, waiting for the ceremony to begin.

Katel-ko-ra positioned himself as the sole witness, sitting nude on the bleachers, watching.

Only one Officiant was needed, the book said, but, in situations like this, when many people had been involved in negotiations, two was preferred. Shukkat hugged Tanji. Tanji would act as her Apriya, a backup, a source of strength, someone who helped prepare her. She would watch from the room. And Rey would be Zehra's

But as Rey followed Zehra into the side room it became clear that Zehra was nearly panicking. Rey could feel her heart race and her breathing. It didn't take long for Rey to realize the cause of her trepidation.

It was Symkere.

Zehra's fear of insects had been triggered by the sight of his four legs, placed equidistant around a central thorax, his mandibles, even his skin. Rey held on to her as Shukkat called for them.

Rey kissed Zehra and sat the taller girl down in the dressing room. She turned and stepped out to see Shukkat sitting on the matts, nude. She nodded at her. It didn't really matter which of the two was the Officiant and which the Apriya.

She could fill in for Zehra.

She moved toward Shukkat and sat next to her, holding hands.

The petitioners stepped out of their respective rooms. They were nude as well. Symkere was tall and quick, wiry, thin all over with leathery thick black skin over muscles that looked far more insect than human. His face seemed attached casually to his elongated head and his arms dipped down, thin and rugged, with sharp claw-like hands at the ends. As he stood, they could see that he had a spikey tube protruding from his central area, with a thicker area at top. It looked like a small baseball bat sporting a dragonfruit tip. He sat across from the two women on a mat.

From another changing room came Plasri No, her face smooth and snake-like. Her body looked remarkably human with the addition of a long trail of green scales at her back and a ridged tail, waving on its own and lifting when she sat across from the taller woman.

Shukkat was amazed at how literally human her breasts looked, the skin only slightly green, with a blue green tipped areola. It was as though she had been made in the same place, yet colored slightly differently with markers on the way out.

Shukkat began reciting:

"Hi. My name is Shukkat and I represent the Octagon, Earth. I welcome you all in love. I have read the agreements and am prepared to defend them or deliver them to my people as Law."

She stood up to expose herself and moved toward the center. "I stand before you without deception or artifice." She sat back down.

Rey felt surprisingly calm. She recited "hello. My name is Reylan Corroba and I represent the Octagon, Earth. I welcome all of you in love. I have read the agreements and am prepared to defend them or deliver them to my people as Law. I stand before you without deception or artifice." She stood up and padded over to sit right next to Shukkat, sliding to the ground next to her.

Plasri No spoke next. She looked at them and at Symkere. "Yulari. My name is Plasri No and I represent the people of the Ahreee"

Out of nowhere, Rey yelled out, "woo." and Plasri No's face lit up. Suddenly she wasn't some stern alien leader. She was another girl playing on the gym matts with her friends, being urged on. Shukkat clapped. "Go, Ahree."

The greenish woman laughed and continued. "I welcome all of you in love. I have read the agreements and am prepared to defend them or deliver them to my people as Law. I stand before you without deception or artifice." She stood up and the two women applauded some more. Shukkat reached for her as if after a game of red rover, and she moved over to the center of the mat and fell down next to her, pulled in and falling over their little group. They grabbed her ass and pulled her closer.

Suddenly, in the back of her mind, Shukkat felt Archie. She could imagine him calling out, loving how all of this could be turned into some degenerate game. He was there, with a whiskey in his hand, his cock out, swinging it around like a helicopter, yelling louder than anyone.

Symkere looked at them. He smiled and shook his head. "Kauthaus. My name is Symkere and I represent the differentiated and disparate worlds." He stopped for a moment, building playful drama. His head dropped. "of the Velios Unity."

The three women cheered and clapped loudly. Rey yelled out "Velios." making a "V" with her fingers. They chanted "V, V, V, V."

Symkere stood up. "I welcome all of you in love. I have read the agreements and am prepared to defend them or deliver them to my people as Law. I stand before you without deception or artifice." He recited the last quickly, waving his arms around his own nudity.

They all cheered and waved him over. His long insect like legs moved unnaturally quickly, bringing him close enough that Rey could pull him down on the mat with them. She pushed him down and brought her face down on his, kissing him with her mouth wide open. He tasted salty and warmer than she'd imagined. She held onto his thin, pincer-like hand.

The four of them laid on each other in the center of the mat now. Shukkat leaned in and kissed Plasri No, placing her hands on both her pretty breasts. Her tongue was quick and darting and it felt alive, like a goldfish. Shukkat tried to capture it. She came up for air.

"Simmy, Plas, millions of years ago, as officiants, We would have offered our lives to you as defense of this contract. But we are a people changed and guided by love, by compassion, by joy. We offer you our ears if you wish to contest it. We offer you every other piece of us both, in passion and acceptance, if you wish to make it live."

Rey slid her hand down Symkere's chest and felt the strength of him. She licked at his mouth. "Ok. Now we get to speak from the heart, right?"

Rey rolled over on top of Symkere and took his hand, placing it between her legs. She could feel herself, wet, losing herself in the ceremony. But not just that. There was more. "This is what's in my heart. This is it. Symkere. I know your people now. I learned everything I need to know when I saw these hands save my life. I will be there, watching your people grow and succeed, every time you let me. I celebrate with you. Thank you for seeing me and saving me."

She leaned into him and kissed him. Shukkat and Plasri No applauded. Shukat turned to Plasri No. "Ok, my turn. What is in my heart. On the worst day of my life, you stood there, kicking ass for me, making it better, taking my side. I will never forget that. I love you."

Shukkat kissed her, wrapping her arms around her.

Plasri No grabbed her arms and wrestled her on the mat until she was on top. She leaned down and massaged her breasts with her lips, forcing Shukkat's back to arch upward.

Symkere lifted Rey's chin with his hand. "What is in my heart. My people consider… I consider… this treaty to be final. Nothing else is needed. You've gone through so much today." He looked kindly at Rey.

"As do I." Plasri kissed Shukkat's head delicately.

Rey looked over at her. "We're the only people in the building. No one will ever know what happens here except Katel and he'll say anything we want."

He called out, "that's true, I will."

Rey cheered for Katel. "Woo!"

Shukkat looked over at Rey and smiled. She crawled toward Symkere and slid in between his four legs. "She's right. Let's celebrate." Rey kissed Plasri and giggled as her tongue flicked across her lips. Shukkat dipped her head down over Symkere's growing cock and licked at the tip of it. She tried to get the mace-like tip past her lips and was barely able to. He moaned as she slid her tongue up and down its length.

Plasri No pushed her way between Rey's legs, sucking on her clit and letting her flickering tongue invade her soft spaces. Rey's head went backward. Symkere kissed her neck, white she grabbed his pincer and placed it in her mouth.

Shukkat sucked him until he was thick and ready as he pressed his face against the smaller girl. The reptilian woman grabbed at Shukkat, pressing her face against her. Shukkat could taste Rey's pussy, even as she saw the dark wet pool under her from Plasri No's darting tongue.

Rey pulled herself on top of the darker insectoid man and slowly slid his spiky member into her wet open cunt. She looked into his eyes, pressing her body down on top of it. "Fuck me, Simmy, fuck me."

He whispered to her, "we should be careful."

"No, it's good. Deeper. Deeper." The spikes were rigid but not sharp. Rey felt them invade her cunt, battering against her spot inside.

He yanked her down hard on his middle, and she dropped her head into the space below his neck. She pulled his pincer into her mouth and sucked it as his Insectoid legs lifted them again and again. Shukkat looked over. The shadow on the wall showed the scene, with Symkere's four legs, as a shadow play of a woman riding a great spider.

Plasri No's tail darted between her legs and slipped into Shukkat's pussy, the knobs at the end of it playing against her clit. Her goldfish-like tongue darted across her breasts, bringing Shukkat dangerously close to orgasm almost immediately. Plasri No held her down with all her strength and whispered in her ear, "yes, I've never fucked an earth girl. Do you want to take it?"

She nodded vigorously, bucking, pushing her ass up in the air. The reptilian woman continued, "do you want me to breed you, little girl?

Shukkat nodded her head. "Please, please, put what you want inside me. Please…"

Plasri No kissed her deeply as she felt it. The tail pressing itself in and out of her widened, opening her. Shukkat let her legs fall to the mat, wide open, trying to relax her womb. The tail grew and opened, pushing out an egg inside her. Shukkat felt so full. She felt the warmth of the solid egg in her belly and screamed out. That was the last straw. She came, pawing at Plasri No for one more kiss, begging her. Just then, Rey called out as Symkere exploded inside her. She slid off his ribbed spiked member to the ground, leaning back against his dark body, breathing hard. Symkere's thick white cum was pouring out of Rey's pussy. She opened her legs wide

Shukkat pulled Plasri No over and the two of them began to lick the cum from Rey. She fell back, pressed against the larger insectoid and let her legs fall open. Shukkat felt like an animal as she and her alien partner swallowed the white goo, kissing and dipping their faces in Rey's pretty cunt.

Shukkat knew that the egg inside her would dissolve harmlessly in a couple of days, but it still made her cling to the Ahreee on the mat, body pressed against her, as Symkere leaned over to kiss her. The two aliens whispered back and forth, laughing until they all fell asleep, wrapped around each other.

***

It was bright When Shukkat woke up. She stepped over the bodies of Tanji and Zehra, who had joined in, with Katel, late last night. She looked down at the two girls, the alien tattoos on their heads and felt free for some reason.

Rey stepped up behind her, pulling on a robe. "I have to feel like that worked." She leaned her head against Shukkat's arm.

Turning to stare at Rey, she started, "you know, you were always so much nicer to me than you needed to be."

"You were the one who took the time to show me around when I first got here. I always appreciated that." She looked at the others sleeping and held Shukkat's hand. "Now what do we do?"

Shukkat looked at her and kissed her, her tongue slowly slipping into the smaller girl's mouth. They stayed like that for a few minutes until she stopped, whispering, "anything we want."

They walked, holding hands, to the infirmary to make sure Vorun was still ok. She'd be sleeping for a few years still, but she seemed healthy.

She seemed ok.

It felt strange putting clothes on. Shukkat and Rey found new black robes in the linen room, soft, with hoods. The warm Mediterranean day let them leave the fronts open as they made their way through the building.

They moved up to the rooftop and looked out. The protestors outside were gone, no doubt terrified. They'd be back. But the rest of the view?

Stunning.

Plasri No opened the door, moving over toward them. She wore her robe. Rey grabbed her hand and pulled her between them. She kissed her on the lips, feeling that perfect little goldfish tongue gliding from mouth to mouth.

"My people are on the way. We'll have this place built up and protected for you. A transporter ring around the whole area will keep you safer than anything."

"That's too much." Shukkat squeezed her hand.

"We have a lot of celebrating to do, coming up, my people. For me, this was the real celebration. I'll be able to get many of them to come help."

"That's…amazing." Rey shook her head.

"It's customary to leave gifts behind for the officiants. Kivak Atel is installing your transporters in the building now."

"Teleporters." Shukkat tried to wrap her head around it.

She turned and looked her in the eye, holding her hands in front of her. "No one will bother you again."

Rey looked across the rooftop. Symkere walked over, back in his robe. The others followed.

Rey reached up and kissed him, sliding her hand under the robe. "Simmy. I like the robe, but…"

He laughed and looked out. "It is a beautiful planet."

"A good place to visit. Sometimes?" she looked up at him. In the sunlight he looked like some great alien god. His skin, impossibly dark and smooth, his head, pulled back into the shape of a weapon.

Rey thought he was beautiful.

Tanji slid in to hold Rey. She wrapped her arms around her. Symkere looked down at the girls. "My gift." He pulled a small disk from his robe pocket, enclosed in a tiny box. It had an engraving on top.

It said "Eren."

Rey looked up. "I don't understand."

Symkere took her hand. "We left tools inside to place this in. It's your sister, her mind, her spirit. This is what made her uniquely her. Through this you can speak to her. You can tell her you love her. And she can talk back."

Rey held tightly to Tanji's hand. "Thank you. I don't know what to say."

Simmy held her face in his hands. "I'm so sorry for everything you went through. I wanted to leave you something in love."

Rey rubbed up against his hand. She pressed the disk against her heart, mouthing, "thank you."

He opened his hand. There were two more.

Shukkat looked up as Simmy came up to her. She leaned in and hugged him, kissing his chest.

He dipped his head. "I have my gifts for you, as well."

"He gave me something, too, Shar." Rey stood by her friend, ready to hold her up.

The disks in his hands read "Dorothy," and "Archie."

She looked up at him and felt the world stop. She could barely hear anything. Not when Simmy showed her how to use the disks. Not when they all scrambled to pack the ship up.

Not when Katel told her that she would need more people – that other petitioners were already on their way.

That there was a lot to learn and not much time before the next group arrived. Not even when the ship took off, leaving Katel behind to help build. And Vorun to be kept safe, to wake up in a place waiting for her.

No, her hearing only returned when she sat in the library, Rey's hand on hers, and asked out loud for a book recommendation, hearing Dorothy's voice over the speakers, connected to the library database, her same quirky sense of humor, her same silly mannerisms...

Her same everything.

It was only then that she heard.

It was nearly a week, though when she laughed again.

When she sat at that giant mirror in her room and flipped a switch.

"Hey."

"Hey there, you." The voice was warm and cocky and mischievous.

It was just right.

"Am I repeating myself if I just say I miss you?" She whispered.

He laughed. "I always liked a little repetition. Let's not go running off crazy new all the time, right?"

She looked around. The light was low. It was easy to walk around and feel like he was there in the room with her, just slightly out of reach.

But when was Archie ever out of reach?

"I think I changed my name."

"Oh, yeah. To what?" He challenged.

She paused. "Shukkat."

She felt his voice get warm. This was where he started hitting on her. Assuming, at all, that he had ever stopped. "Oh, that's pretty."

"Vorun said it means 'someone who wants to know.'" She slid her robe off and sat on the edge of the bed.

She could swear that she heard his breathing. "That's not far off. So, hey, what's your name, again?"

She smiled. "Shukkat."

"I like it. Leave the past behind, eh?"

She closed her eyes and listened. "That's right."

For a moment, he seemed sad. "I wish I were there to see you happy."

Shukkat laid back in bed. She imagined him walking back and forth, pacing like he did before some big event, while she lay there naked on the bed, touching herself until he noticed.

It never took long.

"I was always happy. When you were around. That's the only me you know. Because of you."

"And I'll always be there. But you have to do something for me, Shukkat, who wants to know."

She rolled over on her side, listening. "What, Archie Benjamin?"

He paused. "Find the off switch. And use it. Come back every six months, or every year. Or every time you really need to."

Against her will, her lips pursed. She started to cry. "Why?"

His voice was smooth and deep. Lower than usual. It was a hand holding her. "Baby, don't cry."

She breathed in. There was pain in the back of her lungs as the air met it forcefully, She managed to hold back. She hadn't been a little girl in so long, even when she was one. But she was one now. "You don't want to talk to me?"

As she curled up on the bed, she imagined him sitting just on the edge. He was using his voice to warm her, like he did sometimes, coming in with a hand or a kiss only when it would absolutely make her explode. Only when the need had built up. But Archie never really made her wait for anything.

"You have been every single minute of joy in my life. And now it's time for you to get all the joy you can. You can't live in the past with some artificial version of me. Move on. Fall in love. Be love. Then tell me about it, every once in a while. But live."

She breathed slowly in the warm night air, displacing the oxygen that wasn't her. She realized that she was all the air that would circulate here from now on. This room was hers to fill up. She pulled the covers over her. He finished.

"Promise me."

She whispered, "I promise."

His voice lifted, loudly, powerfully. "But first, tell me about today. Don't hold anything back. And make it hot."

She laughed, pulling a pillow up under her knees. She told him everything, not holding back, because this was Archie.

And that's not what you did.

3 - Change - 2115

"Something like 60 years ago, a small group of Voyagers from different cultures landed on Earth, looking for neutral territory to celebrate and foment their alliance. They found a beleaguered embassy full of people who wanted to do what was necessary to help."

"And they did."

"In the intervening time, everything on Earth changed. The Embassy became the Octagon, neutral ground for any species in the galaxy to work out contracts, to find agreement, and to finalize their associations."

"Ten years after formation, Earth science had been revolutionized by the gifts from cultures all over. Transportation and food were free. Wars fell apart midstream as children were fed and parents lost their drive to fight. Conflicts were paused to find medical solutions to disease, conflicts no one bothered to reignite. Armies became organizations of engineers, moving through countries together building, turning places that had fallen into disrepair or were impossible to live in into gardens that hid technological wonders behind pretty pools and expanses of oxygen rich trees that children were more determined than ever to climb. "

"Within 20 years, the Octagon expanded to a city state of a million people, only a small subset of which were Officiants, working to finalize contracts. The rest were inventors, thinkers, farmers, writers, cooks, anyone who wanted to live peacefully in a place where they could, nearly every day, catch sight of a person from another planet, wandering through their streets, eating in their cafes, swimming in their pools alongside them."

"Almost immediately, The Octagon became the center of a newly burgeoning science fiction community, one that was able to stand up and pat itself on the back. "

"Those books were right all along. They always had been."

"ten years after that, the Octagon had gifted free energy to a world that was now building its own spaceships in earnest to find people they now knew were friendly and waiting. Learning languages became the newest hip trend. That included the native language of the Octagon, Halk – a combination of Turkish, English, Sanskrit, and various Voyager words that had become too valuable to dispense with. Translator tools were everywhere, but let's face it, they didn't always deliver all the meaning you needed."

"Books and films from other planets became Saturday night for teenagers all over the world. And raves that spun extra-terrestrial music went on until early in the morning. Streaming chefs and songwriters went from a million views to a trillion, routinely, as earth signals became trendy for Voyagers everywhere. The now million plus citizens of the Octagon grew into their own nation, served by a council that included Shukkat, the very first Earth-born officiant, in her signature red robe."

"Things that were never possible now are. The Octagon stands today as the center of a planet that has chosen wonder and conflict resolution as its twin navigating stars. And its people have more names for 'joy,' in more languages, than any other word."

"Some people will try to convince you that's an urban legend. But it is factually true."

"For a partial list of these words, please blink twice."

Uher looked up at the swirling black spot above him. The problem with the instruction was that he was doing his best not to blink. His lungs burned in his chest as he tried to ignore them for just a few more seconds. He'd made it through entire histories playing out through his implant while holding the handles at the pool bottom. He could probably handle a word list. No reason to come up.

Except for that black swirl.

Finally, his curiosity coupled with his desperate need for air, pulling him to the pool surface. He inhaled, shaking his head. He never needed to wipe his eyes anymore. He just let them normalize on their own.

"That was impressive." A woman in a black robe clapped for him. Right next to her, a man in a thin floral linen shirt shouted out, "ten, woo."

Uher smiled. He looked around for Gara and Lee.

The man was handsome, possibly Nigerian, with a strong face that looked like a squared off heart. He wore a number of necklaces spilling down into the collar of the bright garden of a shirt, with a ceremonial looking line tattooed down his forehead, drawing the eye down his face to a thin goatee, perfectly groomed. He was definitely no older than 30. Although these days, who could tell?

He spoke. "Oh, yeah, we asked your friends to give us a few minutes in private. Hey, is it cool if I put my feet in?"

Uher chuckled. "Dude, why stop at the feet?"

The brightly dressed man jumped up and made a big deal out of letting himself fall into the pool backward, laughing.

The woman in the black robe smiled and shook her head.

He popped up, pulling his shirt off and tossing it poolside. "I'm sorry. I'm Phoka. And this beautiful woman is Master Qerici."

She put her feet in the pool and kicked water at him, Laughing.

Uher treaded water like he always did, trying to make it look smooth and gliding. He had actually watched videos of fish. In fact, his mirrors, in the house, showed fish whenever he walked away from them.

When he looked in them, Uher could see himself. He had a strong, greek face. The same face as his father and his father before him.

But where his father had a mop of black curls on top, Uher had cropped his hair short, almost bald. His arms and neck were covered in deep blackout tattoos on a wiry, not overly muscled frame.

He looked up at Master Qerici. She was beautiful. And he couldn't fail to notice the Octagon tattoo on her forehead, regal, as if presiding over all her other tattoos, a goddess-like hierarchy. Her lips were beautifully pursed and the violet lip shade she wore looked like it could have been the reasonable true color of a perfect pair of lips on her mahogany brown skin.

"Master Qerici, are you coming in?"

She looked at him. "Okay. Let's talk in the pool."

She stood up and pulled her robe off, folding it and laying it next to her.

She was nude underneath it, except for tattoos and bright silver jewelry, rings and chains that glittered in the sunlight. Her breasts were full and round, dipping into a tiny wave at front, making pace for areolas whose near violet hue seemed to make the case for the reality of her lips.

And beneath a slight and pretty belly, a graceful yet thick penis, stretching down nearly to the center of her legs, swinging casually as she prepared to dive in.

She lifted her arms and made a perfect dive a few feet to his left. Uher couldn't help but clap along with Phoka as she came up for air. She was close enough to him that he imagined he could feel her warmth in the water between them.

Uher floated, his face just a few inches from her. She smelled like cinnamon. He was acutely aware that his body was responding.

It was the lips, he thought.

"I didn't think you guys would come out here. I didn't…"

"I know. The fifth test." She rolled her eyes.

Phoka floated by them. "It took ME a bit, not gonna lie."

Master Qerici swam around. Her movements were smooth and easy. "One of the people you'll probably meet is my friend, Master Gossamer. It took her a year to pass the fifth test. Her college roommate basically had to traumatize her."

"It's a good story." Phoka slowly dropped underwater as though in an elevator.

"I wasn't sure if I needed to, I guess. Because of what I'm looking to do." Uher realized that the end of that sentence went up, like a question.

Master Querici swam up to his face. He could feel her breath on him. Her lips were only a few inches away. "You are wrong, so I'm going to dunk you now."

She pushed down on his head and he slipped underwater. He looked around. It was clear that the closeness was having some effect on Master Qerici as well. That made him happy. He saw Phoka pull his linen pants off. As the three of them floated nude in the pool, Uher noted, right before he rose, how the water disappeared at this perfect temperature. There was no water. There was only body and it was everything.

"I'm sorry, Master Qerici." He wanted to ask her to do that again.

"You can just call me Qerici." She put her hand in his to shake.

The water amplified the electrical connection with her hand. He held it, grateful she didn't take it back. And then something hit him.

"Wait. You said I'm going to meet her, them?" A wave of excitement washed over him.

Qerici smiled, "Yes. You want to, right?"

Uher looked at them. "Yes, more than anything..."

Phoka pulled himself up, shaking his head. "Yes, as soon as you pass the fifth test."

Uher let out a breath. He looked up into the pretty Santorini sun. He wondered if it looked any different above the Octagon.

"Hey, doof. Are you going to introduce us to your friends?" Gara pulled off his sandals. He had a wave of blond hair over a tanned full face. He sported a single tattoo on his chest, a heart with the word "Dad" in it. As he stripped down to a red set of trunks, he slid into the pool.

Next to him was Lee. Her skin was nearly chalk-white in a one piece black suit, covered in pentagrams and playfully satanic figures. She sported a dark black mohawk flopping down over a shaved head. She sat down at the end of the pool, took a deep breath, and then slid in. Lee always felt a bit awkward running around half naked. At 75 kg, she was not large at all, but she never much cared for her body.

The water made her feel more comfortable.

The two swam over and bobbed near Uher.

"These are my roomies. This is Gara, he is an artist. It's technically his family's house. We've been friends for a long time. But they live in Crete. And this is my best friend and first girlfriend, Lee."

Lee smiled and splashed him. "I don't think everyone needs to know that." She looked at Qerici. "I was three."

She shot back, with a faux seriousness. "Still counts."

"I think my girlfriend at three was a stuffed panda," Phoka interjected.

"What can I say? I was an overachiever." Uher winked at Lee.

Gara looked over at Phoka. "Hey, don't pandas forget how to have sex? Like we have to show them, right?"

"It's a dirty job, man." Phoka reached out and shook their hands. "I'm Phoka. I'm a novitae at the Octagon."

"So you're in training?" Lee asked.

Qerici interjected, leaning on her back to float, "liar, he's training me. He's brutal. I can't stand him."

Phoka laughed. "Yes. I'm learning all about it. That's Master Qerici. She is the leader of my thula – it's like a little team."

"So, it's true. Uher, you're going?" Lee splashed over to him.

"This was always my plan. Ever since I was young. This was my plan."

Gara looked over at Phoka, "Except the plan changed a little after the interview."

Phoka perked up. "What interview?"

Lee looked around. "With the fish girl."

***

The house was small, probably about the same size as the pool, if Uher had to be honest. In reality, this entire house had probably started its existence as the pool house. The three rooms were all small, mostly taken up by their respective queen sized beds. The kitchen and facilities were small.

It looked like the only room that was decently sized was the main living area. It was wide open and uncluttered, filled with some pictures on the wall, taped on, mostly, and a large viewscreen, presiding over the space like a priest, with a sectional couch, comfy and overstuffed, dark green and large, its only supplicant.

Qerici looked through the photos on the wall. Picture after picture showed the three roommates out, dancing, having fun, at dinner, at shows. They looked close.

In two of the pictures, Lee was wearing a shape drawn on her forehead. A tiny octagon. Lee walked over.

"Oh, yeah. Is that bad? I didn't mean that to be disrespectful."

Qerici reached down to hold her hand. "Do you know what that is?"

"It's a t'kau. It means you are sexually available…"

"To anyone."

"Yeah, some of us draw those on when we want to go out and get crazy. Is that bad?"

"Do you have fun?"

"Sometimes, yes." She smiled. "A lot."

"Then no harm, no foul." Qerici squeezed her hand. "Do you know what the marks inside are?"

Lee shook her head.

The taller woman pulled out a tiny marker from her robe. "Can I?" Lee nodded.

She leaned in and pointed. Ok, the up and down points stand for giver and receiver. You can be both. Notice mine is a straight line, from top to bottom because I'm both. You can be a range."

"Got it." Lee nodded. Qerici handed her the marker and she filled in the area in her picture. Mostly receiver. But more giver than she thought.

"Now, the side to side line. Host at one side, Catalyst at the other. These are your breeding preferences. Do you like the idea of breeding happening inside you?"

Lee nodded vigorously.

"So fill that in. Good. Now this diagonal. Dominant at top, submissive at bottom. It's a range. Note that mine is full from one side to the other. I switch."

"I think that's me, too," Lee said, filling it in.

"Now, this diagonal here, this side is sensual. That means you are pleasure driven. This side is primal. You know what that means, probably."

Lee nodded, laughing. "Yours is a straight line, again. You're basically an asterisk. What's that called?"

"Well, genders don't really have names, just shapes."

"I like that. A lot." Lee stepped back and looked at her more instructive t'kau. She liked it.

"So, now, when you draw it in to go out dancing, it will be accurate. And it could change. Gender is a verb, not a noun or an adjective."

"You are so cool."

"I was going to say the same thing. Now I seem like a copycat."

Gara stood near Uher and Phoka with the remote, searching. He called out, "ok, people. I found it. The interview."

"It's not that big a deal." Uher held up his hands.

Qerici turned to Gara and grabbed the remote, smiling. "I'll be the judge of that. Everyone come in close."

Uher sighed as she hit play.

The videoscreen lit up. A tall black man with an English accent stood near an opulent black-tiled pool. There was a waterfall dripping down onto lush foliage and filtering into the water. He walked over and a woman's face popped up from the water pulling herself up on the side of the pool.

The man pulled out a microphone.

"All right, our next guest is a woman named Killean and her family. She is from a race called the Xonaxis and is a Master Officiant at the Octagon. How are you, Killean?"

She responded, "I'm good, Verious, we're just swimming." Her face was pretty, with what looked like permanent blue eyeshadow.

Her head extended back further than a human's might, descending into skin that might look at home on a dolphin. She wore sleek silver rings around her neck and a mesh shirt that didn't work very hard to hide her rose colored nipples rising over a slim pair of swimmer's breasts.

Qerici looked at the room. "She's a Taranakah. Officiants at the Octagon who are mostly water-based, who help with all the water breathing petitioners. She looks familiar. But I confess I haven't met every single Taranakah."

Killean spoke for a while, back and forth with the host, Verious Style. They laughed a little.

Phoka looked at the room. "She's very cool. Is this what did it?"

Qerici leaned in closer as Lee slid onto the couch next to the taller woman with a bowl of chips she had gotten from the other room. "Keep watching."

Phoka glanced down at Gara's tattoo. "Hey, why do you have a giant 'Dad' tattoo on your chest?"

Gara looked down. "Oh, yeah. My dad went on some bender one night about how everyone in the comics gets a 'mom' tattoo but you never see a 'Dad' one.

"I've seen 'Daddy,'" Lee yelled out.

"Oh, hell yeah." Gara shot back.

Phoka cocked his head. "So you got a giant chest tattoo to amuse your dad?"

"It worked. He laughs his ass off whenever he sees it."

"I like these guys." Phoka winked at Qerici.

Lee yelled out. "Here it comes."

Uher put his head into his hand as the show continued.

Two other people had popped up from the side of the pool. The first, a beautiful black man with deep skin and tattoos all over. The octagon on his head seemed like a helmet under his small brown and gold dreadlocks. He was covered in tattoos and seemed to wear only a thong. He introduced himself as Kura. And he was from Earth.

But that's not where everyone in that room was looking.

Right next to him was a woman of about 30 or so. Her skin was lightly bronzed and smooth, under long, slightly wavy red hair. They flashed her name under her, "Dannae," and when she smiled, her whole face widened and everything seemed good and warm. She could have been the most beautiful woman in the world.

Or, at least that's what it said all over Uher's face as he watched, hypnotized, unable to move or breathe.

***

"So, you think this is all about the red-haired girl?" Qerici asked Lee while they scoured the grassy area around the house. They'd all been up all night, talking, mostly in the pool and Lee was still in her bathing suit alongside the taller woman in her black robe.

She answered uncertainly, "well, no, not all of it. Hey, is that one?" pointing to a large reddish insect.

Qerici looked closer. "No, we need beetles. The ones we're looking for look like little warriors. Rhinoceros beetles."

"Rhinoceros beetles."

The grass sported thick droplets of water, spread across the green bed by the early dawn. It wasn't easy to see anything in that glare. "They're all black. We want the big ones."

Lee nodded. "Got it. I mean. He always wanted to be at the Octagon. And he loves the water. Until that interview, I think he never realized that, you know, you guys could change him."

"We have some native water breathers, too. But we can change baseline humans. It's an uncomfortable process." Qerici stopped, looking at her expression closely "Do you think that's what he really wants?"

Lee considered. "Once he's changed, he can't be in the air anymore?"

The taller woman waved in dismissal. "No. He can be out of water for about two hours at a time once he's changed. But if history has shown anything, he won't want to be."

Lee jumped up, excitedly, "Got one. "

"Perfect." Qerici looked at her mischievously. "Can you carry it here in your mouth?"

Lee's face lit up, always up for a game, "You want me to?"

"Only kidding." Her robe swam in the morning wind while she cocked her head and smiled. "But you could, right?"

"They don't bite?"

"Or sting." she shook her head.

Lee opened her mouth and put the beetle on her tongue. She held her breath and started walking forward. She put her hand under her chin. As she approached, she made a whimpering sound. It moved backward, towards her throat.

"Ok. Stay like that. It'll come out on its own. Don't panic. Just let it sit on your tongue." Qerici stepped closer and placed her own hand in front of her mouth. The insect stepped out, over her lips, into the open hand. She smoothly slipped it into the bag.

"That felt so weird." Lee skipped. She turned to her. "But cool."

Qerici laughed, staring at the smaller goth girl.

The thick eye makeup she had on the night before had all been worn away by their night in the pool. She seemed brighter. "Good work. So all this is amplified by the red haired girl?"

Lee shrugged. "I guess." She paused. "So, the insectoids? When you have sex with them? Like giant beetles?" She was clearly trying to imagine it in her mind.

"Not really? But some of the sensations are the same. We're sort of naturally conditioned to think bunnies are cute and beetles are, well, not."

"I think these guys are pretty cute." She lifted another one from the ground and held it near her nose. "This one's name is Ringo." She carefully slid Ringo into the bag.

Qerici pushed her, laughing. "Oh my god, you are way too young for that reference."

"So, would you have sex with me?" Lee stopped, looking up at her. "I mean, for fun?"

"Do you want to?" She answered, still searching the ground.

"'I'm just saying," Lee stopped and pulled the top of her bathing suit down over her breasts. They were smooth and white and thick. He nipples were darker than Qerici would have guessed from her bright china skin. Lee put her shoulders back and stood topless in front of her. "Am I someone you would fuck?"

She smiled back. "Oh, yeah. But do you like me?" She let her robe slide back on her shoulders, moving forward, inches from the other girl.

Lee leaned in and licked her breast. "I think you might be the coolest person I've ever met."

She slid her hand into her hair and pulled her in. Lee's mouth opened wider, taking in more of the breast. "I think you're pretty cool, too. I'm wearing a t'kau. When you drew yours on, what would you say if someone wanted to fuck you?"

"Ha. Yes, usually. I'm such a fucking whore." she tried to choke herself on Qerici's breasts, nearly unlocking her jaw to fit their entire mass in her mouth.

She tied off the top of the bag and tossed it aside. Leaning down, she took the girl's tongue in her mouth and sucked. "Do you think I'd rather be looking for beetles than fucking you, you little whore? Do you want to do it here or in front of your friends? Back in bed? The grass?"

Lee pulled the rest of her suit down. Qerici couldn't help but notice she didn't look around first to see who might have been watching. "You are so cool," Lee whispered.

The darker woman grabbed one of her tits, squeezing it hard and dragging her to a spot on the grass near the discarded bag. "Come here." She twisted her nipple.

Lee breathed in, following. "Yes, Master Qerici."

Qerici pushed her down, pressing her head into the grass. She reached into the bag and pulled one of the beetles out, placing it on her nipple. "Do you want to try this?"

"Oh, that feels so weird. Hey, little guy."

She took another one and placed it on her belly, letting it crawl down to her belly button and lower. "This is the fifth test."

Lee clawed at her. "I thought the initiate was supposed to masturbate with the beetles on them." She spread her legs.

The Master placed another beetle right near her neatly shaved pussy, rubbing it against her clit. "Technically, I'm masturating you. It's more fun this way. "

"Fuck." Lee let her legs open wider.

"Do you feel them, climbing on you?"

"More. Are there more...?"

She placed a beetle on her chin. "Hold it in your mouth. I want to fuck you."

"Ahh. Oh. Your dick is huge. Lee could feel how hard she was. She tried to open her mouth, sticking her tongue out for the tiny feet.

"I know." She slapped the girl's pussy. "This thing is tiny. Don't talk if you don't have to. We want to protect the beetles. Not hurt them. I'm going to enter you slowly."

Lee shifted her cunt forward. "They won't stay in my mouth."

"Keep your mouth open, let them just go in. You have to spread your legs wider. If this doesn't work, I may need to use your ass."

The word "use" seemed to work like a switch on a lamp. Lee's breathing went shallow and she stared, hypnotized. "Oh, fuck. Do you want to use my asshole?"

Qerici smiled and licked at her lips, letting the beetle slide in between them. She pretended to be sorry about the mismatch. "I think it might fit better, baby."

Lee moaned animalistically. "It doesn't matter if it fits, just fuck my ass up."

The taller woman slid a beetle in her cunt. "Do you feel that?"

"I do. Do anything. Destroy my fucking asshole. Your cock can do whatever it wants." She pawed at her, pulling her closer.

Master Qerici carefully flipped Lee over, taking care not to hurt the beetles. She placed insects at the opening of her vagina as Lee opened her legs to make room for them. Pulling the bag over, she slid it under her head, pulling it up around her so that her head was in the bag with what looked like six beetles.

"Ok, open your fucking mouth, bitch. Lick them. Feel that? Can you feel the little legs? Don't hurt them."

"I won't. Fuck me with anything you want. Please just don't stop. Oh, your dick is god. This is like being used by god." Lee let the tiny warriors move in and out of her mouth as more scratched lightly inside her.

"Lick these. Open your mouth. I'm going to go deep in your little ass. It's so fucking tiny. Spread that shit. Spread your ass. Hold the beetles with your mouth."

Lee whimpered. "I'm sorry. I'm sorry. I'll do better. Just rip me open, please."

"Lick the bugs. Let them in your mouth. Don't hurt them. I'm putting a few more in your cunt. Do. Not. Close. Your. Legs." She punched Lee's ass in rhythm as she said that.

"Oh, thank you, Master." Qerici's cock pushed its way inside Lee's ass. The girl dropped her hands, spreading her asshole manually while licking at the insects gently. All she wanted was to follow orders. That was the only thing in her mind.

Qerici pumped herself in and out of her in a steady rhythm, interrupted only with a savage jab every time she barked an order. "Don't cum until I get this one in you. Can you feel the bugs in your fucking hole?"

Lee let out a series of plaintive moans. "Yes. It feels so good. The little feet."

"Make it warm for them while I breed your fucking ass. Do you like that giant prick?"

Lee's body shook again at the sound of the word "breed." She slammed herself into the woman's prick while trying to protect the beetles in her mouth. "It's like god. I worship it. I adore that dick. Please breed me. "

She yelled out as Qerici pumped her ass full of thick, hot cum, staying inside as long as she could. She didn't move until she pulled out and returned the beetles to the bag, closing it up and standing up.

Lee rolled over, laughing. "Oh, my god. That was so cool and fucked up."

The Master slid her robe back on. "Was it? What did you like? What didn't you like?"

Lee put her hands over her face and spread her legs in the grass, looking up. "Are you kidding? That was amazing. I liked everything. I never did anything like that before."

The darker woman shielded her eyes from the sun. Lee looked happy lying on the wet grass. She knelt down.

"That was the hardest one. Do you want to do the other four self-tests?"

"Holy shit, yes." She bolted up, screaming. She started running back to the house, stopping for just a moment to run back and grab her bathing suit. Qerici let her robe sit on her shoulders and followed.

***

Uher sat on the couch with Phoka, waiting for them to return. "Are you guys really going to stay here until I pass the fifth test?"

Phoka flipped through the channels, looking for something interesting. "Yep. It won't take as long as you think. I think I have some ideas, too."

"I'm glad you think that. I've always been kind of squeamish about insects." Uher leaned back against Phoka's arm. He pulled him in closer to rest as he channel surfed.

"I get that. It's a lot easier than you think."

Uher paused for a second, "So you've had sex with anthropods?"

"Arthropods. Insect type yolcu. I haven't yet. I want to." He looked down at Uher. "I'm really excited."

Uher looked back at him. "You don't have a t'kau? Is that a line?"

"Yeah, I started tattooing my own on until I found out you have to earn it. It's a ritual. The Octagon loves their rituals." He lowered the volume and kept scrolling.

"Oh, yeah?" Uher tried to imagine what the rituals must be like.

Phoka nodded. "I think rituals are important. They just remind you that you're doing something, finishing something. That you're a part of something."

That sounded really good to Uher. Up until now, he'd had the sense that his life was one solid thing. The self tests were the most interesting things he'd done. "I gotta tell you, I'm really excited about that."

"When you start, you'll be in our thula. With us. Then, once you... change, you move to the Forala." Phoka put his hands on Uher's chest and massaged it, when he said "with us."

He put his hand over Phoka's. "Ok. That's the water area underneath? "

"Yes." He stopped scrolling as his voice got more animated. "It's huge. It's literally nearly 20 times the size of the Korvun – the upper area for air breathers. I've seen pictures, but it's too much pressure for me to go down there."

He leaned back more into the other man. Uher had always dated both men and women, but he tended not to have close, intimate friendships with men that felt like this. He and Gara didn't cuddle on the couch. "So you never meet Taranakahs?"

"Oh, I know a ton of them. Not all. So, check this out." Phoka shot up and grabbed a pen and some paper from the drawer under the view screen. Pulling Uher onto the ground, he started drawing between them. "Here is the Korvun. It's really kind of a big circle. In the center, if you go to the first floor, is this giant area known as the Thessalia. It's like a little town, maybe? Like an area that is half submerged. They have bars and clubs and stuff. It's like the area where us air breathers and the water breathers meet to party."

Uher pointed to the wide connecting area. "So, If I'm a Taranakah, I can spend time with anyone in the Thessalia?"

"Yes. There are even kurges there for connections between water and air species. And then this is the cone, it's the doorway area to the Forala." he made a flourish with his hand that was so dramatic, Uher laughed.

"It's all a lot." He pulled Phoka over to lean against the couch with him.

Phoka whispered as he cuddled him, "you should see it on a saturday night. It's beautiful."

"I bet." He looked at the darker man. He was so handsome. And looked so exotic. "But you're willing to leave and stay here in this dive…"

"In the middle of historically beautiful Santorini Greece," he laughed.

"Ha. Just to hold my hand so I can be a part of it?" Uher pulled him closer in gratitude.

Phoka took his hand. "Yes. Was there a question in there?"

Uher heard splashing in the pool. "Are they back?"

"You want to go see what's up?"

The two got up, holding hands, and made their way to the pool. What they saw was a little unexpected. Master Qerici kneeled nude on the side of the pool while Lee sat crosslegged in a pool chair, her eyes closed, mouth bulging, masturbating while Gara sprayed her with a hose in a kind of rhythm.

Phoka laughed. "No lie, this is my favorite game show."

Qerici yelled out, "welcome." waving her arms.

Gara turned to Uher. "She's holding mealworms in her mouth for two hours without hurting or swallowing them, while cumming at least twice. It's the fourth test."

He looked confused. "I know. Why are you involved? Aren't you asexual?"

"It doesn't mean I can't squirt people with a garden hose." Gara turned the hose on her again to add additional pressure. He couldn't remember whose idea the hose was, but he liked it.

Uher nodded. "Yeah, I get that." He wouldn't pass up hosing someone down, either.

Qerici yelled out, "she wants to take the self tests."

Uher looked over. "She wants to join, too?"

"Maybe. She definitely wants to see if she can." Gara kept spraying. He was wearing the same red shorts as the day before.

Master Qerici yelled at Uher again, "and, oh, she might need your help."

She barked at Lee, "spread those legs. Let the water in. Jack that cunt. Be a good girl."

"Really?" He looked over. He hadn't seen Lee naked since they were little kids, running around after a bath. This was a strange way to be reintroduced to her pussy.

Gara tapped him on the shoulder. "She just did the fifth test, over there." he pointed to the grassy area.

"Holy... Really?" Uher definitely felt the surreality of the situation. He laughed.

Gara continued, "do you want to spray her with the hose?"

Uher grabbed at it. "That's a dumb question. Gimme that thing."

That hose got a lot of use, more than it ever had in that house. Uher watched, fascinated, trying to learn what Lee needed to cum. Qerici grabbed him and pulled him into the water as they watched, submerging him over and over in the warm water.

He slid down her body and sucked her off once, underwater, earning a thick, earnest kiss from her upon his ascent as he swallowed her perfect ejaculate, trying to let it sit in his own mouth as long as possible.

She called out and cheered. With every success, kissing and tickling him as she noticed his efforts to savor her cum.

It took Lee three tries to make it through the two hours and two orgasms. And she nearly swallowed one of the worms. But by the time it was dark, three of them were back in the living room, drying off, lying on the floor in front of the couch, watching tv on their bellies.

"Well, it's pretty naked in here for me and it's bedtime. See you freaks in the morning." Lee threw a pillow at Gara as he left, then settled back in on the floor on her belly between Qerici and Phoka. Uher slid to his knees, looking at the three of them lying there, the two on the outside taking turns slapping Lee's very available ass.

Qerici was fascinating, wild. It was hard for Uher to take his eyes off of her. And after only two days, Lee was morphing into a version of her – wild, free, open, powerful and sexy.

He wondered if he would change that fast when he got to the Octagon. He wasn't afraid of the procedure. He'd never been afraid of change. He wanted to have that thing inside him that let go and let it happen.

Even if that thing was hard to find.

Lee called out, "uh, excuse me, initiate, there is a lot of ass and pussy and stuff in front of you."

Qerici wiggled her ass and lifted it up. "You should start with this one. Let's get that tongue going. Can you get my ass and pussy?"

Lee barked at him, spreading her legs, "And then just move down the line, initiate. Let's get eating." She wiggled her ass.

Uher leaned in, staring at Qerici from behind. Her ass was beautiful, sitting right behind a dark and pretty pussy, pink inside, with full purple lips.

The lips widened toward the font and became round at the bottom. Her testicles, surrounding that massive marvel of a prick.

He leaned in and put his hands on her ass, feeling that electricity he always felt whenever they touched. He slid his tongue inside her, trying to let it move in deeply, to be swallowed by her beautiful bottom. He tried to make it rigid, fucking her with it, listening to the three of them talking about him, talking about the day, ignoring his ministrations until they couldn't. He moved on to Lee, then let his tongue explore Phoka. He sucked on all three of them and then returned and started over, until his jaw ached, the muscles of his tongue revolted, and the salty mist of their cum filled his mouth and ran across his face like ocean water, blown from the top of tidal rises onto the rocks of the shore saying, "I own you today, I have your complete attention. I have everything."

***

Lee held Uher's hand as they made their way down the block through large pastoral houses and big open, wildly unkempt fields. She'd been quick to grab it and he wished he'd done it first.

"Thanks for coming with me." She squeezed.

"Of course. You're still my favorite crazy person." He smiled and swung her arm.

"Aww. that's demented. I wish I'd come with for you."

"Mine was not great. Well, actually, it was. The conversation was worth it." Uher remembered.

"Who did you go to?" she asked, honestly curious.

"Kelly." He winced.

"Oh my god. Did she tear you a new asshole?" Lee bounced up on a group of dirty gray rocks that signalled they were almost there, pulling him up.

"She did." He looked up. "Then she made me strip and slapped me for a while. She almost kicked me in the nuts."

"Oh my god, that's hot." Lee laughed.

"But we made up. We did. This is it." Uher looked up at the building. It was old. There was a covered corridor leading to the back yard, around the stony exterior. For a moment, as they walked under it, the world went dark, brightening back up again as they walked into the back yard. A man in a tan t-shirt stood in the yard, hands in the pockets of his thin white pants, face up enjoying the sun. Lee let go of Uher's hand and walked up to him.

"Hey, Gary."

"Hey. I'm here, like you asked. Is this some 12 step thing?" He cocked his head.

Lee scrunched up her face,. "Ek, gross, no."

Gary nodded at Uher and reached out to shake his hand,. "Hey, U, how you doing?"

"I'm good, man. I'm just being moral support. And a witness."

"What is this about?" He looked over at Lee. Gary was tall and handsome. His blonde brown hair wrapped his face in a soft shag keeping the gaunt cheeks and biting eyes from looking too harsh. He might seem easy going, but In a fight, he was brutal. Lee balled up her courage in her belly.

"I'm leaving to join the Octagon. Before I go, I wanted to come tell you that I fucked up. I was wrong. I wasn't fair to you." That was easier than she thought it was going to be – that part at least.

"Octagon, eh? Well. I guess I appreciate that. It could have been a phone call."

She moved over to him and took his hand. Looking up at the taller man, she continued. "We can go where you want, right now, and take my clothes off. You can do whatever you want to me. And it can be a nice goodbye, if that's what you want, something I can remember. Or it can be a friendship that we can connect on. Or it can be anything you want it to be."

"You're kidding. And why is Uher here?"

Uher started, "I'm moral support and a –"

"A witness, right. That's nuts, you know."

"When I cheated on you and then broke up, I was in a weird head space. My brain was hurting and I just turned it off. I'm not proud of it and it wasn't fair to you."

"Ok." He nodded. "Take your clothes of right here and tell me."

Lee didn't bother looking around, but Uher did. A part of him wondered why that was. Was Lee more Octagon material than he was?

She pulled down her black yoga pants and then in one quick movement, pulled off the black t-shirt, leaving her naked, except for a pair of black canvas high tops. Gary looked at her.

"Damn. You aren't kidding."

"I know that what I did was probably confusing to you. You had to know I loved you and that I cared about our relationship. I promise you it was more confusing to me. I'm sorry, Gary. Is there anything you want to do to me?"

Gary breathed out for a second. "I want to scream at you. But I'm not going to have some kind of non-consensual sex with you. Fine. I forgive you. See you later."

Gary started to walk away. She ran up behind him. "Ok. Gary, according to the rules, I already did what I had to do."

He nodded. "Ok, good."

She held his hand and looked over at Uher, "Is that true, did I do it?"

"Yup, she passed the test."

"Ok, good, see you later, good luck."

She pulled him back. "But I really don't want you to walk away. I want you to smile when you think of me. I want you to remember that I really loved being with you. I loved it when you told stories with your hands like you do."

Gary shook his head and chuckled slightly, staring at the naked girl.

"I loved how your friends looked at you, like you had to be the one to make plans. And I loved how you would touch me in front of people like I belonged to you. I fucked up. I want to be friends for real."

"Friends for real. You're going away." He crossed his arms.

"And when I come back to visit, we can play and have some fun and maybe, eventually, you will think of me that way and not as someone who hurt you. Maybe just as a friend you can tell things to and fuck."

"Is that really what you want?" Gary's face softened.

Lee took his hand and moved it to the spot between her legs. She was wet, nearly dripping down her leg. She locked eyes with him.

Gary smiled. "Are you going to keep the shoes on?"

She reached up and kissed him. "Ha. I knew the shoes would do it."

Lee had forgotten how much she missed Gary's laugh as she slid down him and opened his pants, lifting his dick in her mouth. Uher looked around the yard. It was large and expansive, with a massive tree to one side, with the trademark gnarled trunk of an olive tree. He breathed in, imagining he could smell the new olives on the tree, screaming out to the world where they were.

Gary had pushed Lee to the ground and was pumping inside her now, her arms wrapped around his neck. He couldn't hear what they were saying but he could tell they were laughing. Lee tried to roll over on top of him, leading to a wrestling match she lost. She spread her legs wider and yelled out. The laughing died down as she held his face and tried to use her body to remind him that the past wasn't just full of pain.

By the time Uher dropped down on the grass next to them, they were back to laughing, talking, with Gary's head leaning on her belly.

He lifted himself up on one arm. "So, tell me about this Octagon place. It can't be as pretty as all this." She started talking. This time it was Lee talking with her hands, waving them about. She pushed Gary down in the grass and sat on top of him, her round ass grinding against him, as she spoke. Uher guessed that the conversation would evolve and that he had done his part as witness. He waved at them and set off for home.

Gary wasn't wrong. Santorini was beautiful. All Uher wanted to do was to get home and slip back into the pool. He hoped that Phoka and Qerici would be there already. He stepped into the pool area, though, and found only Gara.

"Dude. They're waiting for you inside. In the bathroom."

Uher nodded and walked into the house. He made his way back to the bathroom to find Phoka and Qerici in there, waiting. They stood around the bathtub that was filled halfway with water.

Qerici saw him and, grabbing his hand, pulled him into the smaller room. The three of them took up nearly all the available space, surrounding a bathtub many times too large to be here. She pulled off his shirt and kissed him hard.

Uher fell into her, leaning into the kiss. His hands massaged her breasts as the warmth from her filled him with a kind of electrical hum. He felt Phoka pull his pants down and off. His body responded when the man's hands started rubbing him down, a sleek oil permeating his skin and cock. He spread his legs as he felt Phoka's hand massage oil into the crevice of his ass.

Phoka pushed his fingers into Uher's open ass and lifted him with the other hand. Qerici held his arms and back and lifted, as well. They slid him into the tub with Phoka's fist coming close to popping through Uher's sphincter. He bore down and let the hand in, feeling a rush of adrenaline as it did, putting his feet up on the tub.

Qerici's robe slipped off and she pushed him down until the water rose to the level of his face. Uher had always liked the tub in this place, even though its three-person capacity took up an awkward amount of space in the bathroom.

"This was Phoka's idea. You're invulnerable in the water. He realized we don't need arthropods from the land. Not when we can immerse you and fill the space with perfectly safe sea spiders."

Phoka continued to pump away at his ass as the sea spiders drifted over his body. He couldn't tell how many of them there were. The bodies of each were about the width and length of a small banana. But their legs were long, extending almost a half a meter from their bodies. They slid over Uher's chest. Qerici spread her legs and straddled the tub, looking down at him, placing spiders all over. He could see her pussy and ass above him as she taunted him, encouraged him.

"Open your mouth, c'mon. Suck on those legs. If you just open, they'll want to explore."

He opened his mouth. The water was warm and good and the spiders smelled briney, like the ocean. This felt familiar and he realized he wasn't panicking.

The woman above him lifted her prick and pointed it downward. A slow trickle of piss built into a stream. "Come on, drink that, open your mouth."

Uher opened his mouth wide. The piss was warm and perfectly matched the brine of the ocean water. The sea spiders followed the warmth to his mouth and began to explore, placing their legs between his lips. He tried to lick and suck on the legs of the sea spiders. He opened his eyes as wide as he could, water and piss splashing everywhere.

His tongue lapped at the bottom of one of the spider's bodies as he felt Phoka play with his prostate. The sea spiders slid over his body and he tried his best to keep them safe and prevent them from being harmed.

He worked to swallow the stream of pee falling onto his face, his hands reaching up to grab her pretty ass and direct it. The sea spiders crawled over his arms and belly, creating sensations he'd never felt before.

"C'mon, lick them. The bugs are so pretty." She laughed as a warmth grew in Uher's stomach. A wave of pleasure ran up his body as Phoka's fingers continued milking him. His prick wasn't totally hard, lying against his belly, but he felt a slow steady stream of cum pouring from it. Uher had never been milked before and the feeling was intense, taking over his senses.

"There you go. Look at that. You're cumming. You did it.

Uher's body shook as she pulled him from the tub. "Oh my god, that was so easy. I did it."

He jumped up and grabbed a towel, starting to dry himself off. Qerici pulled the towel away and grabbed at him.

"No towel. You smell so good. You smell like the ocean." She grabbed his cock and pulled him into the living room. "This is how you're supposed to smell. You're a sea god." She kissed him over and over on the face and lips and his skin exploded with the energy of being this close to her. They rolled over each other onto the floor of the living room and he pushed her down, licking at her lips and tits, his mouth still alive with the taste of her warm piss. She spread her legs wide, pulling him in and arching her back. Her prick was erect, riding up the curve of her belly, exposing the thick purple lips of her cunt behind it. She grabbed at his cock and slid him into her wet and outspread pussy, pulling him in deep.

"Damn." She smiled, holding his face in her hands. "You should have fucked me when I first got here." She rocked her back, pulling him into her in a thick rhythm.

He heard himself slapping against her, and he met the rhythm. "You're so fucking beautiful... so fucking beautiful."

"You're my merman. My fucking Poseidon. You smell so fucking good." She tried to devour him with her mouth, laughing as he pushed into her. Ripping the rug away from the floor, He pounded at her opening like an animal until he came, groaning and grunting. The whole thing must have lasted less than two minutes.

Qerici petted his head and he laid on top of her. She pulled him closer with her legs. "You did it. The fifth test. We did it."

He smiled, pushing his face in her neck. "You didn't cum."

She laughed loudly, grabbing his ass. "I did everything." She pulled his face up. "I like how you kind of forgot language there at the end."

"Me no talk good." Uher whispered.

They were still laughing when Phoka entered the room, having secured the sea spiders.

"Mission accomplished, people. It is now pool time."

***

They were all around the pool at dusk when Lee returned. She smiled and sat on a chair as they all yelled out.

"How did that go?" Qerici asked. She sat nude on the edge of the pool, her feet in the water.

Lee took a deep breath. "It was really good. We talked for hours. We were just...honest, you know. He cheated on me once when we were together, with an old comfortable girlfriend. I told him it was ok. We played around some more. We cried a little. It was actually great."

Uher cheered from the water in front of Master Qerici. "Wooooo! That is awesome. I witnessed the original plowing of the field, as they say"

Lee slipped off her shirt and threw it at him. "Only you say that, nerd." She pulled her shoes off one at a time. "What did you guys do?"

Phoka jumped up like a dolphin. "Uher passed test five."

"He rocked it," Qerici interjected.

Gara was slowly spinning in circles on a giant inflatable seahorse. "And now there is a big tank of sea spiders over there." He tried to stop spinning long enough to point.

Lee stood up. "No way. I missed it."

Uher nodded. "now you have to do test two."

Lee shrugged. "That one's the actual easy one." She stepped up to the front of the pool. Looking over at Gara, she nodded, "Are you okay with this, Gara?"

Still spinning, he called out, "do I get to hose people down afterward?"

Lee laughed, "I think you'll have to."

"Then I'm in. Proceed."

"Ok, ladies and gentlemen, My name is Lee Georgiou and this is my operating manual. First, I want to introduce you to my ass."

She pulled her yoga pants off again and tossed them behind her. She turned around and bent over, spreading the cheeks of her ass. It was large and round and incredibly feminine, Uher thought.

Everyone cheered as she continued. "This is the center of my sexuality. For some reason, whenever I think about hard, real sex, it's in my ass. When I imagine fucking, it's always in my ass. Maybe it's the taboo, maybe it's just the sensation. But this is where sex starts and ends for me." She pushed her hand inside her ass, nearly falling over.

"Get on your hands and knees if it's easier," Master Qerici called out.

"Ok, that's a good point. On my knees is where I feel like I belong. My ass wants to be in the air and my head wants to be down. You can wrap my head up, push it down, choke me, anything when my ass is being fucked. Here." She pushed some more and her hand slid into her asshole.

"I can self-fist my ass, which I have lots of names for, like fuckhole and cumdump and bitchpussy. And I do it when I masturbate."

Phoka called out, "that's hot."

Qerici applauded. "All right. Open up that fucking dickpocket."

Lee looked backward. "I like that name a lot. I'm really into dirty talk. Nothing is too dirty to talk about. I like to gape and I like the idea that people are looking into my asshole." She spread her ass widely and opened it. "If you want to come closer, you can see inside."

Phoka came up close and peered into her wide open ass. "That's cool. I'd love to fuck that."

Qerici jumped in, further objectifying her. "I did. I loved it. It was amazing. You should feel how that little asshole holds on."

"I love being taunted during sex. I mostly cum from anal, but this works, too."

She turned and kneeled, playing with her clit and twisting her nipples very hard. "My nipples like to be hurt. Like almost damaged. And I always imagine stretching my clit out until it's dick sized and playing with it. That'll get me off, too. I like the idea of being used, being available for someone's dirty needs. And my mouth is something that wants to be used, too. Like for pissing in if someone needs or for licking ass or cleaning someone's boot or anything."

"I imagine all the time, being at the Octagon and licking the boots clean for the space people while they talk about their agreement, ignoring me, pissing and cumming inside me until the deal is final. Then I bring them drinks while they celebrate."

"Ok, that's not exactly how it is, but we can work with it." Qerici laughed. "That was great."

Everyone clapped. Gara had climbed out of the pool and started hosing her down. Lee almost fell over. She laughed and bent over, letting the water invade her. He stopped. She looked out in the pool. "Does anyone want to try me?" She crawled to the water and looked at Phoka. "How about you? You're pretty."

"Hell, yeah." He pulled himself from the pool and jumped up. He took the hose from Gara and knelt in front of Lee, pulling her face up. He kissed her. She kissed him back hungrily, her skin even white and more porcelain against his. Phoka grabbed her nipple and started twisting, aiming the hose at her pussy and turning it on. It sprung to life, digging into her clit with a thick white stream that pushed her open legs wider. Lee's breathing increased as he tortured her tits one after another, massaging her pussy with the blast from the hose. He pushed it in closer as she scratched at him and opened her mouth for his tongue.

"Open that fucking pussy and ass," he growled at her. Her legs spread wider than she thought possible under the pummelling of the water as Phoka wrapped his hand around her neck and pulled her toward the pool. He turned off the hose and spit in her mouth.

"Breath in, bitch." He flipped her over and pushed her head in the pool. He pulled her ass up in the air. For a second, she panicked, but then, as soon as his hands came down, slapping her between the legs, she started arching her back. He placed himself behind her, squatting down low, and quickly slid his prick into her asshole, without holding back. She bucked, pushing back on his cock, fucking herself. She let her hands fall into the pool, trusting him as he pounded her asshole again and again in rhythm. She didn't try to escape, shoving her base back into him.

He pumped himself into her, struggling to keep his balance. From the pool it looked to Uher as though it were some kind of bizarre cowboy exercise, Phoka riding her ass while pulling back on her neck and hair as she slammed herself into him. He pulled her head up by the hair and she took a deep breath. "Open that asshole, cunt."

She cried out, "I will. I will, Yes, sir."

Phoka grunted loudly and made noises that everyone could see were bringing Lee closer. She put her head back down in the water and he held it there, ripping into her willing hole like some kind of organic machinery, a piston meant to reduce her to compliance.

Bubbles rose to the surface. Lee let her arms flap to her sides, refusing to lift herself from the pool even as she began to cough and sputter underwater. Phoka nearly rose up, fucking her harder with each push until he climaxed, pouring his hot seed up inside her. Lee's body twitched as she felt it, bringin on her own release as she reached for her clit to hold it and play with it.

She lifted her head, breathing in sharply, water falling down her face, and fell forward into the pool. She floated for a moment and then, as if springing to life, rose to the sounds of Qerici, Uher, and Gara applauding.

Phoka reached for her hand. "Are you ok?"

She pushed over closer, reaching for his hand. "What?"

He saw the mischief in her eyes and pulled his hand back, smiling.

"What did you ask?" Lee taunted.

"Nothing," he started to pull back as she pounced, grabbing his hand and pulling him in the pool. She grabbed him and dunked him.

"Ok, perverts. This is me going to bed. Keep it rough. Peace out." Gara stepped toward the house to get some sleep. Everyone cheered him on as he left.

The other four wrestled in the water as the sun disappeared. Lee laid a towel down at the deep end and spread herself out, naked, enjoying the cool of the night air for a minute, before getting back in.

Qerici swam up to her. Lee rolled over and kissed her. Reaching for Qerici's hand, she placed it on her breast as she laid back down.

Qerici squeezed. "So tell me the truth. Are you looking to change your whole life because of someone you met a couple of days ago?"

"Because of you? Yes. But also no. Not like that. I never really honestly considered it before. I didn't know what all of you people would be like."

"But now?" Master Qerici placed two fingers on her nipple and tightened them.

"You and Phoka and... I didn't realize it would be like this."

"Like what?" she began to twist, but lightly.

Lee arched her back slightly "This feeling I have when I'm with you. Like... It's like, I'm enough. You know."

"Of course you're enough, Leeandrea." She dragged out the sound of her name.

She lifted her head, turning to her. "How do you know my full name?"

"I've been living in your house for three days. You don't have to be a spy. Although maybe I am one." Qerici dipped back below the water for a second.

Lee crawled to the pool edge. "See? This is how I feel around you. "

"Don't you always feel like you're enough?" The Master reached for her hand and squeezed.

"NOBODY out here in the world feels that way. Literally nobody. None of us." She rolled over and kissed Qerici's hand.

Qerici moved up and put her face near hers. "Maybe I've been in that place for too long. "

"Maybe I haven't been there and that's the problem" Lee stared up into the Grecian night sky.

"Ok, you come with, live in my thula, wench."

"Just like that?" Lee smiled.

"You passed all the tests. Except the first one and that's the easiest one. We can do that tonight. And then you apply. We'll just take the application with us. You have an ethics degree and one in conflict resolution. You know what the requirements are."

"Just like that?"

"Ordinarily we would come meet you. So here. Nice to meet you. She extended her hand. "Got that out of the way."

Lee shook her hand. "Good to meet you. That's hot because this time yesterday you were making my asshole bleed by fucking me like a dirty cum pig"

Qerici whispered, "You talk about sex like you want dirtier words than they.ve made so far."

Lee rolled over and kissed her on the lips. "God, yes. Thank you. I need newer, dirtier words. Maybe that could be my side job."

Qerici kissed her back, slowly, pulling her tongue in her mouth. "But first, one more test."

The four of them moved back into the house, absent-mindedly drying off. Lee leaned into Phoka who wrapped his arms around her as she imagined pushing him into the pool at least one more time

They moved the couch away from the center of the floor and sat down, still nude, towels scattered everywhere.

The self-tests to enter the Octagon were designed to show people things about themselves. Many, like Uher, found the last test the most difficult. A few, though, stopped at the first. Lee realized how difficult this test might have been just a few days ago. But how easy it was right now. Her skin felt raw and open. She looked forward to this.

Everyone's eyes were on her.

She started. "This is the first test, but it's my last one. I have to make love to a number of people at the same time and tell them what is really lovable about them. I want to thank you guys for making this easy. I can start with..."

She moved her finger around the room and landed on Phoka. "You."

She moved over to him. She kissed him and massaged his prick. She climbed over him, staring into his eyes, letting his dick fall naturally into the space between her legs. "I love that you are literally one of the prettiest things I've ever seen. But that's just a surface thing. I love this." She slid his cock into her cunt, sliding down on the shaft and breathing in. She moved slowly on top of it.

"I love that you're always smiling at me like it's my fault you're happy. I love that you're obviously book smart but you hate correcting people."

He looked up at her and held her face. "Wait. How could you tell that? That's... How?"

She continued, "I love that you just smile and never correct me when I constantly misuse the word 'literally.' I love how you listen to everything people say and then try to give it back to them. You're kind and fun and you wear bright clothes just because it makes other people smile. I love you, Phoka."

Lee leaned in and kissed him, moving up and down on his member, trying to keep eye contact as he lost focus and came inside her. "I love you, Lee. That was great. I want to see myself like that all the time."

He kissed her and held her close.

She slid off him and made her way over to Uher. She grabbed his face. "You're so easy, Butch." They laughed as she laid down and pulled his head down onto hers, kissing him.

"I love how handsome you are and you never see it. I love how you keep your hair short so that it won't get all curly and crazy like your dad's. I love that you were my first boyfriend."

Uher licked at her lips. "And no one can ever take that away from us." He held her and petted her head, pulling her black mohawk backward into a ponytail. She smiled and continued.

"I love how you tell everyone that like it's the thing you're proudest of or something, like I'm some kind of a great catch."

"Sh. I am. I'm so proud. And you are a catch."

"I love how you only watch tv shows where people are happy at the end and that you'd rather watch the same show over again to see it again."

She spread her legs and pulled him into her. "This is the first time we ever had sex and it's insane how this feels. I love how you've been the bar my whole life for men."

"Is that ok? Are you crying?" Uher realized how vulnerable she was. He'd been given this gift right now, the chance to get inside of her and pay her back for a lifetime of friendship.

"Yes, I'm crying because this is..." She leaned in and kissed his neck. He moved inside her, trying to catch her eyes.

"Let me tell you that I know." Uher looked deeply into her eyes, "My whole life I've lived in this weird privilege because the most amazing person I know loves me. You did that. That's what you do."

"Really?" Lee's eyes filled with water as Uher kissed each one.

"I have never taken for granted what I lucked into. I love you, Leeandrea.

"I love you, Uher."

His eyes closed partially as he felt the warmth inside her.

"We should have been doing this all along."

"Oh my god, yes. This is... oh my god, yes."

Uher leaned in and whispered, "Do you want to put on a good show for these guys?"

Lee's back arched as she nodded vigorously.

Uher started fucking harder, pushing himself into her. Lee felt sloppy and wet all over from Phoka's cum before, mixing with her own. It made it easy for her to put her hands down on the floor and lift her legs, forcing her pussy up and down in a steady but ever increasing rhythm. He pounded at her, as hard as he could, letting go completely. Lee wanted to hear the animal grunts from him, the sign that he couldn't stop. She rolled over and spread her ass as wide as possible.

"Uher, please, don't stop yet. Fuck my ass up."

He fell forward, holding his dick, pressing it into her waiting hole. All of a sudden, everything in Lee's life seemed to make sense. She had love, she had purpose, she was being filled. Everything would be ok. She wanted them to watch this beautiful man force his way into her ass. She felt it dig inside her, deep and hard, squirting all over the carpet as he came in her.

She looked over to see Qerici get up and grab her robe. She pulled a few things out.

Uher kissed the back of her neck and rolled off her. She turned, kissing him and petting his chest.

She got up to kneel as Master Qerici handed her something. Lee looked down, seeing the strap on and dildo in her hands. In front of her, Qerici was pulling black rubber tape out, spreading her ass open and taping it that way with black rubber strips.

Lee leaned on Uher and slid the strap on over her legs, slipping it upward and setting it on her waist. A thick black cock stuck out in front of a harness that felt surprisingly good. As she touched it, it began to vibrate, the rubber protrusion leading downward, spreading the vibration through to her cunt.

She got to her knees and kissed Qerici.

"I love how cool you are and how you see me. I love that I finally met someone I want to be, you know? That I see you and I can see myself as this and it makes me smile."

Master Qerici kissed her back. "I love that. It's really kind. I love how honest you are and how you throw yourself into things. I love that you're so strong but it turns you on so much to make other people feel strong. I love having you as a partner in crime."

"Oh god, yes. I look at you and that's my dream. I want to break some rules with you."

"Me, too." Qerici turned around and bent over, putting her head down.

Lee slapped her ass and moved in to kiss it. She opened her mouth and sucked at her open asshole. Her tongue dipped into the Master's pussy and pulled from her an ample amount of her juice, letting it run all around her lips and mouth. She thought about the taller woman's cock in her ass in the grass before and about how it had lit up her body, making her explode.

Lee massaged the vibrating cock between her legs, rubbing the Master's juices into it. She lifted it and placed the tip right at the opening of Qerici's ass.

"Oh, yes. Fuck my ass. Screw it hard, bitch.

The Master bucked and arched her back, pushing her head down and her ass in the air. Lee dug the strap on into her ass and tried to stay on as she rode the darker woman. "I love you, you fucking cunt." Querici yelled out, laughing at the contradiction, the placement of words, the dichotomy of words of love, coupled with the very dirty words that Lee loved so much, playing out into the night as they said goodbye to Santorini, Greece in the only way that made sense.

***

By morning, all four of them were sitting in the Octagon in a warm pool in the center of the thula, a large and open space whose folds tricked the eye, hiding which parts were inside and which were exposed to the manufactured warm calm of the Mediterranean open air.

The buildings that housed the Octagon were built, at the base, during the Roman Empire. They were expanded on, beautified, rendered triumphant during the Ottoman Empire. And then, each was carefully recrafted, rebuilt, reborn through the hands of the Ahreee, one of the first races to use the structure, and countless other Voyager species, each adding their own unique gifts and blessings.

Lee and Uher were still struggling to not be carried away by the visuals all around them. Despite arriving very early, they'd still encountered hundreds of things in the hallways leading to the thula that seemed to be not of this Earth, objects, rooms, and people that stretched their imagination to breaking.

And here, in the same pool, there was a woman who was born millions of light years away.

The blue skinned bald woman stood up. She was both beautiful and familiar in the shape of her, pretty breasts rising up over a beautiful torso, belly dipping into the gentle V between her legs, with a tiny line of blue hair visible below. It was impossible to tell how old she was, but her skin was smooth and even radiant. In a black and white movie, she might have come off as an Egyptian temple goddess, her eyes with a slight almond shape, her voice, lilting with a slight unplaceable accent, mysterious and ever hiding behind the next word, her hands, so different.

But in full color, she was something even more remarkable, with light blue skin that exploded into a deep, brilliant navy around her lips and areolas, lining the lips of her pussy, too, with a deep and wholy inhuman royal blue. She spoke with a formality that proved to be mostly dry humor in disguise as she proceeded. She wore light silver chains and jewelry and nothing else. And her movements seemed so calculated and perfect that it was easy to believe it when she started to speak.

"My name is Vorun. I'm over 700 years old and a member of a species called the Forsa. The Forsa like to believe they invented the Octagon but I don't think that's true. I believe it's always existed, just as bonobos here on your own planet connect and give each other sexual pleasure in order to foment contracts, make deals, to know each other. "

"I believe that all conflict is a lack of intimacy, a lack of love, a failure to feel compersive, to open yourself to mudita. We fight because we see the ugly in each other while hiding the joy and beauty. We mistrust out of a failure to see and out of a misplaced feeling that there is no joy in the other for us."

"I'm told I slept through the best musical periods of the last century, so you may have to bear with me. I may be the oldest person you've ever had sex with, but that's no reason to hold back or not try. I will accept 'bluey' and even 'baldy' as affectionate nicknames but please, try harder, folks."

They laughed as she continued, waving her pretty three-fingered hands.

"While you are here in this thula, there are no questions that are out of line. This is a place for learning intimacy and it is a particularly intimate space in an intimate discipline. While you are here, you are my people and everything you are is part of us. We welcome you. Especially all of your exceptionally bad choices in haircuts."

Qerici applauded wildly. She and Phoka were familiar with Vorun as part of their thula. Lee and Uher still stared at her as the first Voyager they'd ever interacted with.

Qerici stood up. "None of you know who I am. I am a mystery. I'm Persian and clearly a very grumpy person. Don't cross me or I'll spank HER." Qerici pointed to Lee, who stood up, excited about the idea of being the spanking pony. Vorun clapped, flashing a smile wide enough to let everyone off the hook for any amount of informality.

Vorun stood back up, pushing her down. "All right. Well said. Who is next? Can you tell us why you belong here?"

She sat down and Phoka stood up. "My whole life I knew I would end up here. There are millenia-long wars that are over because of what happens inside these walls. This is my only holy place. And I was told that I didn't have to wear pants. Thank you."

Everyone cheered, in a stunning display of dislike for pants. Vorun nodded.

Phoku took a bow and splashed back down in the water. Next to him, Lee stood up.

"Why do I belong? I'm a complete fucking whore and I hate it when people don't get along. I'm sorry I swore."

Vorun looked over at Qerici, floating next to her. "That works."

She responded, "we should engrave that on the front of the fucking building."

Phoka and Uher laughed as Qerici slid out of the pool and moved into the other room, only to come back a second later with a roll of thick black tape. She motioned to Lee to get out of the water and stand next to her, pulling her legs apart.

She ripped off a piece of tape and set it harshly over Lee's bare pussy, tapping it down to make sure it stuck, before sliding back in the pool. Looking around, she barked out, "this one's anal-only until she's fully accepted."

A visible tremor ran down Lee's body. She looked at everyone with an almost cartoon submission. "Yes, Master."

Qerici motioned again with her hand for her to return to the water. Lee sat back down in the water. Uher and Phoka knew exactly how she was feeling. With a tiny piece of tape her ass had been made available – open – usable for everyone. That four centimeter square black piece of black sticky rubber had given her so much of what she was here for.

Lee's breathing was shallow with desire as she stared at Master Qerici.

Uher was impressed. He stood up and took a deep breath. "I'm going to be changed. Into a water breather. And it's going to hurt, I know that. It's going to be the biggest change anyone can probably experience in their life. And then, there will be Voyagers from a beautiful water world who show up, looking for a solution, wanting to feel like someone cares about the difficult decisions they have to make, the impossible changes they have to make. And I will tell them what I went through just to really see them and be with them and make their problems into something even just a little bit smaller. And they'll know why I changed. And, maybe, other changes won't seem so scary."

The room was quiet as Uher sat down. Vorun looked at him and spoke quietly. "You sound like you practiced that your whole life. And I can't tell you what it means to me that I'm the first person here to hear it." She swam over to him and kissed him on the lips. He felt her hand slide into his and he held it, reveling in the difference of it.

She sat down and looked around. "You're all in the right place."

***

During the day, Lee, Phoka, and Uher spent their time in the libraries in the Thessalia. It seemed to go on forever, the strange mixture of water-filled spaces and air-breathing ones. It seemed like there was a water fountain or waterfall everywhere they looked. It was filled, too, at all times with a combination of Taranakah and Turolo novitae – a term they soon learned referred to air breathers. There were stories about even stranger places being built even now, in the Octagon, to house even more unusual biologies.

It was hard to decide what to learn first. Qerici and Vorun walked them through what was important at night, playfully, with tests and games that were often more fun to lose than win. As the days wore on, each of them became hyper-aware of not only how much they knew, but of how much the universe still had to show them.

Since the gifts of the Voyagers had been spread across earth, people stayed young for three times longer of more than they had. Qerici herself was nearly 65 years old and there would be no way to know she was over 30. Living longer made sense when there was so much to learn.

As they sat, their legs in the water, reading, looking at charts and images, Lee found herself relying on the advice of the disembodied voice that delivered information all over the Octagon, Dorothy.

Dorothy was funny and dirty and quick. She had access to so much information but could also tell a joke in a way that made you realize there was something real in there. And her fantasies about Voyager interactions were often hotter than the actual stories.

Unlike Uher and Phoka, Lee had decided relatively recently to come here. Dorothy helped her cram constantly, to learn the things that everyone else already knew. And she did it without judgment. Dorothy played music for her when her head hurt from too much information, told her dirty jokes when she needed, and took care of her when she felt stupid. And when it was time to see Shukkat, it was Dorothy that told her, excited for her.

Lee dried off and made her way up to the top of the main building, an original conference room Shukkat had turned into her office. It was large and open, with an array of plants acting like a curtain. The woman in the red robe who greeted her had kind eyes. She was dark, like Qerici, and very pretty. She had tattoos all over as well, but on her forehead, where there might have been a t'kau, was an obsidian 8 sided gem, Lit up like a digital t'kau. It was hypnotic.

"You're Shukkat. Wow."

"And you're Lee. You seem nervous. I love your hair. And the insects on the shirt a lot." Shukkat hugged her and played with her shirt. "I hear you killed test five."

Lee smiled. "I think I did. This is sort of. You know. Straight to the top, huh?"

Shukkat hugged her, whispering, "what if I told you that this is just a formality, that you are already accepted. "

Lee hugged back feeling the warmth of the other woman. "Um. Is that what you're... Really. Oh my god. I guess I would breathe again. "

Shukkat kissed her head. "See? Acceptance feels good doesn't it? "

Lee looked at her and smiled. "Damn, that was good."

Shukkat sat back down. "Makes me look super wise, right?"

Lee moved back to the chair. She was about to sit back down. "Absolutely. But, are you...?"

Shukkat waved at her to sit down, smiling, "Yes, You are definitely accepted into training. I'm really excited to get to know you. Dorothy thinks you're wonderful."

"This is amazing. She told you? I don't think I would know anything without Dorothy."

"Of course you would. You're going to be seated with Vorun, right?" Shukkat looked down at the holograph on her desk. Lee couldn't make out what it was.

Lee smiled. "And Qerici"

Shukkat winked at her, "That's good. Qerici definitely makes this fun. And I learned a lot from Vorun."

"You did? It's hard to imagine you learning stuff. That came out wrong." Lee tried to backtrack.

Shukkat stood up and moved to the wall. It slid open, exposing a number of books. "I learn all the time. Let me find this. One sec." She reached up and pulled out a book with a handmade cover. "Here we go."

"What's this?" Lee looked at it. It felt old.

"A notebook. When I first met Vorun, I tried to write everything she said into a notebook." Shukkat sat back.

"I bet this thing's worth a fortune. I mean..." Lee delicately opened it. It was full of precise handwriting and some drawings.

"No, hold onto it. I'll get it back when you graduate."

Lee's eyes widened. "I don't deserve that."

Shekkat leaned into her conspiratorially. "Every once in a while, with Vorun, talk to her using the exact language from that. It'll freak her out so hard."

It suddenly occurred to her how much Qerici and Shukkat were alike. "Omigod, yes. That's going to be so spooky. I literally love you."

Shukkat laughed. "Meh, You got to grab your fun wherever you can."

"I'm learning that." Lee felt grateful. "And I know there aren't a lot of people around here with my shape..."

"Is that what you think?" Shukkat looked at her.

"I don't know."

"You should look harder. There are lots of shapes here. Lots of ways to be desirable, certainly. You belong here. And you're going to help me torture Vorun."

Lee leaned in. "I so am." She hugged the book to her chest, "Can I ask you a question?"

"Of course."

Lee asked shyly. "Your t'kau. It's all black, all filled in. But it looks like a black stone, not a tattoo. Why is yours different?"

Shukkat stood up and leaned back on her desk. Her robe slid open and Lee could see that she was naked underneath it.

Since Qerici had shown up, Lee had come to equate nakedness with honesty. With belonging, even. It made her happy to see that Shukkat was naked.

"Well, Lee. I was in an accident. And it messed up my original tattoo. I figured I could either grow the skin back and redo it. Or I could make something even more permanent."

Lee looked up. "So you doubled down."

Shukkat winked at her. "I really think of it as tripling down. Now, do something for me."

Lee struggled not to say "anything." But nothing else would come out. She nodded.

"Get your clothes off. Leave them here. You don't need them. In a day or two, I'll have some things sent to your thula that you will love, I promise. In the meantime, walk around this place. Meet people. But do it with no clothes."

"In a day or two?" Lee starting pulling off her shirt and the black yoga pants she was always in.

"Spend some time thinking about what you want to wear. If I don't send things you love, you can come back here and spank me."

Lee laughed, involuntarily. "Oh my god, that's hot."

"I had something else to tell you."

Lee sat back down, folding her clothes. "Ok."

"Uher has to be…changed, before the t'kau ceremony. He's going to start in a week. I know he's going to need all of you."

"But then he goes…" Lee's face dropped.

"Yes." Shukkat knelt down in front of her. Lee looked into her face. Shukkat was 89 years old this year, from what she understood. But the treatments here made her look no more than 35.

Or was it something else? She put her head on the woman's shoulder.

"I think this will be as hard on you as it is on him."

Lee thought for a moment about how right Shukkat had been about everything since she walked in that room.

***

The next week was a blur. Back in the thula, there was little sleep. There was celebration and preparation. And in the Thessalia, there was still no sign of Dannae, the red haired Taranakah, despite how Uher had always kept at least one eye open every time they were down there.

Lee spent the next few days naked. As much as she loved the black tape over her cunt, she enjoyed pulling it off finally, accepted completely. Uher was the first person to cum in her newly liberated pussy after what felt like years. Lee gave thanks for both the piece of tape and its absence.

Shukkat had kept her word with a box that showed up three days after their meeting, filled with black scarab jewelry, mesh wraps with tiny insects printed on them and metal skull nipple jewelry. The box seemed endless and each piece was more her than the one before. She dressed up, more exposed than even naked. And when she looked in the mirror, she saw the goth girl from Santorini.

She dressed up for the celebration, where people from the thulas all around them came to celebrate Uher. She watched him laugh all night wondering if he was scared.

And she tried not to be.

The first night in the medbay, they were all able to stay. Vorun laid in a bed near him while the rest of them padded up pillows and blankets to take over half the room and make it into a conversation pit.

Phoka commented on how much it felt like the house back in Santorini and he wasn't wrong.

The first night, he received medication to grow his heart. It would need to pump harder in the pressure of the depths. Uher felt like his chest was about to explode until Lee and Qerici found oil to rub on it, massaging it. That's how they fell asleep, covered in oil, their hands lulling him into a place where the pain didn't matter anymore.

His hands and feet had to be reshaped, to make them webbed, better able to handle his new life underwater, The bones were scaled and thinned, cut down and in a few places, extended. By the fifth day, Uher could barely move.

Human skin isn't made to stay underwater. Uher's tattoos were all removed and his skin prepared. It would dissolve and create the foundation for his new skin. He asked Vorun and Phoka to go back home. The process was painful and there were times he just wanted to scream, to let it go. And alone, that was something he could do. He talked to the disembodied voice of Dorothy, the voice of the entire Octagon. He cried to her sometimes when he didn't want anyone to hear. She talked to him about the other side. She joked with him.

She was there.

He wanted to scratch the red, flaming itch that ran all over his body, but his arms didn't work right now as the muscles were being broken down and regrown in a slightly different shape.

On the sixth day, he opened his eyes and saw Qerici next to him. She looked like she'd been crying.

He looked down, wishing he could touch her. "Are you ok? "

She lifted her head and wiped her eyes. "Yes. I'm good."

It was still dark but it was clear morning was coming. "How long...? Have you been here all night?"

"I was taking turns with Lee. She didn't want to go."

He looked at the door. "Is she ok?"

"Yeah, she's fine." Qerici wanted to touch him but settled for arranging his pillow.

He looked up at her. She still made his heart beat faster when he inhaled around her. "The pain. It's not so bad now."

She smiled, sitting back down, "That's great."

"Hey, why are you crying? You've seen this before."

She brightened up. "Oh, yeah. I know what's on the other end. You're going to love it."

He lowered his voice. "So why cry?"

A tear fell down her cheek. "Just because pain doesn't go on forever, doesn't mean it's not real."

Uher let out a breath it seemed he'd been holding. "Yeah. That's true."

"Right now, you're mine. You belong to me. And I love that. But that means that the pain belongs to me, too." Uher watched as her purple pouting lips and steely eyes, set in a perfect face fell into a racking sob.

He wished he could reach her. "Really?"

She whispered at him, "Is that ok?"

Uher felt so much of the pain fall away. "Yeah. that's ok. It's ok." He realized they were alone. And he had so much to say, " I've really liked belonging to you."

She looked up and nodded, still crying. She breathed in, her face awash with the aftermath of breaking down. She patted down his bedding. "My little sea god. There's a part of you that's going to always be mine. It's like when you mix water and tea in a glass, you can never get them completely unmixed again."

Her voice seemed to usher in the morning.

Uher wondered how he would get by without that voice making fun of everything it could reach. It was a voice that always brought the sun. "That sounds right." He shifted in bed "I love you."

"Oh, I love you, too, Uher."

He paused as the new light started to fill the room. "Which one of us is the tea?"

Qerici laughed in the middle of a sob, her chest momentarily brushing against his arm.

"I'm legitimately 10 shades darker than you, geek."

Uher leaned back

"Got it. I thought that was it."

On the seventh day, the next one, they slid him into a liquid filled tube. Lee came to see him but he couldn't hear her through the glass of the tube. They told her he'd be able to hear her tomorrow but she couldn't wait. She started crying and sat down in front of the tube and refused to leave. He looked at her and hoped she understood how important she was to him. At one point, she ran out and came back with a stack of papers. She wrote notes and put them around the tank. They said:

"I love you, Uher. I'm sorry this hurts…"

"I will kill whoever you want."

"Let me know…"

"I didn't want you to change because you…"

"Are the only thing in the world that…"

"Is stable and real."

"But I know you will always be.."

"Real"

"I could have put that on the last note."

"If I wrote a little smaller"

"You better come see me, fishboy"

"Or we're gonna have some trouble."

 "I wish I could suck your dick…"

"And make you feel better."

She wrote the last note and slid down the tube. Uher looked down. It was almost impossible to move anything. But a part of him wanted to break out and grab her and just carry her home.

Lee was crazy and she was supposed to do anything, literally anything.

She wasn't supposed to cry.

When he woke up the next day, his tube was laying down on a surface. The front of it was open and he could barely breathe. He couldn't tell if it was morning or dusk. He tried to make his eyes work by blinking.

It didn't seem like it was working. As the world came into focus, he saw a flash of red. He wasn't sure if he was still sleeping or not. He spoke, his throat scratchy and evolving.

"Hi."

The red-haired girl leaned over him, her arms on the tube. "Hey, there."

Part of him wanted to cry, but his brain couldn't figure out how that would work. His eyes were confusing to him. "I can't believe you're here. I'm sorry. This all must be really weird."

She smiled just like she did in that interview. "No, I'm flattered, for sure."

Uher tried to control his voice. "It's not helping that you are even prettier in person. "

She leaned in, clearly on her tiptoes. The tank must be up high. "Well, thank you for that, too. But that's just what I look like. I could be a hot mess."

Uher laughed. His chest felt like there was nothing he could do to stop the pain. "Are you?"

"No, actually, I'm cool as hell," she whispered.

He smiled. "Damn."

"It's a lot, you know. What you're going through."

He cleared his throat and tried again, "Why did YOU do it?"

"I love the water. I've had mermaid fantasies since I was a kid."

Uher tried to nod but it didn't happen. "I get that." He breathed in a few times, trying to get the air to talk.

She looked down at him and played with the top of the tank. "Besides, they needed Taranakahs. So many water breathing races in the universe. "

His voice was rough. "It's almost like water is all over."

"Right? Crazy."

He took a deep breath. "Ow."

"Be careful. Your lungs are really confused right now. They're being phased out. Your body hates that."

"I can tell." He managed a slight nod.

"I cried. I'm not going to lie. It hurt." Her honesty was like a salve, a lotion, making him feel better

"This helps."

"I walked in the room here with a t'kau, so i'll help any way you want, I promise."

Uher coughed, "I want to get to know you. But that sounds creepy when I say it. "

She leaned in. "Look, a lot of people saw that interview. I got cards. Letters. You're the only guy who changed your whole life, moved to another country, and underwent painful surgical processes to meet me."

He whispered, "well, I'm not much of a letter writer. "

Dannae laughed. "Ok, that was funny. You're the quietly funny type. I see."

"I can't believe you're here."

"You said that. You're the sick goldfish. I had to at least check in." She ran her fingers over the top of the tank.

"The Master Qerici told me it's ok to do something, change, quit drinking, be better, do something for someone else. It's a myth that you have to do it only for yourself. " Uher sank in the tank, wishing his chest would stop with the fire.

"I think that's true."

"But she said not to expect anything."

Dannae reached into the tank and touched his face. It felt strange, almost as though the nerves couldn't figure out what was happening. "I think that's true, too."

"I want you to know I don't expect anything."

"They told me something. I'm going to tell you. They said I didn't have to tell you. They're letting me decide what thula you're in."

"What place to live?" Uher felt his chest drop for a moment.

"They wanted me to be comfortable. So they're letting me decide. They're all great. Every person in the Forala is amazing. You have no idea. It's like a world of the most amazing mer-people. Even just the colors are beautiful."

He tried to catch his breath. "I'm sure."

She looked into his eyes, "Are you ok with me deciding?"

Uher realized that it took a weight off of him. "I'm more than ok. It helps. Thank you. I'll go where I'm needed."

She got excited. "That's what I said when I got here. And I went with the current. Like when you swim in an ocean and sit at the bottom waiting for the water to tell you which way to go. You can make all the big decisions, but sometimes, sometimes it's best to let the current do the rest. You know. "

Uher whispered, exhausted, "I want to feel that."

"You will. But first, you have to get better, goldfish." She kissed the side of his tank and then looked over. "You know what's great about goldfish?"

Uher tried to shake his head. A tiny nod came out.

"They're small. But they'll grow into anything you put them in. No matter how grand and important. They just silently slowly grow to fill it."

Uher smiled. He tried to take a breath. "Am I going to see you again?"

Dannae looked at him playfully. "Ask me again."

His voice dropped, "Am I going to –"

"Yes." Her face opened up with that beautiful smile. "See how fast I answered that."

He wanted to kiss her, but everything hurt. He tried to stay up but he was asleep by the time she left.

***

Lee sat in the pool of the thula, nude, trying to feel the water. There were days, many days, where she almost could understand Uher's fascination with the water. And days where she didn't

Master Qerici slid into the pool next to her. "Are you doing ok?"

Lee curled up next to her, holding on to her. "I want to be you."

Qerici pulled her closer. "Ok, should we just change places now?"

Lee put her hands in Qerici's lap, holding onto her cock. She kissed her and let her mouth connect to the darker woman's pretty purple lips for a long time. "I'm serious. It's not happening fast enough."

"You want to be me?"

"Like today." The goth girl nearly climbed into her lap.

Qerici rocked her back and forth. "You know, there's nothing wrong with seeing another face in the mirror that you want to grow into. I saw Caleo Cuvo Osa, my Master. She was funny and weird and kind and I love her very much." She ran her hand through Lee's hair.

Lee curled up "That's who you wanted to be?"

"And she saw HER Master, Reylan Corroba, who is, admittedly, cool as fuck."

"And who did she see?" Lee ran her hand over her Master's face.

"Oh, she always saw Shukkat in the mirror. She'll be the first one to tell you. And Shukkat saw Vorun."

Lee smiled, "That I know."

"And Vorun saw T'keil, who is, apparently, by all accounts, the greatest woman who ever lived." Qerici dropped her voice, speeding up at the end.

Lee sighed. "That's a lot to live up to."

"It gets easier when you realize that the mirror is big. And it can contain a lot." She hugged Lee

"You're going to try to convince me that someone's going to look up to me that way?"

Qerici smushed her face. "Nope. Life is going to show you that. I'm just going to float here and play with your boobs."

Lee leaned into it. "Just twist those tits right off."

"I'm trying. Seriously, you're unbreakable. It's impressive." She slapped Lee's breasts.

Lee sighed, "I can't wait until I can work on my first project."

"It's going to happen soon enough. In a few weeks, you get your t'kau. You won't have to ever draw one on again." She raised her eyebrows at her and Lee laughed, moving back in and hugging her close.

"That is amazing."

"You know you've already helped," she said quietly.

"What do you mean?" Lee looked up.

"You interact with people, you work with them, you give them what they need to do this. Back when I was a novitae I helped someone get ready to unite hundreds of worlds."

"Jesus." The goth girl kissed her.

"We can step up the training if you want. Take your mind off things." Master Qerici twisted her nipples harder. Lee's hands dropped to the side as she pushed her breasts forward, trying to just give in.

"Harder. Harder." She slapped the darker woman in the tit. Lee feigned indignation, pouncing on her and pushing her into the water

Qerici smiled broadly. "You did not just..."

They wrestled in the pool until Phoka and Vorun joined them and took sides. Lee looked at Uher's room, across from the dining area, realizing there would be someone else in there soon.

In less than five days, he would be going home.

That night Lee sat outside Uher's room. She couldn't bring herself to go in. But when the red haired girl showed up, she stood up to hug her tightly. She told her about Uher and about how he was her first boyfriend and how he was kind and how he never once made her think that she wasn't still important and the red-haired girl listened.

Before she went in.

Uher's head was wrapped up, but he could hear her voice.

"Hello. It's me."

"You came back." He sighed.

"I told you I would."

"I wish I could see you." Uher thought about what a waste it was. He thought about mentioning that.

"What do you imagine I look like today, Goldfish?"

He thought for a second. "Beautiful, flowing red hair. Big wide smile. Enough to make everything else ugly. "

"I think you're lying. Clearly you can see." For a second, he felt like she enjoyed his adoration. Maybe she did. That made him happy.

He pointed to the bandages. "They took my eyes out to make some changes."

She reached over and grabbed his hand. "You're going to like the changes so much."

"It feels…"

She whispered, coming in closer. "I know. It's so strange, isn't it? And these will go away." She touched the lumps in his belly.

He whispered back. "They move."

"These are new organs you need. They're almost grown in." Uher tried not to fixate on her hand, moving across his belly.

He raised his head. "That's good."

He could feel her breath on his face. "And once your new skin comes in, they can move you to a fresh fully-water tank. It'll feel good. The water is going to make everything feel so much better. It does that."

He breathed in. She smelled like the ocean. He remembered Qerici telling him that. He understood it. It was beautiful. It smelled like mysterious spaces and freedom. It smelled big. "I know you can't stay long."

"I ran up and teleported here so I can stay almost the full two hours. Is that ok?"

He nodded vigorously. Suddenly, the pain rushed up his spine "It really hurts."

He could hear her cry. "I know, goldfish. And you can't cry, which sucks. But I'm going to squeeze your hand really hard. It's going to be brutal. It's going to hurt worse than anything. Are you ready?"

He focused on his hand.

"Ok, go."

***

It was less than a week later when his air-breathing friends all gathered at the Thessalia.

Like most things here, in the Octagon, there was a ritual. He stripped naked and hugged everyone. Lee looked at him, fresh, his tattoos all gone. She saw him again like he was when they were little. When he was her boyfriend and he held her hand, not delicately and carefully, like her parents did, but firmly, with resolve, as though anyone trying to break that bond would fall flat on their ass in the dirt. She realized that those were the hands that had made her feel safest the longest.

Even as she let go.

Uher let himself fall through the center of the cone. The gentle spin of the water was different today, subtly. It was almost like the current itself had a voice, something he could recognize. It was soft and not demanding.

But it suggested. It guided. It even joked around a little. His body didn't hurt at all anymore. And the water made sure of it.

He smiled. The light dimmed as he got deeper and his new cones took over. Suddenly the colors became something profound, deeper. They were rich and effulgent. Everywhere he looked colors beyond what his human eyes could have seen, flowing, moving. Secret colors.

Breathing.

The water showed itself to his new senses. He could feel the temperature, broken down into fractional degrees. He could tell how far down they were and how fast they were going. He realized that, with practice, he could probably just swim without effort by inserting himself into the right current in the right place.

He felt at home.

He took the water in and followed the instructions. It felt strange not bringing anything with him but they had promised to bring all his things to his new thula. So, he took his time. The water seemed open to that. It seemed to be full of distractions and ideas, forces, and solutions.

Not a drop of it was empty.

The descent into the Forala was long, but it was straight and open. Uher could imagine ships descending, filled with water breathing species, full of new people he'd never seen before. People he could help.

As he got closer, it was not hard to feel like a part of something. He swam through a series of vines, opening for him as if on command. The walls looked like dark marble, flowers, and waterborne plants all over. He moved to the doorway, trying to let go of expectations and live for a future he was beautifully, brilliantly unaware of in the expanse of water that had proven to be nothing but welcoming...

And kind.

He thought about Lee and about the thula they'd built up above and how he'd miss the way everyone fit together, about how Lee's change seemed, sometimes, more dramatic than his, and just as perfect. He plotted the next time he'd see Master Qerici, even as he fell away from her, drifting downward.

He spun around in his exact center of gravity in a way he wished he could have in the pool back home, where the water picked up his intent and slipped around him, speeding his rotation like an underwater cyclone. He drifted closer to the massive blue door, shouting shades of itself into the liquid bent light around him, like snaking droplets of paint in a pool.

It was the colors he saw first. Everyone's hair looked different here underwater. This looked more vibrant, more brilliant. She turned as she opened the door and faced him, smiling, her voice filtering through the water like Grecian sunlight.

"Goldfish."

4 - Cub - 2065

Rey took the stairs three at a time, holding her robe up with both hands. Tanji was right behind her as they moved down the corridor from the stairwell to the conference room that had been repurposed as the command center of the Octagon.

Katel-ko-ra stood in the room, looking up at the wall that had been fitted with a massive monitoring screen. He ran his hand through the shoulder length dirty blonde hair that fell down the back of his head, making the lizard-like front part of his face look even more like a hastily put on mask. He moved around the room so easily it was hard to believe he wasn't born here on Earth.

The two women stared at him.

"Are you watching this?" Rey spit out.

Katel took a deep breath. "It's fucked up"

He flipped a switch and the volume rose.

"And from Yemen, the big news, the girl known only as 'Cub', held in captivity by the sex trafficking ring Ghul since she was 10, is scheduled to be hanged tomorrow for the murder of her captor, Andres Al-Azzi."

The speaker cleared her throat and continued.

"World human rights organizations are scrambling to put a stop to it without much time. The girl has repeatedly asked for sanctuary from the mysterious organization in Bursa, Turkey known only as 'Octagon.' A matriarchal group, Octagon, appearing out of nowhere fifteen years ago, is known for its technological gifts to the world and putative associations with extraterrestrials. We have been unable to reach anyone there to comment. Time is definitely running out."

Rey's voice rose but didn't crack. "Where is Shar?"

Katel-ko-ra pointed up at the portion of the screen he had rendered as a map of Yemen. "Where do you think she is? She's there. Yemen."

Rey looked up. "Sonofa…"

Tanji called out, her voice softer, with an accent that she had nearly masked. "Dorothy, can you show us any image or video connected to this?"

The voice of the AI assistant rang out. Dorothy tried to parse through millions of images and video. "Ok, looking. I have a lot on this."

Rey interrupted, "from any posted media, can you see any images or video of Shukkat?"

Dorothy somehow sounded as worried as they were. "Hold one. One second. This could be her."

A video splashed across the screen. A woman under a long sack being dragged into a prison. Rey pointed.

"That's her."

Katel tried to zoom in. He replayed the short clip. "Are you sure? "

Rey moved toward the wall, slamming her palm into a black spot. "I know how she walks. That's her." An armory opened up. She pulled out a couple of streamlined rifles, passing one to her sister.

Dorothy continued, "this picture was taken behind Mansoura Central prison in Sanaa, Yemen, forty seven minutes ago."

Rey motioned to Tanji. "C'mon."

Katel moved to grab a weapon. "I'm coming."

Rey turned to him. "No, you aren't. There are two hundred and fifty people in this building alone still and only you know how all the security works. We'll be right back."

As they ran out, Zehra made her way into the room. Rey grabbed her arm, "Z, you have to take over. We'll be right back, ok?"

"Be careful, please?" Zehra crossed her arms over her red robe as though freezing. She felt unqualified to say anything else as the two women in black ran out of the room. She moved into the room to stand next to Katel. As she looked at him, an idea popped into her head.

"Can you configure their translators to communicate back and forth?"

"From here?" Katel's eyes drifted up as he thought. "Yes I can."

She smiled. "Ok. let's start to figure out what they need."

***

"Jesus." Shukkat jerked awake in the middle of what looked like a prison cell, shading her eyes from a single light bulb placed like an unrelenting sun overhead. Gray walls extended to a metal-barred cage front, complete with massive iron door. Her head hurt worse than it ever had before, and the man crouched over her seemed concerned about that. He was dirty, with mid length stringy brown hair and a black shirt. As she focused her eyes, she could see the tiny white square hugging his neck, sitting in the front of his collar like the diamond in a wedding ring.

"I'm sorry. I didn't mean to wake you up." He spoke quietly, in American English, and she was grateful for that.

She pushed against the wooden bench she was laying on, lifting her back up against the wall. Leaning backwards, she realized her head was wrapped up and someone had placed her in nondescript blue prison attire – a thin, harsh feeling polyester shirt and pants. She looked at the man. "What are you doing? "

He took a breath. "I'm Father Jon. I'm just trying to check that dressing."

"Where am I?" she reached out to steady herself on his arm.

"You are in the Mansoura Central prison in Yemen. Are you ok? Do you remember how you got here?"

She could tell he was examining her for neurological damage. She toyed with the idea of shocking him a bit and discarded it.

She looked around. That felt accurate. "Not really. But I know why I'm here. Where is the girl?"

He made a motion to help lift her up. "She's over here, with the others, but you lost a lot of blood. "

She could feel what he was talking about. She was definitely woozy. "What do you mean 'others'?"

Father Jon looked around. "The other people. The sanctuary people."

Shukkat tried to get up and sat back down immediately. "Uhh."

The man in black helped her back down again, "Be careful."

A new flare of pain washed over her, starting at her head. "It hurts. What did they do to me?"

"You need to sit down. Like I said." He kneeled back down next to her.

Shukkat tried to shake her head to disperse the wooziness, but the pain intensified sharply. "Father, Why is my head wrapped up?"

He whispered. "They do it here now."

"What?" Shukkat squinted, trying to understand. As her hand reached for her bandaged head, the pain shot through her like a gun.

Father Jon's eyes were kind. It was clear he was having trouble talking about this. "When they see the symbol, the one you had on"

Her head swam, "Had?"

"They cut the skin off. "

She pushed against the wall and stood up. "What the fuck?"

He tried to help her step over to the left side of the cell. "I don't have a mirror. Come here."

"What's this?" Shukkat could see that there was another cell to the side of hers, separated by bars. About 20 young girls sat in it, none seemingly older than 25. Some of them also had their heads bandaged, some were bleeding, some looked bruised and hurt. None looked happy.

He pointed to a girl with a beautiful, wide face and long green hair leaning against the bars. She was dressed similarly to Shukkat, in prison attire, with tattoos around her neck and rows of piercings on her face from which the jewelry had been removed. Around her head was a bloody bandage. "These girls. This is Caleo, she's sort of the leader."

Shukkat called out in a whisper, "Caleo, can you hear me?" The girl's eyes were closed and she was leaning awkwardly. "Is she ok?"

"I can get back in there in a couple of hours. They let me go from cell to cell during shift changeovers so I can bandage and care for people." Father Jon reached through the bars to wake her. "Caleo."

She jerked awake and saw Shukkat. She spoke English with a slight Scottish accent. "Who are you?"

"I'm Shukkat." She reached over, trying to shake her hand.

Caleo lifted her hand to her head. "They did it to you, too?"

She kept hold of the smaller girl's hands. "What did they do to you?"

Caleo looked down. "When they see the marks, the Octagon marks. They cut them off."

"Oh, my god. " Shukkat turned to Father Jon as Caleo continued.

"We were just. We were just trying to have a good time."

He tried to explain. "It was a rave. A big dance party in the desert. Every year, there is a big dance party in the desert – the Rub' al-Khali."

Caleo continued, almost as though she were reading from the pamphlet, "It's like the largest uninhabited area on earth. A giant desert. And hundreds of thousands of people show up sometimes."

The man in black leaned against the bars. "DJs, dancing, etcetera."

Shukkat wished she could be in that cell to hug her. "And you drew those marks on your heads?"

Caleo started to cry, "We were just trying to have fun. It's cool and sexy."

Father Jon whispered, "but the Yemenese government considers it a sign of sex workers. Their policy is to cut it off and throw you in jail."

It wasn't hard to imagine what it looked like under the bandages. The pain in Shukkat's head suddenly made sense as she tried to connect with the petite girl one cell away. "Caleo, we're getting you out of here. I promise you."

For a moment Shukkat looked up and appeared to be talking to the sky, "This works. Thank you."

She stood up and reached out to the man in black, "How long until the guards are here – shift change?"

"Soon. Actually, I rely on her for that." He pointed to Caleo.

She perked up a bit. "I have a thing where I can always tell what time it is. So, twenty two minutes."

Shukkat glanced over at Father Jon, impressed. "Good thing."

"What do we do until then?" The man asked.

"First of all," she pointed to the main cell area. "I'm making space."

The man in black was about to say "for what?" when a thick blue light danced over the floor just inside the cell bars, ushering in two nearly identical women in black robes, holding rifles that looked like nothing he had ever seen.

Tanji pulled a device out of her robe, slipped it on the bars and pressed a button.

The bars disappeared throughout the entire cell complex.

Rey looked around and then ran to Shukkat. "Shar, are you ok?"

Shukkat hugged her tightly and then her sister. "Hey, ladies." She held Rey's hand and glanced at the weapon sadly. "I never thought I'd see you with a gun again."

Jon ushered the girls together, moving them into what was his cell space. Caleo nodded to them, helping the ones who needed it. Rey looked up at Shukkat's head. "Why are you bleeding?"

The clergyman crossed his arms uncomfortably "They cut off her mark."

"Let me see." Rey barked.

He pulled off part of the bandage. "They cut the skin off, down to the skull."

Rey's face darkened in a way that Shukat hadn't seen in fifteen years. She tightened her grip on the gun and pursed her lips, her eyes welling up. "I'm going to kill everyone in this building. And then I'm going to kill them again. Then we're going home."

Shukkat reached for her. "We can't do that."

Rey turned and nearly raised her voice. "Watch me."

"Rey?" She pulled the other woman aside.

Breathing heavily, Rey responded. "We're up there in our castle, trying to... And they can do anything they want to us. Nothing changed."

Shukkat put her hands on the woman's shoulders. For a second, Rey recognized the gesture. She knew exactly what it meant. So did Shukkat. "This is the change. What we do today."

Caleo stepped over to the two women. "Seventeen minutes."

"Thank you, Caleo." Shukkat put her arm around the petite green-haired girl.

Tanji walked over and handed Shukkat a robe and bracelet. "A personal teleport band. We deactivated the last one. Your robe."

"Thanks, Tanji. Ok, Caleo, Father Jon, this is Reylan and Etangiel. We are setting up a perfectly safe telepad to get you all out of here."

Father Jon shook his head. "No way. I'm the only one here who speaks fluent Yemeni. No translator bullshit. And you and the girl need medical help. I'm staying"

Rey nodded. "He's not wrong."

A smirk appeared on the clergyman's face. "That is my favorite passive aggressive way of saying I'm right." Rey winked at him.

Shukkat waved her hands. "Ok, stay, everyone else goes."

Caleo pulled away and looked at her. "I'm not leaving."

Shukkat caught her eyes with her own. "We can teleport you anywhere you want."

She lifted her chin and said, defiantly, "this is my fight, too and I'm going to be right here."

Shukkat nodded. "Ok. Tanji, get them weapons. Father, can you carry a gun?"

He shifted uncomfortably. "Yeah, about that. I'm not really a clergyman."

"Is that what you were trying to tell me over there?"

He continued, "Yeah. I was picked up along with everyone else, except I was wearing this black shirt. I buttoned it up with this on the bus." He held out the tiny piece of white cloth he had used to camouflage his outfit.

"Why?" Rey asked.

He turned to her, "If they think I'm a man of God, they let me move around cell to cell on shift changes. I can keep these people from dying. They barely feed them."

Rey put her hand on his arm as Tanji finished the telepad. "Ok, everyone is going back to our home. It's safe. We'll get you checked out and then you can go anywhere you want." She started sending people off with tiny flashes of blue light.

Caleo called out, "eleven minutes."

Shukkat rubbed her arm and called out to Rey. "Do you have her?"

"Yes. I can bring her here?" Rey asked.

"That might really traumatize her. Can you send me and the father there for eight minutes and then bring us all back?"

"Got it."

She motioned to Jon who stepped next to her. "Watch the door, we'll be right back."

The cell holding the girl was much smaller and covered with dirty gray padding all over. There was a steel toilet against one wall and nothing else. Shukkat and Jon appeared by the door and the dirty girl on the floor didn't even look up. She was in a soiled t-shirt and a pair of dirty white men's underwear pants. Her hair was black and cut close. Shukkat suspected she hadn't cut it. She desperately looked like she needed a meal. The room smelled like death.

"Hey, sweetheart. Are you ok?" Shukkat leaned down.

Father Jon tried to inspect her back. "She's a mess. She's worse than yesterday"

The girl stirred, shifting in place. "Father?"

"It's ok. I got you. We're going to make sure no one hurts you again. Ok? Do you recognize her?" He pointed toward the woman kneeling in front of her.

She shook her head. "No. I'm sorry"

The father continued, trying to be cheerful, "well, she's the bigshot lady at the Octagon. She's here to get you."

The girl's eyes filled up. "Thank you."

Shukkat wrapped her arms around her. It's ok. I'm Sharla. Is the Father taking good care of you?"

She nodded. "Yes."

"Well, we're getting him out of here, too, ok?" Shukkat whispered.

She nodded even more vigorously, reaching for him. "That's good."

Without warning, the door swung open and a guard forced his way in, holding a handgun on them.

He fired a shot at Shukkat, who wrapped herself around the young girl, even as Father Jon moved to cover then both.

The bullet went right through Jon's arm and embedded itself in the stone in front of him. Shukkat stood up and waved at the guard, a device in her hand, and he disappeared. The gun dropped to the floor.

"Ow." Jon danced in place for a minute as Shukkat tried to check the wound.

"I'm okay. Aaah. It really hurts. I'll be ok." He moved around for a second.

"Jon, you have a hole in your arm. It's ok to be in pain." She addressed the girl. "We're going to move to another room where no one can get to us and talk. Then we leave. Is that ok?"

Cub nodded again.

Father Jon tried to shake it off. "I don't want to be a big baby. Hey, where is all this stuff going when you make it disappear?"

"There is a lake about 10 kilometers from here with a one-way telepad. They're just a 10-minute swim and a 40-minute hike away." She picked her up and the three of them faded, only to reappear in the other cell.

Caleo moved to Father Jon to wrap his arm while Tanji grabbed the girl and set her on the bench.

Shukkat and Rey faced the door. They lifted the sleek futuristic rifles. Shukkat held her pistol in the other hand. "Time?"

The green-haired girl called out, trying to bandage the father's arm. "A little more than one minute."

"Ok, everyone."

About a minute later, three guards stepped into the room. Shukkat shot the first one in the knee. As he dropped to the ground, Rey used her gun to teleport him away. Shukkat spoke clearly, "I want this prison empty except for us in five minutes or less. You will sound an alarm when it's done."

She pointed. "Or else, that happens to everyone."

The second guard reached for his gun. "You can't –"

Shukkat shot him twice, once in each knee, and he disappeared a second later. "You have four minutes. If you attempt anything, we'll send more people to take over more buildings."

The remaining guard held his arms up in the air, backing away. "Understood." He ran out of the room.

She called out behind her, "Tanji, help me get this room secured. It's pretty well-fortified. I'm going to get rid of a couple of unnecessary walls and take over the room next door. It has food and facilities"

Tanji nodded, petting the young girl on the head and laying her down on the bench with a blanket. "Good idea. "

Father Jon stepped over, sporting a new bandage on his arm. "If you can reach to the room on the other side, I'm pretty sure there is a stand-alone generator, in case they kill the power on the way out."

"Thank you, Jon. And thank you for being shot for me."

"I think I took it pretty well, right?"

"You really did. First time?"

"First time. Really."

Shukkat pulled him into a hug, whispering in his ear, "you'd really never know it."

Rey smiled as she took in the two of them. For a moment. And then she was all business. "Legal, right?"

Shukkat took a deep breath and pulled out of the hug. "Let's hear it."

Rey sighed. "We can leave, but we can't take the girl. Cub. She's technically a federal prisoner accused of high crimes. Breaking her out would be an act of war."

"Well, we're not leaving her, so dig in." Shukkat crossed her arms.

Rey continued, "also, Turkey and Yemen have a mutual extradition treaty, so we're vulnerable after that."

"Hopefully, that won't matter when we're done, right?" Shukkat cocked her head.

Rey nodded. "Right."

Shukkat looked around. "We're going to need to start broadcasting soon. The more we do all this in the daylight, the better."

Father Jon scanned the faces around him. "Wait, what are we doing?"

Rey looked at him. "We're negotiating. It's what we do. Conflict resolution."

Shukkat put her arm around his shoulder, avoiding his bandaged arm. "See, this is a conflict. And we will resolve it."

Tanji added, "permanently"

Jon was confused. "You're not talking about killing anyone?"

Rey shook her head. "No. We're talking about a real solution."

Jon threw up his hands. "I don't understand." His comment was punctuated by an alarm that rang out for over a minute and then died.

Shukkat lifted a finger. "and that's the starting buzzer."

***

Tanji worked with Father Jon to assemble what they needed. The translators helped them all communicate with Katel and Zehra and the telepad let them build a transmitter in short order.

It wasn't long before Zehra's face loomed large on the device.

"It's good to see you, Shar."

"Are all our people there?"

"Yes. No one wants to leave yet. A few want to stay for good." She looked down on a monitor in front of her.

"That's fine. Do you have the signatures?" Shukkat was back to being all business.

"Every one." Zehra was just happy to have Shukkat back in the mix, back in charge. If she had to admit it, she would tell you that she'd spent so much time with Sharla next to her, leading the way, that anything else felt wrong. "We've got about twenty groups of yolcu in the facility right now. All of them say they'd like to help."

"We can't break anyone's neutrality. Anyone who wants to help should pull ships up over the main building complex. I want them to see crazy impressive ships floating above us." Shukkat illustrated with her hands.

"Done. Let me know when you're ready to transmit."

"Roger, sweetheart. And, Z?"

"Yes?" She responded.

"Thank you for being right there."

Zehra smiled and blew her a kiss before the screen went black. Rey walked up behind her with a clipboard.

"Ok, so here are the terms." She handed the papers to Shukkat.

Shukkat reached out and grabbed her hand, scanning the top page. "Perfect. This covers it. "

Father Jon read over her shoulder and his eyes widened. "Holy shit."

She laughed, leaning into him. "If you don't ask, you don't get."

He rubbed his damaged arm, cradling it. "Why would they do any of this?"

Rey responded, looking at his arm. She had a soft spot for crazy men who stupidly jumped in front of danger for her friends. She playfully kissed his arm, and his face opened in a wide smile. She was just an inch or two taller than him and she could see now, through the dirt, what a handsome face he had. He had sharp cheekbones and the lips of an artist, but all of it came together in one piece under his deeply kind eyes.

"The goal here is to force the UN and the whole world to put pressure on the Yemeni government to let us take the girl."

Shukkat counted, "number one."

"And all other people who ask us specifically for sanctuary," Rey continued.

"Number two" Shukkat counted off. "And we've already purchased the plot of land we are on, in Bursa, from the Turkish government. We ask for recognition as a sovereign nation under a strict neutrality agreement."

Rey jumped in, "number three"

Father Jon was overwhelmed. This was so far outside his experience. "Oh my god."

She continued, "this gives us diplomatic immunity when we go places."

Shukkat stepped in. "Right. Four. And one last one."

Rey read off, "a non binding UN proclamation on how the right to safe sex work is an inalienable human liberty."

She shrugged. "It's a start."

Jon ran his hands through his hair. "This sounds great. But why would the UN do it, and why would the world pressure the government here. I'm so confused."

Shukkat scanned their faces to see their reaction. "Because if they don't, we turn off every teleporter on earth, put a hold on all future technology gifts…"She lowered her voice in a matter-of-fact way.

"And leave earth. Entirely."

Jon stepped back incredulously. "That's insane."

Rey nodded and put her hand on Shukkat's shoulder. "Shar, can I talk to you?"

Shukkat nodded and they stepped over to the corner. Rey looked concerned. She twisted her head around and then whispered to the taller woman, "can we turn off every teleporter?"

Shukkat was casual. "With enough time to research, probably. Right now, no."

Rey nodded, thinking. "Ok, could we leave earth?"

She shook her head. "No."

Rey took a big breath. "So this is all a big bluff?"

"It absolutely is." Shukkat affirmed.

Rey's face lit up in realization. "And the ships circling the Octagon…"

Shukkat followed up. "Makes that feel a bit more real."

Rey stepped back and looked at her. "I want to fuck your brain"

Shukkat laughed as Tanji came up behind them.

"All right. We're ready to broadcast." She looked back and forth, "If you are."

A few minutes later, Shukkat sat at a desk near the generator in the adjoining room. She looked into the camera at the blinking red light.

Her notes were sitting in front of her, but as Tanji pointed to her and the light shone steady red, she looked up, delivering it from the heart. She took a deep breath and started.

"Hello, my name is Shukkat. Our technology allows us to broadcast across the entire planet. We are broadcasting from a prison in a foreign country after having accepted pleas for sanctuary from a number of people who have done nothing wrong except to live and protect themselves. We would like your help. But more than anything, we would like your friendship."

"We have placed our terms for the UN and the country we stand in on our website. We have purchased the land on which our community sits in a fair and equitable standard transaction. We have gotten the enthusiastic assent of the 7,524 people who live within the entire area known as the Octagon. And we have met every one of the terms of the Montevideo Agreement, in hopes of being accepted as a free and sovereign nation on Earth, as recognized by the UN and other countries."

"We are neutral, we don't have customers or clients. We have friends. Our only alliance is with peace. Our only attribution is peace. The only firm to which we owe any allegiance is peace. Because peace is the largest living thing in the universe."

"Peace is born pregnant, pregnant with opportunity, with possibility, with life, love, pasion, joy. Peace is not a placid, dull thing. Peace plays, it laughs, it wrestles, it jumps out of planes just for the experience because it can. It explores and takes chances. It kisses hard and rough, bites and makes marks because it trusts that it can. Peace is infinitely variable, with a million faces, and it grows and stretches over anything that reaches for it with infinite elasticity, denying no one."

"We work for peace. And we will work for this one. If the Earth is our friend, we will be very good friends indeed. We will help you usher in a new millenia free of want and suffering. We will partner with you to make this world into the paradise it could be. And we will make sure when you head to the stars that the magnificent people you find will see, in every human face, the face of peace and love. "

"If we are meant to leave, we will. "

"We will wait for two representatives from Earth to meet us here to finalize our contract."

Shukkat looked over to see everyone assembled to watch her. The girl they had called Cub smiled at her. She had put on a pair of jeans and a black shirt, both loose and flowy over her emaciated frame. She leaned against the green-haired girl and said, in a quiet voice, looking right in her eyes, "you did all this for me?"

Shukkat shot up and moved to the girl, putting her arms around her. "This is how we make sure no one hurts you ever again. Or any of us."

She stared into Shukkat's face, wanting marching orders, some way to hold her own and be of some help.

"Now what do we do?"

Shukkat held her hands up, lifting them to her mouth. She gave them a kiss. "Now? We wait."

They all slid into the bench behind them. Rey made a space for the girl between her and Tanji and leaned back, petting her head. Jon and Caleo checked each other's dressings on the other side of the bench as Shukkat paced.

Cub leaned against Rey, her eyes half closed. She was almost 20 years old, but years of starvation and abuse made her look 15. In a healthy place, she might be close to 55 kilograms, but as she was she was probably 10 kilograms less. She spoke haltingly. Rey could tell she was fascinated by the similarity between herself and Etangiel.

"Are you twins?" She asked, shyly.

Rey tried to sound upbeat. "Actually, we are triplets"

That seemed to interest her. She craned her neck around, "Where's the other one?"

Rey caught Tanji's eye. "Our other sister, Eren?"

Tanji answered, "she's back in my room right now, back home."

Rey followed up. "That's right, You can talk to her when you come back with us. She has a pretty accent like Tanji."

Tanji stared off for a moment.

Cub whispered to Rey, "you sound English."

She smiled, "You are really observant. Nothing gets past you."

The girl wasn't really used to compliments and wasn't sure how to take that. "Thank you."

Tanji asked, "do you know where your parents are?" Cub's face darkened for a moment until the robed woman jumped back in, "Ok. I understand. Ours are gone, too"

"Do you know what you want to do when we get out of here and you go home?" Rey asked.

She shrugged. "I don't know."

Tanji asked, "do you know where you want to live?"

She paused. "Can I live with you?"

Rey affirmed, "you can live anywhere you want"

"Do you want to know a secret?" Tanji asked

Cub sat up a bit, "Yes."

Tanji continued, "you're almost the same age as we were when we found each other."

Cub looked confused, "I thought you were sisters."

Rey jumped in, "we are. But sometimes family isn't born all in the same place and they have to find each other."

She reached behind the girl on the bench to hold her sister's hand.

"Do you think I could have a family out there?"

Tanji ruffled her hair. "I'm sure of it, actually."

"We'll help you find them." Rey affirmed.

Shukkat paced over to them, playfully, "What's happening over here?"

"We're coming up with a plan to help Cub choose her family," Tanji shot back.

Shukkat nodded. "I like a good plan."

Jon was back to staring out the windows. "I don't know how much more time we have"

Tanji twisted her head to see. "Ah. Check it out"

He looked back at her. "Wow"

"Every time they move in, I buy us a little time by disappearing a few cars."

Caleo laughed, staring at Tanji. "I'm sorry. I know this is all fucked up, but You are a bad ass."

The screen opened up the room like a window as Zehra's face appeared. She was a pretty Persian woman with a slightly alien look it was hard to pin down. She had a mischievous smile as she addressed Shukkat, "It looked like you have two people coming in, attached to the United Nations. I'm sending them your telepad Code. UN Secretary General Kiann Arjun, and one more person you might know." She flashed on the screen the face of a woman with shoulder length red hair and a business-like expression on her face.

Rey's eyes shot toward Shukkat. They stared in familiarity.

"Holy shit."

***

Rey and Shukkat stood in front of the Teleporter waiting as the rest plowed through lunch behind them in the other room. Shukkat had wrapped a clean black scarf over her head, but it did nothing to dull the pain. They held hands.

Rey leaned in, "You know why they're sending her, right?"

"It's their way to split us up, I think."

"I love you, you know." Rey said.

Shukkat smirked. "Soooo obvious. Is that a gun in your robe or…"

"These things are not made for firearms."

"Nothing is. I love you more, probably. I don't know. It's hard to measure."

"Let me know if you want me to shoot her."

"Deal." Shukkat squeezed her hand hard as the telepad sprung to life holding the UN Secretary General and another person. She was in a grey suit, pale, with short red hair. She was 35, the same as Rey, but unlike the darker woman, she looked her exact age, with stern eyes over pursed lips. She looked at Rey and smiled.

"Reylan Corroba."

She stepped down into Rey's arms and hugged her. Rey cupped her head and rocked back and forth. She hadn't seen her in fifteen years.

"Mera Quinn."

Kiann Anjur, the Secretary General, was a tall, neat Indian man in a black suit.

He wore a dapper, pressed white shirt under a brightly colored tie that Shukkat quite liked. He held out his hand to shake. "You must be Shukkat."

"I am. Thank you for coming, Mr. Secretary General."

He shook her hand politely. "And by what title should I address you?"

Shukkat winked at Mera and smiled. Mera had never hidden her disdain for her when they were at the embassy. "We're led by a council. You can just call me Councilwoman."

Kiann smiled and bowed slightly. "and so I will. I know we have some things to discuss. I figured Miss Quinn and Miss Corroba could become reacquainted while we speak."

"Exactly what I was thinking." She bowed slightly at him and took his hand. "We'll find a place."

The Secretary General looked back at Mera as Shukkat dragged him from the room. Mera shrugged and leaned into Rey. "Is there a place we could talk? Privately?"

Rey nodded and they made their own way out of the room. She realized that while she now knew the layout of the entire building through schematics, that she hadn't stepped out of these connected group of rooms – rooms that were, until about an hour ago, a series of prison cells.

She moved toward what she knew to be a large open cell block, with Mera right beside her. It would give them a chance to walk and talk.

Mera began immediately, "First of all, I'm really sorry about Benji. And the young girl."

"Eren. Thank you. We all loved Archie."

"He was one of a kind, for sure." Mera nodded her head. It was nearly impossible for Rey to separate the red haired girl's judgement of him from those words. Archie was their superior at the Embassy that would, at one point, become the Octagon.

Rey looked up to him. In many ways, he was a genius. He was a statesman. His ability to pull people together from opposite sides of an issue was second only to one person she knew. And Rey smiled, thinking that person was now speaking to Mera's boss. For all that, Mera had always focused on the fact that he was a man who liked to have fun. He would stay up all night playing strip poker, drinking people under the table. He once saw him challenge a dour ambassador to naked limbo. And sure enough, by the morning, the two of them were leaning against each other in their underwear, laughing as they split their winnings. Archie was one of a kind.

But that wasn't what she heard in Mera's voice.

"Have you seen anyone? How are Sean and Ricky, Riley?" Rey asked.

Mera looked over at her. "Well, I see Sean sometimes. When I go back home. I'm assisting the Ambassador. But I think you all broke Riley. He has a small company he runs out of his basement, pricing antique coins."

Rey cocked her head. "That can be rewarding."

Mera paused before continuing. "No. it can't. You know this is insane, right?"

"And yet..."

"We were in school together. Oxford. We wanted to create a new political reality. We wanted to change everything."

"And we are. You and me right now."

"You know what I mean. You want this little cult of yours to be a country, now?"

"I think you know better than that." Rey took Mera's hands and for a moment, they were back at school. Mera had come in here all full of acid. She needed to be reminded that this was her friend under the robe.

Mera took a breath. "That was… I'm sorry about that. I'm just angry FOR you. You're easily the smartest person I know. Here you are with Benji's madam, covered in tattoos, naked under a robe in some foreign prison trying to say – what?"

"It's not a cult. Sharla isn't just someone's Madam. And, yes, I'm super naked under this robe." Rey moved an errant piece of hair from Mera's forehead. "I wish I could tell you one fiftieth of what I've learned. I've seen what political revolutions look like on hundreds of planets. I've read about movements that freed trillions of people in their leaders' own words. I've met people who are a thousand years old, who pioneered ideas in ethics I never came close to even dreaming of. I've helped put together treaties that feed billions of people. This little thing we're doing here. This is just what we need to do to keep working."

"Working. A referendum on sex work as a human right?"

"And fifteen years ago, you would have agreed with me."

"I don't DISagree with you now. I just."

"What? You just want to obliquely support sex workers but not in the same room with them? You want to fight for the people who need it but not associate with them if they need it too much? You want to make compacts and treaties and agreements from a hill somewhere?"

"Yes, Rey, I'm effete. I want to get up and do good things for people in need but I don't want to be dragged down to their level."

"Their level."

"Not everyone wants to be a hooker, Rey."

Rey tried to catch her eyes. She knew Mera well enough to know how sorry she was that she had just said that. She whispered at her. "Maybe they should be."

Mera sighed. "I don't understand you, Reylan."

Rey took Mera's hand and continued walking. "Mimi. People don't follow laws because they're laws. No one, in their heart, gives a shit about a law. They do it because they love something. Order or other people or an idea or someone in need. The rest of the universe seems to have figured out something that we are struggling so hard to realize."

"And what's that?" Mera asked.

"That everything disappears at some point except the connections we make. Time will deconstruct every reason, every thought, every idea, every treaty, every excuse. And the only thing that prevents that is love. I love you."

"Oh my god." Mera's eyes watered, "You ARE in a cult."

Rey laughed and hugged her. "I missed you so much."

They rocked back and forth for what seemed like forever. Mera's face in Rey's neck. Until finally, she lifted her head.

"What do you think Sharla's doing to my boss right now?"

***

Shukkat pulled the Secretary-General into one of the larger spaces. It seemed clean and unused. She maneuvered him into the center of the room.

He looked around and then at her. "So, this is it?"

Shukkat moved over to a row of tables around the wall, and put a device down. "This is what?"

He lowered his voice. "We have sex."

She moved to the center of the room and stood on her tiptoes, as if stretching. "Do you want to have sex?"

Kiann Arjun sighed. "I'm in a little over my head, I think, Madam councilwoman. I don't want to be steamrolled." He started removing his tie as his voice dropped. "You can have what you want. We don't need to go through all this nonsense."

Shukkat leaned in to him. "You can keep taking your tie off." She pointed at the little device and snapped her fingers. A soft rain of guitar strums filled the room.

He looked over at the device. "What's that?"

"Don't tell me you don't know this." Shukkat crossed her arms at him as his eyes drifted up, remembering. He breathed in.

He smiled, "Cuando Pienso en ti."

Shukkat stretched out her arms and put them behind her back, one by one. "Instrumental version. You know, so we can talk."

His head moved to the music and then stopped. "I do remember this. What are you doing?"

Shukkat stepped up to him, opening her arms, putting one leg in front of the other. "Cambridge Dance Society, four years, huh?"

The Secretary-General scrunched up his eyes at her, "Your people researched me. I assumed they would."

"It was me, actually. Is this how we start? The Rumba?" She lifted one arm higher.

He smiled, "That was my dance." for a moment, he forgot himself. He nodded appreciatively. "Good form. Lift your arm a little. "

She lifted her arm. "Father Jon is a dancer. He showed me a few steps." She moved in and he placed his hands on her waist. Their feet slid across the stone ground and then ground to a slow stop as she extended her arm.

"This is more than a few steps." He moved forward, one hand in hers. "He's someone from your Octagon?"

Shukkat closed her eyes and tried to feel the music. "No. We met him here. He was arrested for marijuana at a rave, if you believe it. He's been trying to take care of the prisoners, dressed like a clergyman." They stepped into the tones made by the guitar. She kept the beat in her head, listening to the shaker.

"I see. This is…" He looked down at his feet. "It's been a while."

Shukkat moved back and forth in his arms. "You couldn't tell by me. You're amazing."

"You speak Spanish?" Kiann Arjun prided himself on the list of languages he had acquired. "This is where he would sing 'Me abrazo a la nostalgia por que así soy feliz'"

"I do. This is the core of his unhappiness. He looks backwards, not forwards." She twisted, spinning in his arms.

"I agree completely, Councilwoman." He almost laughed as he moved backward, pulling her with him.

"Or would you rather be having sex?" She caught his eyes and smiled.

The Secretary-General squinted at her. "You are a beautiful woman. You're one of those who would be a beautiful woman even if you weren't."

Shukkat squeezed his hand. "Oh, that's good. I like that one."

They spun together across the floor. Kiann Arjun was amazed at how it came back. When was the last time he'd danced? He whispered, "are you ready to dip?"

She sucked in her cheeks and furrowed her brow with mischief. "A lady is always ready to dip."

He dipped her in a way that made her feel as though she were on a rollercoaster, the illusion of complete abandon, the freedom to fall at any moment, with the hidden reality of machine-driven absolute control.

She wouldn't fall.

She heard the applause in his voice. "That was very good."

"We don't want you to feel steamrolled." Shukkat moved with him.

"You have us over a barrel, Ms. Tuk."

"Ah." She looked into his eyes and grabbed both hands, pulling back slightly. "You researched me, too."

He shook his head "Of course."

She pulled his arms in front of her and backed into him, pressing herself into the man. Looking over her shoulder, she said, "When people agree, it shouldn't be about research and numbers and some law they feel like they have to obey or else. "

He stepped back, removing his suit coat and tossing it on a chair. He reached for her hand again. "Laws are good things."

She spun toward him. using her arm like the string of a yoyo, pulling in closely. "Sure, but you know what is great?"

He laughed. "Ha. good execution."

"You have good hands. I feel like I can't fall." She half bowed at him and resumed dancing

He leaned into her ear. "So, what is great?"

She whispered back. "Shared goals. Walking out of a room knowing that the other person is real. That they're a person. Having a secret with them. Wondering if you can see them again soon."

Kiann Arjun's face looked, just for a moment, like a child being forced to grow up too quickly. "Is that what politics looks like to you, Ms. Tuk?"

"Hrumph. If I nail this spin, you call me Sharla." She pretended to be annoyed with him like women have for centuries.

He set up the spin, leaning back, using her weight as counterbalance. "You're on." She stopped for a moment, on one leg, gravity fell away, and then she rolled up into him in a single beat. It wasn't perfect, but it felt close to him.

"Ha. Sharla it is. What shared goals do we have?"

She continued, "you have a vision for this whole planet. I've read your speeches. You and I have the same boss."

"And who is that?"

She breathed in and out in rhythm. "Peace."

He slowed down and held her hands. "I want to believe that."

Shukkat stopped. She looked into his eyes. "Kiann Arjun. Even if this isn't working for you, it is for me. I'm going to leave this room and want another dance one day. I'm going to smile when I see you on TV. I'm going to remember your hand on this part of my back and think about when I was so close to you, I could tell you were telling the truth." With one hand, she touched his cheek.

Again, she saw the boy. Not the leader, the politician, the statesman. Just a person afraid to be exposed. "I always tell the truth."

Shukkat shook her head and smiled. "No you don't. No one does. This is the truth, though." She moved back and pulled him forward, forcing him to spin into her.

"That was wonderful. I want to believe you"

She felt the sweat seep through the bandage on her head, lighting its own unique fire across her skull. "And I want to dance with you again sometime. We both want something. What can we do about that?"

The song started again as he took her hand. "Would you really leave? The planet?"

Shukkat moved in close to him. "You've seen the ships over the Octagon?"

"I have."

She spoke to the boy she just saw. The young boy growing up in Delhi, wanting to see everything in the world, everything in the universe, entranced with every new place, every new language. Did he have a star chart on his wall?

"When you were 10 years old and someone had offered you a chance to leave in one of those ships, what would you do?"

"I would...weigh my options." he lied.

She smiled. "I have. There are beautiful things here. Especially since I've discovered the rumba."

He paused. "You'll make sure the girl is safe. And has options?"

Shukkat wrapped her arms around him. "Thank you for being who I thought you were. I absolutely promise you."

He reluctantly dropped her hand as he stepped back into a formal bow. "Welcome to the United Nations, Madam Councilwoman."

Shukkat looked up, her arms up as though she could fly. She bowed back. "You're a good man, Kiann Arjun. And I bet you have one more in you."

Kiann Arjun rubbed his hands together and shook his arms. "I absolutely do."

***

Mera was hugging Rey near the teleport pad. She looked up to see Shukkat and the Secretary General return. Moving over to them, she said. "Hi, Shar."

Shukkat wrapped her arms around her and pulled her in tightly. "Oh, Mimi, I missed you so much. You look so good."

"I'm sorry I..."

Shukkat cut her off, reframing today in a way that it would matter to the girl. "I'm sorry, too. Thank you for coming when we needed you."

And they hugged for the first time.

Mera whispered, smiling. "What did you do to my boss?"

Kiann Arjun smiled. "We danced."

"And talked. And agreed on some things" She pointed to the man in the black shirt in the back of the room. "Thank you to Father Jon for the dance lessons."

Jon stepped up and shook the Secretary General's hand as he slid his coat back on. He smiled. "Thank you, son. Good job. That was great."

Shukkat introduced Kiann Arjun to Caleo and Tanji. And then she held her hand out, letting the girl they only knew as Cub step up.

He leaned into her, kindly. "So, you're the one that all of this is about?"

She nodded. "Yes, sir."

He looked at Shukkat. "It's just Kiann. My name. And I have something for you." He reached into his coat pocket and pulled out a small blue book. "This is a UN passport. It says you are one of us and you can travel where you want. Is that cool?"

"Oh my god." Cub reached out and took it. Her hands shook.

Mera reached out to open the little blue book, pointing. "And that's your name. Before they took you, the Ghul people. This is your full name."

The girl looked down as Mera continued. "Noor. Noor Saeed"

Shukkat put her hand on the girl's shoulder. "Noor. It means 'Light'" It's you.

Noor Saeed looked up and shook her head, grabbing onto Mera's hand. Mera held onto it tightly. "You can call me Mimi."

The Secretary-General slid his tie into his pocket and stepped over to the telepad, adjusting his coat. "You know you're going to need to come to assemblies and meetings sometime? Or send someone."

"You wouldn't believe me if I told you how much I was looking forward to that." Shukkat laughed.

He shook his head and smiled.

And after almost two hours of being the center of an international crisis, the prison was empty in 10 minutes..

***

Rey and Katel helped disassemble the mess of electronics that Zehra had used to help them as Shukkat put her office back in order. She reached out to Rey.

"Rey"

"Hmm?"

"Thank you for coming to get me."

"I'll always come and get you, Shar. No matter where you are. I'll be there." She took a deep breath. "And damn. We're a fucking country now." She sunk into the other woman's arms and kissed her on the lips, exploring her mouth, holding onto her out of relief and excitement and not just a little bit of a hundred other emotions.

Shukkat flipped on a holographic projector on top of her desk. It showed a beautiful expansion of the Octagon.

"And we can build."

Rey scanned it. "What's that?"

"It's my plan to grow. An entire world we can share to serve our water breathing friends." Shukkat zoomed in.

"That's huge." Rey moved around. After a second, it hit her. "That's why we can't leave."

"It's going to be so beautiful." Shukkat pointed to the desk. "I want this."

"There are so many people who want sanctuary," Rey mused, looking at the scope of it, building downward for more room.

Shukkat pulled some papers from her desk, in stark contrast with the hologram. "And so many initiates." She pulled two to the top and showed her. "Like these two."

Rey's eyes widened. "Holy shit."

Shukkat shrugged. "They both say they belong here."

Rey Grabbed at the pages. "Maybe they do. Let's find out."

The other woman smiled and kissed her again. "I'll see you in the morning."

Reylan turned to walk out. "You will." She waved the pages in her hand before leaving. "Oh, and the priest and the girl are mine. They belong to me now."

"They're not playtoys." Shukkat called after her.

Skipping once before leaving, Rey called out. "They will be when I'm done with them. Kidding."

Shukkat walked around the hologram. She reached up and touched the obsidian octagon shape on her forehead. She could feel it hum, as though it was alive. But it felt comfortable and flexible. She could almost imagine it as a shield. She thought for a moment and it changed color.

"Do you like it?" Katel-Ko-Ra scanned her face for how she was feeling. His gift to her felt like him. It was strong and beautiful and protective. She threw her arms around him.

"I love it. You gave me my first t'kau. This one is just for me. Plus I'm like a Christmas tree."

He held on to her as though he thought he would lose her. Her fingers scratched his back the way he liked.

"You don't want to hear this, but I talked to her," he whispered.

Shukkat stayed wrapped around him. "I know. I'm about to find her and... I guess talk."

He hugged more tightly. "I'm sorry." For a moment, she was afraid of what he might say next.

She spoke into his neck, the gentle scales moving against her face like a beloved fabric. "I suppose you're leaving, too?"

Suddenly he pulled away. His eyes narrowed.

"I'm sorry, did I accidentally say something to make you think I'm a total fucking idiot.?"

She pulled him in again. "Ha." She lifted her feet up and let him swing her around for a minute." He kissed her on the head and detached.

"I'm going to go find the closest of the 20,000 prettiest warm pools I can, and lay in it like I'm dead for as long as I can because that's what my people do." He moved toward the door as she called out

"Have fun." She thought about for a second. "Oh, Katel?"

He stopped. "Yep."

She sighed, sad about what was coming next. But still. He made a good point. "Save me a spot. I'll be there soon. I think my people do that, too."

Shukkat left not long after he did, making her way down to the lower garden area where she always went. One of the things about wanting to know about people was that, eventually, you know so much that they are there, with you, all the time, even when they aren't.

She was saying goodbye to the flowers, a couple of small bags at her side.

Shukkat sat next to her.

She looked up, reaching for her hand. "I figured you'd come here."

"I wanted to say goodbye. If I have to." Shukkat was still hopeful.

She kissed Shukkat's hand. "I'll be back. Sometimes. I love you, you know."

"I know. Thank you for not leaving me in that place."

Tanji turned toward her. "I could say the same to you, you know. I just. I've been hiding. For fifteen years, I've been hiding in this beautiful hidden away place. Like under a warm blanket. It's time to get out of bed for a bit."

"You're not hiding. You're doing something important." She shot back.

Etangiel took a deep breath. "I am. And I love it. That's why I'll be back. I'm not throwing this robe away. But I have to be somewhere where I can speak out and make a difference out there for a while."

Shukkat nodded.

"Noor. I want to tell that girl's story and hundreds of others like her. I want to write books that change things just like you changed things here."

Shukkat's eyes filled up with tears. "It wasn't just me. You built this place. You came up from the streets and you built this."

Shukkat looked down. "I just want you to remember that."

Tanji sat up straighter. "And I do." She turned to her. "And I want you to remember that you knew my name when I was just a scrawny street kid who barely spoke English."

Shukkat jumped up and pulled her to the grass., kissing her neck. "You were my first Apriya."

Tanji laughed. She looked so much like Rey, but her voice could be so different. "I'm still that." She pulled Shukkat's hair back from her face. "I know what the word means."

They rolled around on the grass. "Eren is going with?"

Etangiel pulled the tiny box from her pocket where her sister's personality had been placed. "She's going to help me write. Her English was always better than mine."

"You have another sister here, you know?"

She nodded. "I do know. And I can't face her right now, doing this. Will you give her this for me?" wiggling to pull a large envelope from her robe, she handed it to Shukkat.

She weighed it cartoonishly. "This is fat"

Tanji responded, "I'm a writer now."

Shukkat pulled her in and kissed her, letting her tongue lazily invade the other woman's mouth. She whispered in her ear. "You are."

Tanji kissed her harder. She slipped her hands under her robe and tried to feel her warmth, pulling the older woman on top of her.

"Do you have time to just talk for a while before you go?"

And Shukkat pushed her down into the grass and they talked about things that didn't matter, things that could have been a text message or an email or even just a drawing stuffed under a door. Nonsensical things and stupid things and things that didn't need to be said at all.

They repeated themselves and misremembered things because it didn't matter. They even talked about Noor Saeed, playing now, like a little girl, in a country that was literally made just for her. It was the talking that mattered, the sounds wrapping around each other, Shukkat's playful half jokes, dancing in the warm wind with Tanji's saffron and cinnamon tinged accent that mangled words just enough to make them something new to the world after hundreds of uses. In between kisses, they shared words.

New and exciting all over again.

5 - Ghost - 2130

"There are at least seven buildings now, representing the Octagon on Earth. Below each one is a secret, an area that allows them to engage and interact with many different species, from water breathing ones to creatures of unusual size."

Caleo Cuvo Osa leaned back against the rocks lined up behind her. If she leaned her head back a few more centimeters, the waterfall behind her would touch the long green swirls of her hair. She sighed and listened. The waterfall would be nice.

"I'm sorry. I can go on, but I thought I'd be talking to Shukkat?"

The green haired woman shook her head, causing the diaphanous dark green robe she wore to flutter in the wind current in a way that made Caleo wish she could just do this all day. "I'm sorry, Shukkat is sort of off the planet right now, looking at possible other locations." She smiled at the girl and continued dramatically. "For expansion."

"She's... on an alien planet?" the young woman in front of her stood up and brushed the beautifully colored red and gold grass from her black jean shorts.

"We like to use the term 'yolcu'"

"Ok, sure. But that's incredible. No one on Earth has done that, have they?" She flipped her notebook to a new page and wrote something down.

Caleo Cuvo Osa sighed. She bent her head to one side trying to really see this girl. She was pretty – very pretty. She was small and animated, with a black, star-shaped puff of natural hair over a beautiful fairy-like face, dipped in rich dark burnt umber. She wore a white half shirt and a pair of black jean shorts that Caleo guessed were the sexiest things she wore, the outfit she put on when someone said "dress sexy." This was brought home by the tall white collegiate stockings, black stripes at top, and the adorable canvas high-top sneakers.

Her name was Corazon and she was a reporter.

"And can you confirm what I started with? The underground areas?"

"Sure. It's totally true. You can see them if you want. You may need special gear to get to some of them." Caleo leaned back all the way and let the water flow over her head. Laughing, she pulled up and shook her hair.

Corazon looked at her quizzically. "Are you really the most senior person here right now? How old are you?"

Caleo's thin face had always been one that threatened to fall apart into a laugh at any moment. Maybe that's what kept her looking so young. Or maybe it was a series of processes, gifted to the Octagon, that were even now tripling human lifespans. She liked to think it was a little bit from both categories.

"I'm sort of a young 85. And, yes, it's crazy, but I actually AM the most senior person here. Trust me, it's blowing my mind, too." A wide grin opened up Caleo Cuvo Osa's face as she reached for the girl's hand. The girl thought she could hear a barely resonant Scottish accent behind her playful banter. It made her voice sound bouncier, even more playful.

Corazon stared at her, "Holy shit. I mean, can I swear here?" She took her hand.

"I fucking hope so," Caleo laughed. Too many people thought that what they had built here was a cult. Or a religion. It made people afraid of them.

"You look like you're 35 or something. You're so pretty. But that's the thing here, right? Everybody's pretty. Like an exclusive club?" Corazon tried to pry. She was clearly still looking for an angle.

"Yes, everybody is pretty here even if they aren't pretty somewhere else. I mean, no one can be pretty everywhere."

"I don't know if that's true." Carazon stepped along after her.

Caleo laughed and looked back, walking backwards, holding her hands. "spoken like someone who's pretty everywhere."

Then she stopped for a moment and shimmied out of her robe, tossing it into the blocked off garden area. "Ok, let's explore."

Corazon stopped and stared back at the space they had just left. "So that is really your office and you are going to walk around naked?"

The green haired woman shook herself in the sun, drying slowly. "I don't love clothes and I don't love being inside."

Corazon looked down at he notebook. "I feel like I could write this whole thing just about you."

"Oh, please don't," Caleo laughed.

The darker girl smiled at her. "Like what does your name mean?"

Caleo loved how passionate she was. Her desire to know seemed so familiar. It felt like an open hand, pulling you close. "When you get your t'kau..."

"That's the forehead tattoo thing?"

She smiled. "Yes. You choose a name that you love. I was born Katherine, which I did not love. Caleo was my rave name, which I do love. And Cuvo Osa is a yolcu phrase that means, "remember the cub – the child." It basically, in English, would mean 'think of the future.' It meant a lot to me from different angles."

"That's a lot." Corazon squinted at the beautiful eight sided obsidian gem-like screen on Caleo's forehead. "Is your t'kau different because you are in charge?"

"No, it's just different." Caleo tried not to think back. She wanted to be honest with the girl, but some things were hers to deal with. "It means the same thing."

"So it means you are accessible, sexually?" This was usually the thing people focused on.

Caleo turned to her and winked. "Yes."

The girl paused for a second. "What if I just took my clothes off and drew one on my head and walked around here?"

Caleo chuckled. "Go ahead. I can draw one for you. Totally freehand."

She cocked her head to one side. "That would seriously be ok?"

The green haired woman leaned in. "So many times, when I was younger, I would draw one on my head and go out dancing topless. Just getting in the zone, waiting for people to put their hands on me while I danced. This was in the early days of the Octagon. But people knew what it meant. They would just grab my tits while I danced. It was hot. I remember dancing to pretty lights while this beautiful stranger just fingered me in rhythm."

"So you guys don't think that it's blasphemous or something?" She wrote in her notebook.

Caleo shrugged, "What are we blaspheming against?"

"How about when prostitutes do it? Do you think that it's wrong?"

Caleo thought for a moment, trying to use her words carefully. "I'm going to put my hand on your arm. I'm going to just fondle your pretty arm. Is that ok?" Caleo smiled at her.

Corazon's face lit up. It was fun to amuse her. Her face was so expressive.

"Sure."

Caleo leaned in and massaged the girl's arm. "Do you feel this?"

"Yes."

Caleo continued, "this is you. It's your body. You own it. You can use it to feel good. You can use it to make someone else feel good. You can use it to make money. You can use it to bring people together." She massaged deeper, pushing her fingers into the muscles that most people carried tension in. The reporter's head lolled a bit as she closed her eyes.

"Oh, that feels nice."

Caleo continued, digging in a little deeper, not so much as to hurt the girl. Just enough to make it feel releasing. "You can use it to solve disputes, to make people see you as a human being, to get out some anxiety, to address depression, to live, laugh, fuck, even to stop thinking about something for a while so you can solve a problem. You can use it to stave off boredom or thank someone for driving you home. You can use it to make a bet. You can use it as a party favor, as a toy. You can let people eat sushi off of it if you're super careful where the wasabi goes."

Corazon chuckled as Caleo went on.

"It's yours. It's a beautiful multi-purpose tool that makes you feel good to use. Morality and ethics have to do with hurting people. Think of all the things you can do with this absolutely perfect, beautiful body of yours that don't hurt anyone."

"It's a lot." Corazon lifted her arm and let it wave around.

"I used to masturbate before tests in college. I can't imagine that's any more immoral than prostitution." Caleo confided.

Corazon looked at the lighter woman, ""Did it work?"

Caleo spun around like a cartoon character, hoping to make her laugh. "Oh my god. It's amazing. I'm so much smarter afterward." She looked right at her. "Like when I read your piece on unions. I was instantly smarter."

Corazon stopped. "Wait, you read my stuff?"

"I wanted to cheer at the end." Caleo tried to look serious, "You know how stupid you look cheering an article?" She pulled her into a large rock doorway covered in vines and flowers. It was often hard, at the Octagon, to determine if you were inside or outside. Hidden weather controls kept the environment always aligned with the Mediterranean area's most temperate days. And the corridors were large and wide enough to host their own airy convergence of breezes, spinning in the air through flowering plants and fountains.

"Thank you. Wow. And this place is amazing. I think I was expecting something different." She looked around and saw that Caleo's dislike of both clothing and closed spaces was shared by nearly everyone. People were nude in every conceivable way, from jewelry alone accenting their private parts to mesh and gauze wrappings that covered nothing. And the variety of people was remarkable. A taller dark haired goth woman, twice as thick as Corazon was wearing only a few strings of clothing and a rope that covered nothing glided by her, winking. A gaunt blue man and a woman who seemed to be part squid, dressed in nothing but open white robes moved past them in the other direction. Maybe this was the angle. The unbelievable variety of people. People from everywhere.

Caleo watched her face. "Let me know if you want to go anywhere."

She laughed. "I want to go everywhere."

The older woman leaned in "Do you want to see where you're going to stay?"

She stopped. "Wait, you worked it out? It's ok?"

"Yes. You can stay as long as you need to write your article." Corazon's enthusiasm was infectious. Caleo felt lighter as the girl hugged her.

"Oh my god. Thank you. This is going to be. This is. Wow."

Caleo put her arm around teh younger woman, "We can start with the main event, first. Let's go see a ceremony."

They had walked for a bit through the warm, surging corridors of the main building when Corazon asked, "so, what am I going to see?"

Caleo pointed and they moved toward an opening in the wall, covered in moss and plants. One of the things that the Octagon was very good at was hiding technology with the beautiful and affirming presence of nature. And this area was no different. The observation area looked like an open air pond with rows of natural rock seating around it. But instead of water, when you looked down, you could see the kurge below, a pretty, padded room surrounded by hanging vines and water fountains, each boasting art that was unique to the space. Every kurge was different and every one built to celebrate the kind of beauty that the worlds across the galaxy had to offer, each pregnant with expressions of natural joy.

"So, there is an ancient race of people, The Vio-Khalera. Nice people. They gave up having bodies about a million years ago."

"So, just ghosts?" Corazon slid into a seat next to her.

Caleo leaned into her. "Well, except they actually exist. They are incredible inventors. They inhabit machines in order to do physical work."

Corazon's star-puff hair bounced up and down as she nodded, making Caleo Cuvo Osa smile. "Ok."

"Now, the Vio-Khalera are coming together with two other species, the Kiener and the Obsuro, to build this beautiful research world to discover new things. To solidify their union, they're going to connect here, with the officiant who helped negotiate. The Vio-Khalera representative has to use the body of one of our people."

The girl shook her head. "A whole world." She stopped and took a deep breath. "That's what we're going to see?"

Caleo nodded.

She whispered. "We have to be quiet?"

The green-haired woman responded casually, "no, they can't hear us up here."

"So, in a way, I'm the ghost. I get to watch and live through you, but no one sees me, no one hears me." Corazon lowered her voice dramatically, like a spy.

Caleo laughed. "I suppose so, little ghost. You'll be free to move around, to find your story to tell."

She waved her notepad and slid it into her pocket. "And I will. I'll find the story."

Turning to her, Caleo pointed down. "That is Master Gadd. And Master Gossamer. They are both amazing people. You are going to stay in their thula."

"What is that?"

"A thula is a small group, usually two Masters and three novitae. It's home."

Corazon nodded to the events below. "They're stripping?"

Caleo explained, "they are opening the ceremony and exposing themselves. Then they have a chance to speak from the heart. This is a little different, since Master Gadd will be embodying one of the petitioners."

Below them, the ceremony started.

Master Gossamer sat cross-legged, nude. She pushed herself up onto her knees and crawled over to M'kira, the Kiener representative, a brilliantly red-and-orange-skinned yolcu who appeared female, also nude.

On her native planet, people of M'kira's gender were receivers and hosts, with a unique physiology. She had breasts to nurse a live birth, as well as a large, appendage resembling a shovel that would enter her partner and, upon climax, shoot a catalyzing agent that would allow her to collect genetic material from them for gestation.

Gossamer pulled herself up next to M'kira and held her hand, speaking to everyone there. "I want to say from the heart that over the last few months, I've seen this project through the eyes of all your people, through YOUR eyes. This isn't just about a few discoveries to you. This is about charting the future and your commitment to sharing that future. I love that. There is no future without friends. And I have come to love you through that."

She kissed M'kira on the lips and ran her hands over her breasts. The Kiener representative's thick, wide, scooplike penis between her legs began to rise like some kind of red hooded snake.

M'kira leaned back and spread her legs. "The Kiener are honored to be a part of this group, made up of millions and millions of years of insights and accomplishments. We are a younger race and yet you met with us as equals. Thank you for letting that be our story. I am so grateful "

She reached a hand out to what looked like Master Gadd. He was a strong-looking Dominican man with short dark hair and a beautiful, squared-off face. Gadd pulled himself to his feet cautiously and walked over to them. The Vio-Khalera petitioner was still getting used to this physical body. Gossamer and M'kira yanked him down into their laps, laughing.

Gadd's eyes rolled back for a moment as he felt Gossamer play with his cock. The sensations washed over him, slowing his speech a bit.

"We aren't a people who are very used to going outside of ourselves for solutions. Getting to know you all has made me realize that every answer we find is going to bring us all together a little. I look forward to that."

He looked back at M'kira who kissed him thickly, opening her lips wide.

"Very much."

Kor-i, the petitioner from Obsuro, rose to his feet and walked over. As he approached, Gossamer reached toward the man. He was more than two meters tall, with skin so black he nearly disappeared, glowing red eyes, and a wide face.

But beside that, and the markings all across his body, he looked remarkably human. Gossamer looked up at him and beamed, slowly sliding his half-tumescent dick into her mouth and pulling him in closer, wrapping her hands around his ass. Kor-i took his time penetrating her mouth all the way, petting her fringe of black hair and smiling.

"I get to speak last. These negotiations have made me realize that there will be a day in the future, where we hold up something remarkable, something that will benefit people across the universe in entirely new ways. And this day, today, will be our origin story. I love you all for that."

M'kira turned to Gossamer and spread the Master's legs. She felt the soft spaces inside, seeing how Gossamer's tiny wisp of pubic hair glistened with strands of liquid that pulled apart as her legs did. Gadd turned to lick her belly, working up to her breasts while Kor-i slid to the floor, moving his prick in and out of Gossamer's mouth tenderly.

The reddish orange yolcu lifted the spoon-like shape of her member and seemed to fold it around itself, sliding it into Gossamer's pussy. "Is this better than practice?" she whispered, a little too loudly while pushing inside of her.

Gossamer stopped sucking the thick black rod in her hands for a moment. "Hey, don't knock practice. It makes everything better."

The Vio-Khalera resident of Gadd's body laughed. "Maybe we should have practiced more."

M'kira kissed him, still slowly fucking Gossamer's open cunt. "I would never say no."

Gadd kissed her harder, moving behind the smooth Kiener representative. He felt his prick, as if for the first time and fingered her little hole. M'kira spread her legs and lifted her ass in invitation. It was round and elegant with red and orange circular swirls across the surface. Through Gadd, the Vio-Khalera pressed his cock into the center and slowly pushed.

Gossamer tried to get Kor-i's member as deeply down her throat as she could, choking on him gleefully. She bounced against the cock inside her cunt as Kor-i leaned forward to kiss M'kira. He pulled at her breasts and bit her lip as they laughed, trying not to cum from the stimulation coming from all sides.

Kor-i smiled and whispered, "is it so hard to hang in there, my little red one?"

M'Kira growled at him with a wide smile. "You're evil." Gossamer could feel M'kira's member growing wide inside her, reaching deeply inside her cervix for genetic material. Her pussy grew warmer and wetter at the thought of being impaled so deeply.

The black yolcu laughed, coming closer himself as Gossamer sucked his dick deeper, opening the space at the back of her throat, her mouth wet and responsive. She prepared herself for the complex configuration of his orgasm as he tweaked M'kira's nipple and put one hand on her face, "You're beautiful."

They all flowed together, Gadd's movements pushing M'kira into Gossamer, whose rhythmic sucking of the Obsura-born petitioner seemed to drive him crazy. Kor-i began to feel his orgasm rising in his gut.

He moaned at Gadd, who began the chain.

With one giant thrust, Gadd came, pouring himself into M'Kira's ass, his hot cum forcing her own orgasm, Master Gossamer's belly convulsed with the gush of the Kiener's thick pink cum, streaming into her as if from a hose. She grabbed at Kor-i's ass and pulled his prick deeper, choking as he let go and came right down her throat, into her center. She could feel the cilia from his cock begin to descend down her esophagus to spread the cum inside her, her mouth locked between his legs by the thick knot that Obsura males created to prevent their partners from detaching until they were fully spent. Millennia of evolution had turned the Obsura male into the ultimate mating machine, one that was relentlessly good at delivering their seed.

It would be about ten minutes until Gossamer could pull herself free from the Obsura petitioner's dick, her belly filled with his cum.

She started to feel the probing tendrils retract, freeing her throat. Many less well-trained kezmaki would panic before that time was up. Gossamer held onto his ass calmly as he played with her breasts and the other two took turns climbing onto her and satisfying themselves in her ass and pussy. She spread her legs patiently and tried to be as receptive as possible. When she finally slipped free of his softening cock, she rolled over onto her side and enjoyed the other three cuddling her.

If it sometimes seemed like the time after the ceremony was when the real bonds were made, that perception wasn't untrue. The time they had spent together over the last few months was coming to a close and all four of them were rejecting that, trying to hold on for one more kiss, one more joke, one more sensation. They talked for a while, laughing and touching until the observation area was long empty.

Caleo and Corazon stepped out of the area into the corridor.

The young reporter seemed to have a new energy from watching. She turned to her. "That was actually beautiful."

"I'm glad you enjoyed it." The green-haired woman smiled.

"Ok, where can I leave my clothes?"

Celeo looked at the darker girl. "You want to take your clothes off?"

She stood up defiantly. "Yes."

Caleo smiled. "For the article?"

She nodded, starting to pull her shirt off. "for the article."

Caleo's lips raised in a grin. "You can leave them at the thula. You'll have your own room." For just a moment, you could hear her slight accent.

"Oh. The thula. Right" Corazon slid her shorts down and folded them, placing them along with her little white shirt.

She was now only wearing her tall white stockings and gym shoes. If anything, she looked more naked for those additions. Her skin was dark and smooth, with beautiful curved breasts and a round, taut ass.

She looked like she would be comfortable naked anywhere. Except for the almost imperceptible, barely visible tan lines in the shape of a one piece bathing suit that suggested a more moderated approach to nudity when in the outside world.

"There will be a lot there you can wear, if you want to just have fun." Caleo took her clothes. "I'll hold that." She could always have them sent to her.

They began to walk. Corazon fairly bounced with energy. She stopped for a moment to stare at two young men kissing a woman in an alcove, naked, their fingers inside her. "I can't believe people can just…"

"Yes." Caleo nodded. "We celebrate openness and we try to learn from it, always."

Corazon looked down at her body, as though for the first time. She examined herself. "I feel so blank, with no tattoos."

Caleo grabbed her hand. "Most of the tattoos you see are from ceremonies. Kezmaki and Apriyas often get tattooed, marked, as part of the ceremony."

Her star-puff hair bounced again as she kissed her lightly. "I can't even tell you how free I feel right now."

"Do you want to hold onto this?" Caleo pulled her notebook from her shorts pocket.

"Hm?"

"Your notebook?"

The girl stopped looking all around for a moment and focused on her, taking the small wirebound notebook and pen. "Oh, right. Thank you."

"You said you wanted to be a ghost, to observe, to find your story. The people in your thula can help you find where to go, what to see. I'm always here for you. Maybe dinner tomorrow?"

Corazon squeezed her hand. "I'd like that."

Neither Gossamer or Gadd were back yet when they arrived at the thula. Caleo introduced her to the two novitae that were there, though.

Terra was was a 25 year old cuban girl with a delicate face and large, wide eyes. She had a lithe swimmer's build with breasts that pointed upward and a persistent arc to her back that rendered her sexy just standing in place. She had a thick torrent of black hair on her head, running down her back, and pretty black untamed hair under her arms and between her legs. The only clothing she wore was a series of bands and necklaces in the same black gemlike material, accenting her mysterious horror-movie based tattoos and smooth light brown skin. Every part of her was something that would have kickstarted a half hour conversation anywhere else in the world. She smiled and hugged the young reporter and pulled her to the pool area to meet the other occupant.

Karesh was a young russet-toned girl with a beautiful, feminine face. Her hair was thick and curly, like Corazon's but shorter, and it played host to a number of bizarre pieces of jewelry that made her look like some kind of hyper realistic android from a sci fi movie. Her breasts were on the larger side, accented by the ropelike grey strings she wore all over, covering small areas of her body while showcasing others.

Karesh leaned against the side of the circular pool that served at the center of most thulas. Nearly six meters from one side to the other, built into the floor and made to look rocky and natural. As she stepped past the vines that surrounded it, Corazon could see that she was cleanly shaven everywhere and had a penis between her legs. It was not large, and seemed feminine in the way it swayed while she walked toward her. The three girls hugged and helped Corazon shake herself free of her last remaining clothes before shimmying into the pool.

Terra leaned back into the warmth of the water, lettering her head fall back as she kicked her legs a bit. "So, you are here to find a story?"

Corazon spun around, letting the water hit her everywhere, breathing in. "I guess I am. I'm feeling overwhelmed, though. I mean, damn" She motioned around her. The thula was beautiful. The large pool in the center was surrounded by a wider circle with chairs and couches. Beyond that, a dining area and a kitchen area. And, on the outside, a ring of rooms, one for each occupant, plus two additional ones. There was no way of telling how high the ceiling was or where the windows were and which were view screens. It gave the impression of being an endlessly large space. She shook her head.

Karesh sympathized. "Yep. I know how I felt when I first got here."

Corazon slid down lower in the water, like an alligator, pointing toward the beautiful woman next to her. "Why did YOU come?"

"Me, I'm transparent. I'm the biggest sci-fi fan in the world. There is no other place I would end up."

"I get that." Corazon moved slowly, just enough to float.

Karesh continued. "The people from everywhere, the inventions, the technology here, the books, the conversation, all of it. There is no timeline where I don't end up here." She smiled at the young reporter. Who spun slowly, using only her hands.

"How about you? " she addressed Terra, who was floating so only her face and the tips of her pretty breasts showed above the water.

"Same, but for different reasons. I love sex and I fall in love about 20 times a day. The world out there doesn't know what to do with me. If you like a lot of casual sex, you're supposed to be cold and unfeeling, jumping from person to person. If you're a romantic, you're supposed to be with one person."

"Not good options," Karesh interjected.

Terra continued, "not at all. I love falling in love. I love everything that goes with it."

"And here?" Corazon asked.

"And here, it's like a calling for people, to see something to love in the people they work with. I heard about that and I'm like, I can do that. I do that every day." Terra splashed and dipped herself underwater.

Corazon floated, nearly submerged. "I love that."

"How about you? Why are you a reporter?" Terra asked in mock seriousness.

Corazon shook her head. "Sitting here right now, I couldn't tell you. I might be right in the middle of you both. At the moment, I'm just amazed by this place." She turned to the girl next to her. "Like, if I walked down the halfway and asked someone to…" She looked around and lowered her voice. "…go down on me, they would?"

"Sure. We would if you wanted. We're both wearing the t'kau." Terra shot back.

"Even if you didn't want to?" She cocked her head and asked.

Karesh made a sound with her lips. "Why would you think we wouldn't want to?"

"I wanted to when you walked in the room." Tera stood up and approached her. "Do you want me to?"

"Is that ok?" She whispered.

"Yes, it's ok." Karesh added. "Do you want me to help?"

She furrowed her brow. "Do you want to?"

"Can I lick you here, from behind?" Karesh swam over and played with her Corazons as she put one leg on the stair descending to the pool.

She arched her back. "Yes."

The other girl ran her tongue over Corazon's ass, slipping it inside and playing. She leaned in and kissed her, making out with her asshole. She asked her, "how does that feel?"

"That is. Oh my god."

Terra put her hands on the darker girl's belly, licking at her pussylips and sliding her tongue up and down her clit. She slid three fingers in her as Corazon spread her legs, her holes being serviced from both sides. She moaned and put her hands on the side of the pool, keeping her legs spread wide open while Terra reached for her spot inside with mechanical precision.

The two girls licked at her, trying to make sure she felt every inch covered. The young reporter arched her back as she sprayed over Terra's face, into her open mouth. Terra dove in, making sure not to miss any. She opened her mouth widely, licking.

Karesh raised her hands to play with the reporter's tits. "Is that your first time squirting?"

"I guess. I've never felt anything like that before." She bent down to kiss the other girl.

Karesh put her arms around her, "That's good. You look a little woozy."

Corazon smiled, reaching around her. "I'm good. I am." She looked down at the girl's cock, hard now between her legs "Can you put that inside me?"

"Do you want that?" Karesh slid the girl's ass down on the side of the pool and kissed her.

She licked at her lips. "I feel like I'm on fire."

"You feel so good" Terra licked at her nipples as she laid back.

"So do you two."

"Is this your first threesome?" Terra asked, kissing her deeply on the lips.

Corazon was breathing hard. Her legs were spread, feet in the water, ass hanging off the edge of the pool. Her breasts lifted up and down with every breath as Terra pulled her hands up over her head. She whispered, "let's assume it's my first everything, in a way. "

"Do you like the way that feels?" Karesh asked.

She moaned, "I really do."

Terra fondled her cunt, feeling the puff of wet hair between her legs. "I love how soft your hair is."

Corazon pulled the other girl over, trying to get her to sit on her face, "I was going to say that to you."

Terra settled over her face, her pussy covered in thick black hair, still wet from the pool. Corazon reached out her tongue and aimed it toward the center of her open cunt, watching as she opened like a flower. "Your parts are all so pretty."

Karesh placed her cock at the opening of Corazon's wet pussy. "Is this what you want?"

The girl bucked, letting her ass rise up off the rock. "I really do. I like how reasonably sized you are. Is that ok to say?"

"Yes, it is. Ha" Karesh started slowly sliding her dick into the pretty reporter, trying to feel every inch.

Terra moved downward onto her face, pressing the lips of her hole against the girls's mouth. "Do you like doing this?"

Corazon nodded, breathing heavily. "I like everything. And you feel good."

She moaned, reaching to pull Karesh in deeper, "Do you fuck her, too?"

Karesh laughed. "Sometimes. When I get lucky."

Terra rubbed her nether lips over the girls open mouth. "Oh, stop, I jump on you, bitch. Who crawled into whose room two nights ago?"

"She IS hot." Karesh stage-whispered, pretending it was only for Corazon.

The girl bucked under the dual assault, trying to pull them both in. "Oh my god. Both of you are on fire."

Karesh pulled out and slid back in again, taunting her, "Do you want her to put that pretty bush on your face while I finish inside you."

"I do. I do."

She ordered the girl, moving in and out of her faster, "Ok, now lick both of her holes. If you want her to pee on you, there's a little hole at the front that you can put your tongue in."

Corazon started moaning louder at that. "Oh. I think I'm cumming."

Karesh fucked her way into Corazon's belly, digging her dick in. "Suck her harder."

Terra glanced over at Karesh as she rode the girls face, "Are you almost there, baby?"

The other girl kept pumping. "I am. Do you think she wants me to fill her up?"

Terra laughed, feeling the girl squirming below her. "She's nodding. Like a lot."

"Ok. I'm cumming." Karesh put her hand out for Terra, who grabbed it, steadying herself on Corazon's face as they both came into Corazon.

They slid off, holding her hands, watching her chest rise and fall.

Terra reached for her cheek. "Are you ok, baby?"

Corazon smiled, staring straight up. "Can you show me my room and do that again?"

***

Master Gossamer sat with Corazon in the living area the next morning, talking, introducing herself, and showing her in detail what they did. She ran through some holos of various negotiations, showing her the complexity of communication.

"Watch this." She flicked on a tiny hologram floating above the couch showing a man covered in a chitinous exoskeleton looking out into a room and speaking.

"Can you hear what is he really saying?" Corazon nodded. She listened as the man spoke.

"The Romahi-Gilea don't want to waste time allying ourselves with species who will misrepresent their other alliances."

Master Gossamer paused the recording, turning to her

"He's pretty straightforward. He's telling us he wants to be associated with people who are honest with him about how they interact with other allies. Right?"

Gossamer nodded. "Yes, exactly. On the surface. Now, look at this face, what is this petitioner hearing?"

She showed the other petitioner on the screen, a man, a member of a smaller chalk-white species. Corazon peered into the hologram, "Um. It's different than what is being said?"

Gossamer zoomed in. "It almost always is. Look at his eyes."

Corazon squinted into the hologram. It hit her. "He's insulted."

"Why?"

The reporter looked up. "He thinks that the greenish one is accusing him of being dishonest without even knowing him."

Master Gossamer lifted her arms, joyfully. "Woo! Right. He feels like he is at a disadvantage from the start. Frustrated, insulted."

"IS he accusing him?" Corazon stared, trying to discern.

Gossamer took a deep breath. "I don't think so. Does the look on his face look insulting?" She zoomed out so that the girl could see both faces.

"No."

The Master leaned in. "What DOES it look like?"

"Is he afraid?" Corazon ventured.

Gossamer nodded. "So. What if you replaced the opening of his statement with 'I'm afraid that...'"

"He would be saying, 'I'm afraid that we will waste time allying ourselves with species who will misrepresent their other alliances.'"

"Right. So what do you think?"

Corazon thought. "He's not insulting."

The Master shook her head. "No, he's expressing his fears and asking for help. 'Allay my fears – help me.'"

"And both of those are positive modifiers."

"Exactly. Your job would be to make sure that the other group sees that." Gossamer spoke in an animated way, with an obvious pride .

The young reporter tried to talk it through. "They need to see that, instead of expressing a negative modifier, he is expressing a number of positive ones."

Gossamer smiled at her. "This can be dull, too."

The girl breathed in. "Oh, no. My mind is just wandering."

"Do you want to do another?" Master Gossamer sat down next to her.

Corazon scrunched up her face in apology. "Actually, I think I have a date."

***

Corazon made her way down the glass-lined elevator banks with Karesh and Terra. Their destination was the half-sunken water playground known as the Thessalia. In the main building, this was the line between the water-breathing species and the ones who needed air. Over time it had become a place to let off steam, to have fun, to enjoy the presence of both air- and water-breathers in one place. Most of the space was filled with pools surrounded by bars and tables, stages, and more. The few dry walkways let people move easily between the many spaces.

As she looked out, it became clear how far this underwater space extended. It was impossible to see the other side. People here wore even less than usual, swimming and paddling in places, wading through water in others. The lights were soft and filled with bright cool blues and greens, filtered through the cascading water, finger-painting on every wall with abandon as though the entire place were submerged.

The young reporter sported an eight sided figure on her head, drawn by Karesh. It looked nearly real.

"It's okay that we just drew this on?"

"Sure. See how the other half lives, right?" Karesh kicked up some water. She was completely nude, except for the sci fi jewelry around her neck and hair. Terra held her hand, nude, as well. Corazon loved the thick hair between her legs and how a line rose up her belly. It made her seem alive, sexy, powerful. Corazon herself wore nothing but a chain around her waist that dipped down in front, occasionally rubbing against her clit when she sat. It felt fantastic. All three felt free without shoes or boots, feeling the warm water against their feet.

"You guys just walk around like this, knowing that anyone can have you?" She could barely breathe, imagining it.

Karesh put her arm around her. "These are all people who are familiar with acceptance and how it works."

"So they wouldn't approach us in a way that made us feel like our agency was rejected," Terra sat back in a tall chair at a bar.

"Over our bodies" Karesh joined her, motioning for Corazon to sit.

The reporter looked confused. "Ok, that went right over my head."

Karesh kissed her hand. "I know. It's something you will learn. If you were out in the outside world, people might come up to you and just grab you, maybe even bend you over at a party."

Terra laughed. "Ok. Which is nice sometimes."

"But here," Karesh continued, "people will try to learn you. They will say yes and play. Affirm and amplify."

Corazon reached for a drink. "To learn me?"

Karesh took a drink, "They'll look at your t'kau, what it says about what you like. They'll try to read what you are interested in, who you are. And they will have fun with you. In a way that makes you feel…"

"Well…" Terra interjected.

"Good. Accepted." Karesh finished.

"They'll find a way to make the first move in a way that makes it easy for you to make the second one," Terra explained.

Corazon shook her head. "How will I know?"

Karesh affirmed, "it will be really clear."

"I'm so lost." The reporter suddenly felt as if she'd never get it.

Terra took a drink, nodding to Karesh. "Watch her."

Karesh turned away, pointing herself at the thin, dark man on the other side of her. She stood with her breasts out and started to talk to him, pointing to her head. "Hi. Is there a mark on my head?"

He turned to her and smiled, looking her over appreciatively. "Yeah. you should be more careful. You want me to get that for you?" He put his drink down

She spread her legs and pointed herself at him, "No. I guess I'm used to it. I have annoying marks in other places, though." She turned, letting him see all of her. He nodded, clearly happy with what he saw.

"That must be rough. I bet I could lick those off." His hand brushed against the front of her belly, right where her cock descended, causing it to twitch.

"Thank you. I noticed that you have two friends." She pointed to Corazon and Terra, "I also have two friends."

He placed his hand on her waist, right below her breasts, feeling her lean in. "Wow. We really have a lot in common."

She pointed at Corazon. "I'm trying to show her how we play here." Karesh could see that the man's cock had lifted up, rubbing against his belly. She rubbed the back of her hand against it. "Oh, like that."

He lifted his hand to her breast and felt it, running his fingers along her taut nipple. "I'm feeling the implications of being naked right now."

Karesh put her hand around his dick, pulling him closer. "Oh, is that for me. It's not wrapped. If you bring your friends, I can put that away for you somewhere." She turned, showing him her ass.

He inhaled deeply, motioning over his shoulder. "That was me getting my friends."

Corazon turned to Terra. "Wow. Now what?"

"Now anything you want." Terra sighed.

She whispered, "we can all have sex together?"

Karesh turned to her. "Is that what you want?"

She laughed. "God, yes."

***

The stayed out a few more hours, enjoying the Thessalia, before coming back and falling asleep, the three of them, wrapped up together in Terra's room. Corazon woke up with the sun and gave Terra a kiss, stepping out into the main area. Karesh had been up for a while already and was standing there, just from a bath. She stepped over and hugged Corazon and grabbed her hand

"Come here, you." She pulled her back into the bathroom. It was large and centered around a tub that could easily fit three people. An artificial waterfall fell against the far wall, brightening the room that still felt warm from Karesh's bath.

"What?" Karesh pulled her over to sit on the tub. She waved her hand at the ceiling and the lights lifted, forcing Corazon to shield her eyes.

"I have to fix your hair. We've been running around so crazy, you forgot to take care of it." She reached into the mirror for her supplies.

"Thank you.

"It's ok." She leaned in. "We basically live in a pool. I'm maintaining my hair every day. It's hard work."

"You have such great posture. It's like you never even think about it." Corazon tried to sit up straighter.

The other girl laughed. "Ha. I do not." She worked on the girl's hair, trying to keep it from frizzing. She pulled out a pick. The reporter kissed her hand.

"I love you, you know."

Karesh kissed her shoulder. "I love you, too."

Corazon looked forward as Karesh pulled at her hair. "Terra was right. Falling in love feels good"

"It does."

She waved her hands. "Just being free to look at the person inside and pick some things and just say, I love these things."

"I think you're getting it." Karesh continued to work on her hair glancing at the mirror occasionally.

Corazon stared at the sci fi baubles that floated in Karesh's hair. One was a beautiful silver spaceship. "Is this what you thought the future was going to look like?"

Karesh breathed out joyfully. "Oh, god. I think I hoped so, you know. Even just a place where people think about love and think about solving problems and try to do it all without blaming anyone." She waved her hands around. "I mean, the technology is great, but when I see people who really know how to love, that's when I feel most like I'm in the future. Maybe that's an angle."

"An angle?" Carazon looked up at her in the mirror.

"For your article?"

She nodded. "Oh, right. Yes. It could be."

Karesh moved to the front of her hair. "Hundreds of years ago, scientists like Einstein warned us of what happens if our technology begins to outstrip our humanity."

"What did they say would happen?"

"That way was certain death," Karesh said with playful seriousness.

Corazon thought for a minute. "I have to say, it's easier to love people when you can just, I dunno, just reach out and touch them, feel them."

"I think that's true. A couple people get together with an officiant. They promise to be sexually available to each other and to tell the truth and to try to see what's to love about the others. They focus on their shared goals. And they feel good. They focus on each other. All of each other."

"Focus." Corazon tried to catch a glimpse in the mirror.

"Yes. Like what I'm doing. I'm spending my time, fixating on your pretty hair. That's love. Making food for someone. That's love. We keep thinking, on this planet, that we're just doing a job, when it's about exchanging love." She put her arms around the girl and looked into the mirror with her.

Corazon saw that her hair looked just like it had when she'd arrived. She started crying and kissed the other girl's arm.

***

Master Gossamer sat outside near the water with Caleo Cuvo Osa. Both had removed their robes to sit on. Gossamer tossed a rock into the water.

"She's definitely interested in what's going on here."

Caleo crawled to the edge of the water and dipped her head in, shaking it off before returning to sit. "That's good. Do you think she's found her story, yet?"

"Well. I don't know."

"What kind of questions is she asking?" Caleo found a flat rock and handed it to Gossamer.

"You know, when I got here, the sex part of it all, I got carried away." Gossamer felt the heft of it before skipping it across the water.

The green haired woman looked up into the sun "I remember."

Gossamer looked around her for stones and continued. "In the outside world, I wasn't the slutty one, my roommate was."

Caleo found another stone and tossed it to her. "Master Zoi, yes."

Gossamer turned to her, catching the stone. "And I never knew how she balanced it. She was bitingly smart, we were one and two in our class, always. But she was also just pure animal, you know?"

"I do." Caleo smiled.

Master Gossamer skipped the stone far across the water. Caleo almost applauded.

"I was the one who wanted to unite the universe and eradicate conflict. She was the one rushing through homework because she didn't want to miss the gangbang in the frathouse."

Caleo interjected, "but.."

Gossamer smiled at her, grabbing her hand. "But when I got here, I went a little nuts. I busted every possible cherry. I think maybe that's where the girl's at right now."

"Is it a problem for anyone?" Caleo crawled back over to the water to dip her head, again.

"No, not at all. I just think it may be a little bit before the balloon comes down and she goes back to being a reporter." Gossamer moved to the water, too, sliding in. She sighed. "It took me a bit."

Caleo dunked herself, looking like a mermaid with clear, light moss in her hair. "Well, what made you level out?"

"I think, really, watching what was really done here, what the benefits of absolute openness were. "She floated a few feet away, thinking. "and That's why you started with the ceremony."

"I think so." Caleo stuffed the woman's head underwater and laughed.

Gossamer came up for air, shaking her head at her. "You're always outside, naked, dancing, soaking wet, watching birds, but I still have this sense that you're the smartest person in the building."

Caleo swam backward, toward shore. "Oh, Jesus that building is huge. And you're in it. So I doubt it. The girl is smart, though."

Gossamer seemed frustrated. "I can't really read her yet."

The green-haired woman floated, face just above the water. "She reminded me of you with the little shorts on. You would always go out into the real world with a little tiny pair of shorts that would look totally normal on anyone else, but were pornographic trying to contain that ass of yours. And pretend you were covered up."

Master Gossamer smiled. "I'll keep watching out for her." She swam over and kissed Caleo.

"Thank you, baby."

***

That night, Corazon moved across the different levels of the main building. She made her way to an alcove near a library and sat down. She looked up at a young man with short hair in an adjoining alcove. She caught his eyes and smiled. He smiled back and stepped over, slowly, sitting next to her.

She looked up and touched his arm. "I'm practicing flirting"

He laughed a little and stood up. "Well, I say 10/10. Good work."

She reached for his hand. "Did you like it?"

He nodded at her. "I'll give you more practice." he pointed a few feet away. "I'll be right there and look over, ok?"

Corazon felt the playful energy and she pushed him. "Yes." He stood shyly and then pantomimed broadly looking back at her. She cupped her bare tit at him, making him chuckle involuntarily. He returned, sliding into a seat next to hers.

"That was even better."

"I'm getting good." She reached over and put his hand in her lap. He squeezed and turned to her.

"You really are."

"I'm Corazon."

"I love that. I'm Migado," he lifted the hand that was in her lap to her breast and pulled her closer.

She whispered, "You have a very pretty penis, Migado."

"Thank you. I made it myself. I love how beautiful and dark your pussy lips are, gently hiding a tiny flash of pink inside that I could see from across the room only for a second. "He leaned in, finishing the sentence almost in her ear.

Corazon smiled widely. "Only for a second. Because I'm demure. That was good. This is not a conversation we'd be having in the outside world."

He pulled her closer and fingered the little button at the top of her pussy. She spread her legs and pointed herself at him, moaning a little.

He shook his head. "No ma'am,"

She put one leg over the arm of the chair, aware that people walking by were watching. "Can you put some fingers inside of it?"

He slid three fingers in her open wet cunt. "I can."

"What do you want to do with this pussy?"

"I'd like to kiss it slowly, hold it in my mouth until it opens up like some kind of crazy yolcu flower that makes you drunk when you drink from it and smells like success and candy."

"Can you fuck it first?" She pulled him in, letting her hands fall to his ass.

"I can." He moved in and pushed the chair backwards, lifting her legs over her head. She put her hands on the back of the chair behind her.

She whispered at Migado, "can you do it so that people can see everything?"

She spent time in the alcove with Migado and then took his hand as he drew her around to explore more. She made her way back to the thula long after dark, moving into Master Gadd's room and sliding into bed with him. She pressed her hand against his chest and he woke up, looking over at her. He lifted his arms up behind him and turned to her.

"Hi. You're back."

"I just got in. I was practicing flirting." She leaned into his chest and cuddled.

"That sounds like fun."

She lifted herself on one elbow. "Can I kiss you?"

"Of course you can. Is there something you wanted to talk about?"

She closed her eyes and breathed. "Kiss first."

"Ha. Okay." He leaned in and took her face in hia hands, kissing her. Her mouth opened and he felt the perfect roundness of her soft wet lips.

"What if I wanted to stay here?" She said, softly.

"In the country? You would be welcome." He put his hand on her cheek.

She pulled his hand closer, kissing it. "How about here, in the center of it all?"

Master Gadd pursed his lips. "That's a big decision"

She nodded, "Kiss again."

He pulled her head in and opened his mouth widely, taking her tongue in and massaging it with his own She leaned back.

"That was nice. What would I have to do?"

He spoke gently, every word feeling like a blanket wrapping around her. "Your degree is in journalism. Which is one of the accepted degrees. Master Gossamer said you have a good head for mediation and conflict resolution. We have tests. There are things to learn. It's not that hard."

"Could I learn them?"

There was a need coming from her that he couldn't identify. He wanted to address it but didn't know how. "I'm sure you could."

"Could you be inside me while we talked?"

"Is that what you want?" She nodded slowly. He put his hand behind her neck and pulled her up on top of him. "Ok, come here, sweety."

She settled in, slipping his cock into her waiting pussy. "Oh my god. That feels so good."

He breathed in, caressing her face. "I like the way you kiss."

She pushed back and forth on top of him "If I did say here, would they put me in your thula? With all of you?"

He held her by the back of the neck. "They would definitely take into account where you wanted to go."

She wanted to tell him her story. "Tonight, I met this guy, Migado. And I asked him about his fantasies. Something even he hadn't done yet. We went to the Thessalia. And we did a water race."

"I've seen those."

She continued, "where you kneel in the water and bend over the vibrating hump. And people shoot you with these kind of waterguns right inside you as you're bent over, trying to get you off. Have you ever done that?"

"I haven't. I'm familiar, though."

She was almost manic now. "And I won, I came last. But then I wanted him inside me and more people and more games. Is that crazy?"

Gadd tried to see what she was experiencing. Something felt off. "It sounds like you're letting go. How do you feel?"

She pulled him closer. "Can you get on top of me? Just fuck me until you let loose. Until you have to get off. "

He rolled over on top of her and felt himself dig deeper into her. "How about you?"

She caressed his face. "I feel like I'm just cumming constantly. Like I want the world inside me. Is that normal?"

Gadd pushed himself into her. "Well, it happens. Maybe that's your story. How easy it is to let go. To lose control"

She put her hand over her eyes. "Am I out of control?"

Master Gadd held her. "It's not really up to me to say."

"Then who? Who could tell me." She pulled away, sitting on the bed next to him with her knees up.

"It's ok. It's ok, sweetheart." Master Gadd tried to speak slowly.

She stood up "I'm sorry I came in here. I can't believe I woke you up."

Gad reached for her, standing up. "It's ok."

Corazon ran out of the room into the living area. "I'm sorry"

She nearly ran into Caleo, standing near the pool, waiting for her.

Caleo spoke gently.

"Hi, you."

Corazon wiped her eyes. "Hi. What are you doing here?"

Caleo Cuvo Osa put a small device on the floor next to her. A delicate piano song flowed from it, barely audible but beautiful. She put her hands out to the girl, "I saw this work before. A long time ago."

Corazon's eyes filled with tears. "We're going to dance?"

"We are"

She leaned into the green haired woman and put her head on her shoulder awkwardly. "I'm a bit of a mess."

"You look great." Master Gadd followed her out. Caleo flashed him a sign and he nodded, returning to his room.

Corazon rocked back and forth. "I'm glad you're here."

Caleo spoke into her ear, petting her hair. "I need to ask you a favor."

She pushed the tears away from her eyes. "What do you need, anything?"

The older woman spun around slowly. "I need you to let the girl go."

Corazon breathed in. "What do you mean? What girl?"

Caleo caught her eye and continued, kindly. "I know you haven't written anything new in that notebook. I'm going to tell you what I think happened."

Tears spilled from the young reporter's eyes, as her back quivered. "Go on."

Caleo's voice was soft but resonant in the room as she explained. "I think that when your people were here, you got caught up in all the excitement. You saw the girl. She is so pretty. And you saw me."

"I do see you." She held Caleo more tightly. "I did."

The older woman tried to sound casual. "And you wanted to have fun."

Corazon nodded, as she cried sloppily on Caleo's shoulder. "That's true. I want to have fun. I want to be with you. I want to be with Terra and Karesh. I want to listen to Master Gossamer's voice and kiss Master Gadd and sit on him, joke around and lick Migado's cock. All of it."

"I know, baby. And there is nothing wrong with that. But you have to let the girl go."

"You know, she was going to leave." She tried to stop crying. "I can tell you like this body."

"It's a beautiful body."

Corazon stood up a little straighter. "I can feel her, in here, part of her loves just letting go. That's what I gave her. The chance to let go."

"It's not her choice. She's not awake in there. She wouldn't have forgotten to do her hair, sweetheart."

The darker girl's eyes closed as tears poured down her face. "I feel her. I know what she wants."

"I'm going to lead, if that's ok."

"Yes."

Caleo asked kindly, "can you tell me your name?"

She closed her eyes. "My name is Vareill."

"It's really nice to meet you." Caleo continued to dance, holding her close.

"How did you know? The hair?"

"You know, Vareill, I've always been able to tell time without a clock. I mean, not perfectly. But pretty close. Usually within a minute or two." She confided in the girl.

Vareill listened, asking, "That's not something your people do?"

"No. But I always was able to. It's like I just listened to my internal rhythms. And got so good at listening to my internal rhythms that I started wondering what other people were listening to. I watched them and tried to see what they could do. What is their superpower? And Corazon is a thinker, a reasoner. Her superpower."

The younger girl sounded afraid. "But me?"

Caleo pulled back and pressed her hands against the girl's face. "You are made of love. You are a lover."

She started crying all over again. "It's not like this where I come from. I'm starving. And no one gets it. It's like I can breathe here. I want to be in love. That's all I want."

She nodded, "I know, Vareill"

Vareill breathed in and out quickly through Corazon's lungs. "I want to stay here."

"What if you COULD stay?"

She put her head down. "How?"

Caleo let her voice sit softly in the room. She didn't push. "What if I showed you how to ask permission from the people here, to spend time inside different people. But only if they said yes?"

"Would they do that?" her voice dropped.

The older women put her hands around Corazons waist as she said matter-of-factly, "let's find out. But first, you have someone to make amends with."

Caleo grabbed Gadd and the three of them made their way outside, to her office area. In her head, she knew it wasn't an office. It was really just a small grotto on the side of the building, something with a waterfall, plants and a pond not 20 meters away.

But, if pressed, the woman couldn't really tell you what an office was supposed to be. Except a place to meet with people.

She kneeled near a chair where Corazon was waking up. She tried to help prop her up.

"Hey, dear."

"What. What happened?" Corazon rubbed her head.

"Do you know the last thing you remember?"

She looked at the green-haired woman. "You and I. We were watching that ceremony. It was beautiful"

Caleo stood up. This would be a long conversation. "Well, something happened."

"What happened? What day is it?"

She held the younger woman's hand. "This is Master Gadd. You might remember him from the ceremony."

"Hi." She smiled. It was bright and, Caleo thought, belonged out here.

She continued, "But, inside him right now is someone who wants to explain to you what happened. Her name is Vareill. Can she talk to you? I'll be here the whole time if you want."

Vareill explained the best she could, what she had done. From watching, disembodied in the observation area as her people finalized their treaty, to her decision to take over the girl's body. To everything that had happened since.

And afterward, Caleo and Corazon went for a walk, leaving Master Gadd/ Vareill in her office.

***

The girl began, "this story might not make you all look very good."

Caleo scrunched up her face. "I know. But it's true. And it's a pretty good story."

"My head is a bit turned around."

"Is there anything you want to talk about?" Caleo asked.

She paused. "Can I come back if I have more questions?"

"Of course. Even if you don't." She reached for her hand.

The girl took her outstretched hand and waved it around, speaking animatedly, "It's so bizarre, talking to him – I mean her. That's a person from a different planet. A whole different kind of organism. Does that ever get old?"

"It never does. Ever." She laughed.

The girl kept moving. "I feel like there are more stories here. Really good ones. Maybe some uplifting ones. "

"I think so."

"And this means I can just come back when I want?" She flashed the teleport code on the metal card Caleo had given her.

"Yes."

She leaned in "Even if i write THIS story?"

"Yes." Caleo nodded.

Corazon looked up, trying to find words. "Vareill told me that I had sex with a lot of people while she was... inhabiting me."

"You did. She went a bit wild. I don't know if I can apologize to you enough. I should have seen it earlier."

She stopped. "Could I interview some of them?"

She glanced over at the girl, and nodded. "Of course."

She reached out, holding the girl's other hand. "She does want to stay here. She wants to learn how to treat people with bodies with respect - with consent."

"Oh yeah?"

"If it's something you feel comfortable with." She looked at her for signs of discomfort.

Corazon stood upright. "Wait– if I do? ME?"

"Yes."

"If I say no, you'll send her away?" She tested.

"I will."

The daker girl shook her head. "Won't that damage relationships?"

Caleo pulled her closer by both hands. "It doesn't matter to me. And it shouldn't to you."

She smiled. "Are you authorized to do that?"

"Ha. Yes. But I won't do anything that hurts you." She tried to read the girl's face to see how she felt.

"Even if I write this story?"

"Even if you do." Caleo swung her around.

"Do you think you can make her understand what she did wrong?" Corazon intoned, her head spinning

"I think I can."

She paused "Then she should stay."

Corazon was anxious to get to the teleporters, get home, and write. It was clear that even she didn't know yet what the story was.

***

Vareill met her back at her office in Master Gadd's body.

"This body is so strong."

Caleo looked into his eyes. "Can you make a hole- in your perception? Can you see him inside?"

"I think so."

She stared at him. "Listen closely."

"Ok."

She continued. "When Gadd first came here, on his very first day, what did he do? Can you feel? Can you ask him?"

Gadd's eyes closed for a second. When they opened, he said, "he says he screwed up all his courage and told you he wanted to kiss you."

"Good. Now listen to him. Touch me in the first place he kissed me." Caleo lifted her arms.

Gadd's body smiled at her as his right index finger reached out to touch her right below the navel in a way she remembered. "Here."

She smiled. "Exactly. Now, open the hole and let him talk to me directly for a minute."

A shadow flickered across Gadd's face. "Hey Green. It's me."

She wrapped her arms around him. "How do you feel, Sunshine?"

"I'm good." He tucked his head in and kissed her neck.

She whispered, "why do I call you sunshine?"

He laughed for a moment. "Because when I was flirting with you I told you I didn't need food, only you and sunlight."

She reached for his face. "That was good, you know."

He shrugged. "Eh, For some people you want to bring the A-tier material."

She hugged him again. "I appreciate you doing this."

He touched her face, "Little duck. Brain or not, my body knows who you are."

"I love you, goof."

"I love you, too."

"Do you want to bring back Vareill?" She took a deep breath.

Again, a wave washed across Gadd. This time Caleo was sure she could see it happen. All of it.

"I'm here," his voice rang out.

Caleo voice was full of kindness. "We're going to spend some time together. And when you learn how to control it, there will be many more people to meet. Many things to do."

"Thank you."

She reached up and put her arms around Vareill. "Now come here."

Caleo lifted up onto her tiptoes and kissed Vareill on Gadd's lips. For the rest of the night, there were sometimes two of them, and occasionally three. And the earth itself had enough water and moonlight and breezes to go around – for all three of them.

And by the time Corazon returned, with a fresh new notebook, Vareill had learned enough to apologize more precisely.

6 - Dot - 2150

Turkey's ultra nationalistic Red Party had just come to power when 20-year-old Azra Badem ran away from home to meet her older sister, Zehra, at a party at the British/French embassy that said would be "wild."

When the hostess at the door asked her name, she hesitated for a moment. Azra means "pure" or "untouched." The pretty girl with long black hair and pouting perfect lips had no intention of following through on that promise, instead calling herself "Dorothy" after the main character in her favorite book, who, herself, was named after the principal in The Wizard of Oz.

At the party, her sister introduced her to Sharla Tuk, a girl just a year older than she was, someone who had already been spending time on the streets as a sex worker, meeting wealthy men from far away places, wearing dresses that someone like her could never afford.

Over the next few years, she grew up a lot, and even tried to reconnect with her family on a number of occasions. Her older brother Gökhan had been her protector when she was younger, always so funny, so willing to spend time with her, even when she felt like an annoying little girl. But as Gökhan became more and more entranced with the increasingly judgmental and religious ideology of the Reds, she found him harder and harder to talk to.

Eventually, he made it clear she was no longer welcome at home.

By this time, though, Dorothy, Zehra, and Sharla had become inseparable. She moved into the embassy where the constant parties soon became the norm. Because of Sharla, she never needed to work the streets.

Men came to her.

She felt safe.

Until she wasn't. Years later, in 2050, When the Embassy was overrun with Red Party fanatics, it was Gökhan who threw the stone that finally killed her. And it was her father's face she saw at the end, enraged, charging, red with hate.

Later, she remembered the last thing she thought, as she died.

What did I do?

***

A little more than 100 years later, there were over 30 people sitting in the observation area overlooking the kurge, here to see the officiation of a contract between the Viraga and the Sarcosians. This particular kurge was one of the original builds on the structure, a room that went back to the time when the Octagon was founded.

But the building it sat in had a deeper history. Originally part of the Roman Empire, built out as a part of the Ottoman Empire, and expanded as part of the nation of Turkey. But, again, as historically far reaching as that was, the principles that the octagon was built on went back even farther.

Across the known galaxy, there were traditions, trends, ways of doing things that seemed to transcend learning.

These were like lines of gold and jewels, hidden in the rocks that anyone, no matter who they were, would find if they looked hard enough.

Cultures that survived tended to use intimacy as a means to build alliances, make agreements, share worlds, building bonds between people that exceeded time and the conveniences of simple politics. The ones that thrived did so by recognizing joy as a right to be shared by everyone. And the ones that lasted were the ones that celebrated the minute flickering differences between people that could be fanned and nurtured to raging flames, tracing sigils of pure dancing art into worlds upon worlds that would wake up gray in the morning and spin with color by the time its sun fell.

The ones that flourished found purpose in art and wonder. The ones that became elevated explored the humane mathematics of the world where solutions were like puzzle pieces, which, when arranged properly, fit together in ways that looked impossibly smooth and machined, ground into a single mirror that reflected their connections like so many lightning bugs in the night.

The ones that excelled found the poignant perfections of touch and the shared wistful allegiances of desire that drew people of all kinds to just want to be near each other one more time. This want became the web that space was built on, and the profound, pretty mysteries of its gravity became the discipline, the calling, of the Octagon.

Most cultures wrapped their beloved dead in white fabrics, white rock, white ore, and liquids. White was emptiness. It was a sign that they were gone. This empty slate let their loved ones mourn, to construct their own version of the deceased, one that could fill that space. To let their own memories write on that blank page.

But, after mourning, they were wrapped in celebratory black, signifying the richness of their lives. Every thread, every drop, every iota filled, as darkly as possible, denoting a life lived richly, so alive with color that every pixel, every piece was filled, saturated. This is how they were remembered – as pieces of art so thoroughly and deeply made that there was no more room for life even. It was now time to become art – to become myth.

At the Octagon, kezmaki, officiants for contracts and agreements, wore black robes, along with the petitioners who entered the kurge to find agreement. These were meant to remind participants that each of them was a rich, beautiful person, with a thriving powerful universe inside them. It was meant to open their eyes and ears, their hearts and senses to the reality of the universes around them, things so full that to learn a fraction about each one would take a lifetime.

But when walking through the corridors and libraries, gardens and pools of the Octagon, you might come across people in white robes. Many were yolcu – voyagers who came from elsewhere. Each of them had dedicated themselves to training officiants in ways that only they could. Some educated Novices – the novitae – on how the bodies of various voyagers worked, how they behaved, what made them feel good. Some educated them on the ways to connect with people like themselves, putting their own world under a microscope for review. The people in white robes promised to be open books, not just to be sexually available, but to be honest at all times about themselves and their people.

Like Reylan Corroba, sitting here, watching the ceremony, all chose to use their experiences, their bodies, their hearts, their minds, as a guidebook, as a storybook that showcased who they were entirely. And the white robe that she wore now, a wisp of material, wrapped haphazardly around her, stood as a warning to novitae stumbling through the struggles of learning the universes of people in front of them. The white robe was the only thing in the Octagon meant to create unease, meant to teach harshly.

It said that the amercement for failure to find agreement, throughout the entirety of known space, has always been suffering and death. The fine imposed upon us by the universe for failing to learn about each other, failing to join and revel in each other's variety and existence is the isolation of the grave and the whiteness of nothingness.

These kheirobos, the ones who wore the white robes, often gave up everything to be read like books by people who needed desperately to learn to interpret the perfect text of each petitioner, every one a rich language of its own.

They sacrificed so much of their own lives so that officiants could learn the one ideal thing that might unite people in that room.

And some, like Reylan's sister sitting next to her, Etangiel Corroba, spent only part of their time at the Octagon. Etangiel lived the remainder at other homes, around the world, writing and documenting everything she had seen and learned, the ugliness that people had wrought in the world and its ramifications, all of it. But more and more, it was becoming clear from her own writings that there was only one immutable law that defined the world they all shared. She soon ran out of horrors perpetrated on a world by broken people and found the not so hidden and full well under them of sincere acts of beauty performed every day by people of every size, color, race, body shape, or world of origin. She discovered that while cruelty was finite, collapsing under the weight of its own stupidity or malevolent incompetence, love had no bounding area and no restrictions, no borders, and needed, sometimes, strikingly little to survive.

She learned that while pain endured, certainly, love thrived and grew, every day, like a magnificent weed.

The third sister you could always find in between them, Eren Corroba, sat around both of their necks, resident in the beautiful steel necklaces they wore. She would speak to both of them, resonant through the bones in their clavicles, watching, learning, cherishing her sisters and linking them in ways that prevented any of them from ever feeling alone. Her body had been gone now for 100 years, but she had chosen to share with them the swell of her fluid liquid wit, speaking to them in a body vibration too dim for anyone else to hear, making each of them break out laughing at the most inopportune moments, building a rope bridge of love that tethered them joyfully together like some wicked mysterious shibari.

Today, as Reylan and Etangiel held hands in the observation space, it was clear that, if the observers had turned around and studied the sisters, they might have commented that they no longer looked quite so identical.

Each wore their robes differently. Rey's, as said, was worn with physically exposed abandon, the thin white cloth almost acting as a pointer, indicating her round, umber tipped breasts, that moved hypnotically every time she laughed. The lithe dip of her beautiful belly, sat over the swell of her pubic area, always open, available, showcasing the rich, dark lips of her pussy, hairless and glistening with the soft wetness that made you want to move in one step closer, to feel the magic of her invitation.

As she stood to cheer you could see her round ass, exposed so willingy, as though she were built to be on display. Even her t'kau, a tattoo on her forehead recently replaced with a beautiful silver matching symbol, drew attention.

And Etangiel shared so many of those qualities, covered as well in tattoos of rituals from around the galaxy, many earned in the kurge during intimate negotiation with a species who considered the marks to be part of the journey to agreement. Her robe, white as her sisters, was pulled close and snug to her body, looking no less sexy for its prudence.

Even their faces were so similar, piercing black eyes wrapped in lashes that needed no encouragement, slightly round heart-shape faces and delicate ears threatening to turn to a point if you looked too hard.

But as time had worn on it had filled Etangiel's lips ever so slightly, pursing them, creating a youthful pout that made her look like the younger sibling. Although, as human lifespans edged at two hundred and seventy years now, neither would be middle aged for decades.

Today, like people in every seat around her, Reylan watched Kashtun, the last novitae from her thula, a massive bear of a man from Boston, Massachusets. He had smooth, Umber skin and, with a black tightly-groomed beard and fade, his head shaved around. His eyes were kind and alive with the chance to joke or play around while his body, built from years of boxing, seemed to want nothing more than to escape the confines of the robe he wore forever. He was quick to laugh and passionate about remembering the lives made better by every agreement he officiated.

Each one lightened his step until he fairly bounced as he walked, lifted onto his toes like a massive panther, every step deceptively light on the earth.

And Rey loved him very much.

But that wasn't difficult. Kashtun's size was an interesting metaphor for his effect on people. He was large, like a planet. And some nights, laughing loudly down in the Thessalia, it seemed like everyone wanted to be in one of his stories, pulled in by the well of his mass, rotating around him. He didn't just draw in fans, he captured satellites.

Kashtun chose to bring his Apriya with him into the kurge. Njeri was a slight girl from Kenya, barely one and a half meters tall. She had a beautiful wide face with elegant lips, much like you would imagine an ancient queen might have had, her upper torso filled with African character tattoos, drawing the eye over her pretty round breasts and neck, covered in silvery rings, under a perfectly shaped head, snakelike dreadlocks falling behind it like a waterfall. She was deaf and spoke in KSL – Kenyan Sign language, which, if she wanted, could be translated by the silver coil around her neck. Njeri was tiny, but she had a feral dominance and a kind of hard to ignore allure that filled rooms. She signed big, her hands reaching outside the square of her body. And she took up space, beautiful, airy, wide open space.

She had earned her t'kau in only six months. Some people speculated it was because of the martial arts training she shared with Kashtun, training that allowed her to be present in a situation like the one unfolding below.

To be clear, the nearly four month long treaty that Kashtun had negotiated between Bracos, the leader of the Viraga, and Gizela, head council person for the Sarcosians, was the real work of art. Three planets sat unclaimed between Viraga and Sarcosian space, hotly contested for decades. Today, all parties were agreeing to use the three planets mutually, as farming planets, with resources provided by both peoples increasing the yields and minimizing the costs to both sides. No one really believed that this officiation would fail. Both sides were exuberant about the deal.

That's not why people were gathered.

And even though the intimate traditions and physiology of the Viraga and Sarcosians were so different that it was difficult to imagine how this might happen – even that fact wasn't why the observation area was full.

It was full because it was rumored that the gift given to the Octagon by the Sarcosians, to be handed off after the ceremony, would flip the entire world on its head and cause many of them to make decisions they never would have thought they had to.

It would change everything.

But right now, they watched.

Kashtun had barely opened the Officiation ceremony when Bracos jumped up and wrapped his left fist around Njeri's Throat, digging his other hand into her cunt and lifting her off her feet. He charged, pushing her against the wall and began twisting his wrist, pressing his claw like fingers deeper inside her.

She smiled and opened her legs, bracing her feet against the wall. She pushed off the wall, using his invading arm to attach herself to his waist, wrapping her legs around his upper torso. His hand slipped further inside her and she grunted and spit in his face, spinning on his wrist and pushing her feet against his chest to free herself.

Bracos licked his hand and smiled, tasting her pussy all over him as he paced. Both his cocks swung in front of him, his anterior one slightly smaller, emerging from further below between his legs, but still impressive. Suddenly Kashtun slammed into him, naked as well, pushing his head face down into the mat. Kashtun pulled Bracos' arms behind him with one hand, punching him hard on the ass with the other. Bracos' thick reptilian horns stuck up in the air as the darker scaled skin of his face was ground into the mat. He roared and bucked under Kashtun as Njeri climbed onto him to flip him over.

She positioned her pussy over his face and pushed downward, trying to cover both his mouth and the flat plane of his nose, represented by just two tiny slits. She rubbed herself on him to suffocate him. In training, they had hoped that the scent would calm him as well as the sex scent of another native Viragan did.

It didn't.

He flipped her off of him, shaking his head. It's possible it was beginning to work. Njeri silently wished she hadn't bathed before she stepped into the kurge today and smiled at that thought. Bracos rose up to his full height, nearly two and a half meters tall, and slammed Kashtun against the wall, nearly throwing him into Gizela. She was completely nude as well. Sarcosians were disarmingly human looking and Gizela was a famously beautiful example of one. She had been a beloved celebrity on her world before being elevated to leader.

She was light brown, covered in white markings and tattoos, slender, with a face that could have made her a fortune on magazine covers across Latin America –smooth, mysterious, with lips that swelled softly on a perfectly heart shaped face when she smiled. Her anatomy was nearly identical to humans except for the slight row of spiky bones lining her spine, carryovers from a more warlike time for her species and her complete lack of hair, from her perfectly constructed head to her pussy, hairless and visible. .

Kasthun rolled over and wrapped his arms around Gizela. Njeri nodded at him and he lifted the yolcu petitioner in his arms, kissing her. She leaned into his kiss and put her hands on his nipples, rubbing them softly. He spun her around, protecting her from the battle being waged behind him, as his hand dipped to her pussy. She opened her legs, letting him gently finger her as he kissed her.

Bracos laughed at Njeri's efforts to hold him down, pushing her to the ground with his arm wrapped around her neck. She fell, hard, on her hands and knees, breathing hard, while the giant reptilian angrily pushed his larger fore-penis into her ass.

She moved forward, feeling his girth invade her smaller hole and let him ride her for a few minutes until he released his hold.

Bracos grunted, letting go of her neck and dropping his hands to squeeze her breasts from behind. He pulled her into him and pumped his member hard into her. Njeri took a deep breath and let out a long, low grunt, reaching behind her to grab his neck behind the horns and flip him over her. He slammed into the wall, breathing hard as she shot up, digging her foot in his neck.

Kashtun slipped between Gizela's legs and began sucking on her. The area right above the pubis, on a Sarcosian, was composed of cells similar to the glans or clitoris in a human. Massaging the area as he licked her gently between the lips of her inner labia was having the desired effect He felt her wetness on his face, hoping Njeri could handle the larger petitioner for a few more minutes

He slipped behind her, still massaging her lower belly, licking her pussy and ass as she arched her back. She tasted slightly of vanilla and something like mint as he dug his tongue inside of her.

Njeri slammed Bracos down on the ground on his back. He started laughing as she kissed him, holding his arms down. She reached up and hit him hard in the face, trying to connect through his thick scaled skin. He bucked, rolling the muscles of his stomach to force her off. She laughed back at him and placed her dark and perfect pussy over the waving head of his front penis, bearing down and impaling herself. He tried to push his ass up, pumping into her, losing control as she hit him again and again.

Kashtun slipped his thumb into Gizela's mouth from behind as she backed into his cock , delicately fucking it with slow and steady, sensuous movements. Njeri shoved her hand into Bracos mouth, wrapping the other around his neck. He squirmed, grabbing at her arms while she dismounted him, dragging him to the center of the kurge by his mouth. She climbed back onto the massive reptilian and held his hands down with her knees as she pumped her cunt with her fingers faster and faster. She moaned and finally squirted into his open mouth.

His breathing slowed and the bucking of his waist became more rhythmic, less violent as he drank her. Kashtun fucked Gizela harder, lifting her forward and pulling her up on top of the restrained Viragan.

She climbed him with a new ferocity, letting Kashtun place the man's fore penis into her undulating cunt. She rode him, at first slowly, but then harder, letting Kashtun lift up Bracos anterior cock and place it in the opening of her ass. She moaned, bearing down on it, until both of his members were deep inside her.

Njeri played with her pussy, digging her fingers deeper, and squirted again into Bracos' mouth as he fucked Gizela's holes in rhythm. She climbed down off of him and reached for her Master Kashtun, kissing him thickly on the lips and climbing into his lap. He leaned forward, pushing her down onto the mat and dug his prick into her wide open pussy, right next to Bracos and Gizela.

Gizela came all over Bracos' members, triggering his release like a floodgate. She licked and bit at his nipples, too petite to reach his face without abandoning the two cocks buried far inside of her.

He pet her hair as Kashtun and Njeri came silently next to them. He breathed out with a playful laugh, "You're a good sport, Gizela."

She licked his chest and smiled. "So I'm not 'Sarcosian' anymore?"

"Ha. I won't be forgetting your name again, trust me." He lifted her up and placed her next to him, Rolling over and playing his fingers over her smooth head.

"I hope not. But I think next time I can do better."

"Oh, next time, huh?" He pulled her closer and kissed her.

She smiled. "Oh, there's always stuff to agree on." She leaned over and kissed Njeri full on the lips as Kashtun bit the larger reptillian's nipples.

Bracos leaned back, hands behind his head as Njeri and Kashtun took turns licking the two all over. Gizela drew on his chest with her fingers, drunk with the aftermath of what the four of them had just done.

"You are a lot tougher than I imagined." He winked at Gizela. He was almost ready for the next round, squirming around as Kashtun took turns licking his cocks.

Gizela pulled Njeri near her, kissing her first and then the reclining reptilian. "I admit this is a Recreator body."

"Im sorry to hear that. Are you all right?" Bracos cupped her face in his hand.

She kissed him hard on the lips. "Oh, yeah, my body was just atomized in a reactor accident."

On hearing that, Kashtun raised his head. "They reconstructed your whole body? With no DNA?"

"Yes. From a personality disc."

Kashtun looked at Njeri. "I didn't think that was possible."

"Oh. It is now. In fact, that's the gift, we're giving the Octagon. It's called Recreator. I think your council has been given it right about now."

Njeri looked up to the observers above. Her face opened up as her eyebrows raised. She lifted her right hand, palm upward and waved it back and forth, then slammed her right thumb over and over again into her left palm.

Reylan looked down, trying to parse what she just heard. She recognized what Njeri was saying and agreed.

"What the Fuck?"

***

Master Leeandrea made her way to the top floor of the central building in the Octagon complex.

The corridors were wide and covered with vines and plants. On most days, the corridors of the Octagon were worth taking your time enjoying. Today, Leeandrea had a single purpose.

Shukkat called out, "come in, sweety." Her gray and red robe was wrapped around her as though it could fall off at any moment, trailing in the air after her with every movement. Leeandrea had never bothered fastening her own robe, choosing instead to walk around mostly naked like a novitae. The gentle, pretty swell of her curves and full breasts always seemed intent on making the case that clothes weren't needed.

"You look wonderful today. Red is totally your color." Leeandrea smiled at the head councilwoman transparently.

Shukkat looked over and sat down. "Oh my god, what could you possibly want?"

Leeandrea fell into a chair across from her and leaned in. "I know what you're doing."

Shukkat laughed. "This is absolutely the most deadly place in the universe for a secret."

"You built a place where everyone is constantly fucking each other and you expect us not to chit chat afterward." Leeandrea's shock of black hair and thick, smokey eyes framed her face so dramatically, while her constantly mischievous smile called them liars.

Shukkat sighed. "That's a good point, baby."

"I want her." Leeandrea pitched.

"You do?"

"You're going to use the Recreator to give Dorothy a body and I want her in my thula. I'll do anything." Master Leeandrea put her hands together in supplication. "Do you want a blowjob? I can arrange it."

Shukkat laughed out loud. "I'm sure you can, you psycho."

"Without Dorothy I wouldn't have made it here."

"Yes, you would." Shukkat remembered the first time Master Leeandrea was in her office and smiled. "You would survive and thrive anywhere on earth. You're a glorious extremophile. You're like those beautiful bugs at the bottom of the ocean that can't be killed."

"Please"

Shukkat cocked her head, realizing how the information had gotten to her. "I keep forgetting Kashtun and Njeri are in your thula."

"And Diallo. We have room for one more." Leeandrea pleaded.

Shukkat sighed, "Everyone wants her. And, honestly, not a single one of you would be a bad choice. Maybe I'm too close to this. Dorothy was like my sister." Shukkat sat back down, looking, for a split second, tired.

"Recreator bodies are tougher, right?" Leeandrea asked. "She wants to Officiate. She'll be able to walk into any kurge with the biggest, strongest, most primal species in the Galaxy?"

"Yes. And yes." Shukkat could see where she was going with this.

"Like I do."

She paused. "Hm. So that's your argument?"

"Yep. What do you think?"

Shukkat thought for a minute. "It's honestly better than most."

"Right?" Leeandrea leaned across the desk.

"But you know what it is? It's a good excuse. It looks good on paper." She nodded.

Master Lee sat back. "Exactly. She's going to walk out of that room and she should know every single thula wanted her. I'm just the tough bitch who won."

Shukkat considered it. It was a solution. "I could say you beat me up."

"I've had dreams about that, "she countered.

Smiling, Shukkat gave in. "I can always spank you if it doesn't work out."

"Or if it does."

She peered closely into her eyes, remembering the young girl who first showed up in front of her. Watching people grow into something remarkable was a particular joy of hers.

"You win. She's yours."

***

For Dorothy, there was no real downtime. Her body was built in the space of a week, through the Recreator. Despite the fact that her personality was originally placed on a single disc, she had, since then, been the disembodied voice of the entire facility, growing and expanding to fill its digital nooks. She was present. She was able to oversee it the entire time. Her body was recreated from her mental imprint, so it relied more on what SHE thought she looked like than on her genetics. Despite that Shukkat was amazed at how true to reality it really was.

Shorter than Sharla, lighter skinned than Zehra, Dorothy was Persian, petite, beautiful, with a body that you would expect from someone who was always the first one naked at parties. Her nose was cute, slightly upturned, with those pouty lips that often made her look like her mouth was always a tiny bit open. Her fringe of thick, black hair always seemed to fall in ways that accented her face. She always looked accidentally beautiful, like she had gotten off a long train ride and just looked like that – perfect.

An AI avatar named Emily took over for Dorothy as she entered the body.

She chose not to allow a copy of her consciousness to live across the computing web of the facility. The changeover was nearly instantaneous

Shukkat talked to her about where she wanted to live, ending the conversation with Master Leeandrea's offer, which she accepted immediately. It seemed that all Dorothy wanted to do was to get back into the world and be like everyone else.

Just a person with a body.

She was anxious to spend time with Shukkat and anxious to see Zehra when she came back.

But mostly she was anxious to live.

***

Diallo was thin, with a beautiful mop of dark hair on top of his head. There was a row of tattoos around his neck and chest under a row of thick rings around his neck. His jaw was square and classically handsome and his lips conjured up rock stars from a century earlier, dancing with the mic, making the girls swoon. His belly was defined and muscular, with an 8 pack descending into a perfect V that women loved to lick the length of. The same modern techniques that hid the signs of his top surgery could have constructed him a penis, built from his own body, but he never needed one to be a man. Twin black wraps around his thighs drew attention to the smoothly shaved virility of his pussy, a part of himself he loved and enjoyed showing off whenever he could.

Today, he stood up in the pool in the center of the thula and made a toast to Master Leeandrea with a wide smile on his face. "To the toughest, most beautiful crazy person I know." He motioned to Njeri in KSL, as he spoke.

Njeri applauded and stood up, the hot water dripping off of her, making a ring of steam.

She put out her left hand, lodging the elbow of her right hand in it, up high, and waving. This was her nickname for Master Leeandrea – Tree. It was common in KSL for people to be referred to with stylized signs as nicknames. Lee's fit her well.

Kashtun mirrored her and laughed. Leeandrea WAS powerful, like a tree. She couldn't be torn down. She was a bad-ass, even in this room. This particular thula was designed for the occupants, with a wide set of circular mats around the pool, mats they used to wrestle and explore ways to officiate with the roughest of species.

Leeandrea lifted her hands, reveling in their cheers. The members of this thula always observed each other's ceremonies, which tended to be more raucous, more intense, than usual. And then they gathered together to celebrate.

Kashtun stood in awe, "First of all, I can't believe you handled two Red Keligs. I thought for a second they were going to fuck you to death."

Diallo interjected, "I have never wanted to jump into a ceremony more than I did today. Except maybe that deal with Bracos and Gizela. That was epic."

Njeri signed that all of her holes still hurt. Here, in her own thula, they had all learned KSL so they could keep her translator off. It was a tiny concession to her but one that paid off. Her signs were often so beautifully stylized and personal that talking through the translator felt like a weak secondary option.

Not real communication.

Leeandrea reached for Diallo. "oh, yeah, come here little boy, let me show you what it felt like." She grabbed his arm and pulled him over. Holding his arms behind his back she took her other hand and spread his legs. She reached in and grabbed his cunt, holding his nether lips and clit in her hand as she twisted and squeezed harder and harder. He kept his legs spread and tried to slow his breathing so he could tolerate it. He leaned his head back and started moaning.

She twisted harder, pulling down on his arms as she kicked his legs open. "Do you like that?"

Diallo moaned and nodded. He spread his legs a little wider. "Thank you, master."

She laughed and pushed him under the water. He burst up and slid in next to her, splashing her. She turned to Njeri. "And I did love watching you take Bracos. I loved how he fucked you like a toy."

Njeri communicated that she was a toy that fought back. Her right hand opened and closed on top of her left hand, then, in a claw shape with her palm facing down, zoomed off in a straight line to the left, suggesting power, agility, speed, greatness, all pieces she added to the sign for 'Toy.'"

As a digital presence, Dorothy had been here before. She had watched Master Leeandrea and her thula come together and become something special.

And as she and Shukkat made their way down the wide-open, flora filled corridors of the Octagon, she couldn't wait to be there.

"You could stay anywhere. You could have a private space. You could run a thula of your own." Shukkat held onto Dorothy's arm as she walked next to her.

"No. I just want to be in the middle of everything. Besides, I might KNOW enough, but I haven't EXPERIENCED enough. This body is so new."

While it might have been new, it felt to Shukkat like the Dorothy she remembered. Petite and warm and beautifully weird. As they rounded the corners and slowly moved closer, they reminisced and talked about times so long ago that surely no one left on Earth remembered them.

Except them.

And when they opened the door, Master Leeandrea was the first to wrap herself around Dorothy, welcoming her into a space full of fighters, ones that had fought for her.

They all fawned over her, dragging her inside, showing her every inch of a place they wanted her to love.

She stood in the pool, hours later, with the four of them, as the descending sun turned the entire space into a beautiful Mediterranean fairy tale, filled with gardens and fountains and every sound you only noticed at night. She addressed the group firmly, her own arms waving wildly as she signed while speaking, trying to match Njeri's massive articulate presence, something that would become her mantra in her new home.

"If I catch any of you fuckers going easy on me, I will hurt you."

***

They spent days at a time on the mats, just wrestling. Dorothy learned about each of them, things she could never have known as a disembodied voice. Diallo, for example, was indestructible. His lithe rock star body seemed to be able to weather anything, and the way he conserved his energy meant he could keep wrestling, fighting, anything, for hours after everyone else was exhausted.

Njeri was small and fast, so much so that she could turn anyone's strength against them. She was never where you thought she would be. Even with terabytes of tactical knowledge in her head, Dorothy couldn't wrestle her to the ground. There were moments, in the middle of their struggle, where gravity itself didn't make any sense as she completed some arcane hold and moved you to exactly where she wanted you.

Kashtun was gentle but strong. Stronger than anyone Dorothy had ever seen. She'd never once been hurt wrestling with him, either, because his strength was so tightly controlled he could protect you while appearing to throw you around like a rag doll. And on days when she just wanted to be loved, Kashtun's bed was sweet and soft.

And Dorothy remembered Lee from her first moments here, at the Octagon, before she was even accepted. The pretty Greek goth girl who would slip back and forth seamlessly between being a ferocious dominant, towering over you, to being the submissive doll, exposed and prepared for any abuse. She could be soft or hard or anywhere in between. The way she read what people needed in the moment was impossible to learn. It came from her. Her love was a radar that reached inside you.

It was Lee that Dorothy took with her most of the times she wanted to explore the place that had been her digital home for so long. They investigated every piece of it. Places that Dorothy saw every day as a digital assistant suddenly came to life complete with sensations that painted them in rich emotional hues she hadn't expected.

Lee brought Dorothy to the underground space below Building Two where kheirobos from sleek wet dirt-filled worlds lived, thriving in a thick, slippery playground of mudbaths and slides. She brought her to the spaces in Building Three where aerial races flew across expansive aeries, owning the sky with glittery, sun-drenched wings and smooth aerodynamic skin.

And she brought her to her favorite place, the Thessalia, an expansive world where Turolo, air-breathing people, would meet and spend time with every kind of Taranakah, the water-breathing people who lived in the spaces below. Dorothy had seen it, of course, as a disembodied presence, but that didn't prepare her for the reality of the Thessalia.

It felt like life. The warm spray of water and sound everywhere, coupled with the swirling smells of fresh water wrapped around her, felt like the birthplace of possibility. Dorothy jumped in to hug Karanasis, a four-meter long Kheirobos from the Ingrassa people, with a beautiful, elaborate set of tentacles below her waist that seemed to move, themselves, like water, reaching up to pull the woman closer into a powerful embrace.

Because this was Dorothy.

This was someone they all knew. Someone that most of them had talked to in the middle of the night when no one else was awake, about things they needed to find words for to speak to anyone else.

But not to Dorothy.

***

She got more and more comfortable in and out of her thula. Some days were easy, spending time with new friends and old ones, exploring and experimenting with the seeming lack of constraints of her new body, stronger and more resilient than her original one.

Some days were filled with reminders of the time she'd lost. Today felt like that as she floated in the pool, thinking. Kashtun stepped out for a moment and she was hit with an overwhelming sense of loss.

Dorothy crawled out of the water toward Kashtun and slid up his body. She reached around and grabbed his cock while she dug her face between his asschecks and kissed him, licking and fucking his hole with her tongue. She seemed to get lost in it, hugging him closer, pulling at his dick with one hand and making deep sucking noises. She ate his ass as though she were starving, masturbating him at the same time, jerking his cock up and down. She pushed him down until he was on his hands and knees, slamming her tongue deeper and deeper, waiting for the thin line of pre cum to come running down his shaft. She pulled the dick between his legs and licked it clean like an animal. His cock was still hard in her hands as she leaned back, breathing in deeply.

"God, I missed the way ass tastes. I missed shoving my tongue all the way up inside someone and feeling their cum all over my hands and face and tits when they finished. I miss the sound they make."

She rolled him over and slid on top of him, wet enough that he slipped right inside her without assistance.

For a moment, she just sat there. Then, she began riding his prick as hard as she could. Kashtun grabbed her around the waist and slammed her body up and down, digging his dick into her like a hammer. She yelled out over and over, cumming on him as he pumped into her only a couple minutes later, sloppily spraying cum all over, inside her and out as she lifted herself up and then impaled herself again and again. She hit him in the chest with her fist and rolled off.

"I missed having a train run on me and crawling around the room, asking people if they wanted to fuck my wide open ass one more time – one more time before they left – and looking at what that did to their faces."

Njeri got out of the water, crawling over to Dorothy. She kissed her and shot up. She ran out of the room. Leeandrea stood up and grabbed Dorothy's hand, dragging her over to the mats area. She pulled off her robe and kneeled in front of Dorothy, who had gotten to her feet, breathing hard above her. Lee spread her legs and laid back, her pussy open and accessible. She opened herself.

Njeri ran back over with a thick black belt, her breathing sharp as she handed it to Dorothy. She drew her eyes in and rubbed her fist in a tiny circle over her left breast.

"Please."

Then she extended her hand, fingers tightly together and made a circular sweeping motion with the other hand over it.

"All."

All of it. She was asking Dorothy for all of it. To let it all out.

Dorothy looked down at Lee, so open, wanting nothing more than to sacrifice herself to the other woman's anger. Njeri dropped to her knees and placed her pretty ass on Lee's face, pushing her down, as she had done so often in the middle of the night, climbing into her room, taking full advantage of her t'kau, along with her lips and mouth, letting them play inside her as long as she could hold out.

Facing Dorothy, she grabbed and spread open the Master's legs even wider, holding her down, exposing all of her to The anger in the room.

Dorothy lifted the belt, feeling its heft, and brought it down hard on Leeandrea's white belly, leaving a dark crimson line down the center. Lee breathed in sharply and sucked Njeri's cunt and ass with a new enthusiasm. Dorothy could hear her licking, breathing, swallowing, over her own hot breaths.

Diallo climbed onto Kashtun's lap, slipping the bear's half limp cock between the open lips of his own pussy, He cuddled closer and nodded at Dorothy.

All of it.

Dorothy turned back to Lee, who was pushing her cunt out at her. She brought the belt down hard, letting it rip into Lee's left tit, drawing a dark thick red line as if by paintbrush.

Leeandrea screamed into Njeri's pussy, begging for it all. The belt came down again on her other tit, threatening to rip it open.

Dorothy called out, "I miss being the first one naked and the last one to get my clothes back on."

She began to slap the dark-haired woman with the belt harder and harder, over and over, painting her breasts and belly in rhythm with her chants. "I miss being a hooker. Not an escort or a lady of the evening, a straight up fucking hooker, that everyone looks at and knows they can fuckstart this ass whenever they want to."

Lee whimpered and dug her face into Njeri's asshole, the pink ips of her pussy glistening with strands of her desire, her want.

Dorothy looked down at her and her pale skin, wanting to paint it all in shades of reds, purples, and blacks, bring the belt down to destroy the woman's inner thighs, to slide brutally across her legs as she continued.

"I miss cock and I miss pussy and I miss shaving my cunt and making it all pretty and smooth and clean and then coming home with slap marks all over it, sloppy and used and smelling like someone's cum and piss."

Njeri lifted her ass slightly from Lee's ravenous tongue, burrowing into her littlest hole, begging for her piss. She started peeing, a slow stream at first, but then a thick clear torrent, pouring into Lee's open, starving mouth. Lee lapped at it and moaned, as Dorothy redoubled her efforts, beating her even harder.

"I miss eating too much with people I love. I miss getting so high that I just say the same thing over and over again to my girlfriend and cry and she's ok with it."

Dorothy's eyes welled up and she began to cry. She wished she were finished and that she could just hold Lee, but she wasn't. She lifted the belt and aimed it between the Greek girl's legs, bringing it down so hard that Lee screamed, choking on Njeri's piss. Begging for all of it. The belt made a wet sound as it slapped greedily into her pussy again.

"I miss masturbating and showing my asshole off to someone for the first time, and swimming naked, pretending it's all friendly when I know it ends up with me being fucked on the dirty beach afterward, with sand in my cunt."

More rhythmically, and harder, she beat Lee's cunt.

"I miss gangbangs and daisychains where we turn the lights off and everyone just sucks each other off. I miss having a body, for gods sake, just lying around naked while Shar and Archie were getting ready to go to some important function, knowing they'd toss me a fuck on the way out."

Doroty let out a screech and threw the belt down. She dropped to her knees and punched Lee in her tits, again and again.

"I miss my friends' dicks and my girlfriends' perfect little assholes and just going to bed in a cold room under a million blankets with the window open."

She used both hands, punching her in the belly, in the legs, beating her already-raw pussy. Lee was red and purple everywhere, spreading her legs now without any assistance, letting the other woman do anything she needed to do.

Dorothy shoved her knee into Lee's cunt, grabbing her throat and choking her, pummeling her with her hands,

"I miss being me. I missed a hundred years of being a body because of Gökhan, because my own brother killed me because I was a whore. Because he thought I should die for his honor because I was a whore."

She dropped down onto the woman in front of her and wrapped her arms around her. Her tears ran over Lee's belly as Njeri rolled off of the Master's face. Dorothy inched up her body, kissing her and holding her until her face was buried in Lee's Neck.

"Because I was a whore." She whispered into Lee's body. She held onto the other woman as though they were falling and between them was a parachute – a lifeline, one that would fall away if they didn't cling together like they were the same person.

The two women held each other barely moving, breathing only air filtered through the other one until morning. That's when Lee noticed a tiny bit of blood under Dorothy's right ear.

She assumed it must have been her own.

***

Many of the people most excited to meet and get to know Dorothy were some of the augmented people. Some had chosen to be changed so as to be able to engage better with the various yolcu races that they would meet and work with. Some had just chosen to change their bodies, to make them into something they saw in their heads.

Dorothy had been present, in a way, for each one. At a certain point, that became a parlor game. Like today, as she sat on the Thessalia, having a drink with Master Leeandrea.

Two young novitae approached her.

The woman was Chinese, with long straight hair and digital looking tattoos all over her chest. Her smile was infectious and slightly silly. Her arms and legs were made from beautiful winding black and silver rods that looked as though they had been designed to be as structurally sound as possible while leaving as much air and space as they could. As Dorothy looked down, it was clear that her legs were perfectly configured to wade speedily through water while still holding her up.

The man was Black, with short blue-black hair and the prettiest lips she'd ever seen, Dorothy thought. His chest lit up with various colorful lights that came from right under his skin. His fingers were wrapped casually in the girl's hand and he never seemed to miss the opportunity to touch her.

They walked up next to Dorothy, playfully challenging her. "Ok, who are we?"

Dorothy hugged them, freeing up two chairs for them. "Master Leeandrea, this is Ako and Imisha Jackson. They were married when they were 10 years old in a pretend ceremony…"

Imisha interjected, "it's only pretend if you were pretending."

She smiled, continuing, "and they came here together. They are part of Master Zoi's new thula."

"It's great to meet you. You can't stump her, you know."

"It's crazy. I remember talking to you all night when I went through my surgeries. When I was scared" Ako was trying hard not to reach out to hold Dorothy's hand. Dorothy looked down and pulled her onto the chair, holding on to her. Ako looked over at Lee.

"I was born without arms and legs. I had extensive surgeries here so I could feel from the prosthetics I have."

"She has like 21 legs at home." Imisha jumped in.

She laughed. "Yes, I definitely have an odd number of legs."

Master Leeandrea reached for her hand and placed it on her breast, feigning amazement. "So you can feel this?"

"Yes. I may need to feel both, though, for the full experience."

Dorothy pulled the man closer, too. "She has an array of very pretty prosthetics, but also a bunch that help her do interesting things. And Imisha has had millions of colored light and temperature plates implanted under his skin. There are over 90 species in the known galaxy whose primary means of communication is through color, light, and/or temperature."

Imisha smiled at Lee. "I'm learning a lot about all of them."

Dorothy continued, "Imisha is the very first earth human in history to become fluent in the language of the Avelaurelis people."

"That is amazing." Lee shook his hand.

"I've been practicing with my Kheirobos coach. She says she wants to see the look on the face of the very first Avelaurelis petitioner I walk into a room with."

Ako beamed. "Me, too. Can you imagine traveling literally hundreds of millions of light years into a room filled with people who look nothing like you and seeing and feeling them talking to you in your own language?"

Dorothy could tell that she had basically communicated Imisha's passion – what he had worked so hard to give. This fantasy was a common one across the entire facility, every building in it. It was the presiding fantasy of the Octagon. How it would feel to make someone feel uniquely understood in a way that really mattered.

And what the look on their face would be at that moment.

Ako and Imisha had dinner with them, introducing them to other Augments who came to the table. Dorothy knew them all. In every case, these were people who had endured some kind of pain, sometimes in a room all by themselves, trying to be strong and self-sufficient to the world around them – lying to everyone that they didn't need anything or that they really felt great.

Lying to everyone but the voice of the Octagon, the voice that was there all night, at their bedside, listening, telling dirty jokes, reminding them of why they endured the things they did...

And what it looked like on the other side.

Lee realized that her experience with Dorothy was one shared by so many people and she felt even more connected. Being where you belonged was such an important part of life. Some 35 years ago, Dorothy had helped her feel like she was right where she belonged.

And she did it again today.

Lee and Dorothy got back home late that night, and somehow it didn't feel right to be alone. Diallo and Njeri had fallen asleep in Kashtun's bed, likely talking about the past or the future or some idea one of them had thrown out, realizing the conversation wouldn't survive the night and would probably have to be revived in the morning. For not the first time, they all climbed in bed together in a giant thula filled with beds and rooms and soft spaces.

Only one room, though, had what they needed.

***

The miniature octagonal shape of the Green Tomb of Bursa was not far from the center of the Octagon complex, although it was separate from the main buildings. It was in the complex of Mehmet Celebim, known for centuries as the Green Complex – Yesil Kulliye, In Halk, the language steadily evolving through the entire country. In the Green Complex, you can find the Green Tomb, the Green Mosque, a madrasah, a bathhouse and an ancient soup kitchen. All of these structures' origins dated back to the early 1400s. Today, they were all made even more beautiful through care and hidden technology.

In fact, planners during the ottoman Empire would likely never have known that the entire area would survive, beautified, covered in flowers and vines, while massive expanses of garden spaces were built out beneath them, with natural sunlight redirected into places it had never reached before.

Kashtun found that even he was impressed by the view as he stepped up the ramp slowly ascending, wrapping around the Green Tomb, into that sunlight, to meet Shukkat. He knew that this was one of the places she went to think, a place that had been special to her since she was a child, homeless, sneaking into the famous mosque to hide and sleep.

To be safe.

She hugged him and grabbed his arm.

"So you are worried."

He breathed out. "Not really. No. I'm not." Shukkat recognized the lie for what it was and moved forward.

"And it's happened twice?"

He scanned her face for the best approach. "But the first time it was almost imperceptible."

Shukkat inhaled the rarified air that had slipped through the cracks in the masonry of 700 year old buildings. "Can you walk me through it?"

"Well. It's like she gets sort of overstimulated."

"And then…"

Kashtun continued. He didn't want to be the one delivering this information. "It seems like a small seizure. Or a series of microseizures."

Shukkat felt his pulse through his arm. "And there's blood?"

"A little bit. Barely any." He downplayed.

She stopped and considered. "But still…"

"Still"

Shukkat sighed. "She doesn't really want to talk about it?"

Kashtun shook his head and held her hand. "No. She says she's just getting kind of re-acclimated. To all of it. Having a body, etcetera."

She stopped, putting her arms around him. In more playful times, she found it fun to try and wrap her arms all the way around this massive bear of a man. She felt him now like a giant fence post, firmly rooted to the ground, immovable. "What do you think?"

"I don't know what to think, honestly."

"Thank you for coming to get me." She kissed him and grabbed his hand back.

The two took their time returning to the main building where Dorothy's t'kau ceremony was to happen in the Bessary. Shukkat thought back to her own ceremony, so long ago. This would be different. The room was filled with people who just wanted to be a part of today. They wanted to touch her, to experience with her, to show her how they felt about her.

She had chosen Master Kashtun to be the one to give her the t'kau and Shukkat could see her perk up when they walked in. She ran over to hug them both, Excited to have them there, with her. Her oldest friend watched her face diligently for some sign of any trouble, some dark shadow. But today, there was nothing but Dorothy there.

There were nearly one-hundred people assembled.

Dorothy stood up in front of them and thanked them for coming, pulling off every bit of clothing she had worn. She advanced to the large seat placed for her in the center stage area of the Bessary and spoke to everyone, as Kashtun lifted the tiny box to her forehead.

"I am called Dorothy and I pledge myself to the Octagon, to listen in faith, to connect in love, to give myself in joy as contract."

Shukkat heard her skip her last name, recognizing the freedom someone could have in that separation. She'd had no love for her own, even way back then.

Kashtun stepped toward her as she pulled his cock from his robe and slid it into her waiting pussy. She wrapped her legs around him, smiling at him while he applied the device to her forehead. Usually, during these ceremonies, the novitae would be the one people would pursue, the one they wanted. Dorothy wasn't going to wait. This was her day and she would choose to use that privilege having fun.

Kashtun's face evolved into a grin as he finished the pretty shape on her forehead. She pulled in his face and licked at his lips, yanking him into her over and over. Shukkat smiled realizing that tiny little Dorothy was essentially fucking herself with the imposing Master Kashtun. Soon, he reached into her hair, holding her head lightly, and came deep inside her.

And people applauded.

The music she had chosen rose from widely set speakers and her friends cheered and applauded some more. Imisha and Ako were among the first to hug her. She kissed her friends, widely, on the mouths. The front of Imisha's chest lit up as he lifted her, carrying her to the round, padded circle in the center of the Bessary. He laid her down and climbed on top of her as she reached her hands out to hug him and pull him in.

Before she could think, he had placed himself inside her and was moving back and forth, his hands playing against her breasts. She spread her legs widely and put her hands over her head, staring up at Ako.

The Chinese girl was wearing beautiful arms and legs that felt like down, soft, against Dorothy's face as her husband fucked himself into her waiting cunt. Moaning softly, she tried to focus for a moment, to lift Ako onto her face, positioning the girl's pussy over her mouth. Ako pressed a button and her prosthetic legs retraced, leaving her open and receptive to Dorothy's tongue, as the girl tried hard to fit all of her into her mouth, opening as widely as she could. She would sometimes play just as herself, without any prosthetics, when she felt safe enough to be vulnerable.

Ako leaned forward and kissed Imisha, who had just begun to cum in his friend's cunt, as a smaller man with a green headwrap climbed onto the padded bed area and slid his dick into her, alternating between her cunt, made open and even more bare by the absence of her prosthetics, and Dorothy's wet mouth.

Ako leaned forward, engulfing the mouth beneath her completely with her spread open pussy as the man pulled out and aimed himself into her ass. Imisha kissed her, sliding off of Dorothy, letting the men behind him have their turn, fucking her pretty holes. Dorothy held Imisha's hand as long as she could before losing him in the mass of admirers who had come to the ceremony in hopes of being close with her.

Diallo and Njeri climbed up on the surface and held her, pressing her down and kissing her while avoiding obscuring her holes for the benefit of potential suitors. Diallo whispered in her ear, telling her about the people lined up to connect with her, the rows of people who wanted nothing more than to be a part of this today.

Shukkat watched closely, but here she was, in the middle of more stimulation than she'd ever experienced, more people, more sensations.

And she was loving it.

***

Dorothy learned how to use her new body. And Master Leeandrea was right to bring her into her thula. The constant wrestling and movement exercises had honed her physical skills to the point where, like Njeri, she could enter the kurge with the most "expressive" of yolcu species without danger. And everyone around her learned from her 100 years of knowledge about people and mediation, conflict resolution, problem solving.

They had sessions in her thula where even Master Kashtun and Master Leeandrea followed her lead. Shukkat could even sometimes be found there, rolling around on the mats with her, falling asleep next to her on days when she couldn't bear to leave.

And sometimes Ako and Imisha would join, Ako wearing a pair of sleek metallic legs that let her launch herself from the ground into a hold, too quietly to stop. Or a special silicon-covered set that propelled her through water so fast Dorothy couldn't keep up. And Imisha would sit on her side, cheering her on, lights buried just under his skin celebrating every time she won.

They wrestled, they learned, they laughed together, and they sat, observing the ceremonies where one or more of them would officiate for a brilliant panoply of voyagers, every conceivable kind of person in the galaxy. Then they'd find their way home and celebrate again. It took almost no time for this thula to become home.

And Shukkat almost forgot there was ever a problem.

***

Reylan stopped for a moment in a tiny alcove off of a wide corridor near her place. The little nook held a few overstuffed couches and an array of bookshelves that could be rotated, exposing thousands more books behind.

The walls were deeply overrun with ivy and flowers and the far wall opened into a waterfall you could walk into, with a pool made for floating and reading these waterproof tomes about politics and society.

Rey had experienced, many times, how much easier complex stories about deadly deep subjects could be made palatable by location. She flipped the bookshelf and it took over, sinking back and spilling out another rack of books. For a moment, she leaned forward to smell, wishing the new book smell were just a bit more intense.

Next to her, a novitae was pretending to look at books. His t'kau was recent, red irritation marks around the blue of the tattoo. He wore nothing but some jewelry and a few blue wraps, one around his head. He was young and curious looking and he couldn't seem to take his blue eyes off of Rey. She caught them and smiled, glancing down at his visible erection.

She felt his hand reach behind her and brush against his ass. Her hand slid behind her for the scraps of her robe and lifted, making sure her ass was exposed and she was accessible. She kept watch on his eyes as his left hand dipped below her, sliding two fingers into her slippery pussy and one slowly into her ass. She pushed against them, her head rolling back a little, eyes still locked with his.

He pushed his fingers in and out for a minute or so and then raised them toward his lips. Reylan intercepted his hand and brought it to her own face, licking his fingers.

Leaning in closer to him, she spread her legs intentionally wider and faced him, devouring his fingers. .

"I'm sorry. Did you want some?"

He smiled wide and dipped his fingers inside her again, this time deeper. Rushing them to his mouth, he tasted her. "You are so fucking beautiful. Oh my god, you even taste good." He seemed lost in the taste of her as he cleaned off his fingers with his mouth. "I'm sorry."

"Sh. Don't be sorry. Do you think I'm pretty?" Rey moved in closer to him.

He seemed bolder, more confident. "I think you're the most amazing thing I've seen here so far."

"That's good." She reached out and held his hand. "You're so pretty."

He leaned in and kissed her, his lips trembling as they touched hers. "Do you think so?"

She kissed his neck and then his chest. Then she slowly kneeled, looking up into his eyes. "Can you get your pretty dick all the way down my throat?" She kissed the tip of his cock and ran her tongue around the tiny hole. "Do you know how to do that?"

"I never, um…" He leaned on the bookshelf next to him. Rey was afraid he would fall.

She grabbed him around the waist. "Come here."

He slid his dick between her lips, pushing slowly "Is that too hard?"

She ran her mouth all over him, holding his balls while she tried to keep him from falling over. Under certain conditions, she thought, it had to be a compliment when someone was so ready to tip over. "That is perfect." She looked up at him, "Do you want to suck on me?"

He was breathing hard. Every time he made eye contact with her, she could tell it was pushing him further. "More than anything." he nodded.

Rey slid his prick all the way down her throat smoothly over and over. It was sloppy wet and her hands playing with his balls rubbed the soft wet into him everywhere. "Do you like that people are watching?"

He nodded, breathing harder. "Do you?" She realized he wanted to look around but couldn't take his eyes off of her. If this were a training session for how to be with a human woman, he would have scored big points with that.

She stage-whispered, licking the side of his dick slowly, stopping at the tip before descending again

"I have to tell you the truth about everything."

He nodded. "Oh, right."

"So you know I'm not lying." She began to pump his cock, slowly, while licking the tip. "I like everything you're doing."

It occurred to him he wasn't doing anything. He felt the redness of the t'kau on his forehead and thought for a moment about how it could have hurt a hundred times worse and it would have been a good deal. He considered saying that out loud. Instead he said, "that's so good."

Rey backed toward the overstuffed chair behind her and flipped around, positioning her pussy in reach as he let his prick slip into her mouth. "Now, can you move in, suck me while you try to get your cock all the way down my throat."

He leaned in. "Is that something we can do?"

She spread her legs and put them over her head, pushing her cunt and ass into the air. "Move it in slowly. I'll make my mouth very wet and pull you in. You keep going until you hear a tiny pop and then you can fuck my throat. Are you ready?"

He moved forward, sliding his dick all the way down her throat, his testicles against her face as it burrowed completely inside. "Yes. Oh my god. That feels so good." He leaned forward and put his face into her slick pussy. She tasted warm and soft and he nearly came the second his tongue moved inside her. "Hm. I think I need to stop. Ooh."

Rey smiled, reaching back to take his balls into her mouth while he covered his face in her. She felt him breathing between her legs, as though the only air he wanted had to be filtered through her. "I could taste your pre-cum. That was great. Do you want to fuck me?" She flipped around in the chair and presented her cunt, holding her legs up.

He looked down at her and saw what was possibly the most beautiful thing he'd ever seen in his life. His dick started to twitch. "I do. I think this is going to be too fast." His eyebrows dropped.

Rey pulled him inside her, placing one hand on his face. "Don't worry about that. If you want to hold on, do it. If you just want to cum, do that? Okay?" She started moving back and forth, letting him slide in and out of her.

"Okay," he moaned.

She could tell that every word out of her mouth was pushing him over and smiled at him while she slowly growled. "Oh that feels good. I love how you fuck me."

The young man tried to close his eyes and bury his head in her neck. But he couldn't escape the sensations. The way she looked, the way she smelled, the way she sounded. He grunted, trying to hang on.

She grabbed his ass and pulled him in deeper. "Oh, yeah, when you push up like that, when you're inside, I feel your prick up against my little spot."

"Ok, like this?" His voice sounded smaller than he likely intended.

"Yes. God. Exactly like that. Do you like how wet I am?" Suddenly, Rey started to feel closer, as well. The part of her that was just enjoying training this polite man began to give way to the part where she wanted it. Where she needed him.

He whispered in her ear. "I do, I wish I could drink it all."

He pushed harder as she shoved her open cunt against him. Oh, yeah, well, that just made it wetter. Ha."

He looked into her eyes. "I like how you hold my ass"

"Have you ever fucked in front of people before?" she whispered.

He shook his head. Sweat ran down his forehead. She pulled his head in and licked it away. He whispered, "Only during the tests."

Rey pointed at the crowd that was beginning to gather, watching them. "Everyone's wishing you were fucking them."

"That's crazy." He tried not to look. His eyes squeezed tightly shut. "I think they want you."

Rey let out a loud moan. "I'm going to cum. Can you feel that squeezing?"

"Yes." he nodded, trying so hard to be what she wanted. Rey felt his face, holding him and staring into his eyes.

"Do you want to cum, too? Look here in my eyes."

"I think we've passed that point." His chest bounced slightly in laughter.

Reylan raised her voice, specifically for the observers. They should have some fun, too. "Cum in me. Oh, that's so warm. Can you feel my pussy contracting, pulling you in?"

The contractions of her climax pushed him over the edge. "Yes, yes. Oh wow."

She wrapped her arms around him, feeling him drain into her. "Oh, that's so good. Can you stay here?"

Rey could taste his sweat as she kissed his face again and again. He nodded, trying to catch his breath.

"I want to feel when you get soft." She settled in. "You've been hard the whole time I've known you."

"Oh my god, that's true." He put his head in his hand.

"It's ok, it's good. Now that you came in me, what's your name, sweetheart?" She slowly rocked back and forth, holding him.

"Oh, I'm Vero." He nearly made a motion to shake her hand, recalled it. And then decided to go through with it. He raised his hand and she took it, shaking it.

"I love your eyes, Vero. I'm Reylan."

"

"I know. Everyone knows. You're the person who wrote the constitution for the whole country." It seemed as though he had almost caught his breath.

She pulled him close and whispered in his ear. "Does me being smart make you hot?"

Vero smiled. "Like I can't think straight. It's crazy." She could tell that he was making no progress in softening up.

Suddenly Rey looked up, a message from Eren in her head "Damn. I'm being summoned."

"I'm sorry." He pulled back, pulling out of her reluctantly, "I know you're busy. I kind of just..."

Rey kissed his face over and over. "Don't apologize for anything to me, Vero with the pretty blue eyes. Can we continue this next time I see you? I'll start." She stood up, pulling the robe around her.

He let her hand slip out of his, trying to commit everything to memory. Vero smiled as she ran off. "Oh, god, yes."

***

Shukkat and Rey stood in her office space on the top floor of the main building. Years ago, it was a conference room for an embassy, the first place they had made plans with people from another planet.

A man with neatly trimmed short blond hair and a wash of silver necklaces walked in, the tattoos on his face following the pretty lines of his jutting cheekbones. He hugged Shukkat then grabbed Rey's hand, standing close to her. She leaned in and smelled him. Priest had always smelled like some kind of fresh wood and citrus to her. She nodded to Shukkat.

In front of them were four more members of the council, as meter-tall holograms, standing on a long stone table. Zehra was at one end, Dorothy's sister, one of Shukkat's oldest friends. Her red and gray robe marked her as a council leader.

Next to her was Caleo Cuvo Osa, a petite green haired woman whose slightly off green color robe might have been missed since so little of it was visible. She had a wide smile and an obsidian t'kau, much like the one Shukkat wore.

Vorun stood next to her. The nearly 800-year-old light-blue-skinned Forsa woman looked like a doll as a meter tall hologram, made specifically for little kids with a sense of adventure. Shukkat was glad she could be in the meeting as she always felt better when she heard her voice.

The final hologram was of Master Killean. Her skin was an iridescent green with a beautiful, human-like face on the front of a porpoise skinned head that bent back behind her in such a way as to suggest real speed underwater. She smiled kindly at Shukkat. Everyone knew this wasn't easy for her.

Shukkat sighed. "Well, seven of us isn't much, but it's enough to make a decision like this."

Priest looked at the green haired hologram as he spoke, with a wink, "look how tiny you all look."

Caleo laughed. "It's a good size for me, I think. Fun-sized."

Rey spoke up. "First of all, how are things going out there?"

Zehra tried to act playful. "Well, Earthing, we are getting lost a lot."

Vorun interjected, "this new facility is huge and there's barely 20 of us here so far."

"We'll fill it." Shukkat looked down at her feet, remembering for a minute how excited she had been about this expansion, one that was 20 years in the making.

Killean smiled. "We're working on your statue now. Should it be gold or like a clear diamond?"

Shukkat appreciated their efforts to play, to joke, to be who they all usually were right now. These were some of her favorite people in the world. "I feel like if it's a diamond, people will just run into it." She smiled wanly.

Rey grabbed her hand. "Roger." She breathed in. "We've been talking about this a lot. Especially now that it's happened again. "

Vorun nodded,. "So have we. Is she ok? "

Shukkat took in a deep breath. "You have all the information we do. She's resting right now. We don't really know what to do."

Reylan continued, "We keep coming back to how it has to be her choice, everything."

Caleo spoke, in an uncharacteristically somber tone. "Yeah. We can't seem to get around that, either."

Shukkat looked up. "Until she's incapacitated."

Zehra added, "if."

Caleo sighed, "Out of love, we have to let her make the call."

Rey stared at the tiny hologram. Caleo Cuvo Osa was her novitae once and now that she was millions of light years away, she suddenly felt every kilometer of that like a tiny knife. "The cute little green one's not wrong. "

Vorun went to reach out and then stopped herself. "I wish we were there. I feel like we're no support over here."

Shukkat looked over at the hologram of Zehra. "I really needed to see your face on this, Z. She's your sister."

"And your best friend," she shot back.

Shukkat nodded. "You too. I mean the three of us... I always felt invulnerable when we were together."

Killean interjected, "I know you hate to see her in pain."

Shukkat nodded.

Zehra looked out at the room. "I remember we were at some fancy embassy event and we got bored and went found a balcony that sat over a pool. Do you remember that?"

Shukkat nodded. "I do."

Zhra continued, "do you remember Dorothy pulling off her clothes without even thinking and jumping into it? Two stories."

"And we followed."

"I remember when Archie defended you, what he said. "Zehra smiled.

"He knew it was Dorothy." Shukkat shook her head, grinning in spite of herself.

"Nothing great in the world ever happens without people like Dot." Zehra said it like it was a line from a holy book.

Shukkat finished, almost as if to herself, "he called her Dot."

Caleo put her tiny hands on her chest. "That's beautiful."

Rey stood with one hand in Priest's and one in Shukkat's. "She loved having a body. She loved being in the world."

"So there it is. We have to let her try" Zehra intoned.

Shukkat looked her in the eye. "Even if it's past the point of no return? Zehra?"

Zehra nodded, wishing she could at least touch her sister's hand right now. "Yes. 100%. I'm the last one of the three of us to ever make a decision, but there it is."

"There it is."

It took them another 20 minutes to end the meeting as they invented reasons to talk, to share some information, even just to hear the other ones speak. Even when there was nothing left to say, it seemed like there was one more thing.

***

The city surrounding the Octagon was full of life, from the wide open herb and vegetable gardens, lit with runoff light from thousands of twinkling beautiful clear solar receivers to bouncy rubberized playgrounds that generated energy with every moment of play from the children who spent so much time exploring outdoors in the enveloping Mediterranean warmth.

Even the sounds were captured and turned to energy with signs all over that flashed numbers to reward the children who could yell the loudest into receiving horns scattered everywhere. Local people rode bikes connected to power multiplying generators charging the projectors that played movies and music for everyone the minute the sun went down.

The city was built for everyone and it wasn't uncommon to see a yolcu visitor walking through the common areas, talking to a group of fascinated local people, pointing to places they just wanted to hear a little bit more about.

And while most of the landing areas were on the rooftops of the Octagon itself, there were a number scattered throughout the city, where some visitors preferred to land. Shukkat made her way to one of them, positioned near a large outdoor garden market. Two teenagers and a young boy watched the ship approach and land. As the door opened, a man stepped out, with sleek, dark leathery skin and an insect-like torso on top of four equidistant legs.

He looked at the children and yelled out in a deep, boom of a voice. "Take me to your leader."

They paused for a minute. The teenage girl began, "booo. Bigger."

The teenage boy next to her shook his head. "It's got to be bigger man."

The young boy, who must have been about nine or 10, clapped his hands. "Again."

Realizing the need for politeness, the teenage girl put her hands together and giggled. "Please..."

The insectoid-looking man stepped back into the ship and then walked out again and bellowed, "take me to your leader." He looked at the children.

The young boy shook his head. "Didn't believe it."

The teenage girl was more clear. "It's better. But it needs to rip your head off, you know what I mean?"

Shukkat stepped into the market next to them. "Phayden. Allessia. What are you doing?"

The kids laughed, pointing at her "Like that. "

"Yeah, loud"

Shukkat smiled and crossed her arms. "Will you stop torturing the man, please?"

The insectoid man called after them as they ran off, "you know I lead over 100 species across billions of light years of known space."

Shukkat reached up and hugged him, whispering, "that's what you get for parking outside."

The younger boy stepped up, before running after his friends. "For real, though, man, this whole thing is razor cool"

He lifted his hand to connect.

The visitor looked down at the young boy. "Thank you, tiny edible human child."

He smiled. "That was good. My man." He saluted the guest before joining his friends.

The insectoid man turned to Shukkat. "See, this is why I park outside. You can never lose sight of what scares children."

"The bar is so high, nowadays." She took his arm as they walked toward the building.

"It's actually hard work," he agreed.

"Thank you for coming, Vikun." Shukkat patted his arm. She squinted, looking upward, "Is he coming, too?"

"He'll be here shortly. He told me to race here with what we have."

She kissed him. "Thank you."

Vikun scanned the building with purpose. "Where is she?"

***

Vikun and his people cared for Dorothy. For a time, it seemed like she would be fine. Shukkat found her confused one day, sitting in front of her door.

From then, It took almost a week for Dorothy to break down. She woke up one morning unable to speak. Shukkat carried her to the doctor herself, refusing to put her down until the doctor was in front of her. She didn't realize how light Dorothy's body was, how impossibly light.

Vikun's people evaluated her, trying to put the pieces together as to why her recreated body was failing.

Shukkat and Reylan sat in an alcove in the corridor as Vikun stepped out of the room to talk. Rey looked up at the new leader, realizing how much he looked like Symkere, who had only recently stepped down. Despite being a few shades darker and a tiny bit taller, he had the same kind eyes as the previous Velios Unity Leader.

And those eyes were in pain.

"Well, as I said, our best people say that her biologic memories aren't compatible. They were just gathered too long ago."

Rey took a breath. "What about her digital memories? The ones she developed as part of the system here?"

"Well, that is a problem, too. There are so many of them. If we had the time, we would parse through them and thin them out. She operated out of every computer node in this facility, for a hundred of your years. There are petaflops of memories in there. No human brain could contain those.

Shukkat stared ahead, her eyes wet and unable to focus. The thought of watching her friend die again was literally shutting her down, as though she were a radio, having her volume turned down. "What can we do?"

Rey held onto her tightly. "You said, 'if you had the time?'"

Vikun breathed in and continued. "Her system is fighting back. It's as if her hard drive was full of compressed files that are all opening at the same time. Her brain doesn't know what to do first. And it's shutting down important systems."

Shukkat's breathing was shallow and her lips were shaking. "What do we do?" She repeated. Reylan rocked her and pulled her closer. For the first time in all the time she'd known her, Shukkat didn't know what to do. Rey felt that in her gut like a punch.

Sharla Tuk had provided the blueprint for everything good she knew in the world, every day, without ever once retreating. And now, for the first time, she needed marching orders – she needed someone to point her in the right direction. Rey felt angry but she didn't know at whom.

Vikun pulled a piece of paper from the white coat he wore. "We told her that we could put her back into a disc. We could wait – try again."

Reylan nodded. "ok."

He continued, "or we could remove all her memories, leaving just her personality, remembering nothing – a sort of blank slate. She would know her name, how to speak, not much else."

Shukkat shook, looking at the piece of paper in his hand. Rey could hear her breathing, intentional and thick.

"Ok, is that dangerous?" Rey asked.

"They're both a little dangerous." He looked at Shukkat. He unfolded the paper in his hand and handed it to her. Shukkat could barely see for the tears in her eyes.

Reylan nodded. Shukkat pulled the paper toward her and closed her eyes.

Vikun breathed out and stood up.

Shukkat's tears blurred Dorothy's handwriting. But Rey could still see what it said, drawn in black, small, yet forceful.

"Take them all."

***

Today had been ten days since Dorothy had made her decision.

Shukkat made her way back into Dorothy's room to find it peppered with blankets and couches, each filled with a person, sleeping, waiting their turn. She shook her head and looked over at Master Leeandrea. "I think the first thing we'll need to explain when she wakes up is why no one else here has a room to go to."

Lee scanned the room. "Looks like that, doesn't it?"

Shukkat kissed her and held her close. "You've spent too much time in this place huddled over sick people."

The dark haired woman shook her head. "Pretty much all my time here has been spent huddled over or under people I adore, and I'm 100% okay with that. It helps with the people who aren't here." For a moment, she seemed sad.

Shukkat put her hand on Lee's cheek. "That's right. Qerici's with some of the others, on Proxima. I bet she misses you so hard."

"She better." Lee laughed. "I think we're all going to go kidnap her at some point."

"Ha. That's hot." Shukkat felt Dorothy's hand, wrapping her own fingers in it. "When we were young, when we were working. Dorothy could turn any party, no matter how stodgy, into an orgy. It was her thing."

Lee dropped her voice. "I love that."

Shukkat remembered so much. "She'd be the first one slithering out of her underwear. She'd make sure not to go off somewhere private with anyone. It was all about getting fucked on the pool table. So loudly. That's when the room would lose it. And even the shy girls in the corner would slide out of their bras. You know, the girls in glasses who love their tits in front of the mirror at home but always felt too afraid to show them. And then the boys, all the boys, afraid to pull their pants off in front of other men. What it took to make them feel safe, too. Like they would be ok."

"I know those people. I know all those people."

She leaned down to speak so Dorothy could hear her. "And she'd bend over the couch, pulling some guy inside her while she climbed over another guy and she'd fake whisper, "Do you want to take this up a notch?""

Shukkat stood back up, "And then we'd be doing something insane and she'd turn and say, "okay, but you know what would be really hot?""

"And then it would be on." Lee laughed.

Shukkat took in a big breath and let it out. "It WOULD be on."

Lee paused. "What do you think she'll remember?"

Shukkat shook her head "I don't know. Her biologic memories aren't compatible. And the AI merged ones won't fit. Vikun said she might wake up with only the most basic understanding of who she is, but with her personality intact. He hopes."

"IF she wakes up?"

"If she wakes up." Shukkat put her hand on Lee's cheek. Lee kissed it, hungrily.

A part of her fell apart at the thought of Shukkat leaving. She whispered, "If you stay for a bit, I'll kiss your feet." She pressed her lips harder into her hand.

She looked into Lee's eyes. She was so beautiful and so transparent. She let her hand slip up into her hair and grabbed it. It wasn't forceful, just firm. "Do you want to work your way up?"

Lee let out a tiny plaintive moan. "Yes, Master Shukkat. I would like that a lot. Please." Her eyes filled up with tears, feelings that had nowhere else to go.

Shukkat lifted her head, holding onto her hair. She pulled aside the black shawl she wore under her breasts and let it drop. Pointing to the rest of her clothes, she said, "Let's get all of this off, ok?"

The dark-haired girl nodded vigorously. "Yes, ma'am," reaching to try and kiss her other hand.

Shukkat slid down into the chair and let her robe fall open. "We'll wait together. I was going to take a bath, but I'd prefer your tongue. Do you understand?"

Master Leeandrea dropped to her knees, nodding. "Of course, ma'am."

She moved in, wordlessly, and put her lips on Shukkat's belly button, letting her tongue play around its rim. Shukkat held her close, pulling her inward into a long hug. Then she slowly pushed her head down, letting Leeandrea lick at her foot. She pressed her bare foot into her mouth, letting it swim in her throat. Lee tried hard to open as wide as possible, giving the foot a home in her mouth.

And she worked her way upward, losing all track of time.

Shukkat tried to take her mind off of Dorothy, lying there, now bereft of all her memories, waiting to wake up into a world that she'd have to learn every part of all over again. She sat with Master Leeandrea watching everyone else drift in and out, and tried to feel positive about what would happen next, sometimes giving her tasks and goals that she knew would fill her mind.

Her friend Dannae came, staying as long as she could, along with Vreill and other Taranakahs. They placed a telepad right by the door so that they could stay for the full two hours they were allowed out of water. The red-haired mermaid held onto Lee and listened to her babble about Dorothy, petting her old friend's hair and whispering into her neck until it was warm and full of secrets.

With her came Uher, Lee's very first boyfriend, quietly helping her care for Dorothy, cleaning her up and moving her muscles so they wouldn't atrophy, looking for a sign that her brain would right itself now and she would wake up. He was in a bed just like this, and he remembered her voice and could hear it in his head, even while she was silent.

Njeri and Diallo did her nails and talked to her while Ako and Imisha rubbed her with oil and talked to her some more.

Shukkat remembered who Dorothy really was and tried not to see her as this small thing, empty, unmoving. All those memories were inside her and each one streamed in front of her face whenever she saw her, whenever she smelled her.

Whenever she heard her voice.

She petted the body that Dorothy was willing to give up everything to keep and realized that this was why everyone was here, gathered every day. This body was something Dorothy loved. She loved being a real person in the world, flesh and blood, loving, breathing, fucking, fighting, eating, floating, alive.

Alive.

They were here to take care of that body until some small part of her returned to it. Any part of her. This was all they could do.

She looked at Kashtun, this giant, growling, fierce bear of a man, changing the incense in the room so that Dorothy would have variety, a different scent for every part of the day so she might feel the passage of time even without opening her eyes, and she felt a swell of gratitude. Dorothy was hers, every part of her. But she was owned by every other person who passed through this room. That's how big she was. That's how many pieces she was made of, so that every one of them could have a piece and know it was something rare and perfect and irreplaceable. And enough.

Reylan and Etangiel brought her news and food, doting on Dorothy's body without thinking, as though they knew, as well, that this was a beloved thing, worth giving up everything for.

The room was still full, 16 days later when Dorothy finally opened her eyes.

***

A week after that, Reylan leaned over the edge of a rooftop with Symkere. Much like Vikun, he was an arthropod, with deep black leathery skin, stretched over a bisected torso on top of four insectoid legs. His skull arched backward in an elegant way, covered in swirls and sigils carved into the carapace to denote his position as the past leader of trillions of people, spanning hundreds of planets. Rey could feel the love in the drawings, the dignity and respect, from the artists who had worked to describe what happens when a good person has the chance to serve so many people. His voice was thick and smooth, with an undertone that sounded like there might have been a violin playing somewhere.

"Do you think she'll stay?"

She leaned into him in the warm dusk, colors changing constantly as the sun descended in front of them. "I don't know. She'll learn about it and she'll choose if she wants to be here or not. Which is funny, because at one point... Well. It's not funny."

"I'm sorry it worked out this way." Symkere reached out a pincer-like hand and placed it over her hand. It was cold and hard, but it never felt like that to Rey.

She kissed his hand, holding it to her lips. "I'm not."

"Really?"

She turned her body to him. "It's ok, Simmy. She has a whole big long life to make new memories. And we can have fun telling her all about who she was."

He wrapped his arm around her. "But she can figure out who she wants to be?"

Rey leaned against the rocky barrier that spanned the rooftop and stood up on her toes. "Exactly. She's alive." She breathed in and smelled the air as the night took over from the day. Symkere thought she might be aging in reverse, from the matter-of-fact, eternally wise 20 year old he first met to this beautiful 120 year old creature of joy that no planet could muster enough gravity to hold down, even for a moment.

"I'm so much older but you look exactly the same."

She winked at him, "I don't see that."

Simmy laughed and leaned into her. "Look closer"

Rey pulled his arm around her tightly. "I always loved these arms. They haven't changed."

The sun finally slid down to its resting place, the death of the day bleeding red and pink into the Sea of Marmara, lighting, for just a few moments, the solar fields of what was once Karacabey, now a city within the Octagon. He closed his eyes and felt her next to him. "You're good to me".

Rey pulled up a tiny hologram showing Dorothy eating, surrounded by people. "Please. Look at her. Look at me. Look at the things that are alive because of you, running around everywhere." She waved her hands. The hologram danced across the rocky shelf silently, but you could see the life in it.

"Ha." He lowered his voice. "This might be my last visit."

Rey let out a long sigh. "I don't know if I want to talk about that."

"We should." His voice still held no sadness. "This is about the life expectancy for my people."

Rey was quiet for a moment, nodding. "I know. Do you think you'll save your mind? You know? Re-implant it?"

Simmy pulled himself up to his full height, as he did whenever he had to say or do anything uncomfortable. He was a man of peace. She remembered how he had stood up tall and straight to fight off people who tried to hurt them. This was his fighting pose. "It's funny. My people pioneered this technology. Hundreds of years ago. We even helped build the Recreator. But we don't use it to prolong life. I have a river to return to and..."

"You are the water that makes it rush and swell." Rey smiled.

Simmy relaxed into her, "You learned that?"

"I read about your people all the time when I miss you." She dropped her voice at the end.

"You do?"

She reached up and put her hand on his gaunt cheek. "It's a lot of reading. You should feel bad for me."

Suddenly the night seeped into the holes in his armor and he let go and laughed, "You have the brain for it. I swear, that thing is bigger than this whole planet." He reached down and massaged her head with both of his pincer-like hands for a minute.

"Hm. Do that again."

He whispered to her, "I'll always be happy we landed here by mistake."

Rey shook her head, careful not to force him to stop. "It wasn't a mistake."

"Do you believe that?" Symkere asked.

Rey reached up and put her hands over his, still rubbing her head. "I believe that the only real thing to know about the universe is that two people born billions of light years apart can love each other. And find peace in each other's presence. And if you hadn't landed here I might not have learned that. And that terrifies me."

He kissed her head. "I was going to look around this place one last time before I left."

She pulled in closer. "In the morning."

Simmy nodded. "Yes. I'm still pretty fast. It might be better if I carried you."

Rey looked up, reminding him she was still that wise girl. "It's funny how all of us, everywhere, we make excuses just to touch each other."

He closed his eyes. "We do."

She smiled. "I think this one's my favorite."

Reylan felt her legs strong and lithe under her as she jumped up onto Simmy. She knew that even the debilitating scars and marks in the backs of them were so old as to be nearly impossible to see and that these legs could carry her anywhere she needed to go without difficulty. But it didn't matter. She was twenty years old again and these were arms that had always carried her toward something wonderful, away from pain.

And she was willing to trust in that one more time.

A few levels below, Dorothy was being reintroduced to the Octagon and everything it stood for. Leaandrea and Kashtun explained everything to her, the goals, the methods

Shukkat and Tanji explained to her the part she played in the history.

Diallo and Njeri explained to her what she meant to them, and to everyone else. Ako and Imisha helped. Everyone did.

And Vikun explained to her why she couldn't remember anything.

While a tiny hologram of Zehra cried with her, explaining how she had died, and how Zehra had felt a little smaller ever since.

She learned why people reached out to touch her everywhere she went. She learned why people closed their eyes and listened perfectly whenever she talked, trying to commit everything she said to memory.

And she learned why no one would dare to contradict her. No matter how silly she got.

She learned who she was from other people. And at one point, she stopped just listening to their words and instead listened to their love.

And every sentence painted her canvas until she was no longer white and clear, like some traditional death robe. But instead black with purpose, deep and rich. She waited until she was filled up and fully black to make a decision about what she wanted.

And when she made it, it was the right one.

7 - Epilogue

Shukkat leaned into the pillow next to her and stared at the face in front of her.

100 years.

The room was as big as the one Dorothy was reborn in. It was white, covered in plants. A warm pool was in the corner, big enough for two people to step into and sit. People used to recover in rooms like this, here in the Octagon, she thought, but recovery times were getting so short that now they were more designed for beauty than for functionality. A pretty place to wake up.

He shifted in front of her and opened his eyes.

Shukkat leaned in and held his hand, her red robe falling open in front, "Hey."

His pearl and bronze eyes opened wider. And there it was.

That smile.

He squeezed her hand. "Hey yourself."

"Do you remember who you are?"

He started to sit up. She stood to help him, but he was quicker than that. Sprightly, even.

"My name. I'm Archie Benjamin. Aren't I? That sounds right," he said.

Shukkat said, maybe a little too loudly, "yes, you are."

Archie's face lit up as he caught her excitement. It was a win. "All right. It looks like I'm one for one. You must be good luck. You LOOK like good luck." His eyes drifted over her. She was covered in tattoos and brilliant ceremonial jewelry, barely spanned by a thin red robe that left her breasts waiting at any moment to slip out. She was 124 years old but she looked 35. He could see the sleek darkness of her skin descend to a beautiful belly button. Archie remembered for a moment that he might have been a belly button guy. He chuckled to himself.

Shukkat felt his eyes on her like warm rain. She breathed it in. "Do you remember anything else?"

He dug back into his memory. It was maddening, but Archie Benjamin lived in the moment, He always had. "Not really. A few conversations." He stood up. He was in a thin white robe that covered nothing as well, it appeared. "You seem familiar."

"I do?" She helped him stand. She didn't really need to bother. He stood up as though he had just sat down for a moment.

Just a moment.

He flashed a familiar grin, merging his unique honesty with the thing you wanted to hear. "But, let's be honest, what man isn't going to say that? Look at you. No offense."

"I'm Shukkat." She remembered Archie looking at her in the eye, one of the few men who was tall enough to do so.

He kissed her hand and moved to the mirror. "That is a beautiful name."

"I always liked Archie." She followed him, watching for signs he recognized his own face.

"Ha. Not much of a name, really." He stared into the mirror and made a face. He ran his hands through his hair and looked at his jawline. "Not much of a hairline, either. Look at that thing. It's absolutely precarious." He bent over, looking up.

She came close to asking him to say the word again. Precarious. The way he said things. "Do you look familiar?"

"Sort of. I like my eyes." He looked back at her. His hand brushed hers. She knew he meant to do it. She grabbed it.

"They're the best eyes."

Archie turned to her directly. He took her in, from top to bottom, smiling. She saw the mischief on his face. The part of him that didn't play by rules. The part she loved.

He spoke softly. "I'm just giving thanks, right now, that they work." He squeezed her hand and winked.

Shukkat kept his eyes locked with hers. "I was hoping to show you around."

He picked up. "Really? So like a little professional tour? Can I afford that?" He winked at her. "What kind of plan am I on around here?"

It was hard for Shukkat to figure out what to explain to him and what to show. But she knew this man. She knew exactly what he would say when he saw this monument to peace. Archie Benjamin was no secret to her, even if he currently was to himself. "I think we built something here you would love."

He caught the pride in her voice, responding quietly, "even more reason, then. Pardon me, what is your name again?"

"Shukkat." her heart skipped as he asked her. She remembered every name she ever gave him. And the one she loved the most. She reached out with her other hand and shook his.

He vigorously, playfully, pumped both her hands until she laughed. "Miss Shukkat. I don't mean to be rude or anything, but what if I already like what I see?"

"There's a lot more. And I'm glad you're here."

He cocked his head. He held on tightly to both hands. "Do we know each other? Because forgetting that would be the real travesty."

She started pulling him through the door. "I can tell you all about it. "

Arche looked around. "Do I get clothes for this adventure?"

Shukkat shook her head and pulled him next to her as she stepped with him into the corridor, laughing.

"Nope."

Appendix

Additional collected information

6

Couplets

The twelve principles, broken down into six couplets, have been passed down from the Forsa, with some minor modifications, and may have existed since before the the dawn of our civilization. They are:

1. We are free, never in requirement or conscription

2. We are powerful, never at the expense of another

....

3. There are no tourists in mediation

4. There are no paychecks in mediation

....

5. Through kindness there is wisdom

6. Through deprivation, there is atrophy

....

7. Perfect acceptance is acceptance

8. All rejection is perfect

....

9. Everyday, We are beautiful, not hiddden

10. Everyday, We are becoming more, not less

....

11. Love is learned through practice

12. Practice is best done in joy

5

Tests

If you are a supplicant, hoping to join the Octagon, there are five tests that you are required to undergo at home before becoming an initiate, under consideration to join. Once you are accepted, you become a novitae and are placed in a thula, with teachers and fellow students.

The tests are:

Imagine:

The very first time you hold a hand in your hand that is completely different – shaped differently – from somewhere else entirely, what would you do? would you be afraid, holding it loosely, without commitment? Or would you hold on tightly, reveling in its difference, loving the parts that were unlike your own, enjoying the diversity?

1. Aatmiyata

Have sex with multiple people that you love very much and explain to them, during the acts, the things you love about them and whey they are important to you.

....

2. Vivruti

In front of friends, prepare your "user manual," stripping and showing them the parts of your body you love, which you do not, and how you need and want to be touched by the people you are intimate with.

....

3. Melamilapah

Visit someone you care for, whom you believe still cares for you, with whom you've had a falling out, and apologize for your part in it. Listen to their concerns, don't defend yourself, and offer to engage in any intimacy that they would like, with the goal of becoming intimate friends who trust each other.

....

4. Muktata

Put a handful of healthy, living food-grade mealworms in your mouth for two hours. Try very hard not to hurt them or swallow them as you masturbate at least twice.

....

5. Anyatvam

Masturbate while covered in arthropods, allowing them access to your mouth and genitals. There is a list of safe arthropods that do not bite or sting on our website.

8

Requirements

If you are a supplicant, hoping to join the Octagon, there are seven requirements that you must meet. On rare occasions, one or more may be waived for people who are a particularly good fit

They are:

1. A degree similar to any of the following degrees or related fields:

Political Science	Mediation	Conflict Resolution
Peace Studies	Journalism	Education
Contract Law	Juris Doctor	LLM - Dispute Resolution
Social Work	Negotiation	Psychology/Psychiatry

....

2. No history of violence

....

3. No history of opposition to sex work

....

4. At least a year of any volunteer work that dealt with interacting and caring for people

....

5. The initiate must have passed the five tests in front of a witness or on a recording.

....

6. The initiate must be pansexual and open to to physical engagement with many different types and shapes of people.

....

7. The initiate must be a kind and loving person, and have been exposed to at least two years of an anger management class.

....

8. The initiate must be xenophilic – attracted to and exctied by otherness, by uniqueness, by people unlike themselves.

20

Genitalia

There are twenty different forms of intimacy building genitalia expressed by visitors within the known galaxy. Some can be used for reproduction but all may be used for pleasure and intimacy.

They are:

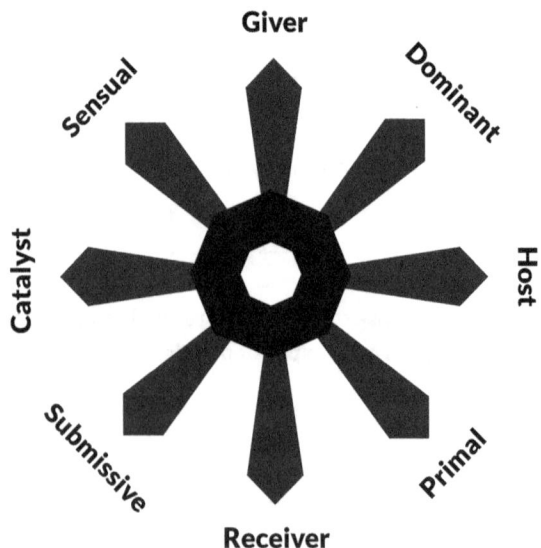

Gender, as expressed on the t'kau

1	**Aatma**	**Mind/Spirit**	the Intellect/ Feelings
2	**Yonih**	**Vagina**	a reproductive orifice
3	**Lingam**	**Penis**	an inseminating member
4	**Gudam**	**Anus**	a non reproductive orifice
5	**Mutramargah**	**urethra**	orifice to expel liquid
6	**Mukh**	**Mouth**	food intake orifice
7	**Stanam**	**Breasts**	reproductive feeding
8	**Angam**	**Limbs**	non-reproductive members
9	**Charm**	**Skin**	non-reproductive surface
10	**Chhidra**	**Cloaca**	multi-use orifice
11	**Dvayam**	**Hemipene**	dual inseminating member
12	**Sparshakam**	**Zakiri**	prehensile tentacle
13	**Kundali**	**Coil**	coiled member
14	**Sarpaah**	**R'kash**	multiple prehensile tentacles
15	**Gruhani**	**M'kara**	multi-holed orifice
16	**Sangrahakah**	**Collector**	egg-collecting limb
17	**Vichedyam**	**Go-Ikiban**	detachable member
18	**Pratyaaropanam**	**Ovipositor**	egg-implanting device
19	**Jihva**	**Jow-kila**	secondary tongue
20	**Vilayah**	**Merge**	giver/receiver combination

12

Kajere

Across the Galaxy, these are the signs of intimacy, the ways people show they love. They are called kajere and there are 12 core universal ones.

1	**Drashtum**	To see someone for who they are
2	**Dnyatum**	To want to know them
3	**Dharyitum**	To hold their hand in connection
4	**Prakashayitum**	To tell them your secrets
5	**Kalah**	To give them your time
6	**Shrotum**	To fall in love with their sound
7	**Gandh**	To revel in their smell
8	**Svadayitum**	To taste them with joy
9	**Saantvanam**	To share their pain
10	**Lingum**	To have sex with them
11	**Tyaktum**	To wish they were next to you
12	**Smaranaartham**	To carry their name with you

Additional Glossary

Some terms that are used throughout the Octagon that may not be instantly recognizable.

Ahreee	A technologically advanced and expansive yolcu group
Apriya	Literally "beloved." the helpmate or assistant for an Officiant
Bessary	A meeting area where T'kaus are often awarded
Catalyst	A gender specifier referring to a desire to initiate reproduction
Cone	The center entry area to the Forala in the main building
Encantada	A yolcu race with very hard white bone like skin
Forala	The underground water space where Taranakahs live at the Octagon
The Form	A yolcu group
Forsa	The group of people who putatively began the method of mediation through intimacy
Giver	A gender specifier referring to a desire to penetrate
Halk	A language evolving in the Octagon mixing Turkish, English, Sanskrit, and some various yolcu languages
Host	a gender specifier referring to a desire to house offspring

Kezmek/Kezmaki	Officiant at the Octagon – person who mediates and finalizes contracts between groups
Kheirobos	A type of Master whose task is to show novitaes specifics about their culture, through sex, truths, or other forms of intimacy
Kiener	A yolcu race who are generally fiery red and orange in color
Korvun	The above ground space where Turolo live at the Octagon
KSL	Kenyan Sign Language, one of the the estimated 6,000 languages spoken throughout the Octagon
Kurge	The space where contracts are officiated.
Novitae	A person in training to become a Kezmek
Obsuro	A yolcu race characterized by obsidian black skin and red eyes
Officiant	Person who mediates and finalizes contracts between groups
Petitioner	A representative of a group, come to have a contract mediated
Receiver	A gender specifier referring to a desire to be penetrated
Romahi-Gilea	A yolcu race

Sarcosians	A yolcu race that leans toward the sensitive and delicate
T'kau	the eight sided tattoo that officiants at the Octagon get that describes their gender
Taranakah	Water-breathing members of the Octagon
Thessalia	The area between the Forala and the Korvun where people go for fun, often
Thula	Home configuration containing two Master Kezmaki and three or four Novitae
Turolo	Air-breathing members of the Octagon
Velios Unity	A large and expansive federation of people.
Vigo	A yolcu race with blue skin
Vio-Khalera	A yolcu race that gave up use of bodies over a million years ago
Viraga	A yolcu race that is fiercely violent during sex
Yolcu	Voyager, the way to reference someone from another planet
Zucaro	A kind of sex gym in the Octagon

■ ‖ PULSEBLACK ‖■